'A truly compelling read, lots of tension and very witty. the scenes, the atmosphere, an public school and modern edu... ...superbly drawn. The characters are interesting combinations of good and bad, light and shade.'

Michael Crick,
Political Editor of BBC Newsnight.

'The dialogue is convincing and the characterisation nicely differentiated. The satire describing the Oxbridge interviews is extremely funny and the close-knit world of a school is convincingly portrayed, the more so as it is subtly connected with the world beyond. Topical, edgy, difficult issues are sensitively handled with a good mixture of comedy and tension, maintaining interest throughout. I cared what happened to the characters, both staff and students.'

Valerie Sanders,
Professor of Victorian Literature, University of Hull.

'Masterly: the best book on public school life that I have read. The novel accurately explores the hysterical reaction to spurious accusations and every-one in the profession will be able to empathise with the dramatis personae. I enjoyed the book immensely.'

Anthony Wallersteiner,
Headmaster of Stowe School.

'The quietly cohesive way in which one scene follows another has a real flow about it. The sophistication of the writing makes for both a stimulating and an easy read. There is a judicious sense of balance. The serious is lightened by the satirical, so that at no stage does the book, though dealing with some big issues, feel heavy. The vivid gallery of characters is brought alive in the lively and revealing dialogue.'

Anthony Meredith, Biographer.

'The story is very compelling, cleverly structured and written with a lot of panache. The twin themes of teenage spirituality and middle-aged sexuality are intriguing and dealt with seriously and intelligently.'

Victor Houliston, Professor of Renaissance Literature, University of Witswatersrand.

'The very topical theme is sensitively handled and a blow against the dangers of Politically Correct obsession. The novel shows well how the motives of flawed, ambitious, ruthless people can be ready to exploit a situation, no matter what it costs to another. The fine, descriptive, reflective passages in the novel contrast with the satirical challenge to Information Technology, contemporary Oxbridge admission procedures, Health and Safety and the stifling regulations which affect the present educational culture. The suicide comes as a genuine shock. This is a courageous book which addresses a Christian's inner conflict between his nature and his faith.'

Walter Eyles, formerly Education Officer for Buckinghamshire.

'A page-turner: a book that involves the reader on so many different levels that we can all relate to with regards to politics, religion and belief, morality, sex and the period of one's life that initiates an all too rapid transition from childhood into adolescence and adulthood. The author has an uncanny way of subtly prodding the reader to take stock of all the above.'

Alistair Lockhart-Smith, National Institute of Adult Continuing Education.

'The pages of this book bring a compelling and pure humanity to the issue of homosexuality and the church, an issue so dreadfully far from resolution and too often subject to hatred and bigotry. This is a controversial book but one that many would be well served to read. The inner torment of the central character and the cool-headed, non-judgmental way in which he comes to terms with his sexuality (without hypocrisy) reflect aspects of Christianity that are not aired in public as often as they should be and introduce and invite the virtue of tolerance.'

Ramsay Fanous, Doctor of Medicine.

'The development and complexity of the characters as the book moves on are deeply, deeply insightful. The level to which one could relate to what they were feeling was without question a highlight for me. A character who faces the dismal despair of being branded a deviant collides with another character whose chemistry, when combined with the misfortune around him, hurls him into a tailspin from which he cannot recover. The novel exposes the anguish experienced between sexual needs, professional responsibilities and the eternal struggle to somehow seek an ultimate guidance and resolution in faith. It illustrates how mundane paradoxes continually haunt our existence and how events throw the gauntlet at how we understand the world as we attempt to find faith and unconditional love.'

Tristan Crawford.

This book is dedicated to

ROBERT WILSON, whose advice, encouragement and proof reading were invaluable.

I would also like to thank the following for all their generous encouragement, advice and assistance:-

Chesney Clark, Ed Colville, Piers Craven, Tristan Crawford, Michael Crick, Greg Cushing, Colin Diggory, Jonathan Elliman, Sam Emery, Walter Eyles, Ramsay Fanous, Ian & Sue Farquhar, Andrew & Jamie Farquhar, Tom Feehan, Tim Field, Bill & Penna Gage, Jamie Gray, Stephen Hirst, Victor Houliston, Robert Jackson, Lucy Jackson, Alistair Lockhart-Smith, Toby Marshall, Anthony Meredith, Will Randall-Coath, Paul Robbins, Crispin Robinson, Christian Roe, Peter Rossiter, Jack Ryley, Valerie Sanders, Richard Searby, Mark Sutherland, Steven Thompson, Nick Thompson, Margaret Tufnell and Anthony Wallersteiner.

Between Boy And Man

Peter Farquhar

authorHOUSE®

AuthorHouse™ UK Ltd.
500 Avebury Boulevard
Central Milton Keynes, MK9 2BE
www.authorhouse.co.uk
Phone: 08001974150

© 2010 Peter Farquhar. All rights reserved.

No part of this book may be reproduced, stored in a retrieval system, or transmitted by any means without the written permission of the author.

First published by AuthorHouse 9/22/2010

ISBN: 978-1-4520-3931-2 (sc)

This book is printed on acid-free paper.

'Not yet old enough for a man nor young enough for a boy............
'Tis with him in standing water, between boy and man.'

(Shakespeare: 'Twelfth Night').

The story is set in a boarding school and the nearby towns and countryside at the beginning of the Twenty-first Century. All characters, locations and incidents are fictitious.

ONE

The streamlined express train, red and grey in livery, was proceeding at high speed from Manchester Piccadilly to London Euston. Passengers dozed, read the morning papers, looked out of the windows at the flat, sodden, monochromatic Midland countryside, tapped information into laptop computers or communicated business through mobile 'phones. The driver sounded the horn as the train approached Midhampton to warn the waiting commuters to stand back from the edge of the platform as the express hurtled through. Suddenly, he saw an indistinct figure detach itself from the mass of onlookers and, incredibly, step into space directly in front of him. The softest of impacts had occurred even before he could reach for the controls. Witnesses said afterwards that the driver's face was frozen with horror as the train screamed past the far end of the platform, finally coming to a halt nearly a mile down the track. In the coaches, plastic coffee mugs and sandwich containers flew off tables; those unfortunate enough to be walking in the aisles were hurled against each other; bags and coats fell from the luggage racks; glasses smashed in the buffet car. There was a moment of eerie silence as shock turned to relief when all motion ceased.

❧

Two shadows blundered about in the cramped, unlit room. There was an impact as one of them collided with the corner of the bed. A male voice cursed. A girl giggled.

'Shut up for fuck's sake! Do you want the whole place to hear?' whispered the male voice hoarsely.

His naked legs gleamed faintly in the moonlight as he struggled into a pair of jeans.

'Do be careful.'

'Yeah, course I will. That was great. Meet again tomorrow night?'

They kissed and he was out through the open window, onto a precarious ledge, down a drain-pipe and landing softly on the ground.

The full moon was a double-edged blade. It helped him to see better but increased the risk of his detection. He raced across a space of open ground, successfully securing cover in a thick copse. The adrenalin was pumping; he could almost hear his heart beating, its rhythm vibrating like a distant bass. He sat on the cool damp ground with his back against a tree and fumbled in the back pocket of his jeans for his cigarettes and a lighter. He inhaled the nicotine deeply and immediately felt his nerves calming. There was a chill edge to the night breeze. His slight form was covered only by a black cotton shirt. He shivered involuntarily and then tensed as something unseen rustled in the undergrowth nearby. Probably only a fox or a badger- or just a prowling cat? Suddenly he exhaled a muted yelp and sat upright. Whatever the source of the noise was, it had disturbed some water-birds on the invisibly dark lake. The silence was riven by a sudden raucous cackling and splashing as the startled fowl broke the surface of the water while taking to the safety of the air. Had the creatures' slumber been interrupted by something else, some concealed danger, more threatening to himself? He relaxed again and, shielding the lighter from an unwelcome, cold gust, he lit a second cigarette, drawing heavily through the filter and feeling pleasantly heady in the luxury of a long, slow, outward breath.

But the red glow of the point of the cigarette could be seen from afar. He was only just beyond the range of the sudden gleam of an electric torch, the invisible owner of which was bearing down on him directly. He stubbed the cigarette out and, mumbling a curse as his hand grazed against a stinging nettle, he plunged into whatever mysterious inhospitality the undergrowth presented. He pushed leaves and branches aside, heedless of any painful opposition. His right leg became entangled with the stem of a wild blackberry bush. Strong, supple, tenacious and thorny, the bush became a man-trap, tripping him over and then holding his leg fast, as it ripped through the thin denim of his jeans, lacerating his shin. The pain was excruciating and the shrub seemed to possess a diabolical ingenuity in its clinging persistence. Tears of pain, frustration and fear filled his eyes as he fought a desperate battle to free himself from this triffid-like enemy. The beam from the torch was on him. He turned his face in the opposite direction in an attempt to avoid identification. With a supreme effort, he suddenly broke free, albeit with the thorns ruining his jeans and ripping vengefully into his thigh. Disobeying a stentorian command to give himself up, he lurched forward and- bliss of all bliss- unexpectedly found himself once again on open ground. He knew that he could probably out-run his pursuer who would, in any case, need to circumnavigate the thorny vegetation. He shot across the field like a hare being pursued by beagles, arriving, panting for breath, at the slightly open window of a hallway. He levered the window upwards, decanted himself onto the floor beneath, shut the window silently behind him, and raced up two flights of stairs to his room. He stripped to his boxer shorts and socks in the darkness, threw his shredded jeans and shirt into a cupboard and, bleeding and sore, scrambled under his duvet and into bed.

Sure enough, he could hear the predictable heavy footsteps in the passage less than five minutes later. The door opened. The light was switched on. He prayed that no telltale signs of vegetation were on his face or in his hair. He turned with his face to the wall, pretending to be peacefully fast asleep. The intruder came right over to the side of his bed and then made a cursory inspection of the room. Oh shit! His trainers- on the floor in front of the desk! The customary dirt would not matter but they were bound to be damp, betraying recent exposure to the wet grass. But the clue went unnoticed. His housemaster switched off the light and left the room.

TWO

'He's in! He's done it! WHAT A GOAL! GREAT LAD!'

'Yeah! WELL DONE, JUDE !' And then, returning to normal volume, 'What a player, John! No wonder you want to keep him sweet.'

'Yes, as a famous manager in this country used to say, 'the lad's done brilliant!'

'COME ON, COLLEGE: TAKE THEM TO THE CLEANERS!' shouted Richard.

'GREAT PASS THERE NICK! DON'T PUT YOURSELF OFF-SIDE ASHLEY!' encouraged John.

John swapped between giving these calls to his players and sustaining a low-key, intermittent conversation with his young colleague.

'Well, we're one ahead now, thanks to Jude. But, to coin another well worn football cliché, 'It isn't over till it's over.' Do you use those phrases in Australia?'

'We certainly know that one. And you're right; there's a way to go yet. How long have you been running the First Eleven, John?'

'Well, I've been here for twenty years. I must have taken it over sixteen years ago.'

'Have they always done as well as this?'

'Yes, they've generally been pretty good. The College has a long soccer tradition.'

'A lot of the credit must go to you John.'

'No, no, no! If you've got a really classy player like Jude Williams in any season it helps.'

'And yet you've not made him captain.'

'No,' answered John, slightly hesitantly, somewhat guarded.

Richard responded with quick reassurance.

'I think you're quite right; I can see why. He wouldn't provide the leadership.'

'I'm interested that you say that, Richard. If one were being nice about Jude, one might say that he was an *individual*.'

'And if one wasn't, one would say that he was a selfish bastard. Oh, I'm sorry, er….'

'Don't worry, Richard. I'm used to worse than that. Actually, I find blasphemy harder to cope with.'

'It's great that the Chaplain takes the First Eleven. The boys all love you, you know. They really respect you.'

'Yes, well, *I* like *them*. They are great to work with. Every year there are pleasant lads. And, for the record, I do in fact like Jude. He can be awkward and cheeky but he's a bright and interesting boy.'

'You've got a gift when dealing with some of these guys. I must confess that I don't take to him quite so well.'

'You find him arrogant?'

'Yeah, that was exactly the word I had in mind.'

'He does have a streak of that within him; there's no point in denying it.'

'He's devoted to you though. Even when he's mouthing off about others, he's always praising you. Oh no! We're in trouble!'

The opposing team's premier striker sent the ball curving straight into the Moreton College goal but the keeper was ready and judged it accurately.

'GREAT SAVE, BEN! GOOD MAN!'

It was a breezy October afternoon. A heavy mid-day shower had washed the landscape and bright afternoon sunlight made the field glisten green, dotted with yellow leaves, below a clear, pale blue sky. Across this open aspect, twenty-two young men competed for possession of the ball, the opposition in red and black and the Moreton College boys in blue shirts, their white shorts irregularly plastered with mud from the soft ground. Good-natured supporters shouted encouragement. Adults stood chatting around the perimeter of the field. Fathers of the team occasionally came up to John to congratulate him on another successful season.

'Thanks, Bill,' responded John to a large, red-faced, enthusiastic farmer, who was wearing a green parka, a shade darker than his Wellington boots. 'It's been good so far but you never know what might happen next week.'

'Well John, whatever: but these boys owe you more than a few. You've given Charlie so much more confidence. You know, Sue and I truly appreciate it. And we're not alone among the parents here.'

'Oh, Charlie is easy; he's a good lad; you know that! Have you met Richard Ellman? He's over from Australia for a year, or, possibly (we hope) longer. He's been a tower of strength with this lot.'

'Good to meet you Richard. I hope you're settling in allright?'

'Yes, Sir, thank you. John's been a big help.'

'What's new? This school wouldn't be the same without John. I hope they appreciate it. I bet they don't. Where's the Headmaster? Why isn't he out here supporting his lads?'

'Oh, I don't know. It's a very busy job, Bill, especially these days. I expect he's stuck in his study with some major problem needing to be solved by yesterday.'

'You're very loyal, John. If you ask me, he's a lazy bugger- begging your pardon for the language. Sorry!'

'You know I'm not that easily shocked, Bill. To be fair, I think that being a Headmaster in the Twenty-first Century is all about management and recruitment and fund raising and P.R. It certainly wouldn't suit me.'

'He might go in for a bit of P.R. by coming out here this afternoon.'

'I don't think he even knows who I am,' chipped in Richard. 'But then,' he added, correcting himself, 'Why should he?'

'Of course he bloody should,' said Bill Blakestone. 'Do you know, he hasn't had a single word with our lad in the four-and-a-half years the boy's been here.'

'That might be to Charlie's credit,' suggested John.

There had been a brief lull when the referee had stopped the match after two members of the opposing team had collided. It had been clear from the beginning that no great harm had been done but the skinnier lad had gone down and a pause had been instigated while he was helped back up and checked for injury. Now, however, as he was limping away bravely, the focus of attention swiftly changed. There was a sudden crescendo of noisy excitement from the College spectators and John, Richard and Bill Blakestone were just in time to witness the electrically fast execution of Jude Williams' second goal. They all shouted glory and then fell to commenting on how gifted the boy was.

Victory was secured. Congratulations offered. The crowd dispersed. The boys came into the pavilion. The College boys hugged each other with joy in their success and John hugged some of them too, as Richard and he went into the changing room to share in breathing in the heady atmosphere of recently achieved triumph.

'Well done, guys!' shouted Richard.

'That was really terrific!' said John.

'Yeah Sir, wasn't it great? Jude's two goals were something again!'

'They sure were. That was a tremendous performance, Jude. Well done!' said John. And then, 'Can you hang on a minute? I'd like a word with you when the others have gone.'

'Sure, Sir, of course.'

'Hey! What have you done to your leg? You've got a nasty cut on the shin there and, look, your thigh's badly scratched.'

'Oh, er, yes, so I have. I took a tumble early in the second half on the other side of the pitch. I didn't realise it had done all that to me.'

'But the ground's soft, after the rain. I don't see how that could happen.'

Jude grinned disarmingly. John noticed some of the other boys shaking their heads.

'Goodness knows what I hit, Sir. There must have been a rough patch out there somewhere.'

'We'll have that cleaned up after you've had a shower, so don't get dressed till then.'

'He'll live,' said goal-keeper Ben.

'No doubt,' replied John, 'but we don't want our best striker losing a leg through septicaemia.'

High spirits. Laughter. Boyish youth.

John controlled his elation.

Richard took his leave, after praising the Moretonians and his older colleague, modestly refusing to take any of the credit himself. Bill Blakestone and Charlie said a friendly goodbye and drove off in their new silver four-wheel-drive. John exchanged courtesies with colleagues from the opposing team. The boys gradually emerged, enjoying all their well deserved praise and either went off with their parents or back to the boarding houses. John noticed again what an amiable, good-looking bunch they were. He felt an accustomed glow of affection for them as he returned to the dressing-room to attend to the injury sustained by the man of the match.

Jude did not see John arriving, as he sat cross-legged on a bench, reading a newspaper. His athleticism notwithstanding, Jude was relatively small for a boy in the Upper Sixth. He was 5'7" and slight in build, though with a neat, muscular body. He had a handsome face, with a fine bone structure, and unexpectedly heavy, careless stubble. He had hazel eyes and light brown hair, cut conventionally short. As on previous occasions, John noticed the copious brown hairs which covered his pale arms and legs, and which contrasted attractively with the pristine, washing powder white of his cotton vest and underpants. John could sense the soft warmth of the texture without actually requiring physical contact. He observed again that Jude had an exceptionally hairy chest for a lad who was still only seventeen.

John felt, as before, a momentarily nervous flurry of confusion when Jude smiled at him. It was a smile which seemed to declare, possibly disingenuously, 'You, Sir, are special in my life. Not only are you one of my best mates; you are my mentor, my top advisor, perhaps even the father I don't have.'

John felt again, as he had done with other boys occasionally through the years, that he could hardly trust himself alone in Jude's half-naked presence. But yet, it was where he most wanted to be and he knew- *before God he knew-* that he had the boy's best interests at heart and that his influence over the lad could only be to the good.

He sat down on the bench beside his pupil.

'That was tremendous, Jude. I'm really proud of you and so must the College be.'

'Thanks, Sir, but a lot of it's due to you, of course.'

'No, Jude, I'm not taking any of the credit away from you. You're very gifted but I do wish you might be just a little more helpful about coming to the weekly practices. Apart from anything else, it doesn't give the right signals to the others.'

'I know. I'm really sorry, Sir. It's these unexpected visits home. As you know, my Mum has this habit of suddenly appearing and dragging me off home for a couple of hours.'

'But, last time, I had the impression that you were here, around the College: or was I mistaken?'

'Last Wednesday?'

'Yes.'

'Oh, that's right. Yes, I remember. I'm really sorry but I had a Mr Scott essay to finish. You know what Scotty's like if it's not in on time.'

'That's not good enough, Jude.'

'I know, Sir. I'm sorry. It won't happen again. I don't want to let you down. I don't think I did this afternoon?'

'No, you know you didn't. But you did on Wednesday.'

'Yes, I'm sorry.' The boy raised both his hands in a gesture of surrender.

'How is your Mother? I notice she wasn't here this afternoon.'

'She's OK. She had to work this afternoon. But I'll see her this evening.'

'Give her my best wishes. I might try to pop over and see you both again some time next week.'

'Yes Sir, why not? Do we have a Chapel Group in your flat on Tuesday?'

'Yes, as usual.'

'I'll be there.'

'That's a nasty cut. Part of it looks as though it has dried up. The blood on the surface has hardened in places and I don't understand how you could have collected those scratches on a pitch like the one this afternoon.'

'Well, I can't explain it either, Sir. I'm probably just some sort of physical freak.'

John laughed as he crossed the room to unlock the cupboard containing the first-aid boxes.

'I washed it in the shower.'

'I'll just put some of this TCP cream on. Goodness knows what infection you could have picked up out there.'

John gently rubbed a little of the cream onto the cut on Jude's shin. Some contact during the match had opened the wound up again quite convincingly. John desperately tried to disguise the erection which he felt beginning as his forefinger brushed against the hairy surface of the youth's leg.

'Oooh, Sir, this is quite cosy,' Jude chuckled.

'All-right, all-right: no need to be cheeky. It just needs a sparing application like that, Jude. I'll let you spread some onto the scratches on your thigh yourself. You had better tell Matron about this. She should know and she'll probably want you to put some more cream on.'

'OK, Sir.'

Jude gave the abrasions on his thigh a cursory wipe with the ointment and quickly put his shirt, socks, trousers and shoes on.

'Thanks again, Sir. I'm sorry I let you down on the practice. It won't happen again. You're a great friend to me. I do appreciate it.'

He then surprised John by giving the older man a friendly hug. In the next moment, he had grabbed his bag and was gone.

John stood alone in the spartan changing room, breathing hard, as he attempted to analyse his own motives, puritanically presuming that sensual pleasure and altruism must of necessity be incompatible, as Eros and self-denial wearily fought their unresolved stalemate.

THREE

AT THE SAME TIME as the First XI was winning the football match, the Headmaster was meeting his two most senior colleagues, the Deputy Head and the Director of Studies. They were discussing the principles behind the new systems management which was to be applied throughout the College.

The Headmaster's study was a splendid room on the ground floor of the Eighteenth Century mansion which was at the heart of the rambling campus which constituted the College. The room had been gothicised at the beginning of the following century by the great London architect, Sir John Soane. The fixed cupboards which formed the walls on three sides of the room were each surmounted by a mock Gothic arch. The southward facing boundary took the form of two sets of French windows which opened out onto the Headmaster's garden with, immediately beyond, a magnificent prospect of the landscaped park, created by Lancelot Brown when the estate was in the hands of the aristocracy of the Enlightenment.

For the past decade, this palatial office had been the domain of Geoffrey Tansley. Accoutred in his pin-striped suit, bow-tie and half-moon reading glasses, he had sat behind his huge oak desk, issuing pronouncements, signing letters, trumpeting his views on a variety of issues (by no means limited to his own school), wheeling, dealing, hiring, firing and drinking copious quantities of gin. His primary interest was so completely with himself that he was unaware that this last mentioned attribute had long since given rise to his universally applied nick-name, G&T, a trick on his initials invented by an irreverent colleague. His booming, brassy voice, little, carefully cultivated, eccentricities, boundless self-confidence and shrewd sense of self-preservation more than compensated for his slender grasp of matters academic or curricular. He spoke with such commanding authority, and at such periphrastic length, that his judgments were as final and irrevocable as those pronounced by any emperor of Ancient Persia. Their appropriateness was never in doubt, except, in tones of muted apprehension, by people other than himself. The entire community had been made aware of his direct descent from a great and ancient West Country family and he regularly reminded everyone that one of his illustrious ancestors had enjoyed the honour of being imprisoned in the Tower by King James II. The ancestor in question had in fact been a misguided Protestant minor squire from the Somerset Levels who had narrowly escaped the deadly cull of Judge Jeffreys after the Duke of Monmouth's rebellion in 1685. There were those amongst Tansley's staff who rather wished that Queen Elizabeth II had accorded the present scion of the family the same privilege as her Stuart predecessor had to his forebear. His wife and he hosted sumptuous dinner parties in this room, to which he invited acquaintances even more distinguished than himself, and for which the College paid. A literary scholar, awarded a third class degree by one of the older universities, one of G&T's favourite indulgences was to impress his staff and Sixth Formers with a variety of quotations which were either inaccurate, invented or celebrated to the point of cliché.

Geoffrey Tansley's two hand-picked senior confidantes

had not been chosen by virtue of age, length of service or even pedagogic or intellectual ability. The appointment of Cressida Fulwell, from outside the College, as Deputy Head, four years ago, had been controversial to say the least. Still only thirty-seven, she had arrived after a short spell as Head of a Department in a well known girls' day school. Twice divorced, she was currently unattached. She openly supported the Headmaster at every available opportunity in public and, in private, guided him during those rare moments when circumstances absolutely forced him to decide instead of pontificate. Vivacious, and often dressed in a manner which bordered on the provocative, Ms Fulwell did not allow the modest handicaps of a nasal voice, slightly protruding front teeth and a size considerably greater than the average, to impede her drive, tenacity and ambition. Her quick temper with the young, however, did not improve her classroom control, especially when dealing with teenage boys, who competed for the honour of getting her to scream with rage when issuing one of her more regular imprecations during Religious Studies lessons:-

'If you don't fucking shut up, I'll put you all in fucking Detention at five o'clock!'

This sport, practised mainly in the Fifth Form, was relatively safe because the class quickly established that the threat was never carried out. They did not, however, realise that this lapse occurred because Ms Fulwell had better things to do with her time than make up for her habitually late arrival in class by providing compensatory teaching later in the day. Jude Williams' esteem amongst his peers had risen a notch two years ago when he had been sent out of the room after enquiring if the repeated threat was being used as a helpful example of alliteration.

If teenagers were not one of the Deputy Head's principal concerns, her colleague, the Director of Studies, did everything possible to avoid them altogether. Lee Crowther was thirty-nine and had been promoted out of the classroom at the same time as Cressida was appointed. The Headmaster had not done this as a sop to the Common Room, by appointing one of their own, so much as in recognition of Crowther's knowledge of computers at a time when the College was required to make the necessary quantum leap into Information Technology. Among the several advantages this afforded Crowther, was the acquisition of ultimate responsibility for the timetable. He had immediately reduced his own teaching commitment to four periods per week. To be fair, his effect upon the one class which he did still teach was quite different from that of Ms Fulwell. His lessons in Mathematics offered a chance to catch up on the sleep missed by those who had spent a portion of the previous night 'skanking' in the grounds. He had an expressionless face, the coded secrets behind which were further shielded by a pair of owl-like spectacles which persisted in slipping down his nose. He was currently working on methods which would put all information- administrative, academic and pastoral- onto a data-base. He was creating a variety of interlocking systems which would record examination results, class and set lists, absences, punishments and even the writing of reports. Cressida Fulwell took an active interest in all this. Although Crowther set the programmes in place, she controlled what went into them.

'There's no arguing with a computer which tells you that you are disobeying its instructions,' she joked to Geoffrey Tansley.

'Quite right,' her boss barked. 'It'll make sure that everybody does their job properly. I myself shall certainly exhort and encourage the staff to recognise that there must be a systIm to follow. This really is terrific! Well done you, Lee!'

The Director of Studies blushed a little and grinned sheepishly as shyness and self-congratulation vied for supremacy.

'Thank you, Headmaster. As you know, I've had the set lists and exam. results on our intranet for two terms now. By and large it seems to have been successful.'

He spoke in a low, bleating voice. This, together with the woolly texture of his full head of blond hair and his mild manner, had resulted in his acquiring the nick-name 'Sheep' from his pupils. Unlike Tansley, Crowther was all too woefully aware of the term of disrespect to which he was consistently referred.

'But, Lee, weren't you saying that some departments had been more co-operative than others?' enquired Cressida.

'Really?' pounced the Headmaster. 'Who has been iffy about adapting?'

'Well, the Head of English doesn't like it and their returns have been a bit slow,' volunteered Crowther in a tone of apologetic diffidence.

'Dilatory more like,' retorted Tansley, grabbing a pen and scribbling a note on a piece of paper. 'Take me through the rest of it.'

'Well, Headmaster, I've got the data-base for the punishment system up and running but I can't really put it to bed until all our colleagues are willing to abandon their own systems. At the end of the day, it does depend upon the Common Room's willingness to be consistent.'

'And, of course, people like the Heads of English and History and the Chaplain don't seem to use any system,' said Cressida, smiling ruefully and gently shaking her head with regret.

'I guess that men of that sort of experience probably don't *need* to punish very often,' suggested Tansley, arching his eyebrows above his spectacles and smiling condescendingly. 'And the Chaplain *is* in a unique pastoral position.'

'The trouble is, Headmaster, that it makes it more difficult for us ordinary mortals when a few colleagues see themselves to be above the system. And it plays havoc with poor Lee's attempts to impose some uniformity of action. Two of the most senior housemasters won't play ball either,' responded his deputy, smiling coaxingly.

'I'm afraid that they want to keep all matters of discipline 'in house',' explained Lee, waving his left hand in a modest gesture of despair.

'Not washing one's dirty linen in public: an old principle and not necessarily a bad one,' mused Geoffrey.

'But it completely skewers the system,' said Cressida. 'These people have got to realise that we are in the Twenty-first Century now. They don't seem to have any notion of accountability. Guidelines must be adhered to, surely.'

'And you have defined offences specifically, Cressida, and prescribed the exact punishments?'

'Yes, Headmaster, and it's all there on Lee's system – if only every-one can be made to use it. Everything can be recorded and verified. And it is another way of keeping staff up to the mark.'

'I see.'

'It will look wonderful when the inspection comes next year: a real feather in our cap.'

'Now that is a consideration.'

'And if colleagues are in doubt about uniform, they can check the requirements exactly by flagging up 'uniform' on Lee's data-base.'

'It is true that our Moretonians do continue to look desperately scruffy. The boys seem to be going through this ghastly phase of wearing baggy trousers that are too big for them so that the frayed hems drag along the ground and one has the unpleasant view of the upper half of their underpants. It is quite embarrassing when parents and other visitors come. The girls aren't much better, showing off their midriffs at every opportunity. Actually,' – with a sudden, fleeting burst of impatient energy – 'it really is all too frightful. Again, colleagues must all be aware of the need for a recognised systIm.'

Some of the more cynical senior members of the Common Room, men like Alexander Scott, the Head of English, and Anthony Ridell, the Head of History, occasionally passed a few leisurely moments musing over the question of whether the Headmaster's mispronunciation of the word 'system' was an unconscious manifestation of his pedigree breeding or a deliberate affectation. Especially when being 'exhorted and encouraged', to quote one of Geoffrey Tansley's regular modes of appeal, as he hectored his staff daily, they were both inclined to choose the option of affectation.

'Have you looked at Lee's guide-lines on our intranet?' asked Cressida.

'Er….no….er, I have been rather tied up with this and that over the last few days.'

'Well, the point is, Headmaster, that all these matters are being confronted, if only, once again, staff would check the regulations and enforce them. We've stipulated grey trousers (not black and not chinos). We have restricted the colour of socks to plain grey, black or navy. They've got to wear plain white or light blue shirts and black shoes with laces. It's all there.'

'That's awfully good. No-one can have any excuse for not getting it right with all this so neatly prescribed.'

'Yes. Everything can be exact. There need be no arguments about grey areas. I also discussed the sports kit with Luke and that should all be clear too now.'

'Well, I think you both deserve a medal. We just can't have a repetition of that ill-fated attempt to get a rugby team together when that Trevor What's-his-name had them all wearing shirts stating that they were going on the 'EdinGburgh tour'. I do wish that some-one had noticed before they got there. We must have been the laughing stock of all those Edinburgh schools.'

'It suited John Donaldson quite well,' said Lee. 'When they lost every match to the Scots boys, and you decided to disband the newly created rugby team, it could only have helped our First XI soccer.'

'Well, quite. I should never have allowed it in the first place. There is no question of our Chaplain doing anything as crass as that with the footballers.'

'But he still doesn't bother with any of these matters,' complained Cressida, not quite happy with the way the discussion was drifting. 'I doubt if he would even raise a murmur if they were wearing pink socks with sky blue stripes.'

Lee Crowther laughed at this witticism more heartily than perhaps it deserved.

'Now, now,' said the Headmaster. 'The next thing is the reports; how are *they* fitting in to all this?'

Lee embarked on some computerspeak which was incomprehensible to his boss. Cressida interrupted him in mid-flow.

'I gave Lee some guidelines about this, Headmaster. You remember that we spoke about it last term. All the reports are now to be written on the computer. The staff have been told that every report must be at least a hundred and not more than a hundred-and-fifty words long.'

'Gosh! For every subject?'

'Yes, Headmaster,' said Cressida, beaming with satisfaction. 'And Lee has built in a locking device which will not close the report until a hundred words have been written.'

'Well, that's certainly going to keep everybody on their toes,' chortled Geoffrey.

'Yes, and what's more, whenever they go into the 'writing reports' entry, they will be warned about this and also told that it is not permitted to paste in pro forma summaries of the syllabus.'

'Music to my ears,' said Geoffrey. 'People won't have the time or energy to do much complaining when they face the rigours of your systIm.' He allowed himself a gleeful smile. 'More importantly, parents will have a greater sense that they have something to show for their fees.'

'And, of course, it *will* look good when the inspection comes.'

'Yes, the inspection is a two-edged sword.'

Geoffrey Tansley leant back in his chair and took a deep breath of satisfaction. He was pleased with his two apparatchiks. They were not a very interesting or inspiring pair, of course, but they were tireless work-horses who spared him a deal of unwelcome effort. Cressida was ruthlessly ambitious to be a Head herself one day (not too soon: he would see to that). She kept up meticulously with all the educational jargon and the plethora of directives issued from government departments and the examination boards. She couldn't care less about trampling on the toes of older colleagues, mainly men, who were all too aware of their own dignity and position, as they tried to continue indulging in gentlemanly restrictive practices. This saved him the bother of engaging in such confrontations himself. Moreover, she would always have to be on his side, supporting him all the way, if she, in turn, at some future date, were to wish his patronage in applications for headships. Having appointed Cressida, he need not worry about being stabbed in the back by some far more senior, settled and formidable colleague, who would never move on and who had become a sort of College institution with the Common Room, the parents, Old Moretonians and even the governing body. There were several of those around and the reality of their power needed circumscription. It was far better to have this brash young woman here to push things forward while remaining entirely dependent on his good will for her own future.

And then there was Lee Crowther. What a dreary chap he was! But the fact remained that he was willing to stay up all night playing around on the computers in a way that enhanced the perception of the College (and its Headmaster) and incidentally called the staff to account in a wonderful new fashion which Geoffrey, in his wildest dreams, could not have conceived. Lee's mathematical brain, allied to his computer, allowed for the creation of an omniscience which, by default, augmented the Headmaster's own omnipotence. And all this without Geoffrey having to move a muscle himself! Moreover, Lee was no political threat. He lived for his systems and was almost cravenly grateful to have been given such a chance to indulge his passion and to do so under the Headmaster's patronage.

Yes, these were good appointments and, if the odd, expensive, opinionated senior colleague did not like them, well, that was just too bad.

It was time for the first gin of the evening.

FOUR

Bernard Bassett, the Housemaster of Blenheim House, had climbed the two flights of stairs to the top storey where the Reverend John Donaldson had his self-contained flat.

Bernard was somewhat over-weight, pale in complexion, with prematurely thinning hair of an indeterminate colour and cold, suspicious, myopic eyes, framed by heavy spectacles. He had been at the College for seven years. Keen to move up the career ladder, he had been appointed as a housemaster two years ago and, at the age of thirty-five, was now looking for further promotion. He had inherited the Chaplain as his under-housemaster (a somewhat anomalous situation, to be sure) and also Priscilla Peverill, the most senior of the matrons. Bernard found it a constant irritation to have these two august personages holding sway within the narrow compass of his own recently acquired territorial authority. He had mentioned to his wife that it could be compared to the Prime Minister being required to have both the Queen and the Archbishop of Canterbury in his Cabinet. He had raised the matter when being professionally appraised by the Headmaster and had felt nettled when Geoffrey Tansley had laughed the difficulty away.

'I'm afraid that there's nothing I can do about that, dear boy. I can't sack the College's most senior and revered matron for you or boot the Chaplain out of the flat he has occupied for twenty years! You should be glad that you have two such experienced folk to support you! Naughtily, I have to say that, although I obviously didn't plan this, it does fit in rather nicely with my unwritten head-magisterial philosophy of *'Divide and Rule'*. When you become a Headmaster one day, Bernard, as I'm sure you will, I bet you'll end up following the same pragmatic wisdom! How's Daphne? All-right, I hope- and the children?'

'Delia, Headmaster.'

'Delia! Of course, forgive me!'

'G&T's a patronising bastard,' Bernard had complained to one of his colleagues immediately afterwards. 'He gives you a job and then leaves conditions in place which make it impossible to carry out.'

And so, like the two young fogies they were, his colleague and he had moaned away about the College going to the dogs. Naturally, they gave no thought to how it had survived for so many generations before them.

Now, Bernard was holding a list of absentees and a note of the duty roster for the house prefects to hand to John who was the duty master the next day. He hesitated at the open door of the flat when he heard John talking and, hearing no reply, quickly established that John was on the 'phone. Bernard paused, initially not wanting to interrupt and assuming that, like most of his own 'phone calls, John's would be a quick and perfunctory matter of business. Then, as he listened, he became intrigued.

'I could pop over on Sunday afternoon. I don't know how that would suit.'

Pause.

'No, of course, I understand. How would you be placed next Tuesday? I could bring Jude back in time for the Chapel meeting in the evening.'

Pause.

'Never mind! Poor you! What a schedule! I could possibly fit something in later in the week…….'

Pause.

'Yes, I can see that. It looks as though we'll have to leave it just for the moment.'

Pause.

'He certainly did very well. As you know, I think that he's a very special chap.'

Brief pause.

'Oh, of course, Lynn. I'm sorry. I hadn't realised. Yes. Well, I must let you go. I might contact you later in the week. It would be good to meet up when you have a moment. I'd better let you go now then. Bye.'

As John put the 'phone down, Bernard coughed and knocked on the door. He handed over the lists, about which they exchanged a few words, and left.

John was comfortable in his eyrie. It looked exactly the same as it had done when he moved in twenty years ago. He had not asked for any improvements and the College certainly had not volunteered to spend money uninvited. Priscilla had bullied the Domestic Bursar into having

John's carpets cleaned once during all that time and the shower had eventually been replaced after its predecessor had given up the ghost. John had not noticed the magnolia painted anaglyptic wallpaper gradually darkening or the curtains fading under the assault of successive summer suns. The armchairs and the sofa were old and comfortable but needed new covers, having been sat on by two decades of grubby Moretonians. Books, piles of paper and letters, some bleached by the sunlight, some yellow and crumbling with age, crowded on a table by the window, spilling onto the sill itself, like a waterfall defying gravity.

John's contentment in such simplicity contrasted sharply with Delia Bassett's insistent demands for a new kitchen and new curtains and carpets throughout their considerable house, adjacent but connected to the boarding house.

For the last few months however, squatting like an altar to an alien god, the neutral light grey monitor of a computer had seized possession of part of John's desk. It sat there, jarringly out of place, like an intimation of doom in a science fiction novel. The computer itself was on the floor. Intended to save paper, it was, ironically, already covered by papers and files. To be fair to John, he had recently become reasonably proficient in the use of a word processor, and even the e-mail, but anything more complicated, let alone the 'Holistic College Intranet' devised by Lee Crowther, might as well have been a process of communication between Mars and Venus, so far as he was concerned.

Charlie Blakestone, the Head of Blenheim House and a member of John's First XI, had called by informally on a number of occasions to teach John the basics. He was a gentle boy, mildly teasing in his friendliness, but, like so many of his peers, holding a profound respect for John and capable of fierce loyalty.

'Oh, Sir, Sir! You forgot to *save* it, didn't you! I've tried to create a data-base for all your documents but you don't seem ever to go to it. Now, Sir, a little test from last week. Send *me* an attachment from a document which we've saved as one of your documents.'

'Er, well, er, Charlie, um…..'

'You've forgotten, haven't you?' Charlie had chortled, with good-natured mirth. 'It's fun, teaching the teacher and catching him out! Never mind, my parents are just as bad. At least Mum recognises that she has difficulty. Dad pretends he knows what he's doing and then just blames the computer!'

This son's patronage was not harsh. Charlie was a tall, handsome boy with a patently honest, open smile. He had his father's easy manner but his mother's gentleness of disposition, her slim elegance and her good looks. They were a delightful family and took no kindness which John ever showed Charlie for granted. A younger brother was due to enter the College next year.

Immediately after Bernard's visit on this particular evening, John looked cursorily at the lists and then turned to a half-written sermon waiting on his desk. Half-an-hour later, Priscilla Peverill knocked discreetly at the door. The Matron of Blenheim House was a grey-haired lady of fifty-eight who, childless and having been widowed early, had been in post for seventeen years. Her mild grey eyes and faintly old-fashioned correctness were somewhat belied by a determined mouth, the fashionable simplicity of her dress sense and the quiet authority of her speech. She was extremely good at her job and was greatly respected by parents who, with varying degrees of apprehension, abandoned their progeny for months at a time. She was kind and understanding in her dealings with teenage boys, while seeing through most of their wiles. Indeed, the boys at Blenheim were fortunate in that they had two adults in whom they could easily confide, although John's brief, of course, extended across the College as a whole. The other matrons at the College naturally assumed Priscilla as a role model and she had represented their common interests with formidable sang-froid to a succession of ex-military bursars. The retired lieutenant-colonel who had shouted at her and banged the table, during his first week in office, never forgot the gravity of the blunder for the rest of his time at the College.

John and Priscilla shared an interest in the opera and classical music. A devout Christian, Priscilla was one of John's most loyal supporters in the Chapel. Their long and enduring friendship combined *Plato* with *Caritas* and *Agape*; from John's point of view at least, there could be nothing of *Eros* and, to his relief, neither did any such response ever seem to be expected. He had great admiration for the wisdom, as well as the humanity, of his neighbour downstairs.

'I've brought you some cakes which I made this afternoon. You can give them to the Chapel Group this evening.'

'Thank you,' responded John, smiling with genuine appreciation. 'Gosh! They're still warm! These will go down well.'

'Well, the wretched College feeds these boys so inadequately at supper; they need something to supplement what they're given.'

'You're terribly kind to them, Priscilla. You're always giving them biscuits and cakes, or even cooking something for them.'

'You know it's my pleasure. Most of them deserve it. And a lot of them are very appreciative. Anyway, you do similar things!'

'Glass of white wine?'

'If you've got a moment, John: thank you very much. The trouble is that half the adults in this College don't seem to realise that they are primarily here for the pupils. I don't think that G&T would know a Moretonian if he bumped into one by mistake and I'm not sure that our young *Obergruppenfuhrer* here in Blenheim even *likes* boys.'

'Oh, come on, sit down. Let's not be too hard on them all. You've got to recall that Bernard does have his wife to answer to as well- and so does the Headmaster!'

She laughed. 'The trouble with you, John, is that you're too good-natured.'

'No. I can get cross too but one's got to try to find a Christian response.'

'Yes, I know. I'm probably too critical but it's just that all the people running this place now seem to be in it for a combination of systems management and feathering their own nests. I think that G&T has a lot to answer for. He actively encourages it.'

'You're beginning to sound just like Alexander Scott!'

'Well! Take him for example! There we have one of the cleverest men in the Common Room, widely regarded as one of the most brilliant Heads of English in the country, and he's passed over and ignored. What must *he* feel? What sort of judgment is that?'

'Alex is very caustic. I suspect that they're all a bit frightened of him. And, anyway, he would hate to be spending his time fussing around with all this modern P.C. stuff.'

'*That's right!* He's a teacher and a scholar. So are you. You're about the only two left (along with Anthony Ridell and Tom Stevens, I suppose). Additionally, you're a wonderful Chaplain. And look at what you do for the Ist XI. By the way, well done on Saturday! Weren't they good? Dear Jude was superb!'

'Thanks, Priscilla. You're so good at coming out to support.'

'Well, in the absence of both his Headmaster and his Housemaster, to say nothing of his mother, some-one should be there to cheer him on.'

'His mother was working,' John sighed.

'Oh well, perhaps I was too hasty in her case.' Priscilla adroitly changed the subject. 'This is very nice wine. What is it?'

'Just a *Pinot Grigio* from the supermarket: I'm quite surprised by it myself.'

'I'm certainly looking forward to 'Die Walkure'. What a treat: Placido Domingo as Siegmund and Bryn Terfel as Wotan!'

'Yes, it'll be great to get away for the evening. It's quite a long way off, though.'

'Well, let's make it seem sooner. The Garden now even sends forms for booking meals, together with menus to choose from. Shall we try the Amphitheatre Restaurant again? I'll bring the menu up and we can make a booking.'

'A delightful idea. Do that. You know, Priscilla, as I struggle with that beastly computer and all these horrible new systems, I feel a bit like the defeated Wotan, finally being driven off to Valhalla: a dinosaur in a new world of electronic technocracy, the language of which I neither like nor understand. Alex, Anthony and I wrote a joint missive about the importance of at least being allowed to retain hand-written reports as an alternative to the computerised ones. The headmaster didn't even reply; we just got a terse rejection from Cressida.'

'How many four-letter words were in that?'

'Oh, come on, Priscilla!'

'Well! How could G&T appoint a foul-mouthed vulgarian like that dreadful young woman over men like the three of you?'

'I don't think any of us would have wanted that job. I'm very happy with my own, if only I could be left to do it in peace. Time for another glass?'

'Yes please, but I'd better be quick. To continue with the analogy, there are certainly plenty of Alberichs around here these days. Anyway, you couldn't be Wotan. He is mercenary and selfish and pagan and you know that you're none of these things! What's more, you've got Charlie Blakestone to help you out with your computer! He gives me a hand with my little tasks on my machine too. He's such a dear! To think he was such a confused and timid little boy when he first came here and now he's developed into this wonderful young man- and he's so gorgeous into the bargain! Oops, the wine must be speaking!'

Even in the company of Priscilla, John was careful not to lower his guard in the event of a remark of that kind. He did not dwell on the attractiveness of his pupils but, yes, he had to admit, Charlie had developed into a very good-looking and personable young man in whose company he delighted.

'Yes, we can be very proud of him,' he vouchsafed.

'Most of it is due entirely to you, of course: along with so many other boys over the years.'

'Other people too: you yourself for instance.'

'Well, none of it is due to the new young Alberich downstairs.'

'Priscilla, Bernard is too tall and burly to be an Alberich!'

'All-right' she giggled. 'And Delia is no Rhine Maiden!'

'This conversation is becoming unworthy, you naughty girl!'

'Yes, I'd better go. Douglas Macintyre put his arm through a window yesterday and we need to change the dressing.'

'Dear Doug: another one who has come on so well: a very nice lad.'

'Except for being entirely mal-coordinated, clumsy, untidy and lazy, yes- I'd be inclined to agree with you.'

John laughed.

'Oh, by the way, Jude Williams ought to be seeing you about a grazed shin. He says that he collected it at the match on Saturday but it looked a bit odd to me.'

'I'll chase him up. Byee!'

Another half an hour later, the Upper Sixth Boys' Chapel Group arrived. They were a bit thin on the ground this week, as the various conflicting commitments of a cluttered boarding school day intruded upon their best intentions. In the end, five boys turned up.

'Hey Sir! Look! Jude's on time! I grabbed him on the way up!'

Charlie beamed with engaging friendliness.

Jude looked faintly sheepish and said nothing.

John could not but chuckle as Charlie's quick eye immediately caught the plate of cakes provided by Priscilla. His friend, Tim, started to pour out glasses of orange juice and Coca-cola.

They had been considering the Beatitudes: Christ's celebrated teaching of Christian attitudes at the beginning of the Sermon on the Mount. This week, they were to discuss the sixth Beatitude:-

'Blessed are the pure in heart, for they will see God.'

'Now, *what* do we think that means for *us?*' asked John.

'It means having integrity,' stated Charlie. 'It means not being devious, not having false motives.' His eyes looked towards John, eyes clear with candour.

'Well,' said Chris, a slightly built cross-country runner, 'So far as us lot are concerned, I think it means that we shouldn't have dirty minds. We should watch it with the girls, a bit more perhaps than we do- or, at least than I do…….'

He blushed as he tailed off. The others laughed.

'Yeah, Chris,' said Tim. 'Tell that to Lucy.'

Poor Chris had committed an indiscretion during the previous summer term, for which he was genuinely penitent, but which his pals would not let him forget.

'Come on: that's enough,' interposed John.

'I'm not sure that I agree with that,' said Jude. 'I think that being 'pure in heart' means being true to yourself. We're all very complex and react at different times in different ways to different situations. Integrity isn't the same thing as simple-mindedness.'

'Well, OK,' said Charlie. 'And I've had my scrape with a girl too, before everybody reminds us. Mr Donaldson here helped me to sort it out. It happened before I really became a Christian. I'll extend what I said. I think that being 'pure in heart' means acting, speaking and thinking in a way that pleases God.'

'And you do that?' asked Jude, with a faint hint of a sneer.

'No, of course I don't,' answered Charlie, well accustomed not to rising to the bait of his cynical friend. 'I'm saying that that is what I *should* be doing. And I suppose that I do try- a bit: more than I used to anyway.'

'And you *are* a good example, Charlie,' encouraged John.

'Every-one knows that you are a Christian and what you stand for.'

'That can make it more difficult,' said Douglas. 'That's why I tend to keep rather quiet about it, I suppose. I just haven't got Charlie's courage.'

'It's not courage,' said Charlie. 'I'm just so grateful to think that God can love me when I'm the way I am.'

'I think that's pretty impressive,' said Tim. 'It must be quite difficult for you, Charlie.'

Jude and Chris both laughed.

'No, shut up!' said Tim sharply. 'I'm being serious. We all know that Charlie could easily pull a whole number of girls- probably more than any of the rest of us here- and yet people know that he doesn't because he's a Christian. And everybody respects that.'

'Well, I don't know,' said Jude more thoughtfully than before. 'It's very difficult. The standards demanded here are impossibly high. It makes me just want to give up.'

'You mustn't do that,' advised John. 'It is impossible for us to be perfect, as Jesus goes on to demand. But that is precisely why He died on the Cross. In doing that, He bore the weight of all our sins. That is the heart of the Christian message. But we've got to acknowledge the love behind that and do our best.'

And so the conversation proceeded for the next half an hour. They concluded with prayer. When they had all gone, John remained seated, deep in thought. After some minutes, he rose, closed the door of his flat, returned to his chair and knelt on the floor in silent prayer. This is what he prayed.

'Dear God, you know what I feel about those boys- about Jude and Charlie and, yes, Chris and Tim too. My own heart is impure, dear Lord; you know all things and you know that. I can't help it. I am flesh and blood and it is the way you made me. But you know too, merciful Father, that my *primary* concern- yes, it is my *primary* concern- is for their spiritual welfare. I thank you for Charlie's faith. I wish my life could be as clear as his. I pray for the others. I ask that you may give them assurance. And, Lord, I pray especially for Jude. He so needs you and he is struggling towards you. Reach out for him, dear Lord. Heavenly Father, you know that I find them beautiful. They're made in your image. I thank you for their beauty. Protect me, Lord; protect them from my baser instincts; confirm me in my ministry to them.'

He paused, sighed deeply, rose and returned to his desk.

FIVE

'Jude! Peggy, the cleaner in your passage, tells me that she changed the sheets on your bed yesterday morning because they had blood stains on them.'

'Yes, Matron, I noticed that she had done that. That was kind of her.'

'But why, Jude, did she have to do it?'

'Yeah, I thought you might be about to ask that.'

Jude switched on one of his most engaging smiles.

'And the answer? And don't tell me it was because of a football injury. Even *you* would not be mad enough actually to go to bed under normal circumstances when you were actively bleeding.'

'No, it wasn't during a football match.'

'And yet Mr Donaldson seems to think that you grazed your leg during the recent match. Does this mean that you lied to him?'

Pause.

'I take it that silence means that you probably did lie to him,' Priscilla continued.

'Well, Matron, I couldn't very well tell him what *did* happen, could I?'

He smiled again in appeal.

'You mean that you were out at night again in the grounds?'

'Yep, Matron. You always see straight through me.'

'But that still doesn't explain the blood on the sheets.'

'I had a fight in the dark with a blackberry bush. The bush won. The Bassett Hound was on the prowl and I took a wrong turning when I was trying to avoid him.'

'Smoking?'

''Fraid so.'

'What am I to do with you? You know what would happen if I were to report this.'

'I know, Matron. I'm very much hoping that you won't.'

'You said that last time.'

'I know. I'm sorry. I realise that it puts you in a difficult position.'

'Were you doing anything else? Or was it just going out for a smoke?'

'Grief! What else would I be doing?'

'I don't know. You tell me!'

'Honest to God, Matron, I swear I just went out for one quiet ciggy. Unfortunately, I chose the moment when the Hound decided to take a midnight stroll too.'

'You live a dangerous life in this place, Jude.'

'Yeah, I know. Sorry.'

He smiled again, knowing that he was going to be let off the hook.

'I'd better look at these cuts. We don't want them getting infected.'

'There's nothing much to them, really.'

'Stop prevaricating. I'd better look at those bony legs.'

Jude sat down and took off his shoes and his trousers.

'My legs are so hairy that it will be difficult to apply the ointment.'

Priscilla laughed.

'Come on, put it on yourself. You're not the only one with hairy legs!'

'True. Charlie and Chris are just as bad. So is Mr Ellman.'

'I'm sure that poor Mr Ellman doesn't want the details of his legs being discussed between a boy and his Matron.'

'I guess that the female members of staff probably fancy him rather a lot?'

'I really wouldn't know, Jude. Now, shut up! Get that stuff on and get out of here!'

'By the way, Matron. Mum asked me to tell you that a pair of boxer shorts didn't come back from the laundry.'

'Well, I don't know what I'm supposed to do about it. Who on earth would want to steal your underpants?'

'Can't imagine. Anyway, I've passed the message on.'

'Did they have a name tag sewn on?'

'Dunno. Probably. It's a bit odd though because Chris said that he'd also lost a pair.'

'I really can't be expected to keep track of sixty boys' pairs of underpants. If each boy wears a different pair every day and the laundry comes and goes every week and there are sixty boys in the House.......'

'That's eight-hundred-and-forty pairs of boxers for you to look out for, Matron,' said Jude, without even a second's delay. 'No need to get all stressed, Matron. I really don't care myself. It's my bloody mother who's making the fuss. How the Hell she knows, beats me....'

'Don't swear in my presence. Your mother is perfectly sensible to keep an eye on such things. It's more than her son does for himself.'

'Okay! Okay! Don't shoot the messenger!'

He pulled his trousers back on, tied the laces of his shoes and began to leave the room.

'Do try to keep out of any more trouble, Jude- seriously.'

'Don't worry, Matron. Nothing will ever go wrong again.'

'In our dreams,' muttered Priscilla.

She checked the hands on the carriage clock on her mantelpiece as he was leaving. She was just in time to switch on the early evening twenty minute programme which BBC 2 were currently screening, when one of a number of art historians presented a famous painting. This evening, the presenter was in the Louvre, commenting on Poussin's series of four pictures depicting the seasons. She found Vivaldi's accompanying music delightful even in its predictability.

Jude sauntered off to meet Olivia, his official girl-friend, under the great cedar tree, three hundred metres from the front of the College and close by the scene of his nocturnal encounter with the blackberry bush.

Olivia Kendall-Reid was, by general agreement, one of the most attractive girls in the College. Among the boys, there had been envy and surprise when Jude Williams had turned out to be the lucky man at the spin of the roulette wheel as the boys in the Sixth Form attempted to select their girl-friends.

'How the Hell did *he* pull *her*?' the aristocratic and wealthy Jasper Russell-Smythe had asked, loosening the top button of a shirt purchased the previous week-end from Pinks in Jermyn Street.

'Jude may not have your pedigree or your cash,' Charlie had pointed out, ever frank, 'but he knows how to get round women, believe me. I wouldn't set myself up in competition against him.'

'Oh, get real, Chips. Look at you, compared with him. Even I........'

Charlie's merry laughter had then goaded Jasper into indiscretion (never difficult).

'When you look at it though, Chips, he's nothing more than a skiv from Midhampton. What's his Mother? Some sort of shop assistant or something?'

'Jasper, don't be such a snob, for Heaven's sake! I'll have to buy you a teddy bear, like Sebastian Flyte! Actually, his Mother works in a doctor's surgery. It's probably a very responsible job. It's hardly their fault that his father took off the moment Jude was born.'

'So, she's a receptionist,' Jasper had mused, possibly even making an honest effort to imagine a role so very distant from his own social circle.

'I don't know what Mrs Williams is exactly. She may even be the practice manager. What does it matter?'

'What's a practice manager when it's at home?'

'We're doing 'Persuasion' in English with Scotty at the moment. You sound just like Sir Walter Eliot. And he had the excuse of living two-hundred years ago.'

'You're always making the point that you're in the top set for everything. Frankly, I think cramming for exams is for plebs.. It's frightfully lower middle class.'

This time it had been a joke, albeit a heavy-handed one; they had both burst out laughing.

'You're just a lazy git,' Charlie had said.

'This place is not for working; it's for networking.'

'Cliché. You'll be telling me again that you're here to walk the walk…….'

'…..and talk the talk. But, seriously, Chips, my parents *know* the Kendall-Reids. They have a flat in Chelsea as well as a house in Suffolk, just a few miles from our weekend place. We meet up with them socially. I can't see them ever sharing a bottle of Tesco's discounted plonk with Mrs Williams in Midhampton.'

'Such considerations don't normally prompt sexual attraction, do they? You are incorrigible, Jasper. My Mum does all our family shopping in Tesco's; there's nothing the matter with it. We don't all live within the calling range of Harrods' vans (not that, personally, I'd want to have much to do with its present proprietor). I do sometimes wonder why you and I remain such good friends. What do you say behind *my* back?'

'Oh, nothing too bad, I promise. I just excuse you for being a country bumpkin who lives on the farm, along with the chickens and the cows, sleeping every night on straw: a bit like Old Macdonald. Being a country bumpkin is certainly one stage up from being a jumped up nobody.'

Jasper had been aware that he was sending himself up quite as much as he was ridiculing Charlie. With his languorous slyness, he was quite prepared for Charlie's good-natured lunge at him. Despite Jasper's vocal detestation of all sport, he was tall and deceptively strong, cool and calculating. It was not the first time that Charlie had found himself held in a headlock, pulled off balance and spread-eagled flat on his back on the floor. With the minimal possible compromise to his own sense of dignity, Jasper proceeded to sit on Charlie and, pinning him firmly to the floor, set about tickling his friend with calm and ruthless efficiency.

'Oh! No! JASPER!' Charlie shrieked, convulsed with hysterical laughter. 'Anything but this! I surrender! You win!'

Charlie's legs thrashed about in helpless, symbiotic response to his captor's depredations. Jasper paused in his torture but still held Charlie's arms firmly down.

'It's *so* important that bumpkins know their place,' he drawled languidly. 'And to think you waste all that time running about in the mud, getting filthy, and finish up being completely overpowered by a London lounge lizard like me. What about under the arms?' Charlie howled with agony. 'Yes, most satisfactory. And further down the rib-cage? Dear me, aren't we ticklish?'

'You know I am, you bastard! Get off me!'

'Language, language, Chippy. A good Christian lad like you! And where did you find that *dreadful* shirt? The Oxfam shop? Or did the Salvation Army take pity on you?'

Jasper settled his substantially superior weight on Charlie's prostrate form, still maintaining an iron grip on his captive's slender wrists.

'God, Chips, for some-one who spends his entire life mucking out barns and rolling about on football pitches, I have to say that you are *so* beautiful- even if you are a wuss.'

Charlie, although still unable to move, had been given a brief chance to recover his breath.

A year or so ago, Jasper had, in a rare moment of anxious confidentiality, admitted his feelings for his friend. Charlie's quick and generous intelligence had absorbed the information with sang-froid. From that time on, Jasper had become another friend for whom he felt protective.

'How come you're so interested in Olivia then?'

'I didn't say that I felt *attracted* to her. How could I, with people like you around? I just disapprove socially of a skiv pulling a girl like her.'

'You know, Jasper, I still can't quite work out when to take you seriously.'

'It's surprising that my metropolitan wit eludes you, since you're Mr Scott's top Oxbridge candidate in English. I wonder if there's a built-in allowance for bumpkins from the provinces when Cambridge Colleges make their selection, even when these happen to come from public schools. This particular Government would surely want to accommodate every kind of social disadvantage.'

'Oh, do shut up! You talk such crap. NO! DON'T TICKLE ME AGAIN!'

After a brief further reminder to Charlie of his vulnerability, Jasper ceased inflicting his disproportionately effective torment but continued to pin him to the floor.

'I do wish that we could continue this conversation in different circumstances,' moaned Charlie, still in commendably good humour. 'I hate being tickled. But, anyway, your prejudice skews your judgment. You know I'm not the top candidate. Jude is light years cleverer than I am. The best I could be is the stalking horse. I work harder- that is true- and I'm better organised but, intellectually, he's certainly got the edge. And that's what gets you into these places.'

Jasper released Charlie and they both sat on the floor, facing each other. Jasper changed his tone.

'Chips! No way! I'm not going to take that! You're my best friend in this place, my only real friend. You *are* a scholar. You *know* you love your work. You're always quoting literature and that's because you know it and you enjoy it.

We have very different views and beliefs, you and I, over many things, but I respect you and……'- suddenly his South Kensington voice began to falter-'……..I love you. Oh, Chips, I'm sorry…..'

Abruptly, tears emerged and a pristine, gold, silk handkerchief was whisked out from nowhere, as if by a magician, as Jasper tried to catch the mixture of salt water and snot generated by this unexpected access of emotion.

Charlie was on his knees immediately and cradled Jasper in his arms.

'I know, Jasper, I know. And, although I can't return your feelings in the same way, I'll always love you as a friend. You know that already. There now, come on; come on.'

The sudden sharp storm had passed. They separated.

'I'm not just saying that to offer sympathy. I'm saying it because you *are* a friend. I love your wit and irreverence- yes, and your bloody cheek. You're huge fun to be with,' Charlie continued.

'Thanks. I'm sorry. I'm better now. I don't know what came over me. But, to go back to what we were saying, I'm *not* going to have you demeaning yourself, relative to that little creep. He might be bright- I can see that he is- but he's just as lazy as I am, with, if I might say so, less reason. And he is *not* a scholar like you. He couldn't care a shit about his work. You're always telling me how he's regularly late with essays and he only does them at all because he's scared of Mr Scott. Good for Mr Scott! They should bring back caning.'

'Oh, come on! You're off again!'

'No, I'm not. OK, forget about the caning- me being silly again- but, seriously, Chippy, I wouldn't trust that little bugger a fucking inch. And neither should you. He's trouble. And as for Olivia, God alone knows what she thinks she's doing.'

'Wow! You're not usually as direct as this!'

'No, I'm not. I'm probably being a silly old queen. Anyway, to change the subject, Mummy sent our driver up the other day with a few goodies. There's a bottle of Plymouth Gin and a bottle of Noilly Prat , both as yet unopened, together with some sort of terrine de canard. Let's go and sample some.'

'Jasper, you are outrageous! And so is your mother!"

'Well, of course I am! That's the only good reason for my being here! And, as for Mummy, she's hardly likely to be wetting her expensive silk knickers because of anything the Hound or G&T might presume to say!'

'We'll get murdered if the Hound catches us.'

Jasper looked at his watch.

'He won't. He'll be in his rugby shorts bathing his brats. What a ghastly prospect!'

'Doesn't Mrs Bassett do that? How come you know all this?'

'No. She hen-pecks him. Linda, the cleaner, told me all about it. She's a mine of useful information. It's amazing what a box of 'After Eights' can do! The Bassett-Bitch will be standing over the micro-wave, sipping her pre-prandial treat of medium sherry, while hubby is trying not to drown the Bassett puppies upstairs.'

'I'm sure she doesn't drink medium sherry! Nobody under eighty does these days! It's what my Granny has, in a tiny glass, before supper each evening.'

'How very bourgeois! And, as you yourself admit, *so* unfashionable.'

'I love my Granny very much. You can piss off!'

'You'll be telling me that it comes from Tesco's next.'

'Of course. Along with the microwave ready meal. Whereas your supplies have come from Harrods?'

'Possibly. Maybe Fortnum's. Anyway, stop holding us up! Let's go and drink to the perdition of all vulgarians- and skivs.'

SIX

'You're late.'

'Yes, Olivia. Sorry. I got held up by Matron. I scratched my leg slightly during the match the other day and Matron decided to have a psychic crisis over it. You'd think I was about to have one of my limbs amputated.'

Olivia did not laugh.

'Hey, Livvy, what's wrong?'

'You know what's wrong, Jude. The whole College knows what's wrong. The whole College knows that you've been two-timing me. I was probably about the last person here to know.'

'What, Olivia? What do you mean? Who with?'

Jude approached her with his arms outstretched.

'No, Jude! Don't touch me! How *can* you? And now you think you can treat me like some sort of idiot, who hasn't a clue about what's going on.'

'Well, what *is* going on- allegedly at least?'

'You *know* what's going on, Jude. You've been seeing….. her….'

Olivia broke off into tears but still she held him off. 'No! Don't *touch* me!'

'Who am I supposed to have been seeing- and who says?'

'You'll only deny it. And I know how you tell lies. You've even boasted about it to me. You were so pleased with yourself when you thought that you'd got away with lying to Rev. D last week about missing the football practice. By the way, did he believe you?'

'As a matter of fact, he didn't. So, you see, I'm not a very good liar.'

'Well, it rather proves the point that you needn't ask me to believe you now.'

'But I still don't know what I'm supposed to have done- or whom I am supposed to have been with.'

'Yes you do, Jude. You've been visiting Emma Morgan at night. All the girls seem to know and I expect that most of your friends among the boys do too.'

Jude gave a little dismissive laugh.

'Oh, that!'

'Yes, that! I like the way you try to laugh it off!'

'Oh, it was nothing- honestly, Livvy.'

A slight whine crept unintentionally into his voice.

'What do you mean, it was nothing? Creeping into another girl's room in the middle of the night! You'll be telling me next that you were just doing your prep. together.'

Jude abruptly changed his tactics. He raised both his hands in surrender.

'Okay! Okay! I did go and see her- just once. I was wrong to do so. I'm sorry. I was really needing some female company…..'

'In the middle of the night?'

'Let me finish, will you? You didn't seem to have been- how can I put it- terribly available…..'

'I bet *she* was 'available'. You won't need me to tell you just how 'available' she has been to most of the boys in the Upper Sixth. A pity that you've been so far down the queue when it comes to her selection. Some of those sweet little boys must have seemed much more desirable to her, with their virginity as yet quite unspoiled. She could have had the pleasure of teaching them what to do. Whereas you….'

'Fucking shut up, you slag!'

Jude stepped towards her in a sudden fury, his hand raised to strike her.

But Olivia was herself now so angry that she neither winced nor stepped back. She tossed her head back and her blue eyes blazed.

'Yes! Come on! Hit me! That's just about your level, isn't it? Why don't you save your slaps for the slapper?'

Jude lowered his hand and paused. His voice was low with restrained rage.

'You don't give me anything,' he said through his teeth. 'You just tease! We've never done it, have we? I've never even seen you undressed.'

'No, you haven't, Jude,' responded Olivia, 'and that's

because, as I've told you before, I'm not giving myself in sex to *anybody*- not until I'm ready. It's too easy to do so and I don't believe it's right. I told you that when we first started meeting and you, of course (as suited your convenience at the time) agreed. But perhaps you don't remember, because your memory operates to convenience too. If that's what you want, we're finished and you'd better go and fix an appointment in Emma Morgan's crowded night diary. She could probably fit you in every so often. You're supposed to be a Christian, Jude. I'm less sure than you seem to be about where I stand over all that but, for you, it should be a clearer case. I wonder what your friend, the Rev. D, would think about this. *I* haven't seen *you* fully undressed either and, frankly- call it immaturity if that suits you- I'm not ready to do so. But,' and here she suddenly softened, 'I have seen you partly undressed, of course, (this sounds so silly!) and you *know* how sexy I find you. That, together with your being such a great footballer and so intelligent and such fun. Oh, Jude!' And now she started to cry. 'I'm really angry with myself but I *do* still love you. I shouldn't, Jude, but I do!'

Jude found himself uncharacteristically moved too. His eyes glistened.

'I know, Livvy. I'm really sorry. I shouldn't have used that filthy word about you. It was horrible of me and obviously untrue. I was just looking for something nasty to say. And, of course, what you say is what we agreed. Please try to forgive me. Emma Morgan means nothing to me. It was just a bloke feeling frustrated and being weak and needing an outlet. It was quite wrong. I promise I'll never see her again. Please try to forgive me.'

They moved towards each other and hugged. He kissed her hair. He could feel her small firm breasts pressed against his chest. Each felt tenderness for the other at that moment, as well as self-pity.

'Yes, of course. I'm sorry too,' snuffled Olivia. 'I've had so much work to do. I've been up late trying to get through it all. I take ages over those English essays and now they're piling it on in History and French too. That's another reason I haven't been seeing you so much. I'm so sorry.'

'I know. I wish I worked as hard as you did. Charlie and you really put the rest of us to shame.'

'Charlie's a good friend. Perhaps you should confide in him a bit. He's such a good person.'

'Yeah, he's easily my closest friend- amongst the boys at least.'

The bell in the clock-tower chimed.

'I'd better get back,' said Olivia. 'And so had you. I don't want you getting into any more trouble.'

'I'll follow. I'm glad we've sorted this out. It was all my fault. See you after supper.'

They gave each other a parting kiss and Jude watched her walk back to Old College. He took a few steps back into the copse and hurriedly fumbled in his pocket for a cigarette. He snapped the lighter on and drew hard on the nicotine. That first inhalation was so good. As he breathed the smoke out from deep in his lungs, he felt headily relaxed. He made an honest attempt to clarify his thoughts, thoughts which, however, were complex and contradictory and elusive.

Jude thought that he loved Olivia. Certainly, she was very important to him. She was a looker, no doubt about that. In fact, she was quite beautiful. And, yes, she was a status symbol in the place. Jude recognised that that consideration was unworthy but he could not deny that its truth appealed to him. She was also clever academically and he definitely respected her seriousness, common sense and moral virtue as strengths. The fact that so many of the lads lusted after her, without her head being turned even a fraction, was pretty impressive. He knew that he should safeguard his good fortune rather more carefully.

Olivia's very purity attracted Jude but it was also a frustrating stumbling block. He tried to rationalise morally his nocturnal visits to Emma Morgan. Yes, sure, they were plain wrong when judged against his relationship with Olivia and also when measured against the Christian faith which he genuinely thought he possessed. They compromised both of these central concerns. And yet, God must know his basic need too. God had made him a creature of flesh, after all. The thrill and, even more, the relief, of sex was something which, once tasted, he could not live without. Moreover, Emma herself was also attractive. He called her into his imagination now. He visualised her dark hair and lively dark eyes and her perfect slim figure. She was tall (three inches taller than Jude in fact) but carried her height with studied elegance. Jude was well aware that, for both of them, their relationship did not extend much beyond carnality. His interest in Emma was erotic, neither more nor (and this was the rub) less. He knew that, beyond that, their lives were very different and that Emma, beyond her appearance, was merely an upper class airhead who lacked the grit even of her socially ambitious mother, who had ditched Mr Morgan to marry into a title. He was fully aware also that Emma had done the rounds with several of his pals. Charlie himself had once been bewitched into swapping his trousers for her well tried bed. It had happened a year ago, on the only occasion when Charlie had been tempted to go to one of the London Exeat parties. It had also been the only time in his life when Charlie had allowed himself to become hopelessly drunk. Unlike Jude, Charlie had then stepped back decisively from the enchantress. Shocked and distressed by his confusion, Charlie had bent his will in a more unitary direction, flinging himself on Rev. D as a launching pad, rather like a Tigger with brains.

Jude's train of association moved on to the Rev. D. What should he really make of him? That he was a good man, who contributed to the moral and spiritual commonwealth, Jude had no doubt. Presumably he was gay, poor old thing, and had had a sequence of crushes on handsome boys year after year. Jude was sufficiently cruel in his adolescence to find that slightly amusing, especially since it could hardly be more obvious that Charlie and he had both, it seemed, been nominated as special favourites. The clergyman tried so hard to cover up his feelings. Jude grinned to himself as he recalled the other day in the changing room. How Rev. D had enjoyed stroking his scratched shin! And yet, and yet: here again was a human being of self-disciplined restraint. Jude knew that Rev. D would never harm a boy, however strong his feelings. Moreover, he, Jude, by nature rather cynical (and proud of it), a boy who, prior to coming within the Chaplain's sphere of influence, firstly through Charlie and then through the football, hadn't given religion more than a moment's thought, had been profoundly impressed by the life and claims of Jesus as these had been presented by Rev. D. Indeed, Jude thought that he probably believed; he certainly was no longer the priggish little atheist which he once had been. Nevertheless, it irked him that, because Charlie Blakestone was his best friend, and he had freely joined the Rev. D's Upper Sixth Form boys' Chapel group, every-one assumed that he shared, unquestioningly, their particular code of beliefs. Perhaps he did; he wasn't sure; other claims on his life suggested perhaps not. Moreover, there was the nagging issue of the Rev. D's motives. Of course they were honourable, and righteously influential, but there was pretty obviously an element of self-gratification there too. But then, so what? Did that matter? Wasn't it true of every-one?

To be sure, Jude was aware that his mother had changed her view of the Rev. D. To begin with, she had been deeply grateful to him for his support for Jude. But, ever since Jude had, jokingly as it happened, suggested the likely truth about the Chaplain's sexuality, she had mistrusted the Rev. D's motives. Jude and his mother had had one of their blazing rows about it. He accused her of being homophobic. The Rev. D, who used to go to the house in Midhampton for supper every few weeks, was no longer welcome. Jude was particularly annoyed about this for two reasons. The first was because his mother had not had the guts to come clean to the Rev. D and the poor man must have felt confused when she kept putting him off over the 'phone. The second reason, which caused a gloomy shadow to cross his face even as he thought of it now, was his suspicion that his mother had been happy to drop the Rev. D when her sudden suspicion of his homosexuality had coincided with the irruption of the dreadful Mike into both their lives. Perhaps, Jude wondered, his own problems with girls had a direct genetic connection to the instability which characterised both his parents: the father who had scarpered when his son was born and his mother, whose judgment over potential life partners misfired unerringly each time. Mike though, Jude thought, must surely have been the worst news yet, a 'chav' if ever there was one. He closed his eyes as he involuntarily brought to mind Mike's patronising interference: the garage proprietor, all weight problem, facial hair and heavy male jewellery, who was suspicious of public schools (Jude, after all, had not asked to come to Moreton College at the age of twelve but had accepted his Mother's bright-eyed verdict when he had won a full academic scholarship) and who regularly proceeded to give Jude dreary lectures about 'the university of life', placing his flabby bulk between mother and son as issues arose, passing on advice to Lynn Williams about how to handle the boy. Initially, Lynn had sworn at Jude when her son had compared Mike's range of vocabulary unfavourably with that of some of the less articulate characters in 'East Enders'. However, perhaps the tide was turning.

'It's not the playing of the game that counts, young Jude, it's the winning,' Mike had chortled, pleased by his own wit.

'Wow! That was as funny as it was original,' had been Jude's riposte.

'Cheeky little bugger! Why don't you let me have a hand in sorting him out, Lynn?' Mike had shouted, glaring wrathfully and making as to raise his large, fleshy hand in Jude's direction.

'Mike! Don't you dare touch him! You'll be out of this house quicker than your shit can be flushed down the lavatory pan if you as much as lift a finger to Jude!'

'Oh, sorry, Lynn!' faltered the bully, genuinely surprised by his own misjudgement. 'No need to take on like that. I was only trying to support you.'

'Well, you can keep your opinions to yourself when it comes to Jude. I know he can be a difficult, lippy little sod but he's my son and it's none of your business.'

'All-right, Lynn, All-right! I've got the message. I was only trying to help.'

Jude loved his mother passionately and he had been grateful to her for that.

Anyway, Mike and his mother were having rows themselves now. Lynn had turned down Mike's kind offer to come and live with them, thank God, and Jude surmised that the fat slob might be unlikely to have a serious future in their lives. He certainly hoped so, at least.

Although Charlie's analytical powers were more consistent than those of Jude, Jude had the intelligence of a poet. Perhaps life *wasn't* all of a piece. Perhaps it was altogether a far more muddled affair, with conflicting realities colliding with each other on a restless and a violent sea. Perhaps all these simple truths could not be confined each one within its own hermetically sealed compartment. Perhaps they were out to get each other by the throat: Christianity, sex, social responsibility, familial loyalty, honesty. Anyway, what is honesty? Can it be simple? Is it not just an acceptance of the muddle, a need to perceive the conflicts that make us what we are? Perhaps the truly honest thing is to prioritise these warring claims and aspirations if one is to approximate a wholeness of response. Perhaps, further to this, priorities must alter, according to shifts in situation.

Jude considered that, in that case, those whose lives were considered to be ennobled by moral clarity (Olivia, Charlie, Rev. D) and who might be inclined, however generously, to judge his inconsistencies, were perhaps themselves dishonest. He sighed as he threw the cigarette butt away. 'What is truth?' Perhaps Pontius Pilate was too easily dismissed when asking that question of Christ. Jude didn't know. Somehow it would all have to work itself out.

Still, there was one point of simple clarity in his life. That was his soccer. Never, for a moment, had his enthusiasm for the game dimmed. Yes, he supported Arsenal and tried to get to the Gunners' home matches during the school holidays, though he wasn't prepared to traipse round the country with all the mindless clones who were happy to sit in 'buses in traffic jams on motorways and hurl insults upon arrival at Old Trafford or Anfield. But his real joy was in the playing of the game and, indeed, for once aligning with Mike, in the winning. The exhilaration of running across the pitch, combining natural speed, co-ordination and foresight in outwitting opponents, with the manoeuvre culminating in an orgasmic delight every time he scored, never dimmed. The adrenaline rush uplifted him into bliss. True, he enjoyed the adulation of his team-mates and the approval of Rev. D and others but the pure immediacy of the action itself often provided a clear, defined focus of happiness during even the most perplexing of weeks. This was the simple, sunlit, breath-taking summit of positive certainty, uncluttered by the competing vegetation and meandering paths which obscured and misdirected in the valleys and foothills of adolescent life. Take that away and it would indeed be difficult to cope.

'Jude Williams!' shouted the Bassett Hound, red with

anger. 'Thanks for turning up! We're only ten minutes into the important House Assembly which I had told everybody about yesterday. See me in my study afterwards!'

'Sorry Sir,' mumbled Jude as every-one turned round to see his scruffy figure sidling into the back of the room. Jude noticed Charlie shaking his head compassionately and Chris's conspiratorial grin.

SEVEN

The Upper Sixth Parents' meeting was in full flow in the Great Hall. Printed notices erected on tall poles indicated the various academic departments. Parents queued to see the teachers, who, all wearing suits and gowns, stood at intervals along the room, with mark-books in hand and grave expressions on their faces, weird personifications of anachronism. This was the image the parents wanted and the Headmaster was only too happy to provide. Many of the parents were members of the same social club and quenched the indignity of queuing by catching up on gossip and comparing notes on their offspring and the College. The braying laughter of pin-stripe-suited fathers wearing distinguished ties mingled with the Sloane Square shrieks of their wives. The mothers teetered on patent leather high heels, their long, shapely legs shown to advantage, as Harvey Nichols skirts, with more or less discreet vents to the side, clung tightly to their thighs. Their breasts were so well formed that some of them at least might have been implanted; costly jewellery adorned their chests. Their faces were immaculately covered in discreetly expensive cosmetics. Some alternative dwellers had deliberately dressed down, self-consciously refusing to be intimidated by the establishment, or indulging in inverted snobbery: thin men, wearing several days' stubble, t-shirts and blue jeans or, not bothering at all, large, horsy women from the county set.

Lynn Williams flitted around, always feeling a bit like a fish out of water but determined to put on a discreetly confident show, while remaining as inconspicuous as possible. Given the press of the crowd, she successfully avoided the Chaplain. She had rejected Mike's offer to accompany her. She felt no loyalty to this place, with its loud, complacent grandeur. Her conversations about her son were clipped and defensive. She was clear that he (and she) were there to receive rather than to give.

Geoffrey Tansley made a gradual and noisy progress the length of the Hall, distinguished from his inferiors by the additions of academic hood and mortar board, his half-moon spectacles dangling across his waistcoat. Parents were eager to catch his eye and he was equally keen to impress and reassure. A certain tribute might well be paid to the man when even people who could afford to hand over more than £20,000 a year could be reduced to a level of servility in his presence.

But here was a thing. In the midst of this populous and claustrophobic social dance, a row was taking place. It was between Lady Wolseley, the Mother of Emma Morgan, and Alexander Scott, the Head of the English Department.

'But *why* do you never give Emma more than a Grade C for her coursework? She finds it *so* discouraging.'

'I'm sorry that she finds it discouraging but I can't invent marks. The examination board would probably notice fairly quickly.'

'But other schools let them write their coursework again and again until they get higher marks. Why doesn't Moreton do this?'

'Lady Wolseley, that would *not* be a good idea for a number of reasons. Other schools which I deal with do not do that. I do meet other Heads of English to discuss these matters. We are generally in agreement about that.'

'But her cousin at St Agatha's was allowed to repeat her work. I want Emma to be given the same chance.'

'I'm not going to alter our policy, Lady Wolseley, for Emma or for any-one else.'

'But why? This is so unreasonable.'

'If you would just give me a chance, I shall give you three good- indeed, compelling- reasons. Firstly, it is specifically against the rules of the examination board. I am not prepared to perjure myself by signing a promise that I have not done precisely what you are asking me to do. Secondly, if Emma spends week after week writing the same assignment, she will get hopelessly behind with all her other work, both in English and in her other subjects. And, finally, a C Grade is (I have to say) a just reflection of Emma's probable ability and it possibly even slightly flatters her effort.'

'She tries terribly hard to please you and gets so upset when you give her no encouragement at all.'

'No. She doesn't try terribly hard. She looks half asleep most of the time, especially first thing in the morning. Only yesterday, I felt constrained to remark about her yawning in class.'

'That's *so* rude! No wonder she's frightened of you. That's really bad teaching. Perhaps she was yawning because she finds your lessons boring.'

Alexander Scott flushed with anger.

'I have no idea why she's yawning. The fact that nobody else in the class yawns suggests that my lessons are not boring. Additionally, the fact that most of the other pupils have scored A or B grades on their coursework does not suggest defective teaching. Given that context, most people would be sufficiently objective to work out that the result points to a deficiency in ability or effort on the part of the individual pupil.'

An immensely rich lady who lunches in high society, Lady Wolseley's bright, dark eyes flashed in mingled contempt and fury.

'That's *so, so rude*. You are one of rudest men I have met. I am going to make a complaint.'

'It is not rude at all. It is a fair, objective and experienced judgment of a pupil's ability and effort. The fact that you don't like it is another matter.'

'I'm going straight to the Headmaster to complain about your rudeness.'

'Yes, well just you do that! There he is, over there, with a long queue waiting. Your silly and insulting threat carries no weight with me. The Headmaster isn't going to over-rule, let alone sack, *me* after more than thirty years' successful teaching.'

'We'll see about that!'

'Madam, you're making yourself ridiculous. Now, you must excuse me; I can see that *I* now have a queue developing. I have no more to say about the matter. I'm sorry that you're dissatisfied.'

And, with that dismissal, the Head of the English Department, glasses glinting, turned to his next interview, seeing, with relief, a grinning Bill and a sympathetic Sue Blakestone, both waiting with discreet curiosity.

An hour or so later, Alexander Scott, who, this exception apart, was generally respected by pupils and parents alike, if slightly feared by the former, threw his academic gown onto a chair in the Senior Common Room, poured himself a stiff Scotch from the bar, added a splash of soda and collapsed into his favourite armchair. He imbibed a generous swig of his restorative and sighed with relief.

John Donaldson revealed himself from behind a copy of The Times.

'Thank God that's over for another year,' said the peppery English master. 'John, you don't still read that rag, do you, now that it has degenerated into a Murdoch tabloid? Just look at that front page, dominated by a photograph of some pop star with dark specs and no tie.'

'Oh dear, Alexander. Have you had a difficult meeting?'

'There are just such a lot of people to deal with when one teaches so many A level sets. But, no, I shouldn't complain. Most of them are nice enough, aren't they, like the majority of their children. I did have a horrible encounter with that Wolseley harridan.'

'Oh her! I think you're joining a fairly large club!'

'I think I'm probably honorary President of it after this afternoon! Anyway, she's off to complain to G&T, ha ha! Good luck to her!'

'What on earth did you say?'

'Just the truth, John! Just the truth about that undistinguished mannequin of mediocrity, her daughter.'

'I can imagine that English Literature probably isn't Emma Morgan's strength.'

'You can say that again! But the Mother! Talk about poisonous pretentiousness, arse-aching arrogance, snobbery and obtuseness and you would still be doing her a favour she didn't deserve! The French are so much better at describing people like her. They have so many different options: *arriviste, parvenu, nouveau*. Mind you, I suppose that Jane Austen didn't do too badly. Lady Wolseley is, I believe, what Mary Musgrove described as 'one of your new creations."

Mr Scott's lashing tongue was famed throughout the College. Most of the girls and the more timid boys were occasionally terrified of him and the most awkward adolescents took no risks in the classroom when he was in charge. One self-regarding, ice cool, pimply, peer group leader in the Fifth Form had lost his status at a single blow when, as an immediate result of being verbally demolished by 'Scotty' for arriving late to the lesson, he had literally begun to wet his pants when standing in front of the class. Far too frightened to ask to leave the room, this stud manqué had sat in dismal discomfort for the next forty minutes, to be mercilessly teased by the boys and shunned by smirking girls thereafter. Mr Scott's aura of authority was maintained effortlessly and entirely without any need to resort to punishment. His colleagues, especially the younger ones, treated him with healthy respect and even the Headmaster was happy to consult him informally behind the backs of his appointed senior drones. Having taken a first class degree from Cambridge, he was one of the last of the Leavisites, albeit more catholic and accommodating in his literary sympathies than the celebrated founder of the Scrutiny School, and his uncompromising rigour in textual analysis had stood many of his cleverer pupils in good stead. For many years, the College's 'Oxbridge' results had been shored up by the English Department. The brighter boys (and some of the girls: those who combined intelligence with a degree of boldness) genuinely appreciated Mr Scott's scholarly range, his immense and serious enthusiasm for his subject and, in the case of the likes of Jude and Charlie, his devastatingly acidic wit. Jude could even rally to this occasionally and draw a wintry smile from his intellectual icon, a risk that Charlie would never consider taking.

Nevertheless, despite his formidable reputation, Alexander Scott (none of his colleagues dared contract his first name), cared deeply for the welfare of his pupils and his judgment of them was unerringly exact. He had, for example, upon taking over the boy's English teaching in the Sixth Form, quickly realised that the amiable and mildly self-effacing Charlie Blakestone was in fact a very clever boy. A month or so into the Lower Sixth, Charlie had been brusquely summoned to Mr Scott's study. The class had handed in an essay on Keats' odes the previous week and had not yet received it back. It had been the sixteen-year-old Charlie's first encounter with the Poet of Melancholy and, always quick to perceive and imagine his own limitations, the boy had wondered what on earth he had done wrong when the minatory summons came. He was so nervous when he gingerly entered the irascible master's study that he was ready to burst into tears when the first shot was fired. He prayed to God to see him through the ordeal (*'Dear Jesus, I know I don't deserve your help and I've done all sorts of wrong things but please, please let him not be too angry with me; you know I did my best; I can't help it if I got it wrong.'*). Charlie's thought that his first serious disciplinary confrontation at the College would be with the most fearsome master in the school, three years into his career there, had filled him with dread all afternoon. He had had one of those moments when he just wanted to go away and live in some other existence. As Mr Scott had swung round briskly from his desk in his swivelling chair, Charlie's bony knees had literally started to knock together. He did not normally stammer but found himself doing so on this occasion.

'Y-you w-wanted to s-see me, Sir?'

'Why, yes indeed! Do sit down! No, no! In that armchair, there!'

Mr Scott had retained his own higher status by remaining in the swivelling business-like chair by his desk, even though the desk was now behind him and he could face Charlie directly.

Charlie had immediately realised that this was not going to be a hostile meeting.

'Jesus, I thank you with all my heart. You heard my prayer. Thank you! Thank you!' Thus had come the silent prayer.

'This essay on Keats now, Blakestone- forgive me, I'm sometimes slow with names- Charles, isn't it?-'

'Yes Sir, thank you, Sir, Charlie Sir,'

'Oh God, I've gone and done it now. That's too informal. God, I'm sorry; I didn't mean to screw up!'

'Charlie- that's what you prefer?'

'Yes Sir, if that's all-right Sir. Thank you Sir.'

'Well, of course it's all-right if you prefer it, Charlie. Please don't be nervous. I asked you to come to see me because this essay on Keats, for some-one new to this work, is really excellent.'

'What?! Sir, I didn't think it was any good. I spent ages on it and I didn't know what the answer to *The Nightingale* was. There didn't seem to me to *be* an answer. He sets the bird up as an ideal and then it flies away. That was the best I could make of it. As you said, Sir, you let us loose on it and we hadn't done it in class yet and it just all seemed quite unresolved to me and so, I'm afraid – or, rather, had been afraid- was my essay. And then the notes at the back referred to 'Negative Capability', without explaining what that was but made a reference to his letter to his younger brother, Tom, and so I went to the Library and found the letter and, although he was writing about Shakespeare, it seemed to apply to 'The Nightingale' and also, I thought- or wondered, rather, to 'The Grecian Urn', but I really wasn't sure and, well, Sir, I was worried about the essay- about getting hold of the wrong end of the stick, but I didn't know what else to write.......' Charlie had tailed off, blushing uncomfortably, conscious of having rambled on far too much.

'But, Mr Blakestone,' (the skilful teacher's quick diagnosis of inappropriately low self-esteem in a pupil being elevated by a teasing little alteration to nomenclature) 'that is *exactly* the point and you, Sir, are one of the very few pupils whom I have had the privilege of encountering who has understood this for himself without any assistance from me and who has done so just a few weeks into his Sixth Form career. And, Charlie, I may say that your written style is a pleasure to read. You make no mistakes and express yourself with poise and elegance. You took obvious trouble over both thinking this quite sophisticated issue through and writing about it. Moreover, you clearly have the literary intelligence to do both extremely well.'

'Well, thank you, Sir! I am enjoying reading Keats and, now that I find I've got it right (or, at least, not wrong), I do feel more confident.'

Charlie then proceeded to check his judgment on 'The Grecian Urn' and was gently led by his teacher to make comparisons between the odes and 'St Agnes' Eve', the only narrative poem by Keats which the boy had so far read. Mr Scott then asked Charlie to note down a line of elegiac melancholy detectable through later poets, possibly all influenced by Keats: Tennyson, Arnold, Hardy, Owen. The schoolmaster was delighted when, within a fortnight, a further, unsolicited, slightly less timid, knock at the door, presented a Charlie Blakestone who had read all that had been recommended and was bursting to suggest perceived comparisons. Thus began the boy's career as a serious literary scholar himself.

Now, however, as a tired teacher, no longer very young, in the privacy of the Common Room, after a long parents' meeting, Alexander Scott could bemoan some of the limitations of modern educational practice with two trusted colleagues. Anthony Ridell had come into the room behind him and had approached the whisky bottle with similar expedition.

'Come on, Padre, we know you don't mind a snifter,' said the Head of History.

John folded the newspaper away and was happy to listen sympathetically (and, in part, at least, empathetically) to them.

'What did you do to the Wolseley woman, Alexander? She was far keener to moan about you than to discuss her daughter's History.'

'Oh, do shut up about that! I'm just trying to put her out of my mind.'

'Oops! Sorry!'

Anthony caught John's faint shake of the head.

'Well, just before we leave the topic, she got into more trouble when she tried to push in at the front of G&T's queue. I didn't recognise the parents but they weren't having any of it! Anyway, Old Thing, your glass needs filling. Here, give it to me.'

'Two pieces of good news within one remark. Thank you, Anthony.'

'Since you're both here, did G&T tell you that he'd got our letter about all the IT nonsense but that he'd passed it on to the Fulwell woman to deal with?'

'Well! Isn't that nice of him!' said Alexander. 'I feel that I've really been taken seriously.'

'And, of course, we got Cressida's reply. So, I guess that that's the end of that!' added John.

'So, here we are,' continued Anthony, 'the three longest serving colleagues in the College and the Headmaster can't even be bothered to send a written reply to the serious points that we've raised about a major change in College policy.'

'At least he deigned to speak to *you* about it.'

'It was just chance. I happened to walk past his study as he emerged.'

'All cynicism apart, I'm afraid that it really worries me a lot,' said John, appealing to his colleagues. 'I just can't cope with it. I'm not 'computer-literate' and I don't think I ever will be. It's just so alien to me. When we've got to do all those things which we've been so used to doing for years, I'm going to get absolutely stuck. Like both of you, I don't like the principle of it anyway but, in the immediate term, I just can't seem to find the basic technological understanding. I've been to Lee Crowther's 'INSET' sessions but, honestly, I haven't understood a word. All the young ones want to sweep on to all sorts of high-powered, complex things when I just want the basics. I think *you've* cracked it, Anthony, haven't you? For you, you are fighting for principle. But how about you, Alexander? Do you actually understand it?'

'Well, a bit, but not really. I certainly have no interest in it.'

'But how do you manage?'

'Ah! Well! That's where Cordelia comes in! She's the computer wizard in our household and so I don't really need to bother. But, listen, dear man! You *must not* worry about it like this. It's all a load of interfering crap and *you* have got far more important things to do and think about. What does it matter if Big Brother's nose is put out of joint because information, much of it entirely pointless in any case, is submitted in the 'wrong' format or is a day or two late? Who's going to do anything about it? You're not here to be an Information Technology guru, thank God. You're here as a Chaplain and, after twenty years, as every-one knows, whatever our own private beliefs might be, you are a very distinguished one. You *must not* get yourself into a state because of a bloody computer and the robotic nonentity who runs it. If Crowther can't explain it adequately to some-one of your intelligence, that's hardly a comment on *you!* Don't you agree, Anthony?'

'Absolutely. You know I do. Honestly, John, I think that loads of people are having difficulty with it. The difference is that you're being honest about it and you're so strictly conscientious. Alexander is quite right. You mustn't worry about it. I'm certainly not as proficient as you seem to think. I just play along with the system as best I can. In any case, it goes wrong half the time! For example, if every-one uses the same programme simultaneously, to conform to these ridiculous, arbitrary dead-lines, it all just crashes; so nobody can do it!'

'Have faith, man!' added Alexander. 'Come on! That's what you tell the rest of us! Entry into the Kingdom of Heaven is hardly going to depend upon careful subscription to a network of tabulated gobbledegook invented by Lee Crowther! Come on! You're behind us with the Scotch! I insist you have another one!'

As Alexander Scott poured out more drinks, he moved onto another vexed question.

'While we're complaining about things, what do you make of the Fulwell woman's new Health and Safety regulations?'

'Oh God!' said Anthony, Ridell, putting his hand to his head.

'Easy, Anthony,' said John.

He was true to his rule of never allowing the name of God to pass if taken in vain.

'Sorry, Padre. I know it offends you. I didn't mean to do that. But it is exasperating. We've just had to write out so much blurb about taking the Fourth Form to the First World War sites for a long week-end. The sheer effort, to say nothing of the frightening warnings of accountability, really make one want to pause about doing it at all.'

'That must be a nightmare. We get all this about theatre trips too. Last week, Valerie Samuels had asked me to give the monthly breakfast lecture at the university. It was on Tennyson and it seemed a good idea to invite four of our chaps who are planning to take English further. When I booked a taxi for them, like you, I had the Fulwell 'Risk Assessment' form. I ask you! Four clever and resourceful eighteen-year-olds, travelling four miles in a taxi, to hear a lecture given over breakfast by their English teacher at the local university!'

'So, what did you write, Alexander?' asked Anthony, smiling.

'Good. I was hoping that you would ask that.'

'I know you were.'

'I'm being perfectly serious:-

1. The taxi driver, despite knowing the road backwards and blindfolded, might cause his vehicle to leave the road and kill them all.

2. Despite being eighteen-year old adults of above average intelligence, they might all step off the kerb in the town centre and be mown down by a bus. After all, it happened to Gaudi in Barcelona, only it was a tram.

3. The university might inadvertently (at least, I hope it would be inadvertent) poison them over breakfast.'

'All this rubbish has, of course, never been read by anybody and is languishing in some file somewhere in the Fulwell woman's office. There again, I suppose it is the sort of fascinating data which the Director of Studies himself might read at night as he sips his Ovaltine. It might even excite him into a cardiac arrest. Here's hoping!'

Alexander Scott raised his glass as Anthony Ridell chuckled. John Donaldson wrinkled his face in tolerant disapproval. Without being smug, he was never willing to go along with snide remarks about colleagues, even the ones he found the most trying.

'The trouble is, Alexander,' mused the Head of History, 'if we didn't fulfil the regulation and something *did* go wrong, we'd be in big trouble. This must affect you with your football, John; doesn't it?'

'Sport seems to be exempt at present. I'm glad about that, of course, but it does seem illogical because the sports field is the most obvious place for an accident. I expect it'll all come.' John started looking gloomy again. 'And, when it does, it will involve some immensely complicated manoeuvre on the computer.'

His two colleagues smiled.

'But, seriously,' said Alexander, 'Isn't it ridiculous that here we are- three intelligent, experienced schoolmasters, who went into the job because we loved our subjects (or, in your case, John, your spiritual vocation) and genuinely wanted to teach the young- here we are, talking about computers and risk assessment forms, imposed upon us by (I'm going to be frank) our intellectual and professional inferiors, in response to the interfering dictates of a philistine government. They all think they're so enlightened and yet Dickens was attacking the same nonsense in 'Hard Times' a century and a half ago.'

'To be fair to our colleagues,' said John, 'they are obeying government legislation.'

'I know,' replied Alexander, 'but how they enjoy it! You're always teaching the rise of Hitler in the History Department these days, Anthony,.....'

'That's not fair. We do other things as well,' interrupted his colleague.

'Well, anyway, the application counts in this situation. If you have an intellectually corrupt system, imposed by ambitious, self-regarding nobodies, whose priorities have nothing to do with cultural, aesthetic or spiritual values, insofar as these can be at all objectively defined, and a government who alters standards to create statistical lies which flatter its own public statement of success, education, as *we* understand it, is placed under serious threat. What do Tansley and the Fulwell woman and Crowther and the Minister of Education and the Prime Minister care about Shakespeare and the Bible and Mozart and necessary scientific exploration and all the rest of it? What do they *know* about them? What sense of a European cultural tradition do they have, based on Scripture and the classics? Next to none. We- the three of us and several others, who have either retired or got out- used to spend time in this room, on these chairs, talking about literature and history and theology and philosophy and the theatre and the opera and the wider political scene. And now, here we are, moaning about the petty stupidities of Fulwell and Crowther and how we hate Information Technology and Risk Assessment and how to dodge the idiocies of Political Correctness and dealing with parents who want their stupid offspring to repeat writing drivel in order to cheat a cumbersome and inaccurate scheme of assessment. Do you know, assessment (as it now has to be termed) is divided into five 'Assessment Objectives' for A level English these days? Each of them is bloody obvious but each box has to be ticked by the 'assessor at the centre'. (We are no longer 'teachers at a school'). The Department is in a constant frenzy of terror in case they miss something out. Tom Stevens, for instance, is up half the night, squandering his First Class Degree from Oxford, agonising over whether or not he has got it all right. He will be wondering at one in the morning whether or not that lazy little tart, Emma Morgan, should be given fifteen or sixteen out of thirty for her badly plagiarised attempt at an essay, for example- as though it matters in the slightest, for Heaven's sake? Even more annoying, is that the pupils pick all this up. A clever, conscientious girl like Olivia Kendall-Reid called the other day, worried sick. Was she coming to talk about 'Mansfield Park', which she has been reading, musing perhaps on the virtues and limitations of Fanny Price? Not a bit of it. She had downloaded the syllabus from the Internet and was concerned to find that Assessment Objectives 2 and 5 were blurred into a miasma of indistinct duplication. Well, of course, she's right; they are. I then find myself refusing to defend the syllabus which the girl is studying because, if I do so, she'll think that I'm a party to this garbage, sharing in all its ill considered lack of clarity. My lack of belief in it all then makes her even more apprehensive.'

'Yes, well, I can assure you that we have similar problems in History,' sighed Anthony Ridell.

But Alexander Scott was not so easily to be stopped when in full flow and the whisky assisted in the sharper articulation of his deep-seated anger over the ills of the current curriculum.

'I'm sure you do. I don't doubt it. But, forgive me; it's hardly a matter for 'assurance', I would have thought. And another thing. John, you mentioned the dreaded word 'INSET' a moment ago.'

'Oh, another dreadful form to fill,' said the Chaplain, despairingly.

'Well, it's not *that* dreadful; it's pretty basic and silly,' snapped Alexander, becoming steadily crosser as he considered the catalogue of ills that were afflicting modern education. 'Did I tell you both about my row with Ms Fulwell over that?'

They both agreed that he had not done so.

'Well, as you know, that cow- stop wincing, John, for Heaven's sake, I can't bear it-'required' all her colleagues to fill up this thing, declaring 'In Service Training' undertaken during the past two years. As you also know, I drive across to the Faculty in Cambridge each month to hear a literary lecture given by some distinguished luminary which they are kind enough to put on for alumni. I sometimes take a few pupils with me (the likes of Blakestone, Williams, the Kendall-Reid girl), depending on what it is, or perhaps Tom S. More often, I go on my own. Anyway, I recorded these and wrote them down on the form and returned them to 'la vache qui ne rit pas'. She then presumed to 'interview' me and had the astonishing impertinence to say that none of that was relevant. Had I been to the I.T. seminars? Had I attended the Head Nurse's talk on Health and Safety given at the Sanatorium (or, as it is now termed, the Medical Centre?) Had I travelled to God knows where to be spoken at about 'special needs'? How was I getting on with the production of a website for the English Department? Well, as you may imagine, after having really let her have it, I went straight to Tansley and demanded that genuine academic further training, like listening to John Bayley drawing fascinating connections between the poetry of Hardy, Housman and de la Mare, or to the creative stimulus of three contemporary novelists discussing their work and offering a prognosis of where their art form might be going in the future, should be included in his protégé's In Service Training form.'

'What did he say?' asked Anthony Ridell with genuine interest.

'Well, of course, the gin came out and the tone of 'aren't we two wise old birds together, each of whom understands the trials of modern life and thought?' was introduced. Then, he immediately agreed that the change should be made- and it was! But then he mumbled on about the alleged importance of all the rest of the nonsense and, with that pained look of appeal that he puts on when it suits him, 'implored' (his word) me to try to support 'poor Cressida' as she wrestled with all the 'necessary evils' which contemporary conditions demanded and which he was too idle to deal with himself (*not* his words).'

John put down his empty whisky glass and rose from his seat.

'You are right in what you say, Alexander, but you shouldn't get so angry about it. It's not worthy of your fine mind. And, in a not dissimilar way, I know that I shouldn't get so anxious about the modern technology. As you rightly point out, it's not worthy of my faith or my witness as a priest.'

The effectiveness of the rebuke, in contrast to the ferocity of its recipient, lay in its mildness.

'Ah, John! You're right, of course!' responded Alexander, relaxing his intensity. 'One doesn't need to be a convinced believer to recognise the authority of a good priest.'

'It does you credit, Alexander, that you can still feel so passionately about these important matters after all this time' said Anthony. 'There are times when I just can't be bothered any more and feel that you two put me to shame.'

'No! No! That has its virtues too,' murmured Alexander.

Lean and immaculate, still with a full head of hair, albeit now grey, Alexander's quick-eyed, bespectacled, scholarly face returned to the composure which befitted one who had inspired so many pupils over three and a half decades of teaching.

The Parent's Meeting was breaking up, heralding the exaggerated anticipation of that over-valued boon to boarding school life, an Exeat week-end. The Volvo Estates of the Nineties had given way to the 4X4s of the new Millennium. These conveyances now filed down the drive to transport their owners for lunch at local hostelries or to take pupils directly home for a forty-eight hour reunion with their families. At least, that had been the intention when the arrangement had been conceived. *Au contraire*, however: the Sixth Form now started Monday morning lessons even more bleary-eyed than usual after an Exeat weekend. There was always an 'Eighteenth' to attend on the Saturday night. These occasions tended to begin some time before midnight and continue until just before dawn. The quantity of alcohol imbibed would have surprised Bacchus himself and the nicotine inhaled would have maintained the planters of Eighteenth Century Virginia in a style beyond their wildest dreams. The possibility of contemporary Afghan farmers and Columbian entrepreneurs also enjoying an indirect share in the enterprise could never, of course, be acknowledged.

Round a corner of the building, Jude Williams and Emma Morgan were having a quick conspiratorial meeting before meeting up with their respective mothers.

'No, really, I can't come to London this week-end. I'm skint. Anyway, I haven't had an invitation. But, look, I'll see you on Monday night. Usual arrangement.'

'Can't wait,' drawled Emma.

Checking that they were unseen, they shared a kiss and a hug before parting.

EIGHT

THE FOLLOWING WEEK, THE football practice was underway. Once again, there was no sign of Jude. Richard expressed his frustration.

'John, the guy's taking us all for a ride. Surely we can't let this go on. What about the effect on the others?'

John was also perplexed and irritated but he did not want to jump into a decision before ascertaining the facts. He realised, with reluctance, that he could not allow his feelings for the boy to interfere with the necessary justice of the situation.

Charlie overheard Richard's remark and made a valiant attempt to rescue his friend.

'Sir, Mr Donaldson, Sir, I *know* that Jude was desperate to get here on time. We were talking about it just at lunchtime. I don't know what can have gone wrong. He knew how important it was.'

'You're always very loyal, Charlie,' said John, smiling graciously. 'You'll be telling me next that there isn't an essay due in for Mr Scott tomorrow.'

'No, Sir. It's not that. I just don't know what can have happened.'

'Is this bloke to be given yet another chance?' asked Richard, directing his question to John.

Charlie felt awkward. He guessed that Mr Ellman judged his uninvited involvement as inappropriate but he did not move away because he was also aware of the danger to Jude in this situation.

'It is obviously serious if Jude has let us down again,' said John to both of them. 'But we'll have to see what this mysterious intervention is, before coming to judgment. Let's get on with the practice.'

In fact, Jude *had* been unavoidably delayed by a circumstance which none of them, including Jude himself, could have imagined. At the same moment as the conversation was taking place between John, Richard and Charlie, Jude was being forcibly prevented from keeping his appointment on the football pitch and he appeared to have no way out of his difficulty. He had, for several minutes now, been lying flat on his back, with his arms pinned to the ground by Victoria Summerthwaite, who was sitting on him. Given the facts that Victoria was five inches taller than her captive, eighty pounds heavier, had a support team of three other girls and was extremely angry, the options available to Jude for his immediate future were constrained.

On this occasion, keen to avoid further trouble and even feeling that he owed Rev. D a favour, Jude had changed into his football shirt and shorts in his study and had set off a few minutes earlier than the others. He had been approaching the playing fields by a different route so that he could drop off two books to the library on the way. He took a path which ran beside a wood. It was a sunny October afternoon and the hedgerows were bright with berries. He saw the light blue flash and heard the raucous chatter of a jay on the wing. The bird rustled in a hawthorn bush and then soared into the branches of a beech tree now more golden than green in hue. Jude enjoyed these moments alone when he could breathe, free from the pressures and expectations which seemed to hem his life in, both at the College and at home. In the immediate term too, he was looking forward to the football: the freedom of fast movement across the wide open space and the thrill, even in a mere practice, of achieving something physical at which he excelled.

Half-way between the College and his destination, he had seen the four girls approaching along the path in the opposite direction, carrying their hockey sticks. They were returning from a practice and were wearing the College blue tops and white slips. When they had noticed Jude, they had waved but then there had been a certain amount of whispering and a few conspiratorial smirks for which Jude felt a light-hearted, breezy contempt which, however, he kept to himself.

'Hi guys!' he had said, as they met, expecting a similar greeting as they passed. Instead, however, they had barred his way. Standing immediately in front of him was the formidable figure of Victoria. Jude's eyes were level with her neck; his chin would have fitted neatly into her spacious cleavage. Her thighs were more than twice the circumference of his and her pale, smooth, powerful legs were significantly longer than his bony, hairy, irregularly scratched ones.

'Hi Shorty! How's the two-timing going?'

Vicky was not smiling. The other three girls crowded around him. He calculated that he might just about manage to push through them but not before his

Amazonian opponent would have caught him. Like most of the boys, Jude, although he would never admit to it, had always been slightly scared of Vicky. He remembered joining in the safe laughter of the crowd some months ago when Tim had, in a fit of particularly stupid bravado, challenged her to an arm wrestle in the public arena of the College refectory. Every-one had been amused to see Tim's face, crimson with embarrassment, as Vicky had effortlessly overpowered him, pinning the youth's skinny frame horizontally to a table and refusing to release him until he acknowledged defeat. That had been in jest. By contrast, it was all too clear that the challenge which Jude now faced was serious.

The next thing he knew, Jude found himself placed in a powerful headlock, pulled off balance and then he was lying flat on his back, with Vicky sitting on his stomach, pinning both his arms to the ground. He was shocked into silence by the suddenness of his demise and by the crushing weight of his captor.

Victoria was head of her House and captain of everything. A country girl from Gloucestershire, plain in appearance, she loved horses. She was respected by the Chelsea set but not really included by them, a situation which caused her no concern. Unfortunately for Jude, however, she was very friendly with Olivia.

'You haven't answered my question, Jude. Tell us about the two-timing.'

A combination of shock and prudence caused Jude to keep silence.

Vicky bent down towards his face, intensifying the grip on his arms as she did so.

'You've behaved absolutely horribly to Livvy,' she said, glaring at him. 'You've been off visiting Emma again at night and you promised her that you wouldn't.'

Jude's face was frozen in alarm.

'See! You don't even deny it! She knows, of course, and she's *so* upset.'

The other three girls were now kneeling round him. He could detect the combined hostility and he felt real fear.

'Come on! Admit it!' said Vicky menacingly.

Jude tried to breathe more freely but said nothing.

'How *can* you treat some-one like Livvy like this?'

'He's such a little worm,' said Christina, a tall, blond, athletic girl. 'Let's teach him a lesson he won't forget.'

'For Livvy's sake,' added Camilla, kneeling beside his head and peering right into his face.

Jude began to panic. As he tried to move his head away, Camilla caught hold of his hair and pulled it sharply. He squealed with pain and his eyes filled with tears. The only other parts of his anatomy that he could move at all were his legs. Unfortunately for him, as he jerked his right foot upwards it caught Christina with a harmless glancing knock.

'Don't you kick *me*! Come on, Amanda! Let's get his football boots off. He's behaving like a donkey. Just you hold his other leg while I undo the laces.'

The boots were quickly off and Christina spitefully pulled the hairs on Jude's right shin. He yelped with pain.

'Shut up!' said Camilla savagely and she clapped her hand over his mouth. 'He could do with a bloody good shave!' she added.

The others laughed.

'His legs too!' chortled Christina venomously.

'They sure are hairy,' opined Amanda in a tone of passing interest. She took her turn in tweaking their victim's leg-hair with forensic delicacy. They all laughed when he emitted an agonised howl and wriggled with momentary hopelessness beneath the massive bulk of his primary oppressor.

'He's got legs like a little monkey,' Amanda added unfairly. 'Perhaps we should find a cage and take him to the zoo and put him in the ape-house.'

'We're waiting for you to say something, Jude,' said Victoria, looking at him steadily.

He was aware that there really was nothing he could say that would serve him any useful purpose. Moreover, he thought that there was every possibility that he would start to blub if he began to make an attempt.

Victoria's anger had in no way abated.

'You're pathetic! You think that you're God's gift to the female sex- a skinny little wimp like you- just because you've got a pretty face and a bit of smarmy charm and the boys rate you at football! The fact is that most of the girls despise you and wonder how poor Livvy can have made such a mistake. And you're conceited enough to think that Emma Morgan thinks you're special too…..'

Camilla laughed mirthlessly. 'I should think he's number forty-three or so in *her* books. Wouldn't you agree, Vicky?'

'He'll do when she's a bit tired,' jeered Amanda.

'And there's no-one better around,' added Camilla.

'What shall we do with him?' asked Christina impatiently. 'Remember we were going to teach him a lesson.' In the absence of finding any fresher thought, she again caused Jude to scream with pain as she tugged at the hairs on one of his trapped legs.

Amanda undid the two buttons on his football shirt and playfully but agonisingly tweaked his chest hair.

'We could wax him,' she suggested. 'he's very hairy all over.'

They all laughed.

'Haven't you got anything to say?' asked Victoria, causing him to wince with discomfort as she adjusted her weight on his slender form. 'You can't just treat people like that and go on as though nothing's happened.'

'I'm sorry,' he mumbled.

'Oh, great! That makes it all fine! I'm sure Livvy will feel much better when we tell her.'

Jude's desperation increased in proportion to Victoria's anger.

Looking down at him with mingled contempt and loathing, she slapped him sharply across the side of the face twice, once from each direction, leaving him with a thick lip. He started to sob.

'I don't know why she wants to have anything to do with you but I'm telling you, if you let her down once more, I'll personally come and break every bone in your body for you, one by one, as painfully as possible.'

Jude believed her.

Jude's trial had nearly ended but not quite. As Victoria lifted herself off his slender, prostrate form, and the girls all stood over him as he sat on the ground, too traumatised and breathless to get up, Christina picked up his football boots and threw them separately into a nearby bed of nettles.

'Come on! Let's leave him to find them!' said Victoria. The others laughed scornfully and they set off back towards the College hoping that punishment, and, just possibly, a lesson, might have been effectively administered.

Jude sat on the path and watched them retreating. The tears started and he made no attempt to hold them back. They were not tears of repentance. It was far too early for any such cerebrally reflective response. He was reacting to the physical shock and the devastating humiliation that he had just experienced. His ribs were aching from being crushed by Victoria. His swollen lip was sore where one of his teeth had punctured it when she had slapped him. He slowly got to his feet and cried in abject surrender to the natural world as he spent the next agonizing ten minutes rescuing his boots from an extensive bed of tall, thriving stinging nettles. By the time he had finished, his hands, arms and legs were throbbing with a series of angry rashes. He limped disconsolately back to his House and explained to Matron that he had unwittingly run into a bed of nettles. There was sufficient evidence of that particular disaster for Priscilla Peverill to believe him and, bizarre though the story might have sounded, she considered that, in its own strange way, this was indeed the sort of thing that could only happen to Jude Williams.

The emotional demands had left Jude too confused to think. What with his mother's choice of boy-friend, an unsympathetic housemaster, barbed blackberry bushes, stinging nettles and girls, he had, at this particular moment, had enough of adolescence and wanted to escape to some state of simple childlike bliss of a kind that he had probably never really known but had sometimes imagined that his greatest friend, Charlie, must have enjoyed.

NINE

Peggy Mullen was the longest serving cleaner in Blenheim House. She had been at the College for more than thirty years. She had lived with her Mother in a 1960s semi-detached house on one of the housing estates which had sprung up round the sedate market town over the past forty years or so. After a long illness, the mother had died two months ago. John Donaldson had conducted the funeral in the parish church. He had returned with Priscilla and a few relatives to the house afterwards for a dismal wake of tea and biscuits.

Peggy was an unhappy lady. Bereft and single, grief and loneliness had allied for victory over her soul. Earlier on this particular day, when Priscilla had asked how she was coping, Peggy had burst into tears. She had wondered, with what she feared might be temerity, if 'the Reverend' might be able to help her. Priscilla had promised to arrange an appointment.

Peggy now sat opposite 'the Reverend', a personification of abject misery, poor woman. She was sipping weak tea and weeping bitterly. The level in the box of tissues provided by John was steadily going down.

'It was such a nice service, Reverend. And Mr and Mrs Bassett sent such lovely flowers. It was all from the boys in the House and that. And they all sent such a lovely card. They all signed it thesselves. I got fourteen cards, I did.

Lovely cards. And that Charlie Blakestone's Mum, she give the boy such a lovely plant, with such nice words wrote on the card, to pass on to me. There's a lot of kindness in the world, Reverend.'

John had heard all this before. And he had prayed. And Charlie, genuinely moved and ever kind, had remembered Peggy in prayer when their Chapel group had met. On this occasion, John had initially thought that he would see her for twenty minutes, before he was due to take the weekly football practice. When it became clear, however, that Peggy was becoming a fixture in his armchair, John had discreetly 'phoned Richard to ask him to take charge, for the time being at least.

'Your house must seem terribly empty, Peggy. It's very hard for you.'

The words of comfort detonated a cascade of tears. She wiped mucous away from her nostrils.

'Oh, it is, Reverend, it is. I sees a picture of her in my bedroom every morning and there she is again, last thing at night. And I'm always getting two cups out to make the tea. It was kind of Mrs Peverill to help me to go through her clothes. She had such nice things: always wanted to look smart, she did……'

Emotion overtook the finesse of language and, removing her glasses, she subsided into another tissue.

'I'm sorry to be like this, Reverend,' she snuffled.

'No, no, my Dear! Please don't apologise. It's quite natural. Every-one feels like this, unless they are a monster. I cried and cried when my own dear mother died. It comes to us all, I'm afraid. But, although one can never forget them, of course, it does gradually get easier.'

'It's an unhappy world, Reverend. And them two little girls getting murdered. And them people with bombs in London.'

'Well, it is, Peggy. And, I'm afraid that it always has been. It was a pretty unhappy place when Our Lord was here on earth.'

'I know, Reverend. A crying shame what they did to Him.'

'Exactly. It was a crying shame. But, look, Peggy, that's why I'm here: to remind you that He is our saviour, yours and mine. It's because I believe in that so passionately that I do this job. I want the boys to know the love of Jesus. I want all the people I know to experience it. I want *you* to know it. That's why I became a priest. It's the *only* thing that can make any sense of all the misery and suffering that goes on. It's always been like this. Jesus knew what it was like to suffer and be alone. That's why He died on the Cross. We've really got to have faith that He cares for us and looks after us. But we've got to have *faith*.'

There was nothing manipulative about John's speech. He spoke with a passion which he felt to be true from the bottom of his heart. He had no doubt about his faith or his calling. He believed that the redemption of Christ applied with as much force to poor, unattractive, dumpy, middle-aged, limited Peggy as it did to handsome, privileged, clever young Charlie or attractive, confused, brilliant Jude. He prayed regularly for the Headmaster, for Cressida Fulwell, for Lee Crowther, for Alexander Scott, for Anthony Ridell, for Richard Ellman. He wanted them all to know the love of Christ. And, of course, he prayed for the boys whom he loved. The fact that they appealed to him in a way that Peggy could obviously never do, did not diminish the *Agape* which filled his thoroughly Christian soul. At this moment, all thought of football and his boys had left his consciousness. He just wanted to bear this poor, wretched woman on the strength of his own faith, to will the peace of God into a life broken and, for now at least, robbed of purpose. He was thoroughly a priest, professionally and by the deepest totality of commitment.

The unanswerable warmth and powerful hope of his declaration had an effect on the afflicted soul in front of him. Peggy stopped weeping. She closed her eyes and breathed deeply.

He prayed for her and blessed her, laying the palms of his hands on the tired grey head.

They talked further and more calmly. He had looked out a booklet for her, one he had used several times before: 'The Christian and Bereavement.' He made a point in his diary to see her in just over a week's time. He did not hurry her away. Eventually, however, Priscilla, realising the extent of the delay, arrived and discreetly offered to drive Peggy home.

When they had gone, John knelt in silent prayer for the soul which God had entrusted to his care.

The football practice would be nearly over. Never mind! John was confident that Richard knew what he was doing. Still, perhaps he would show willing and walk up to catch the end of it. He glanced out of the window. It had been raining all day and there was still no sign of it clearing. They would all be soaked through.

He was just going to collect his raincoat and umbrella when there was a knock at the door. It was Richard.

It was the first time that Richard had visited John's flat. He cut a strange figure, wearing a yellow plastic cagoule, complete with hood, over his sports shirt and shorts.

'Sorry to disturb you, John. I did just want to see you.'

John could tell immediately that something had gone wrong up at the practice and he knew instinctively what it was.

'Don't tell me. Let me guess. It's Jude.'

'Yeah! Got it in one! Let me just take this dripping cagoule off and drop it in the passage outside, along with these filthy trainers. I did towel myself down a bit before coming away.'

'You poor chap! I'm so sorry that you were left on your own on a dreadful afternoon like this. Here, come and sit down, I'll make you a mug of hot tea.'

'No thanks. I need to get back and have a proper shower. My clothes are still a bit damp, I'm afraid. I'm sorry to appear here like this.'

He hesitated, hovering by the armchair. Damp patches were visible on the shoulders of his navy blue sports shirt. He was wearing shorts of a matching colour, which, although now drier, being of a lighter cotton fabric, had been creased by the rain. He stood in a pair of soiled, wrinkled white socks.

'Never mind about that! That armchair's long since past its best, as you can see! So sorry not to have got up there but I had a visitor who was in much need.'

'I fully understand that, John, of course. That doesn't matter at all. I'm not bothered about a bit of rain or being up there on my own: not that you can feel on your own anyway, with the likes of Charlie and Ashley and Tim and Chris and the rest of them. They're great company.'

John had noticed before that homo-erotic temptation often followed hard on the heels of moments of spiritual intensity. Thus it was that, as the twenty-two year old Australian, attired in his damp sports kit, sat down in the armchair so recently vacated by the frumpy Peggy, he could hardly take his eyes off the beautiful young man before him.

'Dear God,' he prayed in silence, '*This seems to happen so often. Protect me from myself or the Devil, or whatever combination it is between us, that teases me like this. I am all unworthy, I know. Thank you for making Richard so beautiful. Sanctify this meeting, I beg.*'

Here on his own, in John's sitting room, Richard, dishevelled and vulnerable in his mild embarrassment, was wholly unconscious of the power of attraction which he was inadvertently exercising. An irresistible compulsion forced John to feast upon every detail of his visitor's appearance. The erotic effect of Richard's presence had been much more diluted up at the football pitch, where they usually met, with its wider space, hurried activity and the presence of so many of John's boys from the College.

Part of Richard's charm was his apparent oblivion to his good looks. He was an athletically slim 5'9", with short dark blond hair and eyes as blue as the sky so often was in his home country. John watched as the young man automatically sought to relieve his mild physical discomfort by rolling his socks down to his ankles and then stroking dry the long, soft hairs on his shins.

The girls were universally in love with Richard, especially when, as a qualified life-saver, he was detailed to supervise their swimming. This change to the timetable could have been misconstrued as a stroke of imaginative genius on the part of the Director of Studies by any-one foolish enough to have thought that Lee Crowther possessed any imagination. Suddenly, all the girls' appeals to their matrons to miss swimming, and all the notes authorised by the Sanatorium, had almost completely ceased. A heart-stopping moment in the week was the appearance of Mr Ellman on the poolside in his swimming shorts (black, with two vertical white stripes on each leg), in accordance with the requirements stipulated by the Health and Safety regulations. And yet, Richard, who could not have been oblivious to the effect which he had upon the girls, studiously avoided taking any initiative in the inevitable attempts at flirting and, temptation notwithstanding for a young man only a few years their senior, he managed to remain commendably professional in his response.

'Tell me the worst,' began John.

'Well, John, you've guessed it. No show from Jude. No message sent. No explanation given. All his mates seemed at a genuine loss about his absence. I'm sorry, John, but I can't take this from him. I know that you couldn't be there this afternoon- I do understand that- but it gets to me even more when I'm up there on my own and in charge of the show. We were all up there in the pouring rain and the lazy little sod just didn't bother to turn up.'

As he became animated by his irritation, Richard's normally

very mild Australian accent became more pronounced. The index finger of his right hand toured the circumference of his elegant waist-line inside the elastic of his shorts. John could see the narrow band of dampness trapped on the sports shirt beneath and could imagine the faintly annoying itching sensation which his visitor probably felt.

'I'm sorry, dear Richard, that you've had such a bad afternoon.'

'It's not just that I've had a bad afternoon. Forgive me, I think you know me well enough to realise that I don't get riled that easily but this guy's really got under my skin. I've got to ask, what are we going to do about it? I just don't feel I can work with the kid any more.'

'Well, we *shall* need to find out why he wasn't there.'

'It's always the same though, isn't it? There'll be some excuse. He's such a devious little bastard. You've got to hand it to him when it comes to having imagination.'

'Be fair. Last week it was the nettles. I know that it seems mad but he'd hardly run into a nettle-bed to avoid football practice. There is no doubt that he was very badly stung. Priscilla saw the immediate aftermath and I saw him a bit later myself, when his arms and legs were livid and obviously still smarting badly. Priscilla had to give him anti-histamine tablets.'

'Yes, I heard. Charlie told me at length. And that's another thing. I feel that the other lads are beginning to see this as a sort of feud between Jude and me and that affects my relationship with them. That upsets me because I've got on with them well. They're a good bunch. It's just bloody ironic that Jude's the best footballer.'

John had never before seen Richard in anything other than a calm state. There was a pause in the discussion.

Richard moved the back of his right hand in front of his own face, first from right to left and then from left to right, as though erasing the bad mood into which he had been settling.

'I'm sorry, John. I've gone on way too much about it. Perhaps it's this place. You get sort of trapped by it as it sucks you inside its own little world and then little things become bigger than they should.'

He sat forward in the chair, pulled his socks up his shins and then lowered them again upon being reminded of how damp they were, and got up.

'I'll leave you in peace,' he said. 'I expect you've had a difficult afternoon too, with whatever it was earlier. I'm sorry to have added to it all with this.'

John also rose.

'No,no, Richard! You mustn't blame yourself for any of this. It is a problem and we'll need to sort it out. Obviously I'll see the boy as soon as I can- straightaway if possible.'

'It's just that we've got this big match on Saturday and he wasn't there for all the sorting out this afternoon. I felt sorry for Ashley Smart. It must be hard being a Captain when your best striker doesn't turn up to the last practice before one of the capital matches of the season. Oh, listen to me! I'm off again! I'd better shut up and get these wet things off and have a shower. I'll feel better then.'

'Richard, I promise you that, unless there is a very good

reason indeed, I shall tell Jude that he's not playing against R.G.S. on Saturday and that he's out of the team. Nick Thomas is very keen. He's always on time and the poor lad has sat around as a substitute for most of the time this term or found himself relegated to the Second XI.'

'But do *you* think that it's right to do that? I recognise that you know Jude far better than I do. It's got to be up to you. I'm just not coping with him.'

'Yes, Richard, I do think it's right. I'll certainly see Jude before the end of the day and I'll let you know. And, be assured that, if it does come to his being dropped, it will be because of his action (or lack of it) and nothing to do with you. Truly. I'm not just saying that.'

'Thanks John. You're a good man. I say it again. It is a privilege to work with you. I feel that I shouldn't really be sticking my nose into decisions about the College First XI, having just arrived in the place. I just seem to have got myself all steamed up this afternoon.'

And then, looking at the rain outside and running both his hands down his uncomfortably sticky football shirt, for the first time during their meeting, Richard's face relaxed into a smile. Instinctively, John moved forward and they embraced. John could feel and smell the warm, perspiring dampness of Richard's supple, muscular frame under his football shirt. He resisted a compelling impulse to hold him far more tightly. He hovered at the door while Richard struggled into his trainers.

'Thanks mate! Take care!' Richard called out, reverting to his cheery normality as he swept up his cagoule and ran down the stairs.

John shut the door and sat down. He prayed. He was a very experienced schoolmaster and he was aware of his responsibility to all concerned. He was also quite clear about the correctness of the likely impending judgment. He could not allow his own feelings about Jude to interfere with public justice or the best interests of every-one else involved. There was no dilemma there. He checked all that through with His God. That was the easy bit. There was no divine call for restraint unless, of course, a truly unforeseen disaster had struck. He prayed that that was not the case. Then, he prayed for Jude in all the boy's needs: for his headstrong, duplicitous nature but also for his genuine attempts to relate to God and for help in the domestic difficulty afflicting the boy's situation. As he had done so often before, over Jude and others, he thanked God for the boy's attractiveness and also for his cleverness and his wit. He asked that, in the event of Jude's being dropped from the team, God might mute the pain of the boy's reaction. He begged, while honestly questioning his own duality of motive, that the relationship between them would not be adversely affected.

Then, he confessed his feelings for Richard, awoken so abruptly on this gloomy, wet, October afternoon. He reviewed Richard's beauty with the Lord in specific terms, while candidly affirming once again that he had no interest in genital contact or inspection. He knew that it would be a total sham- a ridiculous waste of time, a damned lie, the essence of hypocrisy, a hollow shell of a life – if he was even marginally dishonest with the God whose insight is *'sharper than any two-edged sword, piercing to the division of soul and spirit, of joints and marrow, and discerning the thoughts and intentions of the heart.' Before you, O Lord, 'no creature is hidden, but all are open and laid bare.'* He asked God to safeguard him in his feelings for this young Australian who had landed in this strange society of an English boarding school, so far from the sunshine of his own home. He asked, as he had done so often before over the years- the decades- that God, who had made him, John, as he was, would direct these feelings positively, in a way that might only benefit Richard. At the same time, he asked God to let him see Richard more frequently, to have opportunities to appreciate his beauty. He confessed his need for such self-gratification. He reminded his Lord of his human frailty and then he set his mind on the spiritual bliss of the Resurrection and of his part in that in due time. Finally, his thoughts returned to Peggy. What was she doing now? Was she sitting, grieving, at home, with the rain battering against the window? He prayed that the calmness of Christ upon the tempest, the calmness with which she had left earlier this afternoon, might remain with her now.

TEN

Blenheim House was a building three storeys high, utilitarian rather than architecturally interesting in design. John's flat opened onto a spacious landing beyond which was a narrow passage with individual Sixth Form study bedrooms spaced symmetrically on either side. These were small cube-like spaces, just large enough to contain the bare essentials of bed, wardrobe, desk and upright chair, separated one from another by thin, dirty white walls: the sort of rooms the dreary ordinariness of which ironically achieved fame in painting and poetry through the imaginations of Van Gogh and Larkin. At the far end of the passage were lavatories, a shower room, a kitchen area and the Sixth Form Common Room, complete with its own television.

Priscilla's flat was the mirror image of John's on the middle floor. Across the landing from her were two dormitories, separated by lavatories and a shower room. This was the domain of the youngest boys in the house, the ones in their first year. On the ground floor, was the House Room (the general Common Room), a computer room, a further kitchen area and a series of two-bed studies for the Fourth and Fifth Form boys. A broad staircase ran down the centre of the building. The Housemaster's house was connected to the main building by a short covered walkway on the ground floor.

As soon as he had finished his short time of prayer, John

crossed the landing and walked to Jude's room. Jude was not there but John opened the door to the familiar scene of unattended male teenage chaos. The desk, the floor and the single plastic chair were, without distinction one from another, covered with random papers, books, files, cheap pens, dirty games kit, boxer shorts, socks, a towel, a canister of deodorant, a pair of filthy trainers, unwashed coffee mugs, empty soft drinks cans, CDs, and detached sections of yesterday's 'The Times'. Jude's statutory, grey flannel suit lay crumpled on the bed, along with a shirt and College tie. The books on the bookshelf were placed entirely at random, even down to whether or not the spines showing the titles were indicating their identity to the world in the conventional manner or confiding their secrets only to the wall behind. They had come to rest at crazily conflicting angles, interspersed with casually labelled files. Rap music throbbed quietly from a digital radio/CD player on the ledge under the open window. So far as John could distinguish them, the lyrics sounded solipsistically and gratuitously self-indulgent, sexually explicit, humourlessly angry with the world and as repetitive as the rhythm itself. He silenced the simmering machine, cutting short its obscene and complaining declarations to an unheeding world, by pressing the power switch. He pushed the items on the chair to the floor, found a cracked ball-point pen and a sheet of paper and left a note instructing Jude to see him as soon as he returned, anchoring it with a dog-eared copy of 'Measure for Measure'.

It was two hours before Jude came. John had decided not to invite him to sit down. He himself remained standing. Jude was not immediately forthcoming, thus seizing initial higher dramatic status in the scene which they both seemed to sense was about to break.

'You wanted to see me, Sir?'

'Well, of course I did. You must know what this is about!'

'I guess that it's about soccer this afternoon.'

John was very nearly prompted to useless sarcasm by this statement of the obvious but, for a moment at least, resisted the temptation.

'Yes. I was unavoidably held up myself. Mr Ellman was understandably very put out by your absence without notification and, frankly, so am I.' John gave way to his irritation. 'Which nettle-bed did you fall into this week?'

Neither of them smiled.

'I didn't, Sir.'

The politely toned, straightforward, truthful simplicity of the impudence annoyed John, contrived as it was to withhold the basic information upon which the conversation was bound to hinge and serving too as a veiled reprimand. The boy was already winning the game by forcing his superior's next move. John tried to defuse the banality of the question which he was now forced to serve by adopting a tone of hectoring directness.

'Come now, Jude! Why weren't you there this afternoon? This had better be good.'

'I had to finish an essay for Mr Scott, Sir.' The reply was delivered tonelessly from an expressionless face.

'This is outrageous. You promised me before that this would never happen again. You're not being true to your word at all!'

John felt cross about the insulting disregard which lay behind the boy's statement and infuriated as he listened to himself being reduced to the language of a hack schoolmaster.

'Yes Sir!'

'Is that all you can say? 'Yes Sir'?'

"Well, obviously Sir, I'm sorry, and I shall offer my apologies to Mr Ellman, but I don't suppose either of you will want them.'

It was the coldness of it all which maddened John: after all he had done for the boy: the support, the scrapes he had rescued him from, the financial considerations he had eked out for him from the Bursar (as well as, occasionally, from his own pocket), the confidences which he had been invited to share, the time and energy so freely given. He felt like a street lamp-post after it had received the attention of a passing dog.

'Speaking for myself, I don't think I do! Why, Jude? Because they don't mean anything.'

There was no reply. In his anger, John compromised his dignity by making an appeal.

'How could you do this to us? How can you treat your fellow members of the team like this? How can you let *me* down in this way and do so with such dispassionate indifference?'

'Mr Scott would have freaked if I hadn't done it and I couldn't handle that. It had been pretty well all done. I left the disc in Ashley's computer and he accidentally deleted the whole lot. It's no use trying to explain something like that to Mr Scott.'

'Oh, so it's all Ashley's fault.'

'I suppose it is- partly at least.'

'Have you *no* self-critical capacity at all?'

'Yes, I do. I can't help it when something like this happens.'

'But there's always something, as Mr Ellman reminded me forcefully earlier. And how am I to know that you're telling me the truth anyway?'

'That's up to you, Sir.'

'You don't inspire confidence in the light of your record of mendacity.'

The accusation could not be countered. John took the ensuing silence as a manifestation of dumb insolence. Whatever, it lured him into an attack from another direction when it might have been tactically more shrewd to have maintained his newly gained advantage.

'And what *really* happened *last* week? How could you run into a nettle-bed on your way up to the pitch? It's not as though you're an Australian who's just arrived here for the first week.'

(Exactly such a misfortune had overtaken Pete, an Australian gap year student, shortly after his arrival the previous year, to the agonised incomprehension of the victim and the inhospitable hilarity of every-one else.

'Well, Pete, you might have more poisonous snakes and spiders in Oz than any-one else but we've got the English stinging nettle,' Chris had joked, as the unfortunate youth had sworn furiously while fighting back tears of pain in a futile attempt to protect his image.

Every-one knew about the national welcome to Pete because the incident had been photographed and put in *Samizdat*, the pupils' newspaper.)

'No Sir,' said Jude, holding his own by refusing to acknowledge the master's attempt at barbed humour.

'And- I was meaning to ask you- you had a thick lip. You've still got the mark there. How did that happen?'

'It's not connected with the nettles, Sir.'

'That's not what I asked.'

'I had a disagreement with some-one.'

'Can I know whom?'

'No Sir.'

'Schoolboys' honour I suppose.'

'Yes Sir.'

John thought that he had better come to the point. He had taken his decision.

'Well, back to this afternoon, Jude. Can you think of any good reason why we should keep you in the team?'

'Yes Sir.'

'What?' asked John in sharp surprise.

'I'm a good footballer.'

'You're separating your ability from any kind of moral re-sponsibility.'

'If you say so.'

'What do you mean - if I say so?'

'I can't really explain my situation any further, Sir. I didn't miss the practice this afternoon because I couldn't be bothered or anything like that. I missed it because, as a result of an accident on a computer, I found myself in an unforeseen emergency. I am sorry I missed it but I can't pretend that I wouldn't take the same decision again. My work is very important; it's the Oxbridge term; you yourself keep telling me that I'm right to be trying for Cambridge; and, yes I admit it, I haven't got the guts to risk a showdown with Mr Scott. If that last factor is a sign of moral weakness, it's one which is shared by every other pupil at this school.'

'But what about the other people involved: other members of the team? Mr Ellman giving up his time to stand in the pouring rain for an hour and a half? As a Christian, you can't ignore factors like that, can you?"

'I recognise that it's a dilemma Sir.'

'Is it indeed? Well, Jude, it's one that must now be resolved. Soccer is a team sport and you operate with consistent selfishness. You can't say that you haven't been warned. As from now, I'm dropping you from the 1st XI. You won't be playing against RGS on Saturday and you won't be put to the bother of dreaming up excuses for any more Wednesday practices.'

'What?' exclaimed Jude in sudden horrified astonishment. 'Oh, sir, *please* don't do this to me. Football is the only thing that keeps me sane here. Do anything else to me but don't drop me from the team.' For the second successive Wednesday, he found himself beginning to weep.

John did not offer the box of tissues but he was surprised by the intensity of the boy's reaction and the swift change in demeanour. Still, it was certainly best to make a clean break over the matter.

'You should have considered this earlier, Jude. This afternoon's failure must be seen in a wider context. I'm not going back on the decision.'

Jude emitted a sigh of disbelief as the tears started to flow in earnest. He turned on John in fury.

'You promised you'd help me. All you're interested in is appeasing that Australian. He hates me. Everybody knows that. Well, I hope you lose on Saturday! I hope RGS thrashes you! They probably will with me not there. It'll serve you all bloody well right!'

John could not allow the tantrum to pass.

'Don't you dare speak to me like that!'

'Go on! Punish me! I don't care!'

'I think you'd better get out before you make matters even worse for yourself.'

'Don't worry! I'm going!'

And he did, turning on his heel, sobbing in mortified rage.

John felt the calmness of experience in such matters. The boy was wrong. The decision was right. The boy had over-reacted and would calm down. The judgment could easily be reversed in two or three weeks' time if due penitence were to be shown. Given his feelings for Jude, however, he was surprised that he felt quite so clear-headed. Where, he wondered, did this leave *his* moral responsibility to the boy? Was this disinterested professionalism truly honourable in this case? An awkward tinge of guilt coloured the clarity of it all. John wondered if he had found it easier to send Jude packing because of the interest aroused by Richard earlier in the afternoon. As a priest, he felt he knew more about mixed motives than most. Again, he prayed.

ELEVEN

It was noon the following day. The rain had stopped and bright autumnal sunlight pervaded Charlie's study. The boys were all in class. Blenheim House was quiet.

Charlie's study was directly opposite that of his close friend, Jude. Although Charlie's room was identical in dimensions to that of Jude, it could not have been more different in aspect. The occupier's imaginative orderliness had utilised every space. The dingy walls had been obscured by a neatly symmetrical sequence of A4 sheets of paper denoting some of Charlie's favourite texts from the Bible and from his literary explorations, printed in large font. These were interspersed with Royal Shakespeare Company posters and one depicting destitute people in Africa, surmounted by a magnified picture of a white cultic wristband inscribed with the black-lettered message, 'Make Poverty History'. Charlie had killed the worn, industrial cord carpet on the floor by throwing down an imitation oriental rug discarded from home. Books were arranged alphabetically on the shelves alongside carefully labelled files. Charlie's clothes were all in the wardrobe, either hanging up or folded on the shelves provided. A closed laptop was positioned on the right of his desk. Hand-written notes in preparation for next week's essay on 'Measure for Measure' lay in the centre. Behind these, were two framed photographs: one of Charlie with his parents, younger brother and golden retriever, with an elegant, no-nonsense, red-brick, Georgian farmhouse in the background and one of Charlie in sports kit winning a race on Sports Day, with an expectant crowd leaning in on either side of the track. On the wall immediately behind the desk was a collage of photographs taken on various family holidays and an assortment of pictures of Charlie's gang of contemporaries: at parties, on holiday together, posing self-consciously, caught in embarrassing situations. Again, the CD player was on the window ledge, though this one was currently silent. On a small table at the bedside was another framed photograph of Charlie's parents, a copy of the New International Version of the Bible, the quarterly Scripture Union Bible reading notes and Magarshack's Penguin translation of 'Crime and Punishment', Charlie's current bed-time reading.

'There are four great novels which you should read while you're still in the Sixth Form,' Mr Scott had advised. 'They are 'Wuthering Heights', 'Sons and Lovers', 'Crime and Punishment' and 'Great Expectations.' People sometimes forget that the central characters are all young people, much your own age. Try to agree about reading them at the same time so that you can talk about them together.'

Charlie, Jude and Olivia had, among others, heeded the advice and each had so far read the Bronte and the Lawrence. So far as the latter was concerned, Leavis and the Cambridge Scrutiny School were thus living on through the no longer young schoolmaster, despite both Leavis and Lawrence having drifted out of literary fashion. As Auden wrote, posthumously confirming Yeats' misgivings,

'The words of a dead man

Are modified in the guts of the living.'

Jude read in tremendous bursts of a hundred pages at a time, usually during the school holidays but sometimes all through the night at College, a habit now impaired by the advent of Emma into his life. Had Mr Scott known about this development, he might have suggested Jude's dipping into Emma's namesake by Flaubert or identification with Vronsky in 'Anna Karenina'. Olivia read systematically, making careful notes, though she, too, had currently come to a full stop as a consequence of her current anxiety. Charlie was the slowest of the three young readers, though the most consistent in application and the one with the most retentive memory. He was more hesitant in his judgments than Jude though better able to make intuitive connections. He kept a pencil and a ruler by the book, identifying passages for later use and noting the page numbers at the back of the volume.

If the two boys had faults as young critics, they were opposite in nature. Jude was too quickly dismissive if something did not immediately appeal. Charlie was reluctant to make any pejorative judgment at all. When they had been studying Keats the previous year, for example, Charlie was willing to struggle with 'Hyperion' and, when he did not find it rewarding, he blamed himself. Jude, on the other hand, made an early judgment that the odes and 'The Eve of St Agnes' were truly great, accessible without being simple, and that 'Hyperion' was not worth the bother.

They had had an argument after reading 'Wuthering Heights'. Charlie thought that it was the greatest novel he had read to date, revelling in it as a sublime statement of the romantic spirit, where the rugged wildness of the Yorkshire Moors dramatically objectified the tumultuously self-destructive emotions of the characters inhabiting them.

'The rambling excesses of a mad, ranting, sex-starved woman, living in the middle of nowhere,' Jude had pronounced dismissively.

'How can you say that? You're so arrogant. Not only is it the most compelling possible expression of romanticism but the narrative control is something again: the central characters' stories, within Nelly Dean's narrative, within Lockwood's account. That degree of narrative complexity would seem pretty adventurous *now* and yet she did it in 1847.'

'Nelly Dean! What a boring little conformist, inserting her bloody conscience into everyone's business all the time. The best thing that happened to her was when Heathcliff locked her up,' Jude had teased provocatively.

'Perhaps the author meant her to be read the way you suggest. Equally she can be seen as the critical voice of romantic excess,' Charlie had countered.

Soon, however, the argument had lost its impetus, becoming subsumed into the usual good humoured review of College gossip.

On this quiet sunny morning in October however, the door opened and a figure entered Charlie's friendly, welcoming space. The intruder glanced furtively round the room. The only two things worth stealing were the CD player and the laptop but the intruder showed no interest in these. Instead, the wardrobe door was opened and attention was fixed on the shelf containing Charlie's neatly folded boxer shorts. A pair of red and white checked ones was extricated from the others, the presence of the name tag sewn into the back, just below the elastic, inspected, the boxer shorts removed and the wardrobe door closed. The intruder left the room, mission accomplished.

Later the same day, John Donaldson had been invited to share 'simple supper' with Priscilla. Home-made parsnip soup, with cream and butter, was followed by grilled trout washed down with an Australian Semillon-Chardonnay.

'It won't surprise you to know that Jude Williams came and complained about your dropping him from the team,' said Priscilla.

'No, it doesn't but he left me with no option.'

'Every-one other than him must see that. The little turn-coat even went to Bernard Bassett to complain.'

'I wonder what Bernard said.'

'I don't know but I can't believe he would be terribly interested.'

'I'm sorry that it has fallen out this way but, as I've said, dear Jude really gave me no option.'

'Of course not. Anyway, he'll get over it. You know what they're like!'

'I should do by now!'

'Do you know, John, I'm ashamed to say that I've only just discovered some rather good music which I feel I should have known about a long time ago.'

'What is it?'

'Guess. I'll put it on.'

'You know I always get this sort of thing wrong.'

'No you don't. Stop this false modesty. It was, however, new to me.'

'Oh, I recognise this! It's wonderfully melodic. It's one of the waltzes from Shostakovich's Second Jazz Suite.'

'I knew that you'd know it! That's impressive!'

'He's so versatile. It's amazing to consider that the same composer produced the Leningrad Symphony. What a piece of music that is! But this is delightful. Listen to that trombone and horn.'

For a time, the evening left College behind and there was further talk about the impending visit to Covent Garden. After dinner, Priscilla wanted John to hear part of her new CD of 'Don Giovanni' with Bryn Terfel singing the eponymous role. She chose the seduction of Zerlina by the Don in the first act. They both knew it well. Priscilla had a good singing voice and sang with a choir in the town. When Zerlina wavered under the Don's approach, she quietly joined in:-

'*Vorrei e non vorrei;*

Mi trema un poco il cor.'

John joined her in the duet as Zerlina's resistance crumbled:-

'*Andiam, andiam, mio bene,*

a ristorar le pene

d'un innocente amor!'

Just occasionally, at moments like these, John wondered if

there might be a soupcon of wishful thinking on Priscilla's part, even though she must have worked out the unspoken reality many, many years before. But still, how good it was to enjoy the pleasure of adult friendship. 'Innocente amor' indeed, but in no way could it 'ristorar le pene' of the dark and lawless unseen tumult in his heart.

They kissed and parted.

John returned to his flat to try to appease the false god who had demanded a shrine on his desk. He clicked on the 'Moreton College Intranet' icon on Desktop and dug out a scrap of paper containing garbled instructions that Anthony Ridell had hastily given down the 'phone a few weeks ago. He clicked on 'Academic Staff Access' and typed in the password, 'Tansley.' 'Reports' duly came up as an option. He clicked on the box, apparently in accordance with instructions, but nothing happened. Instead of cautiously retracing his steps, he began to give all sorts of other commands, many of them conflicting, and the computer crashed. He compounded the problem by switching the power off. When he tried to start it up again, the screen persisted in accusing him of having committed a 'permanent fatal error'. John wondered if he should be listening for an ambulance siren. Nothing he could do would clear the screen. This particular batch of reports was due in tomorrow morning. Naturally conscientious, he hated being late with things. By now, he would have been well on the way to completing them under the old system whereby they were written by hand. He felt defeated and resentful. Because this was part of a confidential data-base, to which pupils were denied access, he could not cross the landing and commandeer assistance from Charlie or one of the other boys. Priscilla was as useless as he was himself and, in any case, she did not need to perform this sort of task. He picked up the 'phone and dialled Anthony Ridell's number. The voicemail declared that he was not available. He tried Alexander Scott at home but was greeted by the impersonal 'BT service 1571'. He recalled that Alexander and Cordelia were seeing Alan Bennett's new play at The National Theatre, returning on a late train. Cordelia would no doubt have patiently sorted all this out for her husband earlier. In desperation, he 'phoned Lee Crowther who was, of course, close to his own computer and telephone. Lee said that he would come straightaway.

'Dear me! This computer has got itself into a state. What *have* you been doing to it, John?'

'I don't know. That's the trouble.'

'Bill Gates sets up all these clever systems for us and people like you come along and screw them up!'

The remark was intended to be jocular. John found it rude and heavy-handed but, aware of his total dependence on Lee at that moment, he kept silent.

'I'll close down all these false entries and then reboot,' said Lee, warming to the challenge in the way that Pombal might have done when commencing the reconstruction of Lisbon after the earthquake in 1755.

A great deal of clicking the mouse and sweeping the little arrow across the computer screen then occurred, at a pace which it was quite impossible for John to follow. Sure enough, Lee brought 'Reports' up and gained immediate entry. John tried to note down the steps of engagement once again. Lee departed to go and put right some anomalies connected with the omission of Halal food which the catering superintendent had discovered on her data-base. The lock to the file having been unfastened, John dared not provoke the machine by shutting it down until he had finished writing all the reports. These related to a class in the first year at the College that he saw for Religious Studies for one lesson per week and had been teaching for less than two months. The newly devised system would not close an individual report until he had written the required seven lines. He could barely remember who some of the pupils in the class were. Given the nature of the lessons, there was little written work to go by. As class positions were mandatory, the programme refusing to end the report without them, John had to invent an order which seemed not wholly implausible. A large number of pupils were thus placed tenth equal. Naturally economic and stylish in his command of language, John had to teach himself both the art of periphrasis and that of turning a statement of the blindingly obvious into a virtue. Eventually, he had written the final boy's report. It read thus:-

'Oliver has been studying the Gospel of St Mark this term. The emphasis so far has been on faith, miracles and discipleship. Oliver has attended the lessons satisfactorily and, despite his quiet demeanour in class, he would appear to have taken an interest. His map of the Holy Land at the time of Christ was carefully done and well presented. He is diffident about offering comments in public but can sometimes come up with the correct answers if asked directly. I hope that he is enjoying the lessons. Next term, the class will be studying Old Testament history.'

John had attempted to close the report here but the warning block was immediately flagged up:-

'WARNING: -

This report is of insufficient length. You are required to complete a minimum of one-hundred words.'

John could imagine Cordelia Scott kindly padding out her husband's terse remarks with all sorts of persiflage to meet the requirements. He sighed and added the following words at the end of Oliver Yates' report:-

'…..beginning with the life of Abraham and continuing until the deportation to Babylon.'

The computer's verdict was at last favourable and then John very nearly forgot to click in the box denoted 'SAVE', a mistake he had made on a previous occasion, resulting in the loss of a whole evening's work and various complaints from efficiently computer literate colleagues about being late.

He shut the terrifying machine down, hoping that he had made an accurate connection between the name and the actual boy about whom he had just written. The report was inevitably so bland that he realised that it did not greatly matter.

He allowed himself a small brandy by way of celebration. He poured the libation out but, before allowing himself the first delicious sip, he went to his discarded jacket and removed a pair of red and white boxer shorts from the pocket. He spread them out on a chair. Then he picked them up again and kissed the beloved name-tag. The cotton was fine and soft as he inhaled the fresh scent of the soap in which they had recently been washed. He took them into his bedroom and placed them carefully inside the bottom drawer of a chest of drawers. There, they reposed, along with several neatly folded piles of similar articles of clothing.

John sat down with his Armagnac and, for the first time that day, settled to the front page of the newspaper.

TWELVE

LYNN WILLIAMS WAS NOT, as Charlie had generously suggested to Jasper, a practice manager. She was one of a team of full-time receptionists in a large, busy practice in one of the 'neighbourhood communities' of the new and expanding city of Midhampton, some fifteen miles east of the small market town local to the College. Her son had inherited her small neat frame and the colouring of her hair and eyes. Her ill-judged marriage had not left her with an easy life but she had taken care of her appearance and did not look more than her forty years. Like Jude, she was an only child. Her widowed mother lived in Manchester but Lynn had taken a provisional decision to remain in Midhampton when her child was born, despite her husband of one year having taken off to Australia. She had done this to avoid breaking contact with the various agencies which had been supporting her during her pregnancy. To Lynn's credit, her child's welfare had consistently remained a primary concern and the preliminary decision to remain in the area had been gradually confirmed as Jude had grown older. She had worked as a shop assistant to begin with but had taken her present job when the new health centre had been built a decade or so ago.

Lynn's social circle was limited. Sometimes she went out for a drink or a meal with some of the other women who worked at the surgery and she maintained occasional association with staff at the department store at which she had previously worked. But she felt deprived of male company. The range of possibilities was limited and the few relationships attempted over the last seventeen years had ended messily. Having been bitten once in her comparative youth, she was more cautious now but, as the years rolled by and the face-cream had more work to do, she was fearful of remaining single for the rest of her life.

Les had been the first new man on the scene. A supervisor at the department store, he had been kind to Lynn in the early days when she had been coping with her newly born child. A divorcee himself, he had, in the first instance, been generous in arranging schedules and duties and, in due course, he had taken her out for dinner. Lynn's colleague, Debbie, had helped out with the baby-sitting. But things had become difficult when Les had started to arrive uninvited at the house. One evening, after he had had too much to drink, he had become very silly. On his way back from the lavatory, he had invaded her bedroom, unbeknown to her, and then returned to the sitting room waving some of her underclothes in the air. That was the end of Les. Moreover, he was twenty years older than Lynn and she had never found him particularly attractive.

Phil, a regular representative for a pharmaceutical company at the surgery, had been younger and sexier and that relationship had extended to his moving in with Lynn for a while. For the first few weeks, she had been rapturous. Not only was Phil great in bed but he was imaginative in judging her moods and how to please her in a variety of little ways. But then, with the first row, he had revealed his violent temper. Lynn would never forget sobbing on her knees on the kitchen floor after he had struck her and then stormed out of the house. Young Jude, at the age of eight, had stood beside his Mummy, trying to comfort her.

When a newly qualified, single, handsome, Pakistani doctor had arrived at the surgery three years ago, Lynn fell immediately and madly in love with him but, her delicious fantasies notwithstanding, she sensed from the start that Dr Khan was way out of her modest league.

By contrast now, there was fat, flabby Mike. Lynn was becoming very bored with him and resentful of his clumsy attempts to involve himself in her life. The more effort he made, the more obvious the limitations of his understanding. The antagonism between Jude and him was the last straw. Lynn was now working out how to ditch Mike but he was irritatingly persistent. As she drove home from work on this particular Thursday, she brought to mind again the one night when he had been permitted to share her bed and wondered how on earth she could, even momentarily, have tolerated that bulging stomach, those pale, fleshy, hairless legs, the hedgehog-like beard, the glasses with lenses thick enough to stop a bullet, the middle-ranged, nasal whine of the flat Birmingham voice.

When Jude had started at Moreton College, Lynn had felt real gratitude to John Donaldson for taking such an interest in her son. She had been surprised and mildly flattered when John had first visited the house. She had even begun to wonder if, as a lonely, single man, he might have been developing an incipient interest in her. After all, there he was, an ordained academic, presumably celibate, who had lived most of his life in a boarding school. True, he was ten years older than she was, but that might be no bad thing. Moreover, albeit it in a grave and dignified way, he was not bad looking: quite tall and lean, a good sportsman in the past, handsome in the unchanging way that some middle-aged men could sustain for many years. Socially, he would be a catch, with his Oxbridge voice and degree and public school background. Lynn guessed that he was probably not without some private finance. She dared to amuse herself occasionally as she tried to imagine herself in a new identity: Mrs John Donaldson of Moreton College, wife of the Reverend John Donaldson, Chaplain to the College.

'No, I don't think so!' she had thought, smiling ruefully to herself.

And, anyway, she wasn't into all that church business. Without having given it any consideration, Lynn had always regarded religion as obsolete and irrelevant. Mind you, if her son became interested in it, that was his business and it might be no bad thing if it helped to keep the potentially wayward Jude on the straight and narrow.

Furthermore, Lynn began to observe that John Donaldson's interest seemed exclusively to focus on Jude. She did not feel jealous about this but she started to wonder about the schoolmaster's motivation. When, with jocular lack of concern, Jude had chanced one day to suggest similar thoughts, her suspicion increased. She invented excuses when John invited himself across for meals. She felt resentful towards John when, noticing the change in his mother's attitude, Jude had angrily accused her of homophobia.

And then Mike had come upon the scene. She had in fact known him for several years. He was the garage proprietor who had sold her a succession of old cars and, so far as she could judge, had helpfully and honestly maintained them. Six months or so ago, when she was collecting her faded but still reliable Volkswagen Polo from its routine service, Mike had seemed less jovial than usual. Grateful for past kindness, Lynn had asked him if anything was the matter.

Mike had explained that he had been thrown out by his wife who had become bored with him and, despite their having two teenage daughters, had become interested in another man. He had invited Lynn out for a drink, and then a meal, and so it had progressed. But, now, Lynn herself was bored with him, and irritated. She was aware that the point of no return had been reached but that, given Mike's cloying persistence, this would need to be made very clear indeed. She had managed enough rows with men not to feel too fazed by the prospect of this one.

Lynn now collected Jude from the 'bus station. Uncharacteristically, he had 'phoned the previous evening to say that he wanted to come through to see her but, when pressed, had been non-committal about the reason. This had made Lynn uneasy. Moreover, she hadn't seen Jude for at least a week anyway and she did miss him. When she had 'phoned the housemaster, she had been met with the voice-mail message and, not for the first time taking the law into her own hands, had left her own message, stating that Jude needed to come through to Midhampton to see her and that she would keep him overnight and drive him back in time for morning school. After some early skirmishes, following his assumption of responsibility for Blenheim House, Bernard Bassett had given up arguing over this point with Lynn and, frankly, he was happy to get Jude out of the House as frequently as possible. Lynn's call had not been returned.

Jude got into the car and slumped into the passenger seat.

'I've been waiting for ages.'

'Well, I was at work. I can't just knock off early because you announce that you're coming home!'

He didn't reply and looked obliquely out of the window. Lynn realised that something was wrong.

'Do you want to talk about whatever it is now, or wait until we get home?'

'Get home first,' he muttered glumly.

The short journey was completed in silence. She turned into the cramped little cul-de-sac with its modern terraced houses. The development belonged to the West Midhampton Housing Association.

'I left a message with Bassett, telling him that you were going to stay here overnight and that I'd take you back first thing in the morning.'

'Good. Thanks Mum.'

'There's a bottle of red wine in the kitchen. Go and open it while I change into my slippers.'

Lynn put on various lights and drew the curtains. The central heating had been timed to come on.

Jude brought the bottle and two glasses and poured out the wine. Still he said nothing.

'Come on, Dear, what's the matter?'

'I've been dropped from the First X1.'

'What? Why? Who's dropped you?'

'Rev. D.'

'Rev.D?'

'Yes! Rev. D!' he growled irritably.

'But you've got this big match coming up. Against RGS isn't it?'

'Yeah! A fat lot he cares about that.'

'But what on earth has happened, Jude? You're not going to tell me he just walked in and told you that you weren't going to be playing?'

'No, of course not.'

'So what happened?'

'I missed yesterday's practice. Rev. D missed it too. That Australian jerk was taking it. He hates my guts and went on and on to the Rev. D about it. Our special friend called me in and dropped me from the team. End of story.'

'We'll see about that. Have you fallen out with John then?'

'Yes. Anyway, I don't care. He's a perv.; I've told you.'

'Has he lost interest in you or something?'

'Yeah, I expect so. He seems keener on Charlie these days.'

'But how dare he drop you from the team just because you missed a practice?'

'My feeling entirely. God, where did this wine come from? It tastes foul.'

'I don't know. It's something that Mike left.'

'I might have known.'

'So, let's be quite clear about this. You're telling me that, after all this time, John Donaldson has dropped you from the team, before a major match, just because you missed a practice.'

'Yes. After all the goals I've scored for them: after all the gratitude expressed.'

'But this is outrageous!'

'Yes, you could say that. Still, perhaps I'm well out of it. I hate that Australian bastard. In any case, Donaldson's been getting a bit too fresh lately.'

'I thought that you said that he was losing interest in you.'

'Yes, but that's probably because I didn't respond when he made a pass at me.'

'HE WHAT?'

Lynn sat forward and put her glass down abruptly.

'Chill, Mum! It was nothing; it doesn't really matter. Anyway, I can look after myself.'

'I need to know more about this. What happened exactly?'

'It was just the other week, after the match. I picked up a minor scratch on my shin.'

'Well, I knew about that. What else happened?'

'Well, he made me wait behind on my own in the changing room. He told me to shower and then wait for him in my boxers.'

Lynn's eyes had opened wide and her mouth now followed.

'Go on.'

' As soon as all the others had gone, he came in and then made a great thing of putting anti-septic cream all over this little scratch. He sat right up against me and kept touching my leg.'

'He touched your leg?'

'Yes.'

'And no-one else was present?'

'Nope.'

'That's disgusting.'

'Well, he's like that. No-one seems to bother. It's not that big a deal.'

'Not that big a deal?! It certainly is! It's sexual harassment of a minor, followed by victimisation!'

Jude's quick eyes suddenly brightened.

'Well, if you put it like that, Mum, I suppose it is.'

'When I get into the surgery tomorrow morning, I'm going to contact both the Social Services and the police. I'm going to get compensation out of this. And it'll be good to get that creepy priest off our back. When I take you back to that College tomorrow morning, don't you say a word to any-one. Promise me, Jude.'

For a moment, Jude was going to protest and stop her, but then he paused. He smiled slightly. This'll sort those bastards out. The old saying's true: Revenge *is* sweet.

'Mum's the word,' he said.

'And now, we're going out to that new Chinese restaurant for a meal.'

'Great. Thanks Mum,' he said.

THIRTEEN

The soccer match between Moreton College and RGS was one of the major fixtures of the season. This year, it was a bright, sunny day and, at twenty degrees, unseasonably warm for October. There was an air of expectancy around the pitch and, for this match, an army of supporters. This was an occasion when there was a whiff of town versus gown rivalry which was usually (but not quite always) good-natured enough. In the old days, relations had been less friendly but, with the majority of Twenty-first Century public school boys, unlike some of their parents, despising both snobbery and racism, together with the fact that a quarter of the College's intake now comprised day pupils from the locality, there was plenty of reason for the RGS boys to have friendly acquaintance with their opponents on the field.

Lynn Williams had sensibly taken her son to the cinema for the afternoon. If Jude had been thinking that the whole occasion would be blighted by mourning over his absence, he would have experienced the shock of discovering the adult truths that nobody is indispensable and that, when you are out of sight, the memory of you quickly fades. To be sure, within the team, there was apprehension about how they would fare without him, but the College sportsmen's sense of fair play did not incline them to blame any-one other than Jude himself for his exclusion. Charlie felt grieved for his friend but not resentful over the judgment.

Even he thought that Rev. D had had no choice in the situation, a view which, however, out of loyalty to Jude, he kept strictly to himself. The others felt faintly annoyed with Jude, rather than Rev. D, for letting them down.

It was an appropriately nail-biting match. The RGS boys appeared to be taller and faster than their opponents this year and, by half-time, the College was down by one goal to nil. John had, of course, travelled this road before and, in the dressing-room, having got the captain on his side, all his words were of encouragement and confidence. He summarised the familiar story of David and Goliath and made a point of speaking to each of the lads, patting him on the shoulder or finding specific words of supporting advice. No-one dreamt of mentioning that if it had been Jude Williams, instead of Nick Thomas, in possession of the ball at the critical moment, a goal would not have been lost.

Five minutes into the second half, Ashley, the Captain, struck from thirty yards in front of the RGS goal. He had noticed a gap and the opposing keeper scarcely had a chance to see the ball coming.

'Wow! The power behind that!' exclaimed Bill Blakestone. 'And he's only a skinny little lad.'

'But supple and athletic. And he's taller than Michael Owen,' suggested another father.

'Though no heavier. I'd be surprised if that lad was as much as ten stone.'

'Less, less, surely,' agreed his acquaintance. 'It's skill and fitness that counts rather than brawn. We'll see them pull through yet.'

Bill, now standing next to Richard, shouted out in exasperation when his own son, not for the first time this afternoon, missed an opportunity.

'You know, Richard, the trouble with my Charlie is that he's just too nice. He'd sooner stop in the middle of the field to ask them if they're OK than knock the hell out of them to win the match.'

Richard laughed.

'You don't need me, Mr Blakestone, to tell you that Charlie's a great lad. He must be one of the kindest people I've ever met. You must be very proud of him. I believe he's academically bright too.'

'You're right, of course, Richard. Sue and I just thank our lucky stars. This place has had quite a bit to do with it, John Donaldson in particular. These lads owe him so much and so do their parents.'

'So do I, Mr Blakestone,' said Richard.

'The name's Bill- please! Anyway, I hope you're settling in all-right. We must get you round for supper one evening. It's time we had John again too. We'll have you together- some time when we can get Charlie over too.'

'I'd love that. Thank you.'

'Yes. We've been a bit slow about it. Sorry. I'll bully the trouble and strife into sorting something out.'

'Trouble and strife?'

'Wife.'

'Oh,' said Richard, chuckling politely but not understanding.

'Where's young Jude Williams this afternoon? I think the College is missing his input. Injured or something?'

'No. There was some difficulty. He wasn't able to play today. There was a disagreement. I think it's all rather delicate.'

'Oh! Say no more! These things happen! Now then! We could be outflanking them!' and, then, suddenly shouting, 'Oh, Charlie! For Heaven's sake! What are you doing, son of mine? Trying to get him to recite some bloody Shakespeare?' Bill bellowed with good-natured irritation as Charlie politely allowed an opponent to sweep past.

'I don't know why John keeps him in the first team, Richard; I really don't. He ought to make him go and play netball with the girls!'

The College boys had recovered confidence since Ashley's goal but the match remained equally poised for the next thirty minutes. Charlie was not on form. He found concentration difficult. He was worried about Jude and his thoughts were also very much on 'Crime and Punishment'. In fact, in recent weeks, the football had been relegated in Charlie's mind to a low-key relaxation, a chance to run about with friends in the fresh air. Of course, there could be no question of his letting the Rev.D or his own friends down. But, last night, he had been profoundly moved by the fourth chapter of Part Four of Dostoyevsky's novel. He had come to the section where Sonia reads the description of Jesus raising Lazarus from the grave in the eleventh chapter of John's Gospel and he had found himself almost joining Sonia as she willed Raskolnikov into belief.

When the famous, timeless, portentous words of Christ pronounced the twenty-fifth verse, he nearly found himself praying for the salvation of a fictional character:-

'I am the resurrection and the life; he who believes in me, though he die, yet shall he live, and whoever lives and believes in me shall never die. Do you believe this?'

Simultaneously sensitive to the mastery of the great writer and deeply conscious of his own status as a penitent, Charlie had ruled a pencilled underlining below the description of the two young people in the room immediately after Sonia had finished reading the chapter:-

'The candle-end had long been flickering in the bent candlestick, dimly lighting up in that poverty-stricken room the murderer and the harlot who had met so strangely over the reading of the eternal book.'

Now, in the middle of the football pitch, he found himself bringing the words to mind again and resolved to pay a visit to Mr Scott as soon as possible after the match was over. What should he go onto next? He certainly wanted to stick with Dostoyevsky for a bit. Could he take on 'The Brothers Karamazov' yet? Mr Scott had said that some people considered that to be the greatest novel ever written.

'Come on Charlie! Stop dreaming! Get after it! What is it with you this afternoon?'

Ashley's voice was angrily urgent as Charlie had failed to notice the opposing player coming straight towards him at great speed. Too late, the black-shirted enemy raced past with the ball. The RGS boy was four inches shorter than Charlie who should easily have out-paced him.

'Sorry!' shouted Charlie to the empty space as the action rushed elsewhere.

He made a determined effort to pull himself together. He had offended against his own sense of responsibility and was anxious now that he would be letting others down.

Although Charlie then recovered sufficiently to protect his own reputation, the hero of the afternoon was the improbable and slightly patronised substitute for Jude. A few minutes before the end, amidst a tangle of players in front of the RGS goal, Nick Thomas gave the ball an opportunistic flick which the opposing keeper did not spot in time. The College supporters erupted. The referee blew the final whistle and the predictable rejoicing began.

Having been primed about the significance of this particular annual fixture, the Headmaster had arrived to witness the final fifteen minutes. Not naturally a spectator, it did not occur to Geoffrey Tansley to see himself as anything other than an important part of the spectacle. At the end, he posed for the cameras with the team. Richard was displaced so that the Headmaster could stand with John. He was photographed by the local newspaper shaking the hand of the appropriately dishevelled captain.

Bill Blakestone took his chance.

'Bill Blakestone, Mr Tansley. A marvellous team the College's got there.'

'Yes, indeed, Mr Blakestone. We're terribly proud of them all. I think that your son, Alex, is one of the noble warriors?'

'Charlie? Yes, he's in the team. I don't think his mind was sufficiently on the job this afternoon.'

'*Charlie!* Of course! Why did I say Alex? I thought Charlie was doing rather well, from what I saw.'

'*Lying toad*' thought Bill. '*I don't suppose you even know which one he bloody well is and, anyway, you were only here for the last few minutes.*'

Instead, he said, 'I'm aware that a lot of work goes into this. You've got some unsung heroes on your staff.'

'Yes, indeed, Mr Blakestone. We're frightfully fortunate. It might seem like boasting but I must confess to being just a little bit proud of some of the appointments that we've made in recent years. I'm not sure that they go unsung though. I hope not!'

'Well, John Donaldson has been here for over twenty years. I certainly hope that *he's* appreciated. He's done so much for our son and I know that Charlie's one of many about whom that can be said.'

'Yes, indeed. An excellent man. So dedicated.'

'I think it would be fair to say that there are two masters at this College who have transformed Charles.'

'The other one will be his Housemaster. A good man. I'm glad that I appointed him to Blenheim. He'll do well.'

'We're grateful to Mr Bassett, of course. But I was actually thinking of Charles' English master, Mr Scott. Perhaps it's my turn to be a little proud but my wife and I hadn't realised Charlie's potential ability until he got this amazing English teacher just over a year ago. Now, he's trying for Cambridge. We'd never considered such a possibility until recently. We've never had anything like that in our family before and we're very excited about this.'

'It's so good to hear a satisfied customer! I'm glad that we're living up to expectations!'

'They've served the College a long time, those two gentlemen. Anyway, I'm glad to hear that they're not unsung heroes!'

'No, indeed! Let's hope that Charles cuts the mustard for Cambridge. If any-one knows what he's doing over that sort of thing, it's Alexander Scott! I'd better get along and shake a few hands. Good to meet up and hear such positive things!'

FOURTEEN

The bright warm weather continued on the Sunday. The whole College gradually collected outside the Chapel for Morning Prayer at ten-thirty: the girls in their white blouses and grey dresses, the boys wearing grey suits over white shirts, the staff in gowns and hoods. There was a muted buzz as every-one filed in to take their seats. Several rows at the back were occupied by visiting parents and other guests.

The building, plain, grey, long, tall and vast, comprised a neo-gothic nave, without side aisles, of which the chancel formed, without interruption, the eastern extremity. The only item placed on the simple altar table was a plain silver cross. The Chapel would have been cavernous and gloomy had it not been for the sequence of huge, plain, leaded windows on each side, contained within high pointed arches. The October sunlight poured in over the fresh, youthful, morning faces and the mops of uncombed hair, some of them still damp from last minute showers.

A few stragglers sidled in conspicuously, hastily tucking their shirts into their trousers, shoe-laces still undone, ties askew. The Chapel Prefects closed the heavy oak doors. The powerful organ struck up as the Headmaster and the Chaplain made their progress down the aisle, both wearing their plain, white, silk, Cambridge M.A. hoods, in the case of the Headmaster over his black gown and in the case of the Chaplain over his white vestments.

After the bidding, the opening hymn and the prayers, a mighty wave of youthful voices, predominantly male, put heart, if not soul, into the intensely personal, spiritual statement expressed in one of Charles Wesley's great hymns.

'And can it be that I should gain
An interest in the Saviour's blood?
Died He for me, who caused His pain,
For me, who Him to death pursued?
Amazing love! How can it be
That Thou, my God, shouldst die for me?'

Some will have taken the words in; a few will have followed their intent; for many, it was simply the rousing tune of communal worship. Few faces expressed amazement at the paradoxical mystery of 'the Immortal dying' or any serious engagement with 'His strange design'. Mortal minds joined angel ones in 'inquiring no more.' True, Christ's love had 'found out' some in that congregation but, for most, in a secular age, compulsory Chapel was seen, with passive acquiescence, as a gesture of compulsion to conform to institutional requirement, a routine, traditional corrective to the encouragement of individual talent blazoned throughout the College prospectus. Geoffrey Tansley was shrewd enough to know that, with glorious inconsistency, prospective parents, almost without exception, wanted both.

'No condemnation now I dread;
Jesus, and all in Him, is mine!
Alive in Him, my living Head,
And clothed in righteousness divine,
Bold I approach the eternal throne,
And claim the crown, through Christ, my own.'

It now fell to the Deputy Head to read the lesson. Cressida Fulwell strode confidently to the lectern: an immense brass eagle upon which a huge black leather Bible, with gold-leafed edges to its pages, rested open at the page to be used for the morning's reading. In her way, she was a commanding figure. Not far short of six feet tall and weighing over fourteen stone, her shrill, adenoidal voice was relayed by the microphone along the vaulted nave with more than necessary effectiveness. The lesson was taken from the beginning of the eighth chapter of the Gospel of St John.

'Jesus went to the Mount of Olives. At dawn He appeared again in the temple courts, where all the people gathered round him, and he sat down to teach them. The teachers of the law and the Pharisees brought in a woman caught in adultery. They made her stand before the group and said to Jesus, 'Teacher, this woman was caught in the act of adultery. In the Law, Moses commanded us to stone such women. Now, what do you say?' They were using this question as a trap, in order to have a basis for accusing Him.'

'But Jesus bent down and started to write on the ground with his finger. When they kept on questioning him, he straightened up and said to them, 'If any-one of you is without sin, let him be the first to throw a stone at her.' Again, He stooped down and wrote on the ground.'

'At this, those who heard began to go away one at a time, the older ones first, until only Jesus was left, with the woman still standing there. Jesus straightened up and asked her, 'Woman, where are they? Has no-one condemned you?"

''No-one, Sir,' she said.'

"Then neither do I condemn you,' Jesus declared. 'Go now and leave your life of sin.'

John Donaldson bowed to the Cross and ascended the steps to the pulpit. He briefly commended his sermon to God in prayer and began to address the College.

'As I was putting the finishing touches to this sermon last night, I was dimly aware of festive sounds in the distance: mild vibrations from recorded bass drums, merry laughter, the unsteady progress of Blenheim House sixth formers on the stairs outside my flat, even (though, quite probably I was mistaken over this) the occasional, isolated squawk and giggle from the dark bushes below my window.'

He paused as a murmur of expectant laughter ran through the building. An experienced practitioner, well aware of the potential effectiveness of an arrestingly humorous beginning, he had already won their attention.

'And then, of course, I remembered that it was the night of the monthly Sixth Form Dance. I hope that it went OK- and that not too many people disgraced themselves. It couldn't possibly happen at Moreton College, of course, but one has vaguely heard stories from other schools of couples necking in corners (forgive me if my language is out of date), of hugging, kissing and- well, perhaps we'll leave it at that.'

More engaged laughter.

'And, of course, when people are let loose upon even a limited quantity of alcohol after a week's enforced abstinence (in theory at least), any frisson of sexual excitement can be intensified. I know that many of you, during the last few years, have studied 'Macbeth' as a set text for GCSE. Do you remember

the Porter who greeted Macduff before the dreadful discovery of Duncan's murder? 'Drink', he said, 'is a great provoker of three things': 'nose-painting, sleep and urine'- AND, he adds, 'LECHERY'. 'Lechery', he said, 'it provokes and unprovokes: it provokes the desire, but it takes away the performance."

Contented chuckles at this application of Shakespeare's witticism, even from the Headmaster and visiting parents. Lee Crowther, for whom the aphorism was quite new, smiled too.

'But I'm sure that you will agree with me, in the pure light of a Sunday morning in Chapel, that the question must arise in such situations, 'Where should it stop?' The drink, yes, that too, but I'm referring primarily to an individual's response to the reality of sexual attractiveness. We all find certain people (usually, but not always, of the opposite sex) attractive. Any-one who does not have that experience is not human. In Andrew Marvell's poem, 'To His Coy Mistress', we hear of a man's attraction to a woman:-

*'An hundred years should go to praise
Thine eyes, and on thy forehead gaze.
Two hundred to adore each breast:"*

Calculated dramatic pause

"But thirty thousand to the rest."

John hesitated just enough to allow a breath of predicted laughter from the boys. Lee Crowther chuckled a little too loudly. The Headmaster smiled nervously and glanced furtively towards the parents at the back of the Chapel.

'In the Song of Songs in the Bible, we hear of a young woman's attraction towards a young man:-

'My lover is radiant and ruddy,
Outstanding among ten thousand,
His head is purest gold;
His hair is wavy
And black as a raven.........
His mouth is sweetness itself;
He is altogether lovely.
This is my lover; this is my friend,
O daughters of Jerusalem.'

The Bible itself recognises the reality of erotic affection. <u>But</u> the Bible also condemns sex outside marriage. Certain tenets of the Christian faith are not open to negotiable interpretation. For example, no true Christian can reject the divinity of Christ. Now, if Jesus is divine, and therefore to be accepted as Lord as well as Saviour, His moral declarations must be right. With regard to sexual morality, He endorses the Mosaic Law, given to the Ancient Jews in the Ten Commandments and recorded in the twentieth chapter of the Book of Exodus. The Seventh Commandment is decreed in one simple sentence and admits no compromise:-

'You shall not commit adultery.'

So, it is <u>no go</u> for a man to have sex with another man's wife or for a woman to have sex with another woman's husband. Indeed, it goes further. Just in case there is any doubt, let me read the Oxford English Dictionary's definition of adultery:-

'Sexual intercourse between a married person and a person who is not their husband or wife.'

On this, Jewish and Christian interpretations of the Scriptures are in agreement.

This uncompromising denial of <u>adultery</u> is extended in the Bible to *fornication,* which the Oxford English Dictionary defines as 'having sexual intercourse with some-one one is not married to.' Christian morality therefore prescribes the absolute denial of sex outside marriage at any time and *that,* boys and girls, includes pre-marital sex. St Paul insists that either celibacy or the sacred bond of marriage can be the only guarantors of sexual fidelity. He writes this in his letters to the Romans, the Corinthians , the Colossians and the Thessalonians:-

1 Thessalonians 4:3: 'Abstain from fornication'.

Many people who compromise over this would be horrified at the thought of breaking, say, the Eighth Commandment- 'You shall not steal'- or even the Ninth one- 'You shall not give false testimony'. Theft and adultery both involve deliberate physical action. Why, we must ask, should one commandment be arbitrarily selected as entirely acceptable still in the Twenty-first Century when the other one can apparently be relaxed?

People who claim to be Christians, who have accepted Jesus as Son of God, Saviour, <u>Lord,</u> people who have been received into the Church, who go up to accept Communion- bread and wine, symbols of Christ's Body and Blood- people who have been <u>confirmed</u> in the Faith, <u>cannot</u> break a holy commandment by committing fornication, by having sex outside marriage. To do so as a Christian (and many people here, for example, have been confirmed, or intend to be confirmed), is a <u>moral</u> offence. It is far worse than smoking or drinking (though an institution like a school, responsible for minors, must, of course, keep a supervisory eye on those also). But to commit fornication if one is a confirmed Christian is deliberately to disobey the express commandment of the God whom one has accepted as sovereign. One cannot have it both ways. If we believe in Jesus as Son of God, Saviour, we are required to accept Him as

Lord. If we accept Him as Lord, we are required to obey His commands.

Jesus was quite clear about endorsing the Ten Commandments when He Himself was preaching in the Sermon on the Mount.

Matthew 5: 17: 'Do not think that I have come to abolish the Law and the Prophets. I have not come to abolish them but to fulfil them. I tell you the truth, until Heaven and earth disappear, not the smallest letter, not the least stroke of a pen, will by any means disappear from Law until everything is accomplished. Anyone who breaks one of the least of these commandments and teaches others to do the same will be called least in the Kingdom of Heaven, but whoever practises and teaches these commands will be called great in the Kingdom of Heaven.'

And, in verse 27: 'You have heard that it was said 'Do not commit adultery.' But I tell you that any-one who looks at a woman lustfully has already committed adultery with her in his heart.'

So are we then all condemned? After all, if we have reached adolescence, let alone adulthood, each and every one of us has looked at another person lustfully: women as well as men, gay people too. What possible hope can there be? Does this mean that we are all going to Hell?

Let us look at this same Jesus in the story about the woman taken in adultery read to us earlier from John, chapter 8. This is a story which, three-hundred-and-fifty years ago, inspired Rembrandt to paint one of his greatest pictures; you can see it in the National Gallery in London. The woman definitely deserves condemnation under the Law of the Ten

Commandments. She was caught in an act of adultery. She was brought to Jesus. The Pharisees, rather impertinently, reminded Him that, under the Law of Moses, she should be stoned.

What was His response?

'Yes, she has broken the Law; stone her!'?

'No,' He said to the Pharisees:-

'Let him who is without sin among <u>you</u> be the first to throw a stone at <u>her.</u>'

The hypocrisy of the Pharisees was exposed because they will, like all of <u>us,</u> have looked upon other people lustfully. Jesus in fact <u>saves</u> the woman from stoning (the just punishment of the Mosaic Law). <u>But </u>she is told to '<u>sin no more.</u>'

This is the issue and, here, all sin, including adultery, can be regarded in the same light.

Romans 3: 23: 'All have sinned. All have fallen short of the glory of God.'

Isaiah 53:6: 'All we like sheep have gone astray; we have turned every-one to his own way.'

We have all broken the Ten Commandments which Jesus Himself summarised in terms which put them quite beyond our frail human capacity:-

'You shall love the Lord your God with all your heart, with all your soul, with all your mind and with all your strength.'

'You shall love your neighbour as yourself.'

Well, of course, we cannot and do not achieve such imposs-

ibilities.

As Christians, the first thing we must do is accept the <u>reality</u> of our <u>sin.</u> Then we must confirm our acceptance that God's Law, as articulated in the Ten Commandments, and confirmed by Jesus in the Sermon on the Mount even more strongly, since it is not just the <u>letter</u> of the Law, but the <u>Spirit</u> which counts (a message delivered forcefully to the Pharisees who were trying to stone the woman), is indeed right. We must then genuinely repent. We must say honestly to God that we are sorry and promise Him that we shall try to turn away from our sin and, so long as we are genuine, be willing to accept the forgiveness of a loving God.

Moreover, Christians believe that Jesus paid the just penalty for our sins through His death on the Cross. When an act of adultery, for example, is committed, that is another nail in Christ on the Cross. If God is an absolute being, He is by definition perfect. Therefore, His <u>laws</u> are perfect and they must be perfectly maintained. In mere human law, we would all agree that the serial murderer, the rapist, the drunk driver who kills a child, must be penalised. Otherwise, the law does not mean anything. It has been completely devalued. It is a mere option. It doesn't really matter whether we keep it or not- and 'that way chaos lies.' And so, Jesus died on the Cross to pay the just penalty for our sins, and 'yet', in His case, 'without sinning.'

This is very serious for those who claim to be Christians- probably, therefore, for the majority of people sitting here now. The woman was forgiven by Jesus for her adultery but told by Him to sin no more. Here, we see God upholding His own law but we also see His love and His forgiveness, the love and forgiveness which were to take Jesus to the Cross.

I am not, of course, denying the love that people feel for each other and the great joy that this brings. Nor would it be right to deny the innocent fun which, I am sure, characterises most of what goes on at a College dance. But the sin of fornication, which includes the indulgence of pre-marital sex, of all the sins is the sin which, over the last twenty years or so, in my observation has, more than any other, undermined and destroyed the faith of young people, including many at this College. I myself am not pointing the finger at any individuals here guilty of that sin but one would be pretty unworldly not to realise that they <u>will</u> be here. In the recent past, I do know of boys and girls whose Christian lives <u>have</u> been ruined by this sin and the complicated feelings of guilt before God on the one hand but commitment to another person on the other. Well......, as with all sin, 'God is faithful and just to forgive us our sins' and, what is more, 'to cleanse us from all unrighteousness.' There may well be some serious thinking and some significant change of direction required from some people here today.

Now, shortly before I draw to a close, let me remind us that this is a Christian Chapel. This College has a Christian foundation and I make no apology for preaching a Christian sermon. However, I am aware, of course, that attendance at Chapel is compulsory and that there are people here who are not Christian believers and who do not therefore feel that this applies to them.

Well, the <u>love of Christ</u> applies to <u>all</u> who are prepared to take it on His terms and it is, moreover, allied to a great deal of general good sense. Of course one must recognise that people locked into impossible marriages have suffered terribly. But- certainly no less- the sexual freedom assumed by young people in the last two or three decades has caused great misery and instability in society and family life. What it means is that *people feel free to act on impulse if they find another person sexually attractive. Relationships are entered into without trial and without consideration of other factors. One then becomes bored with the other person. His or her looks fade and one finds some-one more attractive, with all the exotic anticipation of a change. And so our society is full of people who have just been dropped, who feel defiled, wounded in spirit, distrustful of entering into any further deep personal relationship, unable to find fulfilment in the giving and receiving of love in its widest sense.*

William Blake used powerful imagery to describe such destruction in his short poem, included in his 'Songs of Experience', 'The Sick Rose', memorably set to music for the tenor voice and the horn by Benjamin Britten:-

*'O Rose, thou art sick!
The invisible worm,
That flies in the night,
In the howling storm,*

*Has found out thy bed
Of crimson joy;
And his dark secret love
Does thy life destroy.'*

One can't have one's virginity back once one has given it away and to do that when one is very young, outside the safeguard of divinely sanctioned eternal promises, is quite wrong if one claims to be a Christian and very probably a bad mistake even if one does not. But what is always available is <u>God's</u> love, provided one acknowledges one's mistake and truly repents.

*'O the deep, deep love of Jesus!
Vast, unmeasured, boundless, free!*

*Rolling like a mighty ocean
In its fullness over me.'*

St Paul said that 'nothing' is able to separate a believer 'from the love of God in Christ Jesus.'

That is love indeed and it puts our lusts and infatuations into a somewhat local perspective.

And now, to God the Father, God the Son and God the Holy Spirit, Amen.'

John Donaldson stepped down from the pulpit, bowed to the cross on the altar and returned to his stall. The large congregation had been quiet. There was never any coughing and shuffling during his sermons. Many of the pupils had been attentive to the challenging and uncompromising words of this celibate Christian priest. He was a popular figure, respected and genuinely influential and authoritative among the young. Not all of them, of course, would heed his words. Some did not accept them.

Soon the rhapsodically reassuring melody of Samuel Trevor Francis' hymn to the tune of Ebenezer filled the vast building.

*'O the deep, deep love of Jesus!
Love of every love the best:
'Tis an ocean vast of blessing
'Tis a haven sweet of rest.
O the deep, deep love of Jesus!
'Tis a heav'n of heav'ns to me;
And it lifts me up to glory,
For it lifts me up to thee.'*

The Chaplain pronounced the blessing and, with the

organ still playing, the Headmaster and he bowed to the altar and processed the great length of the aisle, through the open doors and out into daylight.

'John, congratulations once again,' said Geoffrey Tansley. 'That was so timely and so appropriate. It took some courage too. It needed to be said and it was right to be said. I am immensely grateful to you, dear man.'

They looked each other in the eye and John Donaldson was absolutely convinced that, on this occasion at least, the Headmaster truly meant what he had said.

The staff processed out, the most senior first.

'Well done, John,' said Alexander Scott. 'Almost thou makest me believe!'

'Would it were so,' replied John.

'It *is* so. As I said, *'almost'*. But it was, as ever, a thoroughly intelligent and appealing apologetic. And, speaking as an agnostic, I still agree absolutely that Christianity without evangelism is entirely pointless!'

There was shaking of hands and grateful acknowledgement as other colleagues and adult visitors filed out of the building before the pupils. Several of the latter warmly thanked John too. A few asked if they might come and see him confidentially. He took out his diary and made appointments. It was Olivia who waited to catch him at the end.

'Sir, I really appreciated that. Thank you ever so much. Your comments about pre-marital sex and virginity were really helpful.'

'You're not in any trouble, are you, Olivia?' asked John quietly, with a reassuring smile.

'No- because I had already decided on the approach which you've just been preaching about. But it's wonderful to have it confirmed like this.'

Jude had slipped out through a side door at the other end of the building.

FIFTEEN

Mondays seem to be the least appealing of days at most places of work. Geoffrey Tansley realised, the moment he arrived in his secretary's office, that this was going to be a bad day, even by the standards of Mondays. He usually passed through her office on his way to his own splendid study. Ursula Duncan always arrived extremely early for work. This morning, she was wearing her anxious look. This was a rare event but, when it occurred, it was a troubling sign. It betokened the banishment of a comfortable greeting and a few minutes settling in before confronting the business of the day. The Headmaster tensed expectantly, aware that some new difficulty was about to hit him between the eyes. Ursula did not even produce the usual cup of coffee as she rose from her desk to meet him. She was a short lady with neatly cropped dark hair and quick, intelligent dark eyes. Her spectacles hung on a chain round her neck. She forestalled his enquiry.

'Geoffrey, two policemen have arrived. I've no idea what it's about. I've shown them into your study. Cressida is there but I think that they're all waiting for you. I've told John Donaldson that you won't be in Chapel and I've postponed your first appointment. I'm afraid that there's also been a serious theft in Ramillies House over the week-end. Bill Verney has the culprits in his study. I fear that you'll need to deal with that when you've finished with the police. I've no idea whether the two things are connected or not.'

Geoffrey walked through into his own study. The three people waiting all stood up. The policemen were uniformed: a burly sergeant and a young constable.

'Good morning, gentlemen. Dear me, dear me, what have our Moretonians been up to in the town now?' The genial, patronising tone came easily.

The policemen declined coffee. Geoffrey badly wanted some.

'We've not come about any of the pupils, I'm afraid, Sir,' started the sergeant, speaking in the slow burr of the local accent. 'A serious allegation has been made to the Social Services Department in Midhampton about a member of your teaching staff.'

As Geoffrey Tansley heard the details of Lynn Williams' complaint about John Donaldson, he experienced one of the few occasions in his life when he was speechless with astonishment. He also felt an immediate urge to protect his Chaplain. Yesterday's sermon was still very much in his mind and one of the first things he had intended to do this morning was to dictate a further note of appreciation.

'I don't know what precise action you intend to take at this moment in time, Sir, but, as you probably know, in circumstances of this nature, the usual procedure involves relieving a teacher of any duties involving contact with pupils with immediate effect.'

'Good heavens! Well, I must just consult some colleagues and, obviously, hear what the man himself has to say about this allegation. It is, of course, Officer, only an allegation at this stage. I would point out that the Reverend Mr Donaldson has served the College with unimpeachable integrity as Chaplain for some twenty years.'

'Of course, Sir, but, obviously, there would be serious implications for the College more widely in the event of any repetition of the alleged misconduct during an interval when you yourself were known to be aware of the allegation now standing. And there is no guarantee that the word will not get round anyway.'

Cressida nodded. Geoffrey grimaced under the shock of so immediate a threat.

The police sergeant then laid emphasis on the fact that, under the exceptional circumstances, he was prepared to make a provisional concession by not arresting The Rev. Mr Donaldson there and then. He said that they would be in touch again tomorrow, by which time the Headmaster would no doubt have taken appropriate interim action. The officer also made enquiries about Mr Donaldson's living arrangements and raised his eyebrows when he heard that the alleged child molester had lived for so long within close proximity to minors. The housemaster would need to be involved. The policemen solemnly took their leave.

Stunned and perplexed, Geoffrey picked up the 'phone to respond to an apologetic Ursula's request for instructions about dealing with the two boys currently interned by the Housemaster of Ramillies. He asked Cressida to arrange to meet him later in the morning with Bernard Bassett. No, despite his deputy's somewhat insistent advice, he would not summon John Donaldson yet. He needed to clear his head and, as he candidly explained, to accommodate the shock of the allegation which had just been made. Tansley was an experienced Headmaster and had, on two previous occasions, required junior colleagues to leave for reasons of sexual misconduct but to find himself confronted with such an allegation involving a very senior colleague, for whom he had genuine personal respect, was a real shock, the more so in view of its involving a man of the cloth.

He just had time to imbibe the now vital cup of coffee before the arrival of Bill Verney and his two miscreants. In itself, this was a serious disciplinary matter which would have been quite sufficient to fill a Monday morning. One of the boys, Henry Emsworth, was new in the Lower Sixth Form this term. He had been expelled from another prestigious public school for 'a wholly uncharacteristic and once-off misdemeanour' involving the distribution of cannabis for personal reward. His Godfather was a governor of Moreton, wealthy, well connected and an old boy of the College. Tansley had been leant on during the middle of the summer holiday and the powerful force of apathy had worked in the youth's favour. However, Emsworth's housemaster and other members of staff soon realised that this new acquisition to the Ramillies Sixth Form was bad news. He had been involved in various scrapes, including the bullying of younger boys, before the latest outrage. Bill Verney was convinced that he had brought drugs into the College but, thus far, Emsworth had evaded detection. He had befriended Bas Redmill, a rather unpopular boy, weak in character and a loner within his year group. Emsworth was the dominant partner in the friendship; Redmill was little more than an acolyte.

Yesterday, Sunday, the one day during the week when Moretonians could get up a little later than usual, Emsworth and Redmill had decided to carry through a simple money-making plan, concocted by the former earlier in the week. While every-one else was at breakfast, they quietly stole three laptop computers from their peers.

Emsworth had forged a typed note, allegedly from his parents, asking Mr Verney's permission for the two boys to be absent for the day and adding that, unless there was a difficulty, there was no need to reply. This was risky, of course, but it worked. Having discovered that a new boy in the Third Form was being collected by his mother and driven to London, they had acquired a lift to the metropolis. When the good lady could not but notice the three laptops, they invented a story about having to catch up on prep. all afternoon, after having enjoyed Sunday lunch with Redmill's parents. They explained that the third computer belonged to another member of the family and needed to be returned. Having arrived in London, they took the stolen goods to Portobello Market and were very happy to sell for cash two of the £800 laptops to a shady dealer for a quarter of their value. They then had an expensive lunch in a fashionable restaurant in Knightsbridge before retiring to two pubs where they drank brandy and smoked cigars for a long time. Eventually, they took a taxi to Euston and another one from Midhampton Station to the town near the College. They found a man in the empty darkness of the local 'bus station who was happy to relieve them of the third laptop for £150 as a cash sale. They retained the case of this last one as a depository for the banknotes which they had acquired during the day. They then went to another pub' and, having tucked into a second hearty meal, drank more brandy and smoked more cigars. They took another taxi to a village half-way between the town and the College and thereafter made unsteady progress on foot to a remote corner of the grounds. At that moment, the fickle Lady Fortune deserted them. The Combined Cadet Force was out on manoeuvres that night. Although the grounds of the estate covered eight-hundred-and-fifty acres, the two offenders chanced to clamber drunkenly over a wall at exactly the moment that Captain Clark, the enthusiastic young master in charge of the CCF, was walking past, armed with a powerful flashlight. Asked what they were doing and what was inside the laptop case, their initial hopeless attempts at explanation were brushed aside and their doom was inevitable when, opening the case upon demand, the remaining banknotes fell onto the damp grass, illuminated by the torchlight, to the astonishment of Captain Clark. Meanwhile, back at Ramillies House, all Hell had been let loose upon the discovery of the thefts. At that stage, however, no connection had been drawn with the two thieves and the little boy, whose mother had returned him earlier in the evening, though wondering about it, had decided that the safest course was to keep his thoughts to himself and his mouth firmly shut.

The enormity of the offence and its dreadful clarity did at least allow for a conveniently short inquisition in the Headmaster's study. The grounds for immediate expulsion were beyond dispute. The two malefactors were detained in the sanatorium until their parents came to collect them in the afternoon. Geoffrey Tansley left Bill Verney to carry out the unenviable task of informing the two sets of parents by telephone. Letters were dictated to be handed to them upon arrival later in the day. Ursula provided two further cups of coffee for the Headmaster while this piece of business was carried through.

Now it was morning break and Tansley, having gathered up his academic gown, was due to make his 'Announcements' to the Common Room. This was a source of irritation to every-one except for the great man himself. Apart from providing a not unreasonable respite during a full teaching morning, break afforded an opportunity for colleagues to transact quick but necessary exchanges directly connected with their work. Every morning, ten minutes into break, an inscrutable Ursula would shake a little tinkling bell (joyfully discovered by Mrs Tansley in a box in the attic shortly after their arrival at Moreton) which commanded the silence of eighty busy and, for the main part, intelligent adults. Time would then be spent as the Headmaster organised his scribbled notes in an effort to make his 'Announcements'. Often, these began with the recital of a long rambling letter from an octogenarian commending the behaviour of two boys from the College who had offered momentary assistance on a train, or such like: a 'terrific' example to other Moretonians and good for the morale of the staff who 'were doing a terrific job.' The Headmaster would then air his views (usually a garbled summary of some-one else's) on some current educational issue. Details might then be supplied about momentous events in the College, like the appointment of a third secretary for the Bursar, a lady whom none of the teaching staff would ever see and whose name they would all instantly forget. Next it would be time for the Headmaster to stamp his authority on his subordinates through a hectoring series of minor complaints and warnings. These might involve the observation of car parking regulations, the use of noticeboards or, of course, enforcing the dress code amongst the pupils. Staff were regularly 'exhorted and encouraged' to ensure that the boys in their classes were wearing socks which were grey, black or navy. Evil youths who turned up to lessons wearing chinos, or indeed any trousers other than the regulation grey flannels, were to be sent back to change them and to be reported to their Housemasters *quam celerrime*. (After that phrase had been used a few times, together with a couple of other Latin tags, less accurately, Alexander Scott had whispered to Tom Stevens that the (then new) Headmaster called to mind Chaucer's barbed description of the Summoner in the Prologue to the Canterbury Tales:-

'*Thanne wolde he speke no word but Latin.*
A fewe termes hadde he, two or thre.')

Even this morning, seriously preoccupied though he was, Geoffrey Tansley did not shirk from his perceived duty in speaking at length. He 'requested and required' colleagues to familiarise themselves with all Lee Crowther's 'terrific' work in the creation of data-bases on the College intranet. John Donaldson closed his eyes when the punctuality of reports was declared to be of 'paramount importance'. The Headmaster then informed the Common Room of the expulsion of Emsworth and Redmill, giving a summary of their offence. Young Clark blushed with embarrassment when he was publicly commended for his prompt action.

'Well done, you!' beamed Geoffrey, gazing round the Common Room in an unsuccessful attempt to find the object of his acclamation.

'I have to say that it prompts me to exhort and encourage every-one of us to attend rather more than perhaps we do to the….er… unofficial activities of Moretonians beyond the confines of the College buildings. We might need to consider some sort of night patrol on a rota basis.'

An inaudible sigh was released from his listeners.

Next, as an exceptional, but generally unwelcome, gesture towards democracy, it was the Headmaster's custom to invite members of the Common Room to make any announcements which they felt were important.

In a flat monotone, Luke Barnes, the Head of Sport and Physical Education, proffered a detailed blow-by-blow account of the weekend results. Particular mention was made of the victory of the First XI over RGS on Saturday and Luke, an even-tempered and good-humoured sportsman, still young enough to impress the boys (and girls) with his athletic skills, singled out John Donaldson for special praise. It was widely recognised as a high profile match and his colleagues applauded.

Obeying a genuinely generous impulse, Geoffrey Tansley followed Luke by saying, 'I'm sure that we all agree that it was a terrifically successful weekend for John, with that splendid result from the First XI followed by a magnificent sermon in Chapel yesterday. Chaplain, we salute you!'

He was simultaneously aware of his hypocrisy and his compassion as he spoke. His dark secret, so recent and unwelcome, was a heavy burden to a man normally so capable of throwing weight off his shoulders.

This was followed somewhat bathetically by a young and self-important Classics master, as periphrastic as he was rotund, explaining that he was unable to drive the community service minibus that afternoon because he had a dental appointment. He had made a huge effort to find a different time but, after the dentist's receptionist had tried her very hardest on his behalf, this afternoon offered the only slot available for several weeks. He needed another colleague to do it for him.

Finally, a stridently melancholy young woman appealed to

every-one, for the third successive day, to join in the hunt for her pink umbrella.

Geoffrey Tansley returned to his study with Cressida Fulwell and Bernard Bassett. The latter was put in the picture and instructed to keep the matter confidential.

'Naturally, the police started to probe into the conduct of John living as a bachelor in close proximity to so many teenage boys in a boarding house. The idea of our Chaplain behaving improperly with any of the boys in Blenheim House strikes me as completely ridiculous but I've got to ask you formally, Bernard. Can I take it that nothing of the sort has even been whispered?'

Bernard Bassett was himself surprised by the revelation. How he wished that he could think of something even remotely convincing to help him to secure the *table rase* which he so much desired for his empire! But he was stumped when put on the spot and took modified solace in being able to accede to the unveiled bias in G&T's question.

'I've never been aware of any such problem,' he replied.

'I expected no different answer. I just had to put you in the picture, especially with the boy concerned being in your House too. What's young Williams like? I know that he's a remarkable footballer and a bright lad here on a scholarship. The mother sounds a bit of a nasty piece, going straight off to the Social Services instead of approaching us first.'

'In all honesty, he's not exactly one of my favourites, despite his undoubted ability. I suspect that he goes out at night, though I haven't managed to catch him. He doesn't seem to feel any sense of responsibility to the House.'

'So he probably goes out to smoke in the grounds.'

'Almost certainly.'

'Drugs?'

'No evidence but I wouldn't be surprised.'

'Doesn't he have a sort of special relationship with John Donaldson?' asked Cressida Fulwell. 'One of the 'Chaplain's boys'?'

She was already seeing this turn of events as a golden opportunity.

'They're bound to know each other well if the boy is the most effective sportsman in the team which the man runs,' countered Geoffrey, a hint of acerbity creeping into his voice.

'Of course, Headmaster,' said Cressida, conscious that she would need to make her moves with great care.

'Jude Williams was dropped from the First XI because he habitually missed practices,' volunteered Bassett.

What sort of idiot is this man, thought Cressida? She knew that Bassett wanted Donaldson out of Blenheim House. Here was a chance never to be repeated. She forced herself to keep silent.

'So the boy was dropped from the team by John?' asked the Headmaster, looking for confirmation.

'Yes. I gather that he'd also had a run-in with Richard Ellman.'

Cressida wanted to get up and hit the fool.

'Oh, *I see*,' said Geoffrey crossly. 'So it's quite likely that we're dealing with an act of vindictive spite. John was quite right to drop the little sod if he was wilfully skipping practices. JD knows what he's doing, after all; he's been running the First XI successfully for years. Tell me more about the mother. I seem to recall that it's a single-parent family?'

'Yes, that's right. He lives in Midhampton with his mother. She's a receptionist in a medical centre.'

'And what's she like?'

'Not a great one for communicating. Very abrupt. Takes the boy out of College without permission. Doesn't come to social functions or anything.'

'It all fits rather unpleasantly. Oh dear, oh dear, oh dear!'

'It's all very unfortunate,' assayed Cressida. 'Poor John. Er….Headmaster……would it be right to tell Bernard that John might need to move out of Blenheim temporarily? It's just that Bernard may have a House to run for a bit without an under-housemaster.'

'Yes, this is possible, I'm afraid, Bernard. However, the poor chap doesn't know anything about this himself yet. I'm going to have to break it to him.'

The sudden excitement afforded by such an opportunity galvanised Bassett's memory.

'Come to think of it, Headmaster, I did chance to overhear one end of a rather odd 'phone conversation apparently taking place between John Donaldson and Lynn Williams,' he started hesitantly.

'This could be important,' encouraged Cressida.

'I can't remember the details and it was just a few fragments anyway. But John used to go over to Midhampton to see them from time to time and I'm under the impression that these visits have stopped. It sounded to me as though he was being given the cold shoulder on the 'phone. I was going up to see him on House business. Obviously I made my presence known just after I arrived.'

'Yes, well there's nothing peculiar about that at all,' snapped Geoffrey. 'John is the College Chaplain and I expect that he knew the boy and his home circumstances well and he was probably giving him and his mother the benefit of his wise counsel.'

'Yes, I'm sure,' mumbled Bassett, retreating.

The housemaster was politely dismissed and the Deputy Head was asked to remain.

'This is a very bad business,' said Geoffrey. 'Can you think of any way we can get poor John off the hook? *Prima Facie*, it appears as a piece of vicious vindictiveness and an absurdly exaggerated response to a very trivial incident. Trust the Social Services to waste every-one's time and taxes over this sort of nonsense in the name of political correctness.'

'Yes, I agree entirely. But, in answer to your question, I don't think that the police have given us any choice, have they? I mean to say, they'll be back tomorrow and I'm afraid that they're bound to ask if any action has been taken.'

'Yes, the logic of it is inexorable. I suppose that I had just been hoping that it wasn't. The law cannot be negotiated, I fear. But- one has got to pay homage to the cliché- where is the justice?'

Geoffrey Tansley felt increasingly upset about this turn of events.

'I have no idea about the man's sexuality and, frankly, I don't care. He's still a bachelor at- what is he? Fifty or so? But so what? He's done his job marvellously for twenty years without a whiff of scandal. And then along come a boy and his mother, both of whose morality remind you of the woodlice you turn up under a stone in your garden , and who are here by the grace and favour of the College anyway, and, through this one act of petty spite, can threaten the man's professional life and permanently damage his reputation. In all my time at Moreton, I don't think I've had to face anything as unpleasant as this.'

His private telephone rang. Only his wife, children and the Chairman of the Governors were in possession of the number. He sighed as he listened.

'Yes, dear.' Pause. 'I'm sure all that'll be fine.' Pause. 'Well, that's very kind of Belinda.' Pause. 'No, I won't be late.' Pause. 'I can't possibly get away beforehand, not today, really.' Pause. 'Well, allright. I'll nip into Tesco's for some when I've finished here but it will be at the last minute.' Pause. 'Er…well, it's probably best to go for a Burgundy. Oh, I don't know, on second thoughts there's a case of that Australian Shiraz. That'll do, won't it? It'll go quite nicely with your pork casserole thing.' Pause. 'Ya, it's a Hell of a day.' Pause. 'Oh, this and that. I can't go into it at the moment.' Pause. 'No, I'm not. I've got Cressida here.' Pause. 'Ciao then: yes I'll remember; I'll write it down. Bye.'

He scribbled something on the telephone pad.

The interruption had given Cressida time to marshal

her thoughts. She knew that she could afford to proceed gently because, for the intermediate future at least, there could only be one course of events, the one indeed which *she* wanted, even if her boss did not.

'I mean, Cressida, don't you agree with me about John- about how good he is?'

There was a tactical silence.

'No, I don't think you do. You were hinting that you had reservations the other day. Is your main concern to do with his screwing up all this IT stuff?'

'I don't really want to disagree with you. I can see how concerned you are and I know how deeply you respect him.'

'Oh, come on, girl, spit it out. That's what Deputy Heads are paid for- to offer candid advice to the Headmaster. It doesn't mean that he'll take it!'

The private telephone rang again.

'*Bloody* thing! Normally it hardly ever goes at all. Why it chooses today of all days…..'

He snapped up the receiver angrily.

'Yes?' he barked.'Oh, Chairman, *Hello*! How *are* you?' Pause. 'That must have been a wonderful experience for Lady Francesca and yourself.' Pause. 'No, we haven't been through the Yangtze Gorges: something to save for retirement, perhaps.' Pause. He offered a sycophantic chuckle to a laconic witticism from the Chairman of the Governors, Sir Edward Moncrieff, Old Moretonian, former chairman of a merchant bank. 'Who? Let me write this down.' Pause. While the Chairman spoke, he scribbled down a name. 'I'm *sure* we could arrange that.'Wheelchair access. I see. I'll get Cressida Fulwell or dear Ursula onto the job if that's all-right.' Pause. Another falsely hearty laugh.'No, indeed, that would never do! So- I'm sorry- could you just say again exactly how he's related to Her Majesty? Forgive me; it's being a rather tiresome morning.' Pause.'Well, we'll be onto his P.A., of course. Let me just write down her number.' Pause.'Yes, I'm afraid so. An allegation against a member of staff: it's all just happened; I'll need to be in touch with you about it. I'm just trying to establish the facts now.' Pause. 'No, not at all. I'll probably contact you tomorrow if that's all-right.' Pause.'Best to do it at the Carlton Club. Will do. Many thanks, Edward. Goodbye.'

'Sorry about that, Cressida. He wants his pal, Lord Macclesfield, to come next week some time to see the Samuel Johnson correspondence. Can I leave the nuts and bolts of that with you? Get Ursula onto it as well. You'll need to see Michael B about digging the stuff out of the archives. And we'd better wheel the old boy in here for lunch. Apparently he's nearly ninety but as sharp as a razor. I haven't had my usual morning session with Ursula yet today; I'll go through it with her too. We'd better get Michael B in here for lunch too, and my wife- and yourself, of course, and Alexander Scott and a couple of the brighter Moretonians, a boy and a girl. As it seems to be to do with literature, consult Alexander about which ones to ask. NOT Williams! Now, where were we?'

'You were asking me for my opinion of John Donaldson- and suggesting that I wouldn't be given the sack if it didn't coincide with your own.' Cressida gave a wry, calculatedly coquettish smile.

'*Go on!*' he urged, returning her look with a weary smile.

'Well- I hesitate- but my concern isn't just to do with the IT failures. My antennae do pick up other vibes.'

'Again, that's what a good Deputy Head should be doing.'

'In all honesty, I have sometimes wondered if he's a little too close to the boys emotionally. I recognise that the Chaplain is here to offer pastoral support but he does seem to spend a great deal of time with them and he seems always to have a little group of favourites each year, usually in Blenheim House. There may be no truth in it but I have heard whispers about his possibly hanging round showers a little more than might be necessary......'

'If there's no truth in it and it's just gossip, we can't go with that.'

'No, indeed, but, as they say, it's unusual to have smoke without fire. And don't you sometimes feel that he's just a bit out of date?'

'No, frankly- apart from his inability to cope with Lee's systIms on the computer. I thought that yesterday's sermon was a corker: spot on!'

'Yes, of course, you're quite right to applaud that. I agree with your judgment on that. But, at the same time, it's very difficult sharing R.S. teaching with him. He can be extremely dogmatic and some colleagues find some of his sermons - how can I put it?- too narrowly evangelical for their taste. I know that we don't have many people from other faiths here but there are some Jews and some Moslems and he's very hard-line. He and I have disagreed about the choice of syllabus. Of course, I've given way to him because it's his decision but a very exclusive emphasis is placed on the Bible. There are all sorts of exciting alternatives where the pupils can explore other faiths and, indeed, look at the Bible more critically, or they can spend more time considering practical ethics or such like.'

'This sounds to me like a legitimate professional difference. It seems to me to parallel the moans that you were telling me about, from some of the newer members of the English Department, over Alexander Scott and Tom Stevens both insisting that Chaucer should remain on the syllabus. Personally, I think that they are quite right but I recognise the alternative claim of doing more modern literature. Surely this is just one person's reasonable preference against that of another.'

Cressida was surprised that he was being quite so stubbornly defensive. She had become used to his being so insouciant that she could almost do what she liked, his principal aim being to shelve work for himself, but, suddenly now, he was taking an active interest in something and threatening to dig in. At least he wouldn't be able to resist the police, thank Goodness.

'Yes, I suppose so. I see what you mean. On another matter, there are those who wonder how long he can really keep going as the master in charge of the First XI.'

'What?! After Saturday?!' exploded Geoffrey. 'Who *are* these people? The result was just announced this morning and the Common Room applauded. You heard them!'

'Yes, I know, of course! But, as you said yourself, he's now over fifty and I wouldn't have thought he could keep going for too much longer.'

'It doesn't seem to stop Sir Alex Ferguson at Manchester United, among others.'

'Well, you know far more about it than I do. I'm just conscious that some of the younger members of the Common Room find his approach a little quaint. And there *are* rumours about him hanging about in the changing room more than is strictly necessary.'

'He's bound to do that if he is running the team. I can't see these big strong seventeen and eighteen-year old chaps allowing themselves to be sexually interfered with by the College Chaplain! Anyway, where do these rumours come from? We need to be specific.'

'When I was going round Montague House the other week (I was relieving Alison Pritchard because she had to take her daughter to hospital), I got chatting with some of the girls……'

'Some of the *girls!* What could they possibly know about it?'

'They do have boy-friends, Headmaster!'

'It sounds a bit obscure to me. What did these girls tell you?'

'It was somebody's birthday and I gave them a glass or two of wine. Well, you know how they talk…..'

'Yes, yes.' His tone was becoming mildly impatient.

'Lucy Spalding- she's the captain of the netball team- is practically engaged to Chris Mackenzie in Blenheim. Well, it was Lucy's birthday and they were all being a bit silly and giggly, finishing off the day with a glass or two of wine and being a bit indiscreet in a harmless sort of way. Anyway,

Chris had told her- Lucy, that is- that, during the soccer practice that afternoon, he had had occasion to return to the changing room after all the other boys had run onto the field and had discovered John Donaldson alone, holding his (Chris's) boxer shorts up for examination. Apparently John had said that he had found them on the floor and wondered to whom they belonged. Chris had found this strange because his name was sewn into the garment and he knew that he had folded them up along with the rest of his clothes.'

'I can't see a counsel for the defence having too much trouble in shredding that piece of flimsy so-called evidence!' And then, 'Goodness, if John is to be off limits for a spell, who's going to manage the First XI? Does any-one help him these days?'

'Richard Ellman.'

'The Australian lad who's just joined us?'

'Yes.'

'What's he like? Would he be able to handle it for a spell?'

'Oh, he's very good indeed. As a matter of fact, I happen to know that *he* took the critical practice last Wednesday before the great match *himself*. I think that John must have been called away for some reason.'

'Gosh! You're a mine of information, Cressida. How do you know that?'

'I met the poor boy on his way back, soaked to the skin! Should I approach him to ask him if he might be up for it?'

Geoffrey Tansley was feeling tired of all this.

'Well, yes, I suppose so. It is just one of many things we'll have to sort out. Of course, you mustn't be specific about the reason. You'll just have to say that John Donaldson *may* need to be relieved from it temporarily. Wait till this afternoon because obviously I need to see John first.'

'Richard Ellman is said to be a great asset. It would be good if we could keep him.'

'Well, that's encouraging at least.'

'It will be difficult to avoid telling him something if we're going to be asking him to take responsibility for the First XI.'

'Well, try and be as discreet as possible and do emphasise that these are only allegations, almost certainly unfounded.'

'And then-I hate to say it again- but there are the IT difficulties. Lee had to go up to John's flat the other evening to take him through it all yet again. We do have this scheme up and running now and the Chaplain really is one of the most reluctant colleagues to fit in with it. It's awkward when you yourself have authorised it, Headmaster.'

'I really think we must put that on one side for the moment. The poor devil's going to have more than enough on his plate.'

Cressida paused. Then she said, 'Let's hope that the press don't get hold of this. It wouldn't do our reputation any good.'

'I know. That grubby little thought had been lurking at the back of my mind too. I don't know how we're going to keep it all 'in house'. Anyway, there isn't much more that we can do about it at the moment. It rather horribly looks as though events are going to propel themselves. I'll see John this afternoon and we'll take it from there.'

'And I'll see Richard. I suppose that there's now going to be a temporary vacancy for an under-housemaster's post at Blenheim?'

'Oh dear, I suppose so. Do you think that young Ellman might fit the bill for that too?'

'I'm sure he would.'

'Well, sound him out- but you'd need to consult Bernard Bassett first.'

'Of course.'

As she got up to leave, the Headmaster put his hand to his eyes. Now standing, Cressida felt that she should offer a final remark to help in clarification.

'It does seem that John Donaldson *did* touch the boy's bare leg.'

'That's the allegation. We'll have to hear what *he* says. You'll need to be on hand because this sordid type of thing must have a witness present.'

Then he looked up sharply.

'Has it not occurred to you that he might deny it? If he did deny it, it would be one unreliable pupil's word against that of an ordained schoolmaster of more than proven integrity, strongly supported by a character reference from the College.'

SIXTEEN

Middle age had come early to Bernard Bassett. Bespectacled, podgy, pasty-faced, balding, dressed in a baggy greenish sports jacket and grey flannel trousers which were too small at the waist, his watery blue eyes were bright with excitement as he hurried back to Blenheim House.

Delia, to whom he confided all things, however secret, was writing a cross e-mail to the bank manager about a late statement. Thin, blonde, nervous and miserable, she was nursing her first cold of the season. She was surprised to see her husband in the middle of the morning, even during a free period. Their three children were at the primary school in the village. Some crayoned sketches of entomological people perched on psychedelically green grass festooned the walls. There was a grey Formica table in the kitchen with some pale, wooden, blandly unforgiving, upright chairs grouped around it. A small notice-board had a shopping list, various memos and sets of keys severely pinned to it. The computer – *her* computer- was on a surface below one of the overhead cupboards. She clutched a box of tissues as she swung round on her swivel-chair to greet her husband. Bernard put the kettle on and quickly made them both a cup of instant coffee.

Their very obviously naked ambition had prevented them from ever being one of the more popular couples within the College community. Before they had moved into Blenheim, they had lived in one of the College houses in the grounds. During this time, Delia, always supported by Bernard, had regular skirmishes with the three young bachelor masters who lived in the house next-door. On one occasion, the latter had been throwing a party. The Bassetts were, of course, not invited. In offering directions to the appropriate venue on the sprawling campus, the printed invitation had contained the words 'a stone's throw from Bernard Bassett: bring own stones.' Unfortunately for the perpetrator, one of the invited guests had slipped his invitation anonymously into Bassett's pigeon-hole in the Common Room. The missive had then appeared on Geoffrey Tansley's desk, clipped to a furious note from Bernard, dictated by Delia. A briefly grave word of admonition had been extended to the culprit. A few days later, Delia had returned from taking the children to school in her Fiat Uno to find a neat sign nailed to a stake on the driveway to their house declaring

'HOUSE OF THE HOUND

CAVE UXOREM'.

She had 'phoned the Domestic Bursar in a rage to demand its immediate removal and was fortunate in the maintenance men's ignorance of Latin. Some days after the offending sign had been removed, an anonymous, word-processed missive had arrived with the morning post, comprising two lines only very slightly adapted from Ben Jonson :-

'Come, my Delia, let us prove,
While we can, the sports of love.'

Bernard and Delia had met as undergraduates at Oxford. Delia had acquired a good Second in Greats and Bernard a less good one in History. At Moreton, Bernard was regularly heard to be airing his modesty about his wife being 'so much cleverer than he was,' suggesting that, at home, there was an immense repository of scholarship and acumen upon which he, unlike others, could always draw.

These days, during the hours when the children were at school, Delia spent much of her time bullying the Domestic Bursar to send people across to do her housework, spying on the boys in Blenheim in the hope of detecting misdemeanours and, as Bernard was constantly informing every-one, reading several contemporary novels each week, possibly in a desire to inhabit existences happier than her own and to be able to do so without commitment. Apart from doing the necessary shopping, her most frequent visits to the town were to the library and to the doctor. She had started a few secretarial or public relations type part-time jobs at the College but had always fallen out with the people to whom she had been accountable, returning home in a sulk and requiring her husband to issue a reprimand to whomsoever had delivered offence by failing to see the good sense of the alternative *modus operandi* which her superior intellect had perceived. Above all else, she was even more ambitious for her husband's preferment than he was himself. When out for one of their walks in the grounds, Alexander Scott and Tom Stevens had wondered whether she was more like Nagiana in 'The Jungle Book' or Mrs Proudie in Barchester.

('There's always Lady Macbeth,' Tom had suggested.

'No, Tom, the Bassetts are not nearly grand enough to be tragic,' Alexander had corrected.)

Placing the two mugs of coffee on the table, Bernard now

sat down and relayed the details of his conversation with the Headmaster to his wife.

Delia sneezed into a tissue and then sniffed before saying, 'If you ask me, the best thing that could possibly happen would be for Donaldson and Williams both to be kicked out of this school. The boy is surlier and scruffier even than the rest of them and that man upstairs has always given me the creeps.'

'As we've said so often, it would be good to have a younger under-housemaster, perhaps an NQT. John Donaldson's profile is too high in the College.'

'Of course it is. It's maddening that G&T should have left us with some-one who can threaten our status. Frankly, we need a young chap who's very obviously your junior- the same as all the other housemasters have- some-one who could give proper support, instead of being called away to so-called more important things. You never know what Donaldson might be saying to G&T behind the scenes whereas a junior wouldn't have that access.'

'It would be easier for me to demand more from some twenty-two year old. I would be much more exclusively his line-manager.'

'It would also put an end (not before time) to that snooty alliance between Donaldson and Madam High-and-Mighty on the floor below him. Priscilla's always resented our taking over Blenheim.'

'It would be good to get some-one of our own in here. Apart from anything else, this whole smelly business might attach a stigma to our House.'

'So Donaldson's been touching up boys has he?'

'As I said, Jude Williams' mother alleges that he stroked his son's bare leg.'

Delia shuddered.

'It really churns me up, that sort of thing. It's disgusting, just the thought of it: that lecherous man lusting after boys. It's not natural. They should never have repealed the law which decreed homosexuality as a criminal offence.'

'There's no suggestion that he did anything more than touch the boy's leg.'

'Even so. We've got to think of young Rupert. Just imagine Donaldson interfering with him.'

'I don't think he's interested in five year olds.'

'You never know. I know what I'd do to his type.'

The secret of the horror was, however, not vouchsafed. Delia was interrupted by the 'phone. It was Cressida sounding out Bernard about the proposed appointment of Richard to replace John as under-housemaster in Blenheim House.

Meanwhile, Geoffrey Tansley's day showed few signs of improvement. He had arranged to see John Donaldson at five o'clock, with Cressida Fulwell and Bernard Bassett, the boy's housemaster, present as witnesses. He had decided to do the deed at that time because he knew that he would absolutely have to leave before six o'clock in order to drive out to Tesco's and back, having collected the smoked salmon, olives and assorted cheeses about which his wife had now 'phoned twice, and still be in time to assist with the final preparations for the dinner party which they were holding that evening. His wife, Calpurnia, could not drive at present, on account of a sprained ankle, and had refused to take a taxi for so trivial a purchase. She also felt that, since she was doing nearly all the work, the undertaking of some such small task was the least she could expect from her husband.

However, there was respite for half an hour or so before lunch. Bryan Briggs-Johnstone, the Marketing Director, had had his early morning appointment with the Headmaster postponed until noon. An old boy of the College, Briggs-Johnstone was a large, rather loud man of about forty. Having married relatively late, and now with two young children, eighteen months ago he had decided to leave his job as a stockbroker and sell his house in Fulham, attracted by the prospect of living in the country. Even so, on a salary of £75,000 a year, he had not exactly signed up to a monastic oath of poverty.

Still dressed in his city pin-striped suit, and sporting an OM tie, he now breezed into Geoffrey's study.

Geoffrey was glad to see him and rose from his desk.

'Good to see you, Bryan. Look at the clock, old chap. It's exactly noon. The sun's at its zenith. Time for the first G&T.'

'Hello, Geoffrey! You know me! A G&T never knowingly refused! How are you?'

'Oh, don't! It's been a bugger of a morning- and there's more to come. It's good to stop and talk about something else, I can tell you!'

He mixed two stiff gins, feeling a frisson of anticipatory

pleasure as the sunlight coming in through the great south window of his study illuminated the sparkling bubbles of the tonic water as it hit the gin, a foaming transparency of sensory delight, felicitously punctuated by the bright yellow slices of lemon kept in his private refrigerator. He never failed to enjoy the moment's music when the ice cubes chimed against the glass in harmony to the fizzing liquid.

The purpose of the meeting had been to inspect the proposed logo for the 'Campaign for College' stationery. They spent a merry forty minutes examining the different positions where the College crest could be placed on the notepaper. There was the matter of size of font, too, to be considered. Geoffrey felt it important that his own name should appear with appropriate prominence.

'Far be it from me, of all people, to sound pompous but I suppose it *is* the name which people tend to associate most immediately with the place.'

Then, what colour should the paper itself be? White? One of several shades of cream? Some sort of blue, in recognition of one of the College colours? Blue on white perhaps? Blue on cream? Black on blue? They pored over the various prototypes which Briggs-Johnstone had brought as they sipped their gin. They looked at cards as well, and compliment slips. Briggs-Johnstone had a friend in the Golden Square Mile who could float several designs for a modest consultation fee. He might call upon some expenses to travel up to London next week to see this friend and report back. Tansley thought this a capital idea.

By the time Briggs-Johnstone had left, the first gin of the day had soothed Geoffrey's nerves and he began to view the afternoon a little more philosophically. Whatever happened, in five hours' time it would all be over. He would still be where he was on the planet, with a nice dinner party to look forward to. Tomorrow was another day.

Ursula 'phoned through. A persistent journalist from a national daily paper had been trying to speak with him for the last few days and was now on the line. Would he take the call? Anxiety and irritation competed. Tansley had sufficient experience to know the dangers involved in refusing the press. Surely the Donaldson affair couldn't have got to them already. Or was it going to be about the computer thefts? It turned out to be neither. The enquiry related to an ongoing saga about the summer's examination results. No pupil from the College had been granted an A grade in the AS level examination in History and some genuinely bright and conscientious boys and girls had been awarded Ds. The results were an obvious nonsense. Anthony Ridell and his Department had been understandably upset, as had the pupils and their increasingly angry parents. This was the term of UCAS applications and Durham, Bristol, Nottingham and Leeds, let alone Oxford and Cambridge, would not look at candidates with a single poor result, even if they had achieved top grades in their other subjects. The injustice was palpable but, in best New Labour form, the administrative complexities and layers of self-protective appeals procedures made access to remedy virtually impossible. Brief summer deadlines had been missed while people were on holiday and the switchboards at the examination board were either jammed or being answered by office juniors completely out of their depth. Tansley himself did not return to the College to take ultimate charge of the examination results, remaining strictly incommunicado at the ancestral home in the West Country. Crowther had all the statistics but hadn't a clue as to what to do with them. Fulwell fussed and bossed and finished the day in a cascade of tears as a particularly furious and articulate mother destroyed her down the telephone. Alexander Scott, who had problems of his own with some of the English results, as did most Heads of Department that summer in every secondary school, independent and maintained, finally put Anthony Ridell in touch with one of the former's contacts in the press. The journalist was sympathetic. Moreton College found itself on the crest of a story breaking which dominated the national news for nearly a week. Other journalists came and both Riddell and Scott were interviewed for the six o'clock television news. In the end, justice was only done for candidates when it was too late to influence decisions already taken by the universities. The row and its ramifications were still rumbling on. When he had finally returned to the College, other journalists, not initially involved with the College, had contacted the Headmaster himself. At that safer stage, Tansley had been happy to acquire a little extra personal publicity but it became a nuisance when some of the enquirers wanted details and seemed to have a more exact grasp of the new curriculum than he did himself. Moreover, this particular journalist, Kieran Morrell, was from a left wing broadsheet and was developing his own angle about what he saw as the disproportionate clamour which had been voiced by independent schools, the implication being that poor children in state schools had had to suffer in silence.

The present initial enquiry seemed innocent enough but Tansley's self-protective antennae registered the need for caution. In apparent politeness, suggesting that he was simply warming up, Morrell's introductory gambit was to ask what the teacher/pupil ratio was at the College.

The Headmaster spied the trap. If the figure seemed *favourable*, his pupils could be represented to have had an unfair advantage. However, if it was *unfavourable*, such an assertion would contradict much of the spiel in the College prospectus and invite losing out to Moreton's competitors when new parents might be making a choice. Although none of *them* would be likely to read Morrell's newspaper, regarding it as a left-wing rag, the journalist's spin on the statistic might attract dangerous copy elsewhere. In fact, Tansley was saved by his own vagueness. He told Morrell that he was not quite sure what the figure was 'at this precise moment in time' and, realising that the enemy had, in all probability, got it in front of him anyway (Crowther and Briggs-Johnstone had between them updated the College's website), Tansley magnanimously offered to send a Moreton College prospectus which would provide Morrell with 'all the latest statistics about everything here'. He ran this straight on to a smooth apology which explained that he had some-one with him and that his next appointment was already late. After putting down the 'phone, he poured himself another gin and tonic and turned to the window where he looked out at the sunshine smiling upon the vast extent of Lancelot Brown's magnificent endeavour.

Mary, from the catering department, brought him his light lunch. He uncorked a bottle of chilled Sancerre in the refrigerator and drank half of it before Ursula brought in his post-prandial cup of coffee. Feeling suitably fortified, Tansley took on the afternoon's business. At last, Ursula could come in to take him through the correspondence.

'A bit of a backlog I'm afraid, Geoffrey.'

He sighed. 'Where do we start?'

'Lady Wolseley. I thought it might be a good idea to write to her quickly to try to prevent her 'phoning in.'

'Heavens, yes: quick thinking, Ursula. What is it this time? Another complaint about Alexander?'

'No, not this time. It's about Alison Pritchard. Lady W is complaining that she's out of the House too much.'

'The poor woman's daughter's in hospital for Heaven's sake. Alison was in here, fighting back the tears, just a week or so ago. I understood that all the duties were covered. Come to think of it, Cressida told me that *she* had just recently done a stint for Alison. What's supposed to have gone wrong?'

'Emma needed help with a History essay during prep. and apparently no-one was around to provide this.'

Ursula handed over the thick cream parchment with the Lady's title printed boldly on the top, above the mews address in Chelsea.

'Cressida knows the score over in Montague. Get her to palm the woman off with something.'

But, suddenly, he remembered Lady Wolseley's mention of an intention to do something for the 'Campaign for College' appeal. He didn't know whether it had come to anything or not but, more conscious of the extent of her wealth than of the degree of her meanness, he thought it better that he spent a few minutes placating the woman.

'No, on second thoughts, I'd better write. We can't afford to upset *her* too much.'

A bland letter of assurance was dispatched. Tansley scrawled 'with best regards, Geoffrey Tansley' at the end.

Several letters then needed to be written in connection with a master who was dismissed last term. The man had been a housemaster who, through a combination of negligence and deceit, had firstly failed to detect, and then attempted to conceal, a particularly nasty incident of buggery. It had seemed an open and shut case but it also appeared that Tansley had accidentally contravened some small-print in Employment Law. The teacher had consulted his union and both the College and the Headmaster now found themselves being sued. They were insured, of course, but the general rule under such circumstances is to be seen to fly the flag for moral rectitude if only to counter any adverse publicity. All this took time and temper.

The Bursar came and took Tansley through a recently published document about teachers' pensions which Tansley pretended to understand. This was followed by some discussion about charging for staff accommodation, catering costs and 'colleagues' extravagance in the use of electricity and telephones.'

Some prospective new parents arrived and were given a cup of tea and a sandwich.

The time was fast approaching for the meeting with John Donaldson. Alone again, Tansley rose and stood by the window. The capricious October weather had altered. Dark clouds were rolling in from the south-west. It was going to be an early dusk with no sunset. Migratory water-birds circled over the distant lake which would soon be immersed in shadow. He turned back into the room and switched the lights on.

As arranged, Cressida Fulwell and Bernard Bassett arrived a few minutes before the Chaplain. Tansley heard that

Bernard had been 'most understanding' about the proposed change in under-housemaster at Blenheim.

'Temporary change,' Tansley had corrected.

John Donaldson was, of course, incredulous when he heard about the allegation. The four of them were sitting on the two comfortable settees which faced each other in the Headmaster's study. Geoffrey and Cressida faced John and Bernard.

'Tell me that the boy is making the story up,' said Geoffrey, smiling with genuine kindness and looking at his Chaplain intently.

Geoffrey truly did not care whether John had touched Jude Williams' leg or not. He was willing John to say the right thing.

'It is only his word against yours, John, and I can leave you to imagine which would carry greater weight.'

In a momentary reversal of roles, the Headmaster stretched both his hands out in a gesture of hieratic reassurance.

John gulped as he blushed with shock, humiliation and confusion.

'Poor chap,' said Geoffrey. 'I am so sorry that you're being put through this. Just say the word and we'll defend you to the hilt.'

'The word?' asked John, not understanding.

'Yes, the word THAT YOU DID NOT TOUCH THAT WRETCHED BOY'S LEG,' said the Headmaster, with formidably steely emphasis.

John put his hands to his head. It was not clear whether he was distraught or wracking his brains and, if the latter, whether he was working out what to say or delving into his memory. For a moment, all activity was suspended in the silence of that room, a silence punctuated only by the hum of Geoffrey's computer and the ticking of a great clock on the Robert Adam mantelpiece.

Cressida Fulwell attempted to speak. Geoffrey stopped her abruptly with a sharp movement of his right hand. His natural authority made it clear that they would all wait until John was ready to respond.

Returning the Headmaster's direct gaze, John spoke with an even, if slightly puzzled, diffidence.

'It is true that, after the match a couple of weeks back, I applied some antiseptic cream to Jude's leg. He had grazed it. I remember being surprised because the ground had seemed too soft for that degree of abrasion. I told him to see the matron and, a bit later, Priscilla Peverill confirmed that he had done so.'

John smiled faintly towards Geoffrey, slightly relieved to have been able to recapture the facts with appropriate precision. Geoffrey closed his eyes and took a long inward breath.

'My dear John, I do know, with all my heart, that, in essence, it was a trivial and harmless thing to have done but I have to tell you, with the greatest possible reluctance, that this allegation has made the incident very, very serious.'

The Headmaster's tone, as well as the words just used, caused John sudden and profound alarm. He felt suddenly out of his depth. He glanced towards first Cressida and then Bernard. Both averted their eyes. He felt the panic of dangerous isolation. It did not even occur to him to pray.

'I'm truly sorry, John, but you're digging your own grave in this. The police will be back tomorrow. Now that you've confirmed the fact material to the allegation made by Williams and his mother, we'll just have to hope that a sensible judge sees the whole thing for the nonsense it is and that, if it comes to it, he will direct the jury accordingly.'

'Judge? Jury?' whispered John in horrified disbelief.

'Well, at worst, possibly, yes. Of course, the Williamses might withdraw before it gets to that stage. Whatever happens, I can't see them coming out of it too favourably.'

'But isn't it the Social Services now who'll prosecute, through the police, rather than Mrs Williams?' asked Cressida.

Geoffrey said nothing but sighed and looked down at the floor.

'The trouble is, John,' Cressida now took up, 'touching the boy's leg was badly out of order. In the staff handbook, which we revised two years ago, it expressly states that a teacher is forbidden to touch a pupil.'

John blinked at her uncomprehendingly.

'And,' Cressida continued, pressing home her advantage, while trying very hard to achieve a tone of the gravest regret, 'a public confession has now just been made before three witnesses.'

John looked at all of them in undisguised amazement.

'I am obliged to have Cressida and Bernard here, John,' said Geoffrey gently, kindness now merging into self-defence. 'The Deputy Head must witness a conversation of this kind. It is a requirement. And Bernard has to be here in his capacity as Jude Williams' housemaster. And that, I'm afraid, brings me to another very painful matter which needs immediate address.'

John darted a look of frightened enquiry towards the Headmaster as the latter told him with terse compassion that the police were insisting that he could have no contact with pupils while the allegation was under investigation.

'Obviously, you will remain on full salary while all this is going on,' said Geoffrey, trying unsuccessfully to find a reassuring tone while John looked on in mystification, 'but it will involve your moving out of Blenheim House with immediate effect.'

John gasped with incredulity.

'I know; it's terribly hard; I'm *so* sorry.' Geoffrey paused. 'Have you anywhere you can go, John?'

Now on the brink of breaking down, John explained that both his parents were dead and that he had no siblings. He did indeed have friends away from the College but he didn't feel that he could arrive on their doorstep at this sort of notice and under these circumstances.

'You have no property of your own?' asked Geoffrey in a tone of gentle surprise.

'Yes, my parents' house in Sussex. But it's let out to tenants for months ahead.'

'This has come upon us all so suddenly,' mused Geoffrey. 'I don't know if any of the College properties off campus are vacant. We'll have to ask the Bursar.'

'Matthew and Tamsin Edwards have just moved out of the house down in the Meadows Estate,' said Cressida, finding a bright, helpful tone. 'They've moved into their own house on Moreton Hill.'

She smiled reassuringly at John.

'That might be the answer,' said the Headmaster. 'Between these four walls, I shall twist the Bursar's arm to see that no rent is charged.'

John found himself thanking them for all their kindness and thoughtfulness. They all rose. Geoffrey was keen not to be left on his own with John, partly out of embarrassment and partly mindful of the need to negotiate the rush hour jam on the ring-road as he drove to Tesco's and back to find the olives, smoked salmon and assorted cheeses required by his wife. He candidly announced this pressing schedule, turning it into a sort of rueful joke. On cue, Cressida offered a merry little laugh.

'Life goes on,' Geoffrey said to John, looking at him directly in the eye and putting his hands on each of John's arms.

The others were keen to take their leave hurriedly, too. Neither did they want to be the one left with the victim. Since they were not the one nailed, they turned to their affairs. Bernard bounced off eagerly to tell Delia the news. Cressida left quickly, full of the delightful prospect of taking largesse to Richard Ellman.

John was the last to leave the room. He returned to

Blenheim in a daze. One mercy was that he did not meet any boys. He unburdened his misery to Priscilla who wept first of all with compassion and then with rage. The Bursar sent one of the porters over with the keys to 29 Curlew Close. Patricia helped John to pack all necessary essentials and, between them, after a few journeys and a hasty meal in her flat, they moved John into a featureless, modern, semi-detached house in the least expensive of the three private housing estates which surrounded the town.

And so, having been evicted abruptly from the place which he had for two decades assumed as home, where he had been cocooned by all the reassuring comfort of the community which he had served with such passionate loyalty, John Donaldson found himself in a strange bed in a strange house, invisibly surrounded by total strangers, and without any knowledge of what was going to happen to him in the future, just six hours after his life had been so suddenly and completely turned upside down.

SEVENTEEN

RICHARD LIVED IN A bed-sitting room at the top of four long flights of stone stairs. His room was really a rectangular attic above the boarding house which comprised part of the Eighteenth Century mansion which was the heart of the College. The door was in the centre of one of the longer walls of the room. When entering, the ceiling was horizontal for four metres or so and then sloped downwards, in line with the eaves of the building. Richard's bed was against the wall at this lower side of the room. To the left, on the opposite wall, was a cooker with two electric rings and a stainless steel kitchen sink and draining board above which were some cupboards which contained a limited quantity of crockery. Beside that, was a surface on which stood a kettle, underneath which was a small refrigerator. Between the cooker and the door were a bookcase and a table with a television on it. Facing them was a single armchair. To its right, was a small table with an upright wooden chair.

The only window was at that end of the room. It was small in size but Richard had been rather pleased when he discovered that it afforded immediate, exclusive and secluded access to a flat section of the roof of the mansion. When he had arrived at a nearly empty College in the bright warmth of August, he had enjoyed crawling out of his dark quarters onto the roof where, undisturbed and invisible to others, and wearing nothing more than a pair of boxer shorts, he could lie on a bath sheet and soak up the sunshine while taking in one of the most magnificent vistas in England.

To the right, as one entered the room from the stairs, on the wall facing the bed, was an elderly oak chest of drawers and a heavy, freestanding, matching oak wardrobe. At the far end of the room, opposite the window, was a partition wall behind which a small bathroom and lavatory had been inserted. Richard's desk and accompanying upright chair were below the window. A computer monitor and keyboard rested on the left-hand side of the desk.

Richard was fairly self-sufficient for a very young man straight out of college who was finding his way at the opposite end of the world. Although irenic by nature, he had had moments of home-sickness and loneliness. These were not assisted by the College's isolated situation, made the more pronounced if one did not have a car at one's disposal. However, after they had settled in for the September term, some of the other young men on the staff had come to know him and he had quickly been included in trips out to the pub' and the cinema. His primary qualification was in Sports Studies and he had come to Moreton to teach Physical Education and to help with College sport. Athletically slight in build, Richard was extremely fast, with an unerring eye for a ball and an equally rapid intuitive intelligence when responding tactically on the games field. He was popular with the boys, attractive to the girls and polite and well-mannered when dealing with senior colleagues in the Common Room, who quickly discovered him to be conscientious and reliable. He found an English boarding school strange in concept, but in some ways appealing, and he was keen and well suited to fit in with the house style. He was concerned if he made a mistake and quick to apologise.

Now, at six o'clock in the evening, Richard sat, slumped in the faded armchair, watching the television. The news had just started, having followed an episode of an Australian soap opera which generally seemed to have involved supposedly everyday characters looking shocked each time they answered the 'phone and opening fridge doors in a limitless pursuit of orange juice. Richard was in his socks and wearing a white t-shirt and a pair of blue jeans with fashionably ragged hems and appropriately positioned tears in the denim fabric. His left leg was crooked over the arm of the chair and he was holding a half-empty tinny in his right hand.

Richard's Monday had, not surprisingly, been very different from that of Geoffrey Tansley. As a temporary teacher and considered to be a part-timer, for reasons of economy rather than fairness, Richard was not expected to attend Morning Chapel. Neither could he face a public breakfast. Like many active young men, he required many hours of sleep and tended to fall out of bed at the last minute, grab some orange juice, pour some milk over some cereal and quickly pull on either a track-suit or a pair of shorts and a sports shirt over his underwear. Fifteen minutes after getting out of bed, he was supervising a class of boys in the gym.

Today was no exception. After lunch, he had taken two more classes. Then had come the most trying moment of Richard's week: Upper Sixth Girls' Swimming. Some of the girls flirted with him shamelessly. Richard was easily embarrassed and it was a source of amusement to some of the naughtier girls that he blushed quickly if they looked at him too brazenly when he was in his swimming shorts or if they paraded themselves too obviously in front of him. He was, of course, out-numbered by twenty or thirty to one. The girls competed fiercely to avoid being scheduled for Mrs Froggarty's Tuesday slot, desperately trying to find legitimate reasons which meant that they absolutely had to attend Mr Ellman's swimming class on Monday. Richard was, however, saved partly by the fact that they had all fallen in love with him, partly because he was always very nice to them, instinctively finding just the right tone, and also because he was a good teacher, who knew exactly what he wanted from them, in terms of swimming, and could explain this clearly. From the beginning, he had explained that the whistle commanded total silence and attention. Because the girls so wanted to please him, and Richard called out his instructions authoritatively but pleasantly, this simple system of discipline worked well. Moreover, this year, for the first time ever, under Richard's tutelage, the girls of Moreton College were competing favourably against other schools and so, for many of them, the swimming itself became a serious pursuit. There were times when he found it faintly trying, taking a team off in a College minibus, being driven ferociously by Felicity Froggarty, a busty married woman in her late fifties, and arriving, the only male, at an all girls' school, but he had a sense of humour and a capacity for detachment which saw him through.

Still, these interludes with the girls were a trial. The most difficult thing was the management of his own response to a concentration of scantily clad, nubile young women, all confined, together with him, inside the steamy parameters of the swimming pool. Obviously, he could not but notice their firm, curvaceous breasts, shapely, fully exposed legs and tresses of long hair (especially, for him, the blondes) as he sometimes saw them winding the pale golden strands inside their swimming caps. This had been more of a problem for him even than the few occasions when he had been caught by some of the girls in his boxers, while changing in the small staff room to which the key had been mislaid and the door of which refused to shut securely. He still blushed when this occurred, despite telling himself (and, on one occasion, them) that it was no different from seeing him in his swimming shorts. Such mildly expressed rationality did not prevent the shrieks and giggles of thrilled delight at the sight of sexy young Sir in his underpants and Richard's assumed sang-froid was betrayed by his inability to stop blushing at such moments.

It was always a relief to leave the noisy, claustrophobic humidity of the swimming pool complex with its direct and torturing fleshly temptations and to step out into the cool fresh air. Richard would then meet some of the other young masters taking games of various kinds over tea and sandwiches in the Common Room, before leaping up the stairs to his garret to 'shower, shit and shave', as his grandfather back in Victoria quaintly described the process of ablution. He would change into the clothes he was now wearing, before changing again into a jacket, tie and flannel trousers, as protocol required when dining formally in the Common Room.

Twice a week, Richard spent evenings on duty in the House. He enjoyed going round, chatting to the lads and listening to the issues which concerned them. They, in turn, appreciated his cheerful, informal friendliness and were grateful for his trust. During break of prep., he would pick up a table tennis bat and gleefully thrash any one of them at the game. After prep., he was happy to crash out in front of the House television with the Sixth Formers.

On the evenings when he was not on duty, Richard went out with the other young teachers. He was developing a taste for 'real ale' and was happy to extend his already informed enthusiasm for the cinema. Among other associations, he was striking up a friendship with Rosie Innes, a young teacher of Biology who was the under-housemistress at Montague, one of the girls' houses. They got on well, meeting generally in the company of the others, and, despite it being observed by the Common Room gossips that they were 'a handsome couple', each seemed to appreciate the unspoken willingness of the other not to press for further commitment. There was no question of any more formal liaison or compromise to autonomy.

Now, Richard was sprawling on his armchair, being bored by a political reporter who was standing in front the Houses of Parliament, speculating over the future of a member of the Cabinet. As he absentmindedly put his tinny down on the table in order to scratch an itch on his stomach, there was a knock on the door. Assuming it was one of the boys in the House, he yelled out an invitation to enter. Such was his surprise at the prospect of the Deputy Headmistress entering his humble dwelling, that he leapt off his chair and stood up to greet Cressida.

'Oh! Hello!' he said emphatically. It was all that he could think of, especially as he realised that he didn't quite know how to address so eminent a personage within the hierarchy of the establishment. He pressed the button on the remote to switch the television off, at the same time deftly kicking his tracksuit and trainers away from the spot on the carpet where he had dropped them before taking the shower.

'To what do I owe the pleasure of this?' he asked, smiling politely.

It took Cressida a moment to find her breath, in the wake of having transported her considerable bulk the height of the building.

'Goodness! How many stairs are there to get here?' she asked.

'Seventy-two,' came the quick, bright response. 'Here, do sit down.' Richard motioned her to the armchair. He scooped up the upright chair by his desk and dropped it lightly two metres or so in front of his visitor, placing the back of the chair before him between his legs and grasping it within his arms.

'So you have to climb all those stairs every time you come to your flat?'

'I timed it to begin with. My fastest was twenty seconds.'

Richard grinned ingenuously. Cressida was charmed.

She looked round the room.

'I've never been up here before. It's a bit dark, isn't it? We've obviously not pushed the boat out when it comes to furniture either.'

'It suits me,' replied Richard. 'It's bigger than anything I've had before and I can be in the Common Room in less than a minute without having to go outside.'

'But all those stairs!'

'It gives me exercise!'

'Don't you get enough with all you do during the day?'

'Another twenty seconds doesn't make much difference!'

He smiled again. What beautiful blue eyes he has, thought Cressida, and such finely sculpted cheek-bones.

'Well, you must be wondering why I'm here. I've come as an ambassador for the Headmaster,' she began portentously.

'Ooh…..Err! What have I done- or not done?'

'It's not that at all: quite the opposite in fact. Every-one is saying how good you are and they're all commenting on how quickly you have adapted to the College.'

'That's very kind of them all.'

'I know for a fact that the Headmaster himself thinks that.'

'Really? I'm surprised that he even knows who I am.'

Richard then quickly hurried on, not wanting his comment to be misconstrued as impertinence.

'There's no reason why he should. Mr Tansley shook me by the hand when I arrived and we've not had occasion to speak since. After all, I'm just the young chap who's here to give an extra hand with the sport.'

'Oh, he certainly knows who you are, Richard,' said Cressida, beaming warmly. 'And *I* can tell *you* that he very much likes what he hears- as I do!'

'Right! Well! That's very nice,' said Richard, slightly at a loss.

'I've come about a rather serious matter which involves a degree of confidentiality.'

'I can't imagine what it is. I'm intrigued- but of course I'll keep it confidential,' he added hastily.

'It's to do with the Chaplain, John Donaldson. I believe that you've come to know him a bit, through the First XI Soccer.'

'Yes, indeed. John's a great guy. I really appreciate working with him.'

'Yes. Quite.' She paused. 'But John's no longer very young and the Headmaster is just wondering how long he can go on running the first team of such a physically demanding game.'

'Oh, I see! Well, I do know enough about *that* to set the Head's mind at rest. John is tremendously fit and *very* good at that job. You've only got to consider the results to make that judgment. And, as I've said, he's such a great guy; he's got all those lads eating out of his hand. So the Head needn't worry about that! That's one of the very few pieces of advice I probably *am* qualified to give anybody round here!'

'You're very loyal!'

'No! It's true! Every-one who knows anything about it will tell you the same!'

'Richard, I've got to tell you something which you mustn't repeat.'

Richard looked puzzled as Cressida continued. When he heard about the accusation and its source, he could not disguise his shock and anger and was instant in his condemnation of Jude Williams. He rapidly filled in all the details of the boy's negligence, finally stressing that the break had come because of his, Richard's, insistence.

'So, you see, Mrs Fulwell......'

'Oh, dear Richard- so formal and polite- do call me Cressida, *please!*'

'Sorry....er....thank you....er....so you see.....er.... Cressida, the whole thing's probably *my* fault. Well- it's really Jude Williams' fault but, of all the people involved, *John's* certainly not to blame. I know for a fact that he bent over backwards to help that lad.'

'Exactly that might be the nub of the problem. The unfortunate fact is, Richard, that John has admitted- in front of the Headmaster and me and the boy's Housemaster- that he *did* touch the boy's leg after the match three week-ends ago. As you yourself will know, as a new teacher, that action breaks the rules. I'm sure that you will have noticed that it's laid down clearly in the staff handbook, a document which reflects the law of the land.'

Richard, however, though young and a long way from home, lacked neither a sense of moral direction nor the courage to articulate this. His reaction took Cressida by surprise. Blushing, this time with anger, he got up abruptly from his chair. Taken aback, she also rose.

'I don't know how you normally do things in this country but I've never heard of anything so bloody ridiculous!'

'Calm down!' commanded Cressida assertively.

He faltered; they both sat down as before.

'I realise that this must come as a bit of a shock; it's very unpleasant for every-one concerned. The fact is that John did put himself in the wrong by touching the boy. There's nothing the poor Headmaster can do about it. The police came to see him this morning and they will return tomorrow. There may be nothing in the allegation- there probably isn't- but the grimmest part of all this is that they are insisting that John lives off the premises and has no contact with pupils until the matter is sorted out.'

'But this is mad. What if John did touch Jude's leg? They're both sportsmen. It was in a changing room. The lad had a cut on his shin. It's perfectly natural to put some antiseptic cream on it. If John hadn't been there, I'd have probably done the same thing myself. So would anybody else.'

'Oh! Did you see it then?'

'No, I didn't. Why should that be important?' And then, 'Don't think I'm going to stick anything on the poor bloke.'

'Indeed not, Richard. I've not come here for that purpose. The events are as I have described and there's nothing you or I or the Headmaster can do about it. It's all very sudden and very sad.'

She shook her head gravely and then continued.

'The Headmaster asked me to come because we've got to turn to you to help us out of the immediate jam that this puts us in.'

Richard looked puzzled again.

'We need your help in two ways. Firstly, we've got to keep the First XI going and want you to take it over.'

Richard frowned and said nothing.

'For the time being, anyway,' added Cressida.

'I'm not sure that that's a good idea. I didn't know anything about soccer until a few weeks ago. Every-one plays rugby in Australia. I was only slotted in to help with the football because there was a manpower shortage. I couldn't replace John.'

'I'm sure you'd cope very well. I'm under the impression that John, like every-one else, thinks very highly of you, Richard. Look at it this way. Some-one *must* take it over- for the time being at least. Who do you think John would most want to step in? It points to you for the sake of continuity, if nothing else. In fact, you'd really be doing it *for John's sake.* Consider that you'd be looking after it for him for a little spell. And, I'm afraid to say, there just isn't anybody else.'

He agreed, of course, 'for John's sake', and then wondered what the second item for consideration might be. Cressida introduced the matter of the Blenheim under-housemaster's post, stressing the improved status, accommodation and allowance in salary. When Richard demurred, having been taken even more by surprise, she again fielded the argument about *'who John would most want to be there in this, his hour of distress.'* Richard agreed with even greater reluctance but only on two conditions: that John could leave anything he wanted to in his flat and that he, Richard, would move back into his present accommodation when the Half Term break came so that, in the absence of any boys, John would be free to come and go as he liked. Cressida immediately regretted prompting such scrupulousness, through having pointed out how nice it would be to be in the Blenheim flat over Half Term, but agreed all the same.

'I still can't believe that this has happened,' said Richard. 'To think that he's being thrown out after all these years just because he touched a boy's leg. Anyway, Jude Williams is seventeen: hardly some little dewdrop!'

Cressida gave an exaggerated little laugh in response to the mild witticism in the metaphor and then reverted swiftly to serious mode.

'I realise how ridiculous it must seem but the boy is still a minor in *locus parentis* and John really should have known better than to put himself in the wrong by touching him, however innocently.'

She rose to go.

'It all seems pretty crazy to me. I'll do these two things but I'm only doing them to help John out,' replied Richard, also now standing.

'Of course. That's understood and it does you great credit. One would have expected no less from you.' She hesitated. 'Half Term's coming up. What are your plans?'

'I'm going to London to stay with a couple of other Australian guys who are working in schools there.'

'That'll be a good break. Are you off straightaway?'

'Almost- but I'll probably spend the first night here and get going the day after that.'

'I'll be here then too. I'd be so glad if you could come for dinner that night. I might ask some others. It'll be very informal.'

Richard was rather taken aback but could find no reason for declining.

Cressida took her leave. As she made her way down the steep, dark stair-case with due caution, she felt pleased with her day's work. The police had forced Geoffrey's hand with regard to the Chaplain whose departure she very much favoured. She felt that she herself had gently steered the head magisterial ship in the right direction when it had threatened to lose its way. What a happy chance that Donaldson had touched the Williams boy! And what a bonus just now to involve Richard Ellman! What a lovely boy, with his slim, athletic figure- and so handsome! How delightful that she should have the good fortune to bring him the favourable news of his double promotion! The football might be off womanly limits but she would make it her business to see that the young man was settling happily into Blenheim House. She would make personal visits from time to time, as was appropriate to her position as Deputy Head. Now, she could look forward to Richard's coming for dinner really quite soon.

Cressida had received good news of another sort in the post that morning. Details of the settlement of her second divorce had come through. Her marvellous solicitor, Heather Wilding, had secured everything which they had hoped for and more than she, Cressida, had really expected. Tony would now have to leave her the house and all that it contains, as well as rather a lot of money. It amused her to think of him renting a miserable flat, making weekly visits to the launderette and living off ready made supermarket meals cooked in a microwave. His fling with the art mistress at her previous school had come to nothing but it had provided Cressida with a flawless excuse to get rid of the slimy sod.

Yes, it had been a good day and now she could look forward to dinner with the Tansleys. She would listen attentively to Geoffrey's monologues, laugh at his repeated anecdotes, enquire about Calpurnia Tansley's sprained ankle, praise her for her cooking, helpfully carry things between the kitchen and the dining room and enjoy meeting the other (possibly influential) guests. She wondered enthusiastically who these might be.

EIGHTEEN

It was the Tuesday morning before the Half Term Break. Capricious late October had slumped into a surly slough of leaden skies and drizzle. The Rev. John Donaldson had endured a difficult night but had finally descended into a fitful doze at about five o'clock. He was brought back to consciousness by the unfamiliar sound of car doors slamming as his still faceless and innominate neighbours set off for work. During a brief interval of semi-consciousness, he had been waiting for the shouts from boys below his bedroom window and in the passage behind the internal wall. Awake now, he lay still in the darkness, conjuring them up individually in his mind's eye: Charlie, Chris, Ashley, Tim and then, inevitably, Jude. His imagination, temporarily in free fall, presented Jude as he had been on that fateful day, sitting on the bench in the changing room in his underclothes. John's supine, futile yearning in the empty darkness of the alien little bedroom was suddenly jerked aside as the imaginary prospect of Jude's underpants assumed a dreadful concrete reality. They, or an identical pair, were now resting, neatly folded, in the bottom drawer of the chest of drawers in John's bedroom at the College, along with several others, each with a name-tag neatly sewn onto the elastic at the back by Priscilla. He sat up in miserable consternation and snapped the bedside light on. What on earth would Richard make of that discovery? Indeed, what on earth would Richard *do?*

Still in his pyjamas, John stepped into his slippers and hurried to the telephone in the hall. What a dreadful start to his unwelcome new situation!

'God, I don't merit any favours from you over this but please, please, let Priscilla be in. And, Lord, if she is in, PLEASE let me not lose her support and her respect. It's unreasonable to ask, Lord, I know, but I am a sinner and I shouldn't have done it and I'm probably only offering this petition out of fear of discovery, I know. Oh, God have mercy ,PLEASE!'

His mind was racing. He was, of course, immediately aware of the bearing that this might have on the case. And what of all the other boys whose intimate sartorial possession he so wrongly held? What degree of disgust would Charlie feel when faced with so squalid a revelation? Horrors flashed across his mind's eye in a nightmarish kaleidoscope: the revulsion and disbelief on Richard's handsome young face as he makes the shocking discovery, the disdain of Geoffrey Tansley as the Headmaster coldly turns against him, the smirks on the faces of an unknown jury as the counsel for the prosecution calls for 'Exhibit A' to be held aloft in court, the wagging heads in the Common Room as his last great sermon is consigned to the dustbin of hypocrisy. Towering over this collage of Bosch-like horror was the image of Christ on the Cross, let down totally and placed there to suffer by this, his disloyal priest. Most assuredly, if and when he ever returned to the College, he would not be indulging in that wrong-doing ever again.

The 'phone was dead. Of course, it had been disconnected when the previous tenants had moved out. He had a mobile 'phone which he hardly ever used. Charlie had helped him to buy it over the internet. It was several agonising minutes before he found it and several more before he remembered that he had to dial the full STD number.

The reassuring, cultivated tone of Priscilla's voice was rehearsed on the answering machine. She would be going round the House, getting them all out to Chapel. *Chapel?* Who would be taking that? The Headmaster would need to give the entire College an explanation for the Chaplain's sudden and unanticipated absence.

'Priscilla. It's John. I need you to 'phone me urgently.'

Unaware of the number of his mobile, and forgetting about the 1471 service, he had to check in his wallet and 'phone a second time with that information. Then he fell on his knees in a silent, inarticulate prayer of confession, repentance and begging supplication.

The 'phone rang a few minutes later.

'What's wrong, John? Oh, my Dear, what can I do to help?'

He told her his pathetic, lamentable tale about the boxer shorts.

'Goodness! Well….er, John- this is a bit of a surprise….To think…. I'm sorry; I'm momentarily lost for words….'

But then, deciding her attitude to the situation and quickly making a firm resolution about how to deal with it, she was able to speak with her accustomed self-possession.

'Right!' She paused for breath. 'I'll go in straightaway. Richard hasn't moved in yet. I'll rescue all the offending items and slip them into the laundry room. They'll be returned to their owners next laundry day along with the rest of their stuff. These boys won't even notice and, if they do, it will simply be assumed that there was a hold-up in the laundry and that some items had been misplaced on a previous occasion. That's always happening.'

'Oh, Priscilla! You are an angel! You've saved me!'

'Now, John, before you embark on a tortuous explanation of it all, there is no need. I understand and it *simply doesn't matter a jot*. Everybody has fantasies. All these adolescent boys do. I sometimes indulge in them myself. What you did is so innocent! And you're under great emotional pressure in your job. God understands that we're human and this was a very trivial little outlet for natural and pent up feelings. So, accept His forgiveness and don't torture yourself a second longer. You've got enough to think about without this.'

'Oh, thank you! Thank you, my dearest, darling friend! I thought that probably you'd never want to see me again!'

'Don't be ridiculous! After a friendship like ours! After all these years! Over a few pairs of boys' underpants! Come on, now! Don't let paranoia get into all this! I'm coming round for a couple of hours this evening. I've got a nice fish pie in the freezer and we can put it in the microwave. If you haven't got any with you, you go out and buy a bottle of white wine.'

'Oh!' he gasped in wordless gratitude.

'Also, I've been thinking. Might it not be a good idea for you to go and see Maurice Stantonbury about all this? Hasn't he got some authority anyway?'

'Well, yes. He's the vicar of the parish church and he's the Rural Dean.'

'And isn't he a friend of the Bishop?'

'I think they know each other pretty well. I know the Bishop a bit too, though not as well as he does.'

'Maurice and you have worked together all the time you've both been here.'

'Yes, of course. I haven't started to think straight. I'll give him a ring now.'

'Yes, I'm sure that that would be a helpful thing to do. And you'd better contact a solicitor. You do have one?'

'Well, I used Timothy Watson in the town for probate when my parents died and then again when letting the house in Sussex.'

'He's local. Are you confident that he'd be discreet?'

'Oh yes, I'm sure.'

'You're not in any union, are you?'

'No, it never crossed my mind.'

'Well, you'd better make an early appointment with this Mr Watson. Now, don't you dare tell any-one else about the underpants, not even Mr Watson, not even Maurice. They're an incidental side-show which will have finished in five minutes' time when I have removed the offending things. Have you had any breakfast yet?'

She reminded him of the bread, milk and croissants left in the refrigerator and obtained his permission to give his mobile number to the Headmaster and the two senior colleagues, Alexander and Anthony, who had both been enquiring after him, but not to any-one else, including, it had to be reluctantly agreed, to any of the pupils. Before he could embark on any analysis of the situation, she repeated that she would be round at the beginning of prep. and that he had better not delay her now as she set about her immediate quest. The 'phone went silent. Again, he dropped to his knees, this time with thanksgiving.

He consumed some coffee, toast and croissants and then resumed his normal discipline of prayer, reading his portion of scripture for the day. The Scripture Union calendar was taking him through Isaiah and the verse which leapt off the page this morning was strangely apposite and very comforting. It was from Chapter forty-two and verse three:-

'A bruised reed he will not break, and a smouldering wick he will not snuff out. In faithfulness he will bring forth justice.'

He then 'phoned Maurice Stantonbury who suggested that he came round in an hour's time. Next, he spoke with Timothy Watson's secretary and arranged an appointment for the following afternoon.

He drew back the curtains and explored his new domain. The house was antiseptically impersonal but it had been newly furnished for the previous occupants and it had been professionally cleaned after they had left. There were two more bedrooms and bedding and blankets in an airing cupboard. There was a sofa and two armchairs in the sitting room and even a television. He could leave his own T.V. for Richard. The kitchen was modern and well appointed. In terms of creature comforts, he was better off than he had been up at the College. He did not, of course, have access to the Common Room dining facilities and, anyway, all this was beside the point.

Unusually these days, the Vicar of St Mary's still lived in the Victorian vicarage near the church. Both were built on the summit of a steep rise just west of the centre of the town. The house was a rambling, red-brick affair. Shortly after their two daughters had grown up and left home, Maurice Stantonbury and his wife had confined themselves to the upper of the two storeys. This had been converted into a spacious, self-contained flat. The ground floor, which included two arbitrarily planned Edwardian extensions, was now divided into three sections: a flat for the unmarried female curate, the parish offices and a small self-contained flat let out for rent.

John had decided to walk to the vicarage. By the time he had arrived, the drizzle had reduced to a fine mizzle and the sky, though still lowering, conceded a lighter tone of grey.

Maurice and John were old friends and longstanding colleagues whose business over the past two decades had regularly overlapped. There were thus no formalities when they firstly went into the kitchen to make some coffee and then into Maurice's capacious study, with its bright bay-window commanding a southerly view across the town. Even on this gloomy day, the room seemed to exude a contented and protective guardianship over its prosperous, restlessly extending parish.

Since his arrival at Moreton College twenty years earlier, Maurice was the only person to whom John had confided what he saw to be the guilty secret of his sexuality. Maurice had been unruffled and supportive and, on the few occasions when John had felt the pressure too intensely, he had visited the Dean to ask for prayer.

Maurice, some ten years older than John, was quite a large,

comfortably upholstered man, with a full head of brushed back grey hair. He had a smooth, polished face, upon which reposed a pair of tortoise-shell framed spectacles. He was wearing an elderly tweed jacket which had long since lost its shape and had brown leather patches at the elbows and in reinforcement of the cuffs. His waist had expanded since he had bought the grey flannel trousers which he was wearing. The brown brogues and green woollen tie seemed unnecessary accoutrements for indoors.

While they had been moving between kitchen and study, there had been the customary easy chat. John was relieved that Pauline was away visiting one of their daughters. He reserved his achingly bad news for the moment when they were sitting facing each other in the comfortable armchairs in Maurice's study.

A patient and practised listener, the expression on Maurice's calm face could nevertheless not disguise his consternation at the sad tale which his fellow servant of the Almighty was unburdening. John was close to tears by the time he had finished. Maurice lent forward, keen-eyed behind his glasses, to express his concern and dismay.

'This is a terrible thing to have happened to you, John. Whatever the College might do, the church has an involvement in this too and it must move to protect you. The Bishop will need to be informed. I'm sure that he will have something to say about this malicious nonsense in a way that might cause a few of the people involved to think about putting their feet on the brakes.'

'I don't think it's the College's fault. Geoffrey Tansley seemed genuinely upset and I got the impression he wanted to do anything he could to help me. The trouble lies with the boy and his mother and, it would appear, the police and the social services.'

'As though we don't have enough *real* problems in the country, without wasting time and taxes over idiocy like this.'

'And it's my *work*, Maurice, my *work with my boys*……'

John could contain himself no longer. He apologised as he pulled out his handkerchief and wept at last.

Maurice rose and went to his friend. Bending down, he placed his hand on John's arm.

'I know, John. I know just how much it has meant to you over all these years- and, of course, even more, how much it has meant to so many others. You've helped so many people, especially young men, over the years. I'm sure that, when the wood is seen from the trees, this incident, so wickedly wrong in itself, cannot possibly outweigh all that.'

'Oh, it might; it might. I can see it all unfolding ahead of me now,' muttered John.

'No, don't say that. This is a terrible trial for you but think of the comfort which you've given other people during *their* terrible trials. Think of the divine promises which you've led them to, in full conviction of their truth. Now, dear brother, you yourself need faith, great faith.'

The lashing intensity of the storm passed for the moment. *'A bruised reed he will not break, and a smouldering wick he will not snuff out. In faithfulness he will bring forth justice.'*

Maurice returned to his chair. He agreed to bring the matter to the attention of the Bishop on John's behalf. He also thought it appropriate that he, as area Dean, should contact the Headmaster.

'Geoffrey's an awful old poseur and windbag, John, but he's not without a soul and a certain worldly shrewdness (no bad thing in a Headmaster) and I know that he holds you in great personal regard.'

'I've never had any reason to think otherwise, Maurice. He's always been considerate and gracious to me, as has Calpurnia- and, *the great thing is- was- he's let me do my work unhindered*.'

Again he broke down.

Maurice kept quiet, thinking it best to let this next squall take its natural course. As John became calmer again, they discussed various aspects of it all further and Maurice committed the matter in prayer. In due course, they returned to the kitchen where Maurice made them a tomato omelette and some fresh coffee. He pointed out that John lived within easy walking distance of the vicarage and insisted that, whenever his new situation became unbearable, he was not to hesitate to be in touch.

It was the early afternoon by the time John left the vicarage. The rain had now stopped altogether and the sun was even struggling to dispatch a few fitful rays to cheer the scene below.

He found himself on Market Street, amongst busy shoppers. It seemed suddenly strange to be included within the normality of this ordinary, real world, inhabited by young mothers pushing infants in buggies, elderly couples stopping to pass the time of day, young estate agent clerks in cheap pin-striped suits carrying envelopes to the Post Office, delivery men hoisting their wares across the pavement into shop entrances. It was as though he had dropped in from another planet as cars and vans trawled their interrupted way along the thoroughfare.

He went into Tesco Express and bought a newspaper and an assortment of basic groceries. He selected a bottle of Australian Semillon-Chardonnay to drink with Priscilla's fish pie this evening. A few of the townspeople recognised him. He returned their greeting while succeeding in avoiding conversation.

Upon arrival back at the house, he noticed that his mobile 'phone, left beside the dormant land-line installation on the small table in the hall, was indicating receipt of a single message. It was probably Priscilla, possibly the Headmaster, or maybe even either Alexander or Anthony.

His heart leapt when he discovered the message to have come from the police and that they required his immediate attendance at the police station in the town. Of course, the Headmaster would necessarily have had to tell the police where he was, passing on the mobile number, and- again of course- it was obvious that the police would need to speak with him. Still, it was another shock and it underlined the horrible change in status which had so suddenly and dramatically overtaken him.

John had dealt with the police several times but always as the professional clergyman who was providing information, assistance and reassurance when attempting to bridge a gap between a youthful miscreant and a respectful officer, grateful for his presence. The last occasion had been eighteen months ago, when Kevin Dobson, a young resident member of the kitchen staff had committed a minor motoring offence. It was entirely due to the presence of the Rev. Mr Donaldson that Sergeant Hawkins had smiled indulgently and let the agitated young man off with a paternalistic reprimand.

Now, however, as he sat on the other side of the table from a strange sergeant, in a bleak, windowless room, it was all palpably very different. John enquired after Sergeant Hawkins, only to be told briskly that he was on leave. He felt an unprecedented and humiliating intensity of self-loathing as he absorbed the unpalatable truth that, on this occasion, he was there as the suspect in an alleged crime rather than as a dignified and secure member of the social establishment. The interviewing policeman was a portly man with thinning hair and expressionless, prominent, cold blue eyes. Without anything explicit being communicated, John sensed the homophobic disgust which his interlocutor felt. A young W.P.C. sat on a chair some distance to his left, out of eye contact. He was required to write a statement before he left. He described the incident exactly as it had taken place. He was instructed to read the document through after he had finished. The policeman spoke in a tone of patronage which Tom Stevens might have used to a boy in a bottom stream in the Third Form who was struggling to write an essay describing his summer holiday. It was suggested that he sought legal advice.

At what he thought was the end of the ordeal, when they all rose from their seats, John's customary sense of courtesy prompted him to extend his hand to the police sergeant. Far from being reciprocated, the gesture was received with disdainful surprise. He was formally advised with minatory coldness that he was being charged with the sexual harassment of a minor and that he must attend at the magistrate's court in the town the following morning. He was asked if he understood the charge and reminded that anything he might say could be used in evidence. John reminded himself with disbelief that, little more than forty-eight hours earlier, he was being praised by the Headmaster and his senior colleagues and several Moreton College parents for preaching a spiritually authoritative sermon to more than seven-hundred people and that, the day before that, he had been sharing the glorious success of his boys on the football pitch. Only yesterday, he had been pleasantly embarrassed by Geoffrey Tansley's public plaudits in the Common Room. Cowed with humiliation, he looked at his shoes and made an ungainly exit, wondering if he was indeed the criminal which they suspected.

When he arrived back, he noticed with apprehension that his mobile 'phone was holding a second message. Listening fearfully, he felt relief upon hearing the distinctive, self-confident, academic drawl of Alexander Scott.

'John, old chap, it's Alexander. Look, I'm just horrified to hear about this nonsense. Priscilla has put Anthony and me in the picture. I'm 'phoning to say that Anthony and I have booked a table for three at The Wheatsheaf the evening after tomorrow. We'll go by taxi and we'll pick you up at seven-thirty on the dot. We can talk further then but I thought I'd just try to offer a word of comfort by letting you know that G&T has, so far, in public at least, handled it surprisingly well. He told the College in Chapel this morning that you would be away for a bit. He didn't go into any details and managed to sustain a pretty convincing tone, suggesting that it was an entirely ordinary situation which should attract no special interest or concern. Quite the right way to play it, I'm sure you'll agree. I suppose that some degree of rumour is inevitable because the bloody boy's involved but it was faintly amusing when the ghouls in the Common Room all turned up for G&T's notices in Break only to hear him repeat exactly the same thing and then rabbit on for seven or eight minutes about shirts and trousers. I guess that he probably did it deliberately: not a bad ploy, huh? Anyway, put your feet up while you can. In one way you're a lucky sod. Only joking. See you tomorrow evening. Bye, meantime- and your friends are with you; you know that.'

Despite his misery, John could not restrain a smile. Dear, cynical, compassionate, acute Alexander: always the same. What a friend! What a colleague! It was reassuring at least to know that G&T had not been away at some conference, leaving Cressida Fulwell to present the information to the College, no doubt far more explicitly.

NINETEEN

The Sixth Form Common Room was crowded with pupils during morning break while Geoffrey Tansley was lecturing his colleagues in the Common Room. Margaret and Gloria, faithful servants of the College over many years, were selling hot and cold drinks, biscuits and chocolate over the counter. Ashley and Charlie were chaffing Gloria.

'Go on, Miss G,' said Ashley, switching on his most appealing smile. 'I can see that box of crisps down there on the floor. They're only going to go back to the kitchen. Have pity on two poor, hungry, penniless young lads who are starving to death.'

'You two would sell your grandmothers for more food,' replied the amiable Gloria, laughing as she handed over two bags of crisps free of charge.

'Look at what she's charging for Mars Bars, Ashley,' teased a grinning Charlie.

'I know, Charlie. It's daylight robbery. Miss G'll be on the town tonight at our expense.'

'Now get along with you, you two; there are other people waiting while you're clowning about.'

'Oh no! She's getting cross!' declared Ashley in mock anxiety, pretending to bite his nails.

Gloria chortled merrily as the two relatively slightly built boys were pushed aside by an irate Victoria Summerthwaite who was next in the queue. Ashley raised his hands in surrender as Victoria loomed over him. Although Charlie could just about look her in the eye, she was half his weight again and could easily have knocked him down.

'Move on. Stop holding everybody else up,' reprimanded Vicky bossily.

'OK, Vicky. Cool it. Don't get stressed,' said Ashley with good-humoured wariness. 'We're your male slaves.'

'Like in Ancient Rome,' Charlie added merrily.

'You will be in a minute, if you don't shut up,' said Vicky, smiling despite herself.

The homeless chic fashion of the day coincided with Ashley's natural scruffiness. The muddy, ripped flannel trousers which he was wearing clung tenuously to his hips. They would have been rejected by any remotely self-respecting inhabitant of the developing world. Vicky now grabbed the elastic of his exposed navy blue underpants at the back with both hands and yanked them sharply upwards. Ashley yelled in shock when the most sensitive parts of his anatomy were suddenly constricted in pain as Vicky locked them in a powerful 'wedgy'.

'No! Vicky! Stop! Let me go! You're destroying my manhood!' He gave a little falsetto gasp when she released him. 'You ball-crusher!' he said, gasping again and grinning ruefully as every-one around laughed.

'I can't really see you as one of the *castrati*, Ash,' commented Charlie.

'You very nearly are doing. God knows what she's done to me.'

'Next time, she'll put metal collars round our necks and chain us to rings which she'll have hammered into the walls outside Montague.'

'Good idea,' said Vicky 'and then I'll pour boiling pitch on you both from my window and record the screams of agony.' She turned to greet Gloria who was a favourite lady amongst all the boys and girls and whose friendly, motherly face locked away many adolescent secrets never to be disclosed.

In another corner of the crowded room, Olivia was asking Jude about the Rev. D.. They had had two further rows about Emma but, angry with him though she was, Olivia could not cure herself from being in love with Jude. Despite her friend Vicky's sane advice, she found that she could not easily let him go.

The Upper Sixth, in particular, realised that there must be more behind G&T's bland announcement earlier in Chapel than the Headmaster had chosen to declare. Moreover, enough hints had already been dropped suggesting that the Chaplain's absence might be connected with the row which everyone seemed to know had taken place between Jude Williams and him. There is no more efficient rumour factory than an English boarding school. Charlie, Ashley, Chris and Tim had already visited Priscilla to find out what was going on. Suspicion had immediately been generated when Jude had coyly declined to join them.

'I'm very sorry, boys, but I can tell you nothing,' Priscilla had said, feeling much more unhappy than she hoped she had appeared. 'Please don't press me any further.' And then, feeling that she had to give some tiny concession away to their troubled young faces, she added 'I'm as worried as you are,' before turning away so that they could not see the tears coming to her eyes.

'Look, Livvy,' Jude was trying to speak in *sotto voce*, 'the bloke's a pervert. He made a pass at me in the changing room. It was disgusting. My Mother's taking him and this bloody College to the cleaners.'

'I can't believe it! The Rev. D?'

Olivia's voice was shrill with incredulity.

Jude hissed at her to keep her voice down but it was too late. The gang of friends was bearing down upon them, laden with soft drinks, crisps and chocolate biscuits.

Olivia was truly shocked.

'Jude says that the Rev. D's a pervert and that apparently he had touched him up in the changing rooms.'

'I might have known that you'd be behind this,' said Jasper menacingly.

'Yes, why am I not surprised either?' added Vicky.

'You'd better come up with some evidence, mate,' said an unusually troubled Chris.

'I'm not allowed to say anything,' said a rattled Jude. 'It's all *sub judice*.'

'*Sub Judice!* Fuck that!' said Jasper. 'You'd better tell us what's going on before we get it out of you.'

'I'd like to see you try,' snarled Jude. 'Donaldson's a screaming queer since you all want to know.'

'Don't you dare speak about the Rev. D like that!' shouted Jasper in a sudden fury.

'Why not? As the old saying goes, I thought it took one to know one,' sneered Jude.

'Fuck off, you treacherous, malicious little bastard!' yelled Jasper, lunging at Jude.

'He's pretty good at doing just what you've told him to do, Jasper,' said Vicky, glaring at Jude.

Jude was fortunate in successfully dodging Jasper's weighty blow.

'Come on, Nancy Boy,' he said, his eyes calculating Jasper's likely attack. 'I'm ready to give your balls an experience they've never had before.'

But Charlie and Ashley had both put restraining arms on Jasper and Olivia had moved in front of Jude whom Chris had also stepped towards.

Every-one was astonished, and not just by the shocking allegation. Fights were quite exceptional at the College. Bitching, slandering, foul language- all of them perhaps, but hostile physical violence, no.

For a moment, all movement and conversation froze.

'Now, cool it everybody!' commanded Ashley, the Captain of the First XI.

He released Jasper, patting him gently on the arm, but he

was looking directly at Jude as he delivered the instruction. Olivia had moved aside again. Charlie still kept his hand gently on Jasper's other arm.

'Now Jude: what exactly are you accusing the Rev. D of? You might as well tell us after all this,' demanded Ashley with authority.

'It's as she said,' mumbled Jude sullenly, pointing his elbow at Olivia, without looking either at her or meeting Ashley's gaze.

There was another uncomprehending silence.

'I don't believe it!' said Tim quietly, his face reddening with self-conscious dismay.

'You nasty, lying little runt!' said Camilla, with manifest dislike.

Olivia started to weep. Vicky moved to put her arm round her.

Then, silent until now and white in the face, Charlie, moving a little away from Jasper, spoke.

'Jude, this is a terribly serious allegation. It's incredible! What exactly are you saying the Rev. D did? Did he really touch you where he shouldn't or was it just a permissible, friendly sort of touch? You *know* the difference.'

"*Demand me nothing. What you know, you know. From this time forth, I never will speak word,*" replied Jude.

'*Not* the time to quote Shakespeare,' said Charlie, the colour returning to his face with unaccustomed anger. 'And, if you must be so melodramatic, I would hardly have thought that Iago was the most suitable character to choose at the moment.'

Jude had never heard his friend speak in such a tone. That, more than anything that had happened before in the confrontation, brought tears to his eyes. Continuing to indulge his sudden, irrational, crazy fix on Shakespeare, for some reason he now thought of King Lear. He thought but did not speak the words:-

'No, I'll not weep. I have full cause of weeping.'

He met Charlie's clear gaze in the dreadful realisation that their long and enduring friendship had suddenly terminated.

'So he's trying to show off even to the end,' said Vicky with disgust, her arm still round the shoulders of the distressed Olivia.

'Ya,' said Jasper, trying to recover his self-control. 'Still, we all saw that he couldn't put one over on you, Charlie.' And, then, having not in fact recovered as well as he had imagined, 'Those things he was saying about me. It's true.....'

As Jasper began to lose his self-control in indiscretion, Ashley moved back beside him and once again squeezed his arm.

'Never mind, Jas. We don't need to know about all that.' He looked Jasper in the eye. 'You and me are mates. Right? So's Charlie your mate- and all the rest of us. You're OK, Jas.. Don't say anything else. Just calm down.'

Yes, thought Jude. Let them all close ranks: bunch of posh, rich kids. I've never been one of them. The sooner I get out of this fucking place and off to somewhere else the better:

somewhere bigger, more real. Even Charlie: he's the same as all the others when it comes to it. This last thought caused him a pang of regret but he felt that the newly exposed gulf between him and his closest friend was widening into his past with measureless rapidity. The future would be a newly peopled territory.

The five minute warning bell, announcing the imminence of the next lesson, shrilled through the crowded room. As no-one could think of the next appropriate move or comment, the group dispersed raggedly.

'Are you coming to Scotty's classroom?' asked Charlie quietly.

'In a minute. You go on ahead,' responded Jude, not meeting his eye.

Charlie shrugged his shoulders and set off alone.

One person who had missed all the drama was Emma Morgan. Glistening with the dampness of the morning, she emerged from the bushes in response to the distant bell. Accompanying her was her latest conquest, a boy in the year below, the son of a Conservative M.P., who was clumsily tucking his shirt into his mud-stained trousers.

At lunch time, Charlie, Ashley, Chris and Tim met in Ashley's study to consider the situation. Charlie persuaded Ashley that it might be best not to invite Jasper. Jasper seemed busy anyway, engaged in a protracted telephone conversation with his Mother. Presumably he was telling her everything.

'The first thing we've got to decide,' began Chris, 'is how far we believe Jude.'

'I don't believe him,' said Tim. 'I just cannot imagine the Rev. D doing anything wrong like that. After all, he's been at the College for ages. Why would it suddenly happen now?'

'I agree with you, Tim. I don't believe it either,' said Charlie in a low voice. 'Which means……' His voice tailed off.

'Jude is lying,' said Ashley with flat firmness.

'I don't like saying this,' said Chris, 'but we can't pretend that that's entirely new. I mean, he did lie to the Rev. D over coming to some of those practices.'

'Did he though, really?' asked Charlie, desperately trying to be fair. 'I thought that the last straw was that he was a bit *too* frank. Another person might have concocted some excuse. Jude was honest about taking time out to complete Scotty's essay.'

'So he says,' said Chris.

'No. It was true. That *was* what he was doing,' insisted Charlie more firmly.

'Okay! Okay!' continued Chris. 'But you've got to admit that he *did* lie when he was doing one of Scotty's essays on a previous occasion. He said he was with his mother. Rev. D caught him out.'

'Yeah,' said Ashley, 'and everybody knows that he's lied all the time to Livvy. He's been two-timing her. He keeps making up and then doing it again. It would be quite funny if people weren't getting hurt!'

'And he lied about those nettles,' added Chris. 'Okay, so Matron and Rev. D believed him but all the girls have told everybody what really happened.'

'That *was* quite funny,' said Ashley, grinning, never able to be far from laughter, even in a situation like the present one. 'It must have been really embarrassing for the poor guy. I wouldn't want Vicky Summerthwaite sitting on top of *me!*'

'No,' said Tim, sheepishly.

They all turned to him and laughed.

'That was *so* funny,' said Ashley, 'when she pinned you down in the refectory.'

'After you lost the arm-wrestling match,' added Chris.

'To which *you* challenged her,' came back Ashley in chorus.

'And she wouldn't release you until you admitted that she had won.'

'And she forced you to tell everybody that you were a wuss while she had you there, lying flat on your back on a refectory table.'

'You looked so funny!'

'You went so red!'

'Like now!'

By now, Ashley and Chris had worked themselves up into a state of mild hilarity.

'You two wouldn't have fared any better,' Tim said in an injured voice, blushing crimson as he was forced once again to live through his moment of abject public humiliation.

'That's true- but we weren't stupid enough to challenge her,' replied Ashley, rocking with laughter.

'Anyway,' responded Tim, rallying, 'who was squealing with pain when he was put in a 'wedgy' this morning in front of everybody?'

'Okay! Okay! Quits. Actually, it's still bloody sore. I hope she hasn't done me any permanent damage.'

Now it was Tim's turn to join with Chris in merry laughter.

'It's not *that* funny,' said Ashley, nursing his crotch.

'Oh, come on guys!' interposed Charlie, who had himself been unable to repress a smile at the recollection of the hapless Tim lying prostrate and mortified on the table. 'We're supposed to be thinking about Rev. D and Jude. This is a serious situation. *Come on!*'

'Yes! Charlie's right!' responded Ashley, quickly recovering seriousness.

'So,' Chris said, 'are we agreeing that we don't believe Jude?'

'S'pose so,' said Ashley, suddenly gloomy. 'I guess we are. And yet…..'

'What?' asked Charlie.

'We're his mates. I'm not sure that I'm really into doing down a mate. It doesn't seem right- meeting altogether like this to call the poor bugger a liar behind his back.'

'That's an unfortunate word to use under the circumstances,' said Chris.

'Oh God!' said Ashley, putting his hands to his face.

They both started to snigger again.

'Look, shut up, you two!' interrupted Charlie crossly. 'I count myself as one of Jude's best friends- perhaps even his closest friend,' he continued, 'but, if he has been telling lies, which, as you say, Ash, have really hurt people, then a judgment has to be made. Isn't it time we started thinking about Rev. D? Presumably he's out of College because of all this. Goodness knows where he is or what state he's in. Matron was very tight-lipped this morning and I could see she was upset.'

'Yes,' agreed Ashley, 'you're quite right, Charlie. I suppose though, in fairness, we've got to consider whether there might just possibly be anything in what Jude is claiming. I mean- do you think it possible that Rev. D might be a closet perv.?'

'Well- *I* don't,' said Tim.

'I guess that 'perv.' isn't at all the right word,' considered Chris.

'I know what you mean, Chris,' said Charlie. 'It suggests some-one who is capable of molestation. Personally, I'm with Tim. I just cannot imagine the Rev. D doing that.'

'You're so great with words, Charlie! You're dead right; that's exactly what I meant.'

'As Tim said earlier, he'd have been kicked out years ago if he'd been up to that sort of caper,' said Ashley. 'Have any of you had reason to suspect him? Speaking for myself, I haven't.'

There was a brief pause.

'Definitely not!' said Tim.

Chris drew in his breath.

'Well, Chris?' asked Ashley.

'Well…… I've sometimes wondered, in all honesty. There was a weird moment earlier this term.'

'What?' asked Ashley.

'It must have been at the beginning of term. It was during a footie practice. I noticed that I had forgotten to take my watch off and so I ran back inside the pavilion with it. As I came into the changing room, Rev. D was standing there holding my boxers. He appeared to be studying them. He put them down very quickly when he saw me. I may be wrong but I though he looked a bit guilty- just for a moment or so.'

Each of the other boys silently considered how to react to this piece of information. Chris quickly regretted having imparted it.

'It was probably nothing,' he added, shaking his head.

'What do you make of that, Charlie?' asked Ashley.

Charlie took a deep breath. He felt that he had been asked to deliver judgment on the Rev. D. Modest by nature, he was, however, not so ingenuous as to imagine that the opinion now being requested might not have an influence upon his entire year in the College. They were four socially influential boys. This was especially true of Ashley, the person who had asked him, who, as well as being a close friend, was also the highly respected Captain of the prestigious First XI. Charlie surmised, moreover, that it was probably generally felt that he, Charlie, was closer to

Jude than any-one else in the year. He was reluctant to submit an opinion which might influence them all. He knew that Ashley and the others respected his judgment far more than he ever did himself, his robust intellect, strong faith and bright personality notwithstanding.

'Dear God, give me the words. I must get this right- for your sake, for the sake of truth.'

'I think you're right, Chris, when you say that you don't want to make too much of a momentary incident like that.'

'Yes, Charlie, I wish I hadn't mentioned it. It was nothing.'

'No, I wouldn't go that far but it's not enough, in my books, to make a definitive judgment on a man whom hundreds of Moretonians have come to know and respect over many years, ourselves included.'

'Yeah,' said Tim, pulling a face. 'And who'd want a pair of *your* knickers anyway, Chris? They probably had holes in them and he was doing the decent thing and thinking of buying you a new pair!'

Ashley started to laugh again.

'Getting your own back after being reminded about Victoria,' said Chris with a knowing smile, shaking his head.

'All-right! All-right,' said Charlie. 'So, we're agreed that we're not going to make too much of any passing interest which the Rev. D might have taken in a pair of Chris's boxers some time ago?'

'No, of course not!' said Tim.

'In which case, though I really don't think it was wrong

to mention it here, Chris, I think we should all promise now never to relate the incident to any-one outside this room. It would do Rev. D no good at all and I sense that we're coming to a consensus that we feel we should do something to help him.'

Every-one promised and Ashley made them do so individually.

'But what can *we* do to help him?' asked Tim.

'Let's go to the Head Man, to G&T, straight after afternoon school. We'll all meet and go together. Charlie, you'll have to be our spokesman,' declared Ashley.

Charlie looked distinctly uncomfortable at the prospect but his silence was assumed to signify assent.

The bell summoned them and they could hear the hectoring voice of their Housemaster getting people out of the House and on their way to the next lesson.

Charlie had a study period. He knew that it coincided with one of Jude's. He waited until his friends had gone and the House was quiet before crossing the passage. Normally, he just walked in to Jude's study. On this occasion, he knocked on the door, only entering after Jude had called out an invitation.

Jude had kicked his shoes off and was lying on his bed reading a book with a series of critical essays on 'Measure for Measure.' He showed neither surprise nor pleasure at the arrival of Charlie. He said nothing. As was his custom, Charlie tipped an assorted load of papers, books and clothing off the plastic chair by Jude's desk and, turning it round, sat to face his friend.

'Jude, this is a dreadful business. Can you tell me what happened?'

Jude shrugged his shoulders.

'I've said all I've got to say when we were in front of the others at Break.'

'I realise that you couldn't say everything that you might have wanted to then. There were so many people and you were suddenly put in an impossible situation.'

'Dead right, man and, when I said that I wasn't going to say any more, you gave me a public reprimand because I did it through Shakespeare and took the opportunity to show them all how smart you were. You impressed everyone, I'm sure.'

'Quoting 'Othello' did seem a bit over the top under the circumstances.'

'Well, great! That's your opinion. If you've come here to tell me off again, you can piss off.'

'Don't be like that. Of course I haven't 'come here to tell you off'. I just wanted to know what on earth's happened. It's pretty shocking, Rev. D not being in College and what you said about him.'

'Very clever; you're trying now to shame me into justification in the hope that I'll tell you more.'

'It's not like that at all. I just wonder what has suddenly come between you and Rev.D. I realise that it's not just the football. Jude, what did he do to you to have caused all this?'

'You heard at break. I'm not going into all the gory details just to gratify your imagination. I shall not be saying anything more about it to any of you. You patronised me publicly when I told every-one that. I meant what I said then and I mean it now.'

'Olivia's telling every-one that you're taking him to court.'

'Is she now? Well, there's a thing to get you all gossiping.'

'That's not fair and it's not in the spirit of our friendship.'

'God! You are such a fucking moraliser! You think you have some sort of God-given right to stick your nose into every-one else's business, to judge it and then to treat it to a piece of your own over-simplified, rehashed Rev. D-style advice. Rock of Ages Blakestone! Well, you can go back and tell them all to go to Hell! I'm sick of all of you! I'm sick of this fucking school! I'm sick of you and your patronising presumption! Why should *you* be given some special knowledge into what happened so that you can salivate over the precise details of attempted buggery? Does it excite you, Charlie? Is that it? Wish it was you? Now just piss off and leave me in peace. We're through.'

Charlie was used to making allowances for Jude's sudden tantrums but he had never ever been spoken to like this. He sat ashen and dumbfounded for a moment before getting up and hurrying from the room.

He fell on his knees by his bedside. He was too shocked even to pray. He started to tremble as a reaction set in. Being Charlie, he brought every word used in the attack to mind and considered each in detail. Of course Jude was furious and upset and some of the things said, though cruel, were mere lashing out and even the self-critical Charlie could immediately dismiss them as nonsense: nasty nonsense but nonsense all the same. However, was there some truth in the character assassination just delivered? No smoke without fire? Did he really go round being 'holier than thou' in Pharisaic hypocrisy? What indeed was the distinction between the legitimate exercise of faith and intellectual cop-out? But then, surely that is a question for everybody, Jude included.

He had known that Jude had had a less fortunate and happy home background than he had enjoyed himself. And, with that thought, Charlie's lucid integrity began to bring the tide of assurance back in. No, he had never patronised his friend and he had always wanted to share what he had with Jude, including his home, and to do so for the mutual benefit accordant to true friendship. Neither had he imposed any views he had ever held on Jude. Indeed, he had often remained silent when Jude himself had made provocative final pronouncements over literary matters and people. Yes, true, possibly he, Charlie, was more simply definite when expressing his Christian commitment but that was after all a matter of faith, a faith which emanated from Charlie's certainty of the love of God expressed through the Crucifixion and the Resurrection, events which were, for Charlie, sufficiently well attested to justify building a life view around. Charlie felt that if Jude could not accept some clear starting point, perhaps that is why he had got himself into his present morass. He knew that Jude was a profound and intelligent thinker and could only assume that he had not been able to make any anchoring commitment. Even Tim and Chris had been able to do that, without being able to give it quite the analytical examination available to Jude. It was true that Ashley had no such commitment but Charlie judged his cheerful agnosticism to be the superficial response of a carefree, happy disposition putting off such gloomy profundities until later. That could not be true for Jude. As he teetered on the precipice, he would be aware of the vortex of conflicting options whirling around him in his vulnerable isolation. He had now, for some reason, possibly responding to a momentary fit of pique, taken a decisive act, almost certainly the wrong one, and the consequence would be unimaginable. Dostoyevsky's 'Crime and Punishment' came back into Charlie's mind. He thought of Raskolnikov drawing back from the parapet of the bridge across the Neva. Was Jude to be compared with the *alter ego*, Svidrigaylov, who, having descended to a nadir of despair, rashly blew his brains out?

Charlie rose from the floor and sat on his bed. He had, even at this early stage, found it easy enough to forgive Jude for his outburst. However, the more he understood it, the more he felt deeply troubled for his friend. Jude had cut himself off from every-one. Charlie was sufficiently realistic to understand that he himself could not approach Jude again. Forgiveness is pointless if the recipient rejects it because he sees no need to have it offered in the first place. Jude had pulled up the drawbridge and Charlie had no power to lower it again from his side of the chasm. Having danced dangerously on the edge for so long, Jude was now becoming a personification of alienation. He did indeed mirror Raskolnikov in the novel, Raskolnikov, the heretic. However, Raskolnikov accepted salvation and, after due penance, achieved redemption. But then, Charlie thought, although Raskolnikov had eschewed the fate of Svidrigaylov, he had committed a double murder for motives of greed and self-protection. Whatever Jude has done wrong, to whatever extent he has turned Rev. D into a martyr, Jude can surely still be saved.

Now, his mind turned to Rev. D. Jude had once mentioned that he thought that the Chaplain might be a closet gay: middle-aged, unmarried, close to the boys, though never, up until now at least, improperly so. Charlie had deliberately shut such a possibility out of his mind. It had complicated things too much. Now, however, he considered the matter afresh. Yes, if one thinks about what one sees of the Rev. D's life, during the College terms at least, it was quite possible that he was homosexual in orientation. But then, Charlie felt with sharp conviction, so what? If that is indeed part of the Rev. D's motivation, he directs it most positively with kindness, generosity and genuine concern for the spiritual and moral welfare of the boys at the College. Actually, Charlie thought, his consideration is not only for the boys. Olivia spoke highly of him when, anxious about her work (and possibly her relationship with Jude?), she had taken Charlie's advice to go to the Rev. D for counsel. And he is so wonderfully discreet. No, Charlie decided, there could be no doubt about it; the Rev. D must continue to be regarded as a highly professional man and a very significant friend. Unless clear evidence emerged to the contrary, Charlie would not believe that the Rev. D had compromised years of self-disciplined celibacy in an illicit encounter with Jude. Very possibly, Jude was simply elevating the grievance he had felt over the football and- unfortunately it had to be admitted- both Chris and Ashley were right when they pointed out Jude's mendacity. Yes, he, Charlie, would speak up for the Rev. D to the Headmaster. How could he have ever thought otherwise? The idea of sitting about doing nothing was unthinkable.

Now Charlie wondered what the Rev. D was doing at this moment. He would be devastated by this. Charlie desperately wanted to make contact with him. Should he bring his parents into it? Perhaps he would go and see Matron on his own. Might he even dare to broach Scottie over the matter? After all, he was a friend of Rev. D and a powerful master in the College. Yes, he might try all of these things. When all is said and done, Jude had rejected him, something the Rev. D would never have done. Charlie prayed for the Rev. D in his need. He asked God to remember all the good things which the Rev. D had done and he prayed that, at this very moment, Christ would grant his friend and mentor peace and, in the very near future, justice and restoration.

The next bell sounded. Charlie felt clear in his head as he picked up his carefully typed essay on 'Measure for Measure' and set off for his second English lesson of the day, this time with Mr Stevens. It had long been Charlie's custom to call in on Jude so that they could walk to class together. He hesitated for a moment outside Jude's room. There was no sound of movement. Charlie decided to go to Stevo's classroom alone. Jude would no doubt be late and would invent some lie to offer Stevo, a master just as scholarly but somewhat less severe than Mr Scott.

Forty minutes later, the four friends met, as arranged. They paused outside the Headmaster's Secretary's office to tuck in their shirts and do up their ties properly, a somewhat novel endeavour for Ashley in particular.

Ursula Duncan always made an effort to be polite and helpful when she had any contact with the pupils. She was not expecting the four boys but she had had dealings with both Ashley and Charlie and could see that they were worried. She immediately guessed the reason. When they asked to see the Headmaster, Ursula explained very pleasantly that the Headmaster's schedule was so busy that people normally had to make appointments. Their faces fell. She went on to say that, if it was an emergency, she could usually arrange something but that, at this moment, the Headmaster was attending a meeting elsewhere in the College. Observing their continued expressions of disappointment, she suggested that the Deputy Head, Mrs Fulwell, might be able to see them. They all tried to conceal their lack of enthusiasm for that idea, shuffling hesitantly, saying nothing. Ursula smiled reassuringly, picked up the 'phone and was immediately speaking to Cressida Fulwell.

'Yes, boys. Good news. Mrs Fulwell is free and will see you straightaway.'

They thanked her very politely and went off to the Deputy Head's study.

Cressida Fulwell remained at her desk and kept them standing. Ashley's tie, always an alien appendage to him, had succeeded in slipping down to the second button on his shirt in the few moments the short walk had taken. His falling-down trousers had responded symbiotically.

'Do up your tie!' Cressida shrieked. 'You look a wreck! And look at those trousers and your shoes!'

Ashley looked down at the frayed and muddy hems of his trousers, one of which sported a uselessly deployed safety pin, and at a pair of shoes which had never been polished since they had been purchased.

'I'm sorry, Mrs Fulwell,' he mumbled.

'Report to me at eight o'clock tomorrow morning, wearing a clean pair of trousers and some properly polished shoes.'

'Yes, Mrs Fulwell.'

'The Headmaster is getting extremely angry about boys like you looking so disgracefully scruffy and, I must say, so am I! Now, I'm busy with some very important work. What did you want to bother the Headmaster about?'

She addressed her remark to them all.

As agreed, Charlie spoke.

'Thank you for seeing us, Mrs Fulwell. We realise that you are very busy and don't want to take up much of your time.'

'Well, get on with it! I haven't got all day!'

'We wanted to come and see you about Mr Donaldson. We are very concerned about his absence. We were wondering if the Headmaster might have been able to give us any further information. We are keen to help Mr Donaldson and to speak up for him. He's been very good to us and to many others.'

'Good Heavens, no! What outrageous impertinence! I am certainly not going to discuss other members of the teaching staff with pupils! Now, clear off and get on with some work! And you, Smart, don't forget to see me at eight o'clock tomorrow morning.'

TWENTY

Priscilla Peverill was deeply upset by the sudden turn of events. Her friendship with John was one of great affection. She had gradually and carefully developed some understanding of his character and, in due course, she had privately made a shrewd assessment of the nature of his sexuality and the positive role that that probably played in his work at the College. Nothing was ever spoken between them about this, nor did she discuss it with any-one else. It is true that she did find John attractive but she was so satisfied with the terms of their friendship that she did not want it complicated by lust any more than he could have done. They shared a common faith, common interests and a common concern for the young. For different reasons, there were streaks of loneliness and sadness in each of their lives but, instead of yielding to any sense of deprivation, Priscilla silently commended both herself and John for turning circumstance into a friendship the focus of which was pleasurable service for others. Her interest in the boys in Blenheim House was professional, maternal, lively and dedicated. She loved their bright youthfulness and humour, understood but did not tolerate their nonsense and took a genuine and personal pleasure in their success. She felt for them in their sadness and shared in their gladness.

As Senior Matron, Priscilla took an equally responsible interest in that area of operation across the College as a whole. Over the years, she had defended two matrons against bullying housemasters and their wives and had prevented two others from being swindled by the Bursar. She had been centrally, and unhappily, involved when a glamorous young woman (initially appointed against her advice) had attempted to seduce some of the senior boys in another House and she had defended a colleague in court who had been wrongly accused of theft. She was the scourge of the catering manager, tirelessly campaigning for more nutritious food for the pupils. She would go up to the refectory at lunch-time and her gimlet eye would spot any sloppy short-cuts, disguised re-heating of yesterday's food or attempts to palm off the pupils with cheap lumps of carbohydrate.

Priscilla was careful over her appearance without being vain. Always immaculately presented, she preferred subdued colours: pale greys and blues and fawns, woollen in the winter, conservatively but elegantly cut. She did not favour wearing trousers. Her oval face was gently but firmly pretty, free from make-up, her grey eyes usually calm, sometimes faintly wistful, her hair, turned grey with sorrows long ago, neatly permed and left in peace from any attempt to dye it.

The day had been predictably difficult. She had had no problem with the business-like exchange with Bernard Bassett over the crisis and she had been impressed by young Richard Ellman's tact, and evident concern for John, when obeying Cressida Fulwell's repeated prodding to take himself over to inspect his 'lovely new flat'. Both Priscilla and Richard had quickly established that the other was aware of the details of the allegation made against John and each of them had found it reassuring that an immediate confidence could be established between them. With commendable diplomacy, Richard had asked her to pass on his best wishes to John if she happened to be in touch.

Dealing with the senior boys, however, was another matter. The relationship between them and John and herself was a closely defined triangle. She had felt particularly dreadful when she had turned her back on Charlie, Ashley, Chris and Tim that morning. It was as though she had refused to accept their humane and self-evident trustfulness and a wall of ice had descended upon the relationship. Of course, in their goodness, they were concerned about their friend and pastor! It was deeply upsetting that she was unable to tell them what they would almost certainly soon discover for themselves anyway. It would have seemed the most natural thing in the world to have invited them to sit down, as they so often did, and talk about the injustice over a mug of coffee. The ripples emanating from a single act of evil rapidly extend across the lake of a society.

Her first encounter with Jude had been when she had passed him on the stairs. Each of them had averted their eyes. She supposed that she would have to deal with the boy at some point. Something was bound to crop up. In such an event, she had decided that she would simply do her job and, beyond that, avoid any communication with either him or his mother. Priscilla was profoundly and terribly angry with them both. She had felt a physical revulsion just at the sight of him. Even if the whole thing were to be exposed as the spiteful lunacy which it undoubtedly was, huge damage would have been done. She found it impossible to imagine that they could both behave in such a way towards some-one from whom they had accepted so many acts of kindness, some-one so gentle in his goodness and so manifestly clear in his probity as John. Additionally, she felt offended on behalf of the College which she loved. The College had taken that wretched boy in, paid for him, given him the best all-round education available in the world, only for him to turn round and spit in its face. How otherwise would he have benefited from the teaching of Alexander Scott, Tom Stevens, or Anthony Ridell? How realistic would his chances have been if he had been applying to Cambridge from the local comprehensive school in Midhampton? Such a thing might not have been impossible, of course, but, obviously, he had been given a great and wonderful advantage in coming to *this* nationally renowned and beautiful school. Even as she thought about it, Priscilla clenched her fists and groaned with fury. Moreover, she could also see that, single-handedly, Jude Williams had ruined the community amongst the boys of that year in the House. They had been a particularly happy, decent, well integrated bunch of lads but their troubled faces this morning had demonstrated the destruction of all that at a single blow. And that germ of infection, Jude Williams, would still be living amongst them, continuing to benefit from all that the College could offer, while dear John was mouldering away miserably in a strange house in the middle of an estate, unable to do all his good work! Dear God, how she would like to go upstairs and wring that bloody boy's neck!

She had said that she would drive over to John at seven-thirty, when all the boys in the House had settled down for prep.. Although she had of course been thinking about John, she had not really had a chance to feel the personal loss of his absence until she paused at about six o'clock. This was the hour when they sometimes called upon each other for a drink. Suddenly, after a particularly stressful day, she found herself craving for this meeting. But, no, she was not going to open a bottle of consolatory wine for herself; she would wait until she saw him later; in any case, she must be careful because she was driving.

A fleeting look of vexation crossed her face at the sound of a knock at the door.

It was Charlie. He closed the door behind him and stood facing her. A space of fifteen feet divided them. He looked down at her with eyes of wounded amazement. He said nothing but spread both his hands out. Suddenly the wellspring of tears which she had been nursing all day forced its way through. She turned away from him abruptly, at the same time putting her handkerchief to her face. It was over in a moment. She blew her nose, dabbed her eyes and turned to face him.

'Charlie, I'm sorry; it's just suddenly caught up with me.'

Perhaps he was in a similar situation. Normally so articulate, bubbly even, he just shook his head slowly and sighed. For a moment she was at a loss to know what to do.

'Forgive me. Do please sit down.'

She motioned him to one of the armchairs.

'Oh, for Heaven's sake, Charlie! Let's have a glass of wine. I'm sure we could both do with it.'

'Yes, thank you,' he replied, in a voice of muted tonelessness.

He waited until she had poured out two glasses of white wine.

'Matron, *What* is happening? Where *is* Rev.D?'

She took an immediate sip from her glass. Charlie had put his glass down untouched.

'Charlie, Charlie! I'm sworn to secrecy. I can't tell you! I'm not allowed to!'

'But is he all-right?'

'Yes- at least I think so. I'm going to see him this evening after prep. has started.'

'Please could I come with you.'

'I've said, no. Charlie, please don't make this harder than it is.'

'Why do adults imagine that they can keep everything a secret? We all know what's happened. Jude was shooting his mouth off in the Sixth Form Common Room at break.'

This really was the last straw. It was exceptional for Priscilla to be wrong-footed by a pupil. How formidable Charlie had suddenly become! Where was the smiling, appeasing lad of yesterday? She had never heard the remotest tone of truculence emerge from his lips before. Well, of course, they do grow up. She was conscious that, instead of facing a joking, pliable adolescent, a highly intelligent, morally authoritative, self-possessed adult was confronting her in the opposite chair. He was not going to take 'no' for an answer and why on earth should he? Well, since he was now a young adult, she must be free to express herself in a less guarded way than usual.

'Look, if you've come here to tell me off or to try to bully information out of me which I'm not at liberty to give, I really can't stand it! You're not the only one who's upset by this, Charlie!'

She made a superhuman effort not to weep again.

His eyes softened with concern. He got up to go.

'I'm sorry Matron. I shouldn't have come. It was wrong to distress you further.'

Priscilla also rose.

'No, don't go, Charlie! I'm sorry to snap at you of all people. My nerves are just all over the place today. Aren't you missing supper?'

'I'm not going. I can't face everybody in the refectory. They'll all be gossiping like mad, enjoying all the juicy details of the scandal. Can't you hear Jasper now?'

She desperately wanted to hug him- at least she thought so. Or, did she want him, standing at over six feet tall, to hug her? She could certainly have used it but both were options best avoided. She needed to *do* something; it was always the best remedy.

'You're not going without food this evening, Charlie. Bring your glass of wine into the kitchen. I'm going to make you some scrambled eggs. I won't be joining you because I've got a fish pie to take over to Rev. D later.'

He acquiesced without any further fuss. Long, slim and elegant, he leant against the kitchen wall while she busied herself cracking three eggs and scrambling them. What a handsome boy he has become, she considered. She put the meal on a tray and refreshed his glass of wine. They returned to their seats.

'Forgive me, Charlie. *Of course* I'm happy to talk about it with you; it would do *me* good as well. I wish I could tell you where he is. I discovered this morning that not even Richard Ellman knows that and he's taking over from John- er, Rev. D- as under-housemaster of Blenheim until Rev. D returns.'

'Well, that seems pretty ridiculous- that they don't tell *him*.'

'I'm afraid it's one of these situations where the decisions are not ours, Charlie. But I can tell you that I helped Rev. D to move last night and that he is not living too far away in quite a comfortable little house. Mr Scott's keeping an eye on him as well. Of course, John is very shocked by it all. Since you've heard about it from Jude, I expect that, like me, you can draw your own conclusions.'

'Poor Rev. D.. None of us boys can imagine that he would do anything wrong.'

'Well, it goes without saying, Charlie, neither can I.'

'What do you think's going to happen, Matron?'

'I wish I knew. I have no more idea than you have. Surely good sense will prevail, Charlie. Rev. D will have so many people speaking for him. After all, he's led an unblemished (not to say, distinguished) career at this College for twenty years.'

Her concern was not diminished when Charlie told her about the abortive visit to Cressida Fulwell. She kept her real thoughts to herself but said that she was sorry to hear that they had got no further.

In due course, Charlie left, but not without getting her to

promise that she would take his very best wishes to Rev.D and, he was certain, those of his parents too, as well as the regards of Ashley, Chris and Tim.

The evening prep. began. Priscilla got the fish pie out of the freezer, found her coat and slipped out to her car.

It was a surprisingly cheerful meal. John had brought his CD player. They listened to some optimistic Baroque music and watched a detective drama on the television. He told her about his visit to Maurice Stantonbury and then, less happily, to the police. She, of course, told him how shocked everybody was back at College and how much he was missed already. She highlighted the positive visits of Richard and Charlie and faithfully passed on their regards.

'I suddenly missed you at six o'clock, John- just when we often meet for a glass of wine. That was when the shock-wave struck. As it happened, Charlie dropped by. As you might expect, he is very cut up about it. Again, as you might expect, he is totally loyal to you. It didn't take *him* long to make up his mind about who was right and the same is true, he tells me, about the others in that group. He was extremely keen to pass on everybody's good wishes. They all know something about the allegation because apparently Jude was being less than discreet in their Common Room at break. It sounds very much as though his slander had a boomerang effect, loathsome little creep.'

They hugged. He pecked her cheek with a discreet kiss. She left with a heavier heart than she disclosed.

The appearance before the magistrate the next morning was perfunctory. John did not know the presiding magistrate and neither Jude nor his mother nor anyone from the school attended. The surly police sergeant who had administered the charge was present with the W.P.C. who had been taking the notes. John confirmed his identity and his understanding of the charge which he did, of course, deny. The magistrate said dispassionately, but not unkindly, that she had no discretion in the matter and that the case would be referred to a Crown Court. John was placed on bail and informed that the Crown Prosecution Service would take the matter forward in due course. Maurice accompanied him to and from the court and took him home for lunch. John felt profoundly shaken and could not avoid, even in the company of his friend, a steep descent into a morose silence.

That afternoon, the solicitor confirmed the situation as John himself was already beginning to understand it. He promised to procure counsel for John. Although, employing all the instinctive caution of a lawyer, Timothy Watson could not, of course, foresee the outcome of the impending trial with certainty, nevertheless, on the basis of the information which John had given him, he thought that the chances were pretty good. The barrister he would employ on John's behalf was a specialist on such matters and had successfully defended far more tricky cases than this one appeared to be. John's mood lurched back into a more favourable zone. Nevertheless, he felt a sharp pang of loss when he remembered that it was Wednesday afternoon. He wondered how his boys and Richard were performing at the football practice

By Thursday morning, the initial impact of the disaster had passed and John was beginning to find a second wind. He had slept better and, after a light breakfast, had drawn inner strength from his faith. He was wondering how to spend the day when his mobile rang.

'John, it's Priscilla. Listen Dear, I think that you ought to go out and buy this morning's edition of *The Daily News*. I'm sorry to add to your burden but I thought that you'd better hear it from me and see the article yourself before you might be confronted with it in even less favourable circumstances. There isn't that much to it, though you won't like it. It's on one of the inside pages. It's an awful thing to say but mercifully that smutty rag has, rather predictably, devoted the front page to salacious gloating over the sacking of that cabinet minister for being caught with his trousers down with a rent-boy. The Williamses must have contacted *The Daily News*. No doubt they will have been paid. It was Jasper of course who found it a short time ago and naturally they have all been poring over the rubbish. Apparently *The Daily News* had been trying to get hold of you. I 'phoned Ursula to find out what was going on and she said that there was no way the College was going to pass on your number. They didn't get much out of G&T. They've got things wrong, including G&T's name! Don't worry about it, John. It's a piece of smut that'll blow over quickly. I'm sorry that it's happened.'

Dear God, this is quite a trial you are letting me go through. I'm not resenting it now. I know it's just about a poor misguided boy and his unfortunate mother but, sweet Jesus, please help me to cope. I claim your promise that you won't test a believer beyond what he can endure.

Before going out, he looked up the verse of comfort: 1 Corinthians 10 v. 13:-

'No temptation has overtaken you that is not common to man.

God is faithful and he will not let you be tempted beyond your strength, but with the temptation will also provide the way of escape, that you may be able to endure it.'

He had turned to the text often enough when tortured by the temptation of lust. Now it would need to arm him against the temptation of despair.

He put on his coat and set off to one of the newsagents in the town centre. Once again, it felt odd to be walking amongst all these ordinary, bustling people, like a stranger in a foreign land. He was going to collect a national newspaper in which he featured. None of them had such distinction! The irony of it!

Arriving back again, he spread *The Daily News* out across the table. He soon found the article. It was in the lower right-hand section of a right-hand page in the middle of the newspaper. It was longer than he had imagined from Priscilla's 'phone call.

He started to read the article quickly but found himself slowing down as his apprehension increased.

Gay Sex Scandal Rocks Top Toffs' School

Shockwaves are engulfing one of the country's most famous public schools, as teachers, pupils and parents reel from the disclosure that the Chaplain of Moreton College (fees £23,000 a year plus extras), Rev. John Donaldson (55), allegedly attempted an indecent assault upon a 17 year old boy. The student, who cannot be named, is Captain of the College's First XI Soccer Team and is currently applying for admission to Cambridge University. His single-parent mother, a

Primary Care Trust administrator, is taking the Rev. Donaldson and the College to court over an alleged incident in the changing room after a match. 'It's in the public interest for people to know what goes on behind the scenes in some of these places,' commented the boy's mother, adding that she did not want others to have to go through the trauma faced by her son. The Headmaster of Moreton College, Mr Gerald Tanswell (57), said in a statement: 'The Rev. John Donaldson, Chaplain of Moreton College for the past twenty years, is currently suspended from duty pending an allegation of improper conduct made by one of the pupils and his mother.' It was only last year when Moreton College was at the centre of another scandal involving gay sex. On that occasion, a senior pupil molested some younger boys. The case, which was first reported in *The Daily News*, resulted in a prosecution and the dismissal of a housemaster. Former pupils at Moreton College include Sir Edward Moncrieff, Chairman of Delmundo's Bank and a prominent figure in the Lloyd's crisis of 1988 when he came in for criticism for allegedly failing to support the interests of some of his fellow 'names.' Also among the role of former pupils is the singer and television personality, Jonny Jamieson, who claims that the College had been well known for homosexual activity when he was a pupil there in the late 1950s.

John felt momentarily faint and needed to sit down. Then he felt consumed with rage. The newspaper's entire representation of him limited him to some sort of paedophile. He knew that the circulation of *The Daily News* was enormous and now some two million people up and down the land would be introduced to him in those terms. He thought with mortification about all his colleagues, and the boys and girls, and their parents, reading this trash. What a terrible and insulting travesty of a judgment upon all that he was and had done over so many years! His identity had been reduced to a smutty allegation pronounced by a mendacious and spiteful boy. Dear God, talk about trial by the press!

If it were possible, his anger intensified when, leaving himself aside, he started considering the damage done to the College. In the interest of meretricious sensation, some hack of a journalist had done everything possible to vilify a magnificent and noble institution. The place wouldn't be 'reeling' with shock anyway. For the great majority of people up there, the daily routine of lessons, games, marking, trying to keep up with administration and all the rest of it would be continuing as normal. Even the Headmaster would have new issues dropping on his desk all the time to consider alongside this problem. Even those closest to John- Priscilla and Alexander and, more recently, Richard and some of the pupils – boys like Charlie- would, quite rightly, be getting on with the quotidian demands required from each in their different ways. They couldn't even get his age right, or the Headmaster's name, and, of course, Jude Williams was *not* the Captain of the First XI, part of the whole issue in the first place. The newspaper had even attempted, quite unnecessarily, to slur the Chairman of the Governors, digging up, entirely irrelevantly, the row involving Lloyds of more than a decade and a half ago, when, in any case, Sir Edward had arguably done the right thing in pointing out that the expectations of some of the 'names' were unrealistic when measured against the financial realities of the crisis. At the very least, there had been nothing either corrupt or foolish in assuming such a position. What on earth did it have to do with this present situation anyway? And trust *The Daily News* to bring in that unsavoury reprobate, Jonny Jamieson, from amongst the thousands of OMs around the place! The man was known to have hated every minute of his time at boarding school, except when he was illegally indulging his own homosexual promiscuity. This projection of his personal experience as a universal truth was a blatant misrepresentation.

John was acutely aware of just how very much he loved the College for itself. He was so angry that scalding tears of rage ran down his face. He folded the paper up and then found his attention turning to the front page.

STAVELEY'S SECRET SEX WITH RENT-BOY

Simon Staveley, the chief architect of the Prime Minister's 'Return Morality to Britain' campaign, resigned from his post yesterday after having his double life exposed when Gary Hassell, a 22 year old rent-boy from Tottenham, North London, told *The Daily News* about the Minister's twice weekly sex sessions with him. It is alleged that Staveley (39, married with three children and a £2.2m house in the Cotswolds) would take a taxi to the seedy terraced house, where Hassell rented a furnished room, direct from the House of Commons or Downing Street. The first thing that he required Hassell to do was to change in front of him into one of a number of different football strips, all of which Staveley had bought for this purpose. Hassell claims that Staveley elected to play the role of the dominant partner, sometimes using handcuffs to bind the younger man to the bars of the bed- head for various sadomasochistic activities before engaging in oral sex with him. Staveley had become a close aide to the Prime Minister and was widely regarded as a rising star within the government, even tipped by some as a possible future contender for the leadership. A statement issued from Downing Street spoke of the Prime Minister's 'profound sorrow' at the disclosure, adding that it was a 'personal tragedy for Simon Staveley and his family.' Political commentators have little doubt that this latest scandal further embarrasses an already beleaguered administration.

Two photographs of equivalent dimensions filled the space below the reportage. On the left, the very personification of affluent respectability, the Minister was seen posing with his wife, family and golden retriever in an elegantly furnished drawing room. To the right of this, this time in colour, a good-looking young man, with dark hair and eyes and a sallow complexion tinged with stubble, stood with his arms folded, wearing a plain yellow football shirt and a pair of navy shorts. The captions stated the obvious and there was a promise of more pictures inside. These comprised a serious and responsible Simon Staveley having a tête-à-tête with the Prime Minister during a busy conference and two further studies of Gary Hassell, both again in colour. In one he was sitting on the floor hugging his bare knees, clad this time in a red football shirt and white shorts, socks wrinkled round his ankles. In the other, where he was wearing a light blue shirt and black shorts, he was shown manacled to the bed head, lying in the prostrate form in which he had allegedly permitted himself to be enjoyed by the Minister of State.

The self-congratulatory delight in this journalistic coup oozed from the pages. John felt sorry for both protagonists.

Of course, the public had a right to know that a potential future Prime Minister was guilty of more than usual hypocrisy, and more obviously open therefore to the threat of blackmail, but the newspaper's blatant pleasure in ruining a man's political and domestic life at a single devastating blow should surely be mitigated by compassion for the painful emotional deprivation which lay at the sad heart of this aspiring, ambitious, public man.

John also felt for the young male prostitute. He could see at once that the lad was attractive but felt sad that such youthful beauty should be squandered so unworthily and that, behind the handsome, ostensibly guileless, face, there should be so much cynicism and greed. What horrible need or social circumstance had driven the boy to this? He composed himself to pray for each of them, both within their present situation and, thinking of their salvation, looking to an eternal context. There but for the Grace of God, he thought- but stopped abruptly when he realised anew that he had been placed in a comparable situation by the very same edition of the same newspaper and, in his case, surely with no justice at all.

He noticed with disgust that a terrible massacre at a market in Iraq had been compressed into a space of four square inches at the bottom left hand corner of the front page.

He needed to clear his head and so he decided to drive out into the countryside. He checked on a local Ordinance Survey map and took an unfamiliar two-hour circular walk, which he followed with a sandwich lunch at a pub', where he could benefit from anonymity while reading a broadsheet paper (in which he mercifully did *not* feature) and which, for today's edition at least, had been published too soon for the Staveley scandal. Normally he found walking in the countryside exhilarating but not on this occasion. The air was chill and still, the sky uniform and leaden, the flat ploughed fields a neutral brown. The footpaths had been rutted by tractors and were disfigured by patches of adhesive mud and filthy, opaque puddles which reflected the dull sky. A mile to the east, the silence was punctuated by the urgent whisper of high-speed trains rushing people north and south, between London and Birmingham, Manchester or Liverpool, peremptory streaks of red, fleetingly assertive as they crossed the unremarkable landscape. His mind travelled across the county to the green fields around his beloved College.

When he arrived back, he had a further conversation with Priscilla on the 'phone and returned a kind enquiry from Maurice Stantonbury. They both continued to express generous concern but, obviously enough, neither could wave a magic wand to release him from his misery.

The taxi bearing Alexander and Anthony arrived promptly. John's two friends and colleagues insisted on buying him a delicious meal at the Wheatsheaf. They both sought to reassure him and Alexander railed against the Williamses, mother and son, the social services, the police and any-one who might have had anything to do with 'this scandalous iniquity' with a coruscating and caustic brilliance which soon had even John smiling.

TWENTY-ONE

Alexander Scott walked along the empty passage removing the crudely scrawled notices with their filthy sentiments and placed them in a bin at the end of the corridor. The malignant juvenile retard who had anonymously perpetrated them would not, of course, be aware that he was guilty of libel. They had probably been seen by too many people already but at least his good friend, John Donaldson, would, he very much hoped, be spared any knowledge of them. Alexander was not a believer himself but the contrast between the cheering crowd who greeted Jesus on his entry to Jerusalem on Palm Sunday and the mob who jeered at Him on the Cross shortly afterwards came to mind. At least this litany of semi-literate obscenities could not have been written by Jude Williams, unless he was even more devious than one could reasonably imagine.

Half Term had begun, much to the relief of every-one, and the College had emptied with the usual quite extraordinary speed which, given the leisurely pace which characterised its pupils during the working day, never ceased to amaze their teachers.

However, the place was not totally deserted. Circumstances had forced Richard to alter his plans. Since John's abrupt departure, he had been sleeping in the flat in Blenheim House and had conscientiously attended to his duties as under-housemaster. However, true to his word, Richard had kept most of his possessions in his own garret room. He felt deeply concerned about John and had never for a moment doubted his innocence. Still, it was awkward being in the House when dealing with friend and foe alike. The Bassetts had made rather a fuss of him, inviting him to supper twice, but Bernard Bassett had warned Richard straightaway that communication with John was strictly forbidden. Richard had privately wondered whether such an edict could be legally binding but had felt that it would be in nobody's interest, least of all John's, to make an issue of it, for the time being at least.

His most significant ally was Priscilla, whom he soon came to trust absolutely. It was she who truly explained the running of the house and who provided necessary information about individual boys.

The Donaldson affair made his relations with the senior boys tricky and he often consulted Priscilla about this. Having always disliked Jude, it was, ironically, easier to deal with him on strictly business terms than it was to judge how far to relax with some of the others. To be fair, Ashley and Chris, had, in their open, friendly natures, made an effort to welcome him and it seemed to be tacitly agreed that the dreaded controversy was off limits. It suited Richard that the agile Ashley could find a worthy challenger at table-tennis and the easy sort of friendship available to two accomplished sportsmen was soon established. Doug Macintyre had dealt with the change in a clear, decent, boyish sort of way, telling Richard that they would miss Rev. D while he was away but that, if anyone had to come and replace him, Richard could not be a better choice. Tim immediately erected a reserve which made Richard feel slightly uneasy but the most difficult boy of all turned out, to his surprise and regret, to be Charlie. Not that there was any overt hostility: indeed, a polite formality and even a regular smile of greeting was flawlessly maintained. But Richard was a sensitive young man and he guessed, without anything being said, that Charlie resented his presence in the House. It was the one study (along, more predictably, with Jude's) which he never felt at liberty to sit down in uninvited- and the invitation never came. Richard wondered if he was imagining it but sensed (he did not know how accurately) that to broach the terrible subject might be to invite a devastating snub. Indeed, it seemed to Richard that Charlie had treated him with sudden caution when enmity had first broken out between Richard and Jude on the football field. Now, he felt that Charlie saw him as an interloper in the House, the cuckoo in the nest from which Rev. D had been forced to fly. Charlie was, of course, far too mature and morally sound to create any difficulties. Indeed, when Charlie was on duty as a house prefect, the evening was far more efficiently administered than when Richard found himself in the casual hands of the friendly, chaotic, laid back Ashley. If it had been anybody else, Richard felt, it would not even be a detectable lack of warmth. Perhaps Charlie's reputation for spontaneous and imaginative kindness had caused Richard to expect more than was reasonable: at least so the new young teacher wondered.

Now, at the beginning of Half Term, Richard had taken himself back to his original room and he was most unhappy. An influenza virus had hit the College early in the season and, having not built up immunity to local infections, he had fallen victim and was therefore unable to go to his Australian friends in London. The College was almost deserted. Priscilla had gone to stay with a friend in Cheltenham. The Bassetts had retreated to their cottage in North Devon. Richard's young friends in the Common Room, including Rosie, had disappeared to parents or friends. For the first time since those early days in the summer, he felt home-sick. At the outset of the illness, he had gone to see the doctor who visited the sanatorium each morning. The doctor had been able to do little more than prescribe an analgesic and advise the frequent consumption of fluids. Richard languished in bed, feeling too hot but shivering whenever he got up to go to the lavatory or replenish the glass of water at his bedside. As soon as the medicine started to wear off, the fever and head-ache returned. His head was filled with catarrh but felt too light whenever he tried to rise.

However, Richard was not entirely alone within the sprawling campus of the College. Cressida was also around for the first few days of Half Term. The intimate dinner which she had planned to have with Richard had been cancelled because of his illness. Priscilla had telephoned her on Richard's behalf, adding that she was concerned about leaving him. Thus it was that, on the first full day of the Half Term holiday, the afflicted young man was surprised by an unexpected visit from the Deputy Headmistress. He was aware from a repeated knock at the door that his croaking invitation to enter had not been heard. Wearing only a t-shirt and boxer shorts, he was swinging his legs out of bed to admit the visitor when Cressida entered the room. Instinctively obedient to social ceremony, he stood up. His legs, normally so capable of amazing speed on a games field, could hardly support him after the sudden movement. Cressida put down the plastic bag which she had been carrying and advanced upon him. His physical discomfort notwithstanding, Richard felt acutely embarrassed. He blushed under a two day stubble.

'My poor boy! Priscilla told me that you had caught the 'flu".

'I'm sorry that I couldn't come for dinner- and, er, I'm sorry that you have to see me like this.'

He found himself trapped between the approaching schoolmistress and his bed. Cressida was slightly taller than Richard, even without the additional advantage of shoes, and she was nearly half his weight again. She was wearing tightly fitting black slacks and a mauve pullover over a blouse. In mortified discomfort, Richard found himself enfolded in a hug which he was far too weak to resist.

'This is when you'll be missing home and your mother to help you,' said this unanticipated and self-appointed benefactor.

Richard's crimson face looked disconsolately across the room, his chin wedged on Cressida's left shoulder. His collar-bone was pressed against her bosom. Her powerful, fleshy arms embraced his back as she held him tightly. His boxer shorts were rucked by her left thigh, constricting his genitals. He was more aware of a sense of humiliated panic than he was even of his illness as he recognised the total helplessness of his situation.

'I'm sorry; I'm afraid I need to sit down,' he mumbled, desperately trying to think of a route of escape.

'Of course you do, you poor dear lad!'

She released him and he sat down heavily on the side of the bed. However, Cressida sat closely to him and again put her left arm round his shoulder. She felt his fevered brow with her right hand. Unable to attend to decorum any longer, Richard edged away from her. The exertion of the last two minutes now precipitated a coughing fit and, despite the excessive heat of the room, he started to shiver. For a moment, Cressida was about to suggest that he might benefit from finding a shirt or a jumper but she checked herself in time as she considered how attractive he looked in his underclothes.

'Let me make up your bed properly so that you can lie down again.'

Richard considered that he might be even more at risk in bed.

'No, thank you. It's good for me to try to sit up for a few minutes. I can then appreciate going back to bed all the more.'

'I've brought some goodies. You sit down in your armchair while I straighten out the sheets and duvet on the bed.'

'Thank you. I'm sorry that you find yourself doing this. I'll just try to find some trousers to put on at least.'

'It's terribly hot in here, dear boy.'

'My feet are like blocks of ice,' he said disconsolately as he subsided into the armchair.

'Where do you keep your socks?'

'I'll find a pair,' he said, beginning to lever himself up.

She insisted that he remained seated while she opened the drawer which he indicated.

'Well, Richard! This is a contrast from running up and down all the stairs – in how many seconds did you say?'

'Yeah, I know,' was all that he could manage as he started to cough and sneeze again.

Cressida enjoyed the frisson of opening the drawer and seeing and touching the intimate collection of underwear and socks which it contained. The brushed cotton underpants were all white or black or conservatively masculine shades of grey or blue. She envied the thirty-two inch waist-line. She extracted a pair of short black woollen socks and took them across to her patient, so endearing in his vulnerability. He refused her offer of help and lust masqueraded as compassion as she watched his minor struggle to put the socks on. What beautiful legs he has, she thought, so slim and so hairy and what a perfect figure, with his neat torso tapering to a slim waist.

She emptied the plastic bag which she had brought, presenting a box of tissues, some apples and bananas, a bottle of lemon barley water, a jar of honey, a packet of Paracetamol and half a bottle of whisky. She switched the kettle on.

'I'm going to make you a hot toddy.'

Seeing his look of incomprehension, she explained what this was. Richard found it impossible to feel enthusiastic but he dared not refuse, expressing dull gratitude. The influenza was now reasserting its primacy over his embarrassment as the dominant evil.

Nevertheless, the old Scottish remedy, consumed with two Paracetamol tablets, had a rapidly ameliorative effect. The coughing, sneezing and shivering eased and a more welcome exhaustion took their place. He allowed Cressida to supervise his return to bed, asking her to put the light out as she left. She said reassuringly that she would return to see how he was in the morning.

TWENTY-TWO

It was the first Monday morning after the Half Term break. Richard had recovered and, if not quite his usual vigorous self, he was fully up and about and glad to see everyone back. This real world of limitless space, inhabited by a host of busy, often smiling people, was a welcome and airy contrast to the dark, airless, claustrophobic underworld of sweaty sheets, fever, head-aches, catarrh and miserable isolation to which he had so recently been condemned. Even now, however, he had retained the cough, if less acutely, and had lost much of his appetite. Moreover, this morning, to his chagrin, he had discovered that he rapidly became exhausted in the gym' and was simply unable to run up and down at his accustomed speed. He was easily outpaced by even the feeblest boys. He was reduced to controlling the lesson by moving as little as possible and he felt profound relief when he was able to sit down. At Priscilla's insistence, he now agreed to commit himself to staying in the flat in Blenheim House. Indeed, he was glad not to spend any more time in his original quarters than was strictly necessary, at least for the moment. Priscilla was, of course, accustomed to the ailments of young men and, during the week, she made him digestible but appetising meals which gradually helped to restore him to full health. Rosie visited most days and put a bunch of large, dark crimson chrysanthemums in a vase in his bedroom.

A major bonus was Charlie's apparent change of heart.

Richard had deliberately asked Charlie about his Half Term, anticipating a politely laconic answer. However, not only did the old warmth seem to return, but Charlie expressed immediate and undisguised concern at the news of Richard's fate. It would seem that Charlie had thought matters over during the recess and was no longer blaming Richard, not that he had ever *overtly* done so. The next day, Charlie arrived at Richard's flat with a magnificent box of chocolates, beautifully wrapped by his mother, and a bag of huge, sweet, rosy apples gathered earlier from the orchard at the farm. Richard was genuinely touched and felt that it was the moment to clear the air. He invited Charlie in and they sat down.

'Charlie, I know how difficult it must be for you having me here instead of Mr Donaldson.'

'Sir, I'm sorry if I gave you that impression. Honestly, it was nothing against you personally. I was just upset about the way Rev. D seemed to have been treated. In fact, I still am. I think that what they've done is horrible- and so do my parents. We all know- the lads here and Matron and my parents- that Rev. D is innocent. Sir- believe me- he would never have done anything – er, like that.'

'Charlie, man! You don't need to convince *me*! I feel just the same way mate! I've never doubted it. When that Deputy Head asked me, I told her just that. In fact, I got very angry when she told me about it. If you don't believe me, you can ask her. I'm on your side over this mate, honestly- and on John Donaldson's. I just wish it could all be sorted out so that he can come back to us all. It's kind of important to me that you believe me, Charlie!'

'Sir, of course I do and I'm really sorry if I gave you any

other impression. As I say, it wasn't so much you being here as Rev D *not* being here.'

Charlie had a beer (to be more precise, a 'tinny', as Richard described it; he didn't bother with glasses). The prospect of alcohol was temporarily repugnant to Richard in the aftermath of his sickness and so he knocked back half a litre of orange juice. A professional relationship which had been put under strain now became a friendship for which they were both grateful.

'And you don't need to call me 'Sir', mate. Ash calls me by my first name when the younger lads aren't around,' offered the young Australian as Charlie was leaving.

'OK, Sir- I'll bear that in mind,' replied Charlie, the old grin returning as they shook hands.

He can still wrong foot me, thought Richard but he did so with charity. He felt sure of Charlie's good will again.

Cressida had visited Richard twice more before carrying through her arrangement to take a low-cost flight to Paris for a few days. Her attraction to the good-looking young man did not diminish. She would dearly have liked to have pressed home her advantage and to have exploited the dear boy's temporary vulnerability further, even at the risk of catching the 'flu'. However, self-advance was just as strong a motive as lust in her character. Although she might have just about considered sacrificing a cheap holiday in Paris, she most certainly did not want to do anything that might even remotely threaten her career. After all, when evaluating risk assessment, one need only consider the sudden and very recent fate of the Chaplain.

Indeed, this restraint, however motivated, had earnt Cressida unexpected credit. Richard, realising that he was not going to be the victim of molestation, had come to feel grateful to her for her practical assistance. It had been a relief to see another face, even hers. He had said as much to Priscilla who, while expressing surprise, had privately rebuked herself for possibly judging Cressida too harshly. To Cressida's delight, word had even reached Geoffrey Tansley, who expressed his own gratitude to a 'Deputy who can hold the fort in one's absence; with a person less competent and concerned, a detail like that could easily pass unobserved.'

Now, at ten o'clock, she was sitting in the Headmaster's study as the third member of a meeting with the Rural Dean.

Geoffrey Tansley and Maurice Stantonbury had dealt with each other quite extensively over the years. The latter came to preach in the College Chapel once a year. There had been occasional invitations to dinner. Relations had been good, albeit in a somewhat distant way. Although Cressida and Maurice had coincided at functions two or three times, she only really knew the local vicar by sight.

'This is a dreadful state of affairs, Geoffrey. I had thought that in this country a man was innocent until proven guilty. After all, we have both known John Donaldson for a great many years. He's a dedicated priest of immense integrity. He's hardly going to molest a boy at this stage. In any case, I understand that it was a senior boy. A seventeen-year old sportsman isn't just going to sit there and let himself be seduced by a middle-aged clergyman. Surely the whole thing is nonsense!'

'But it's the police. We had no choice,' Cressida intervened.

Maurice bridled.

'Forgive me, Mrs Fulwell, but I was directing my remarks to the Headmaster. He and I have conducted business with each other, some of it confidential, since he first came here.'

He smiled severely.

'I'm sorry, Maurice, but when we are up against a situation like this, bristling with legal implications, it is now accepted practice to have a third party present. That is why I asked Cressida to join us,' explained Geoffrey Tansley, trying to find a mollifying tone.

'Well, I'm a little surprised that you and I can't just talk it through informally on our own, to begin with at least, but if this is what political correctness and risk of litigation combine to require these days, I suppose I'll have to live with it.'

'Would you like me to leave, perhaps, Headmaster?' asked Cressida, all sensitivity and discretion.

'No, I would not, Cressida,' replied the Headmaster, slightly nettled by what he took to be a rather confrontational approach on the part of the Rural Dean. 'This is a College matter and, however regrettable in nature, it is official business.'

'Whatever people prefer,' said Cressida demurely.

Geoffrey Tansley then outlined the legal straitjacket which he saw himself to be in. He felt weary as he went through it all yet again but he tried hard to assume a tone of patience which was in no way patronising.

'I can see the difficulty which you and the College are in, Geoffrey, but it is *not*, contrary to what you said earlier, entirely a 'College matter'. John Donaldson is an ordained man in the Church of England and he is answerable to the Bishop.'

Geoffrey closed his eyes and sighed gently. He had travelled this path before with Maurice. It had always led to the inevitable impasse. Whereas former conversations had been in the spirit of friendly debate, there was now, suddenly, the potential for real conflict.

'Maurice, we've been through all this, *en principe*, on other occasions, as you know. The fact remains that the Chaplain was appointed to work in this independent school by the chief executive of the institution, the Headmaster- in this case, my predecessor. We employ him and we pay his salary, which, incidentally, we are, of course, continuing to do in the present situation.'

'I should certainly think you would! The man has not been proved guilty of any wrongdoing and I am sure that you agree that it is very unlikely that that eventuality will occur.'

'What would you do in my position, Maurice? I haven't wished this and God knows (and I use that phrase deliberately) I don't wish John Donaldson any harm: hand on heart, quite the opposite. I was as shocked and dismayed as I can see you are when all this blew up without warning.'

Maurice chose to ignore Cressida's vigorous nodding of her

head. He had decided at the beginning of the conversation that he did not take to her.

'I am not in *your* position, Geoffrey. *I* am also in a difficult position. As Rural Dean, I have a responsibility to the ordained ministers of the Anglican Church within the Deanery. As far as I am concerned, that includes John Donaldson. More significantly, I hold him in exceptionally high personal regard and consider it my duty- indeed, my sacred duty- to do everything possible to defend him against the injustice which I am convinced is currently being perpetrated against him.'

'Well, don't blame me!' responded Geoffrey crossly. 'You had better tell all that to the police, or the social security blockheads in Midhampton, or to the infernal Williams woman and her blasted son.'

Cressida drew breath to speak but Maurice cut across her.

'This is so serious, Geoffrey, that it is going to have to go to the Bishop.'

'Oh God,' said Geoffrey.

'I'm sure that Bishop Michael would only regard himself as God's humble servant,' replied Maurice with a donnish sarcasm which did nothing to improve tempers.

Maurice knew that Geoffrey would be fully aware of Bishop Michael's national reputation for publicly challenging homophobic elements within the Church. The brilliant Bishop was something of a celebrity on the media, regularly offering 'Thought for the Day' on the 'Today' programme on Radio Four and often serving on the panel of 'Any Questions'. With news of this incident having already appeared in the press, the last thing that the College Governors would want would be the campaigning Bishop turning Moreton College into a whipping boy across the national press.

Really, thought Geoffrey, one couldn't win. Either he, Geoffrey, is to be lambasted for harbouring an alleged paedophile on the staff or else he is to be denounced as an example of homophobic prejudice.

He decided that it would, upon reflection, be better if Cressida left him on his own with Maurice. The meeting was not going well and Maurice had effectively gagged her. She left the room with exaggerated compliance, taking care to avoid Maurice's eyes, not that he was bothering to look in her direction.

'You're making this incredibly difficult for me,' Geoffrey said irritably. 'As I keep telling you, it's not my fault that all this has happened.'

'I'm sorry, Geoffrey, but my primary concern and sympathy is for John. If you think that *you're* having difficulty, I wonder what *he* is feeling at the moment.'

'I can't think that it will be helpful for the Bishop to be dragged into this.'

'I can readily see that it might not be helpful to you, or indeed the College, but it could only be advantageous to John, especially if, as now seems probable, the matter goes to court. It could be jolly useful for judge and jury to have seen recent television footage of Bishop Michael inveighing against homophobia. Anyway, all this is making assumptions about John's sexuality which people have no right to make. Not that there is anything wrong in being homosexual, of course, but John can't even be labelled in that way just on the say-so of a boy with a grievance who is supported by his mother.'

For once in his life, Geoffrey Tansley could think of nothing useful to say. He knew the truth of all that had just been said but, in all honesty, he could not think that there was anything more that he could do. There was, however, a pressing practical matter which he did need to broach.

'One of the many difficulties with all this, Maurice, is that we don't have an acting Chaplain on the staff. I know that you are very angry with me but I'm going to have to turn to you to ask for help with this. John is the only ordained person on the staff.'

'Oh, really, Geoffrey! You have some nerve! I have a big parish church to run, as well as the need to deal with all my responsibilities within the deanery!'

'Well, at least try to give me some advice!'

'Well, you're going to have to depend on the good will of Christians on the staff to take services and preach sermons. You do have some good folk who are both spiritually experienced and competent. I suppose that I am going to have to come and dig you out of this pit when it comes to celebrating Holy Communion. I'm afraid that that will need to happen at times when I'm not occupied elsewhere.'

'Well, thank you for that, anyway. It sounds as though we might probably get by until the end of this term, by which time let us hope that we'll have a clearer picture of the future. We are desperately trying to get some-one in to take over John's teaching. A helpful young Australian is filling the slots with Blenheim House and the football.'

'As a Christian priest, it is my responsibility to say too that, if there is any specific case of urgent spiritual or pastoral need amongst the College community, pupils or staff, they must feel free to approach me in total confidentiality. Perhaps you should advertise that fact.'

'That's very generous,' said Geoffrey.

'It is my responsibility as a priest,' corrected Maurice.

Not wanting any small talk at this juncture, Maurice declined coffee. They shook hands and he left.

TWENTY-THREE

NOVEMBER DOES NOT ALWAYS receive a fair press. There can be sparkling days of unexpected brilliance when the trees in the landscaped park around the College exceed the attempts of any artist in their evanescent display of crimson, orange, gold and purple, framed against an azure sky. This year, however, November was in a protracted and sullen torpor, coldly perspiring in grey days of lowering cloud and chilly drizzle. One dank, monochromatic day lapsed indecipherably into the next as the dark evenings stealthily encroached into the sunless afternoons.

With an almost imperceptible gradualness, the alliance between the senior boys in Blenheim House weakened. After Half Term, it was agreed that Jude would go home to his mother every day at the end of afternoon school. The good sense of such a compromise was clear but for Jude it was a mixed blessing. It was, of course, desirable to leave the now hated boarding school at every available opportunity. On the other hand, the crisis had provided an opening for the despised Mike to come to Lynn's support. For instance, she could not always free herself to collect her son from the College in the afternoon. Jude was therefore forced to endure Mike's laboured attempts to relate to him conversationally for the duration of several car journeys each week.

Richard had refused absolutely to allow Jude back into the First XI. This had prompted a complaint from Ashley on the grounds that such an exclusion did not benefit the team's prospects of success. Ashley and Chris, both ever easy-going and accommodating by nature, had drifted back into an association of superficial friendship with Jude. Richard was surprised and irritated that he needed to point out the moral perspectives behind what he saw to be an obviously just decision. However, never one to seek confrontation, Ashley had been quick to back down,

'Point taken, Sir.'

'Good man, Ash! You're a top captain, mate!'

'Thank you Sir.'

Ashley had averted his eyes. It wasn't the moment to grease up to a master. Richard was still learning where to draw the fine line between friendship with lads who were only a very few years younger than himself and the distance sometimes required from one who is in authority.

Tim remained quietly but consistently loyal to Rev. D. Like Charlie, he refused to let time or distance mute the bold clear colours of moral outrage into the pastel shades of compromise. He found that Charlie was the only person with whom he could discuss the matter safely or, occasionally, in the company of Charlie, Matron.

Charlie's icy relationship with Jude had never recovered. The decisive fracturing of a close friendship combined with a rigorously imposed self-discipline, as he prepared for his interview at Cambridge, to develop a greater seriousness and self-confidence. During these days, he lived for literature. He saw Alexander Scott almost daily, usually staying after both Jude and Olivia had left, after one of the 'Oxbridge sessions' which the three of them were freely given. Charlie alone had been allowed totally free access to Mr Scott's extensive library of over two thousand books. Alexander had even lent him a key to his study, situated at the top of the English Department classroom block. Occasionally, at week-ends, or during evenings when the boarding house was noisier than usual, Charlie would escape to this heaven and sit alone at his master's desk, surrounded by all the books, each one placed with exact accuracy on the shelves, many of them valuable editions, some of which Alexander had purchased, at what would now seem laughable prices, from a market stall in Cambridge nearly forty years earlier. Sometimes, Alexander and Charlie would coincide. Each would work in silence, Charlie sitting in a comfortable chair, reading, Alexander working at his desk. After a long period of time, when Alexander had come to the end of marking, or some necessary piece of 'desperately dreary data distribution', there might be half-an-hour or so before Cordelia would arrive in the car to take her husband home. On such occasions, Alexander would open a bottle of wine, pour out two glasses and, sitting in the opposite armchair, engage his pupil in literary conversation. Charlie was profoundly conscious of the privilege of such education and on each such occasion he had several new questions in his head which he had been keen to ask.

Alexander enjoyed these interludes with no less satisfaction. No longer young, and after a twelve hour day of diverse and sometimes stressful demands, he could freely share his intellectual passion with a young scholar who was himself capable of genuinely personal literary perception. As he listened to Charlie's informed enthusiasm, he thought with pleasure of the contrast between this young adult, capable of humane, balanced and imaginative judgment, and the nervous, stammering youth who had first appeared in this same room to discover Keats' odes just fourteen months earlier. What a privilege it has been to have spent thirty-five years contributing in partnership with one's pupils to success like this. Sometimes names and faces from the past glided benignly across his inner vision: all bright young men and women whom he had had the immense privilege of introducing to literature, each one of them different, many now themselves serving in academe, some working for the BBC, some serious journalists for broadsheet newspapers, a few successful writers, at least three notable critics and two actors who were now household names. He wondered how long it might continue after he had gone. Would these books surrounding this boy and him now, each one tangible and distinct, mean anything to a future age which could download everything in piecemeal and transitory fashion from the Internet? Would the critical intelligence which this young man was now so assiduously cultivating remain relevant in an information gathering age so smugly self-congratulatory in its passion for cripplingly ignorant and arbitrary evaluation, where the language of discernment was reduced to an abstract cacophony of ugly jargon: 'norm related assessment criteria', 'whole folder coursework band descriptors', 'dominant assessment objective weighting', 'quality of written communication descriptors (QWCD)', 'relationship of assessment objectives to specific units' – this and so much more, to a point where even Gradgrind and M'Choakumchild would have drawn a blue-pencilled line one-hundred-and-fifty years earlier? *'You are to be in all things regulated and governed by fact:'* except, mused Alexander, that the interpretation of language by language admits of no such reduction. The truth of fiction cannot be reduced to facts, not even by the Schools Curriculum and

Assessment Authority and the Minister for Education. No, Alexander thought, he was an old timer and no mistake. There would be no place for him in the teaching of the future: two years to retirement: not before time, if so much that he valued most was to be discarded.

Teaching that particular trio at that time, in relatively intimate circumstances, might have presented a lesser teacher with insurmountable difficulties. Olivia had finally broken with Jude. Alexander himself had, unsurprisingly, sharply altered his moral judgment of Jude after the Donaldson affair. He noticed that all three of them arrived separately and split up the moment they left the room. Charlie and Jude avoided each other as far as possible and Charlie, ever sensitive to decorum, did not feel that it would be appropriate to escort Jude's very recent girlfriend through the College in full view of his own erstwhile closest friend. In any case, Charlie invariably wanted to stay behind and talk further. Olivia, still a little nervous in the presence of Mr Scott, especially given the complication now with Jude, hurried back to the safety of her friends at Montague House. Despite his own well hidden anger with Jude and his awareness of the tensions which must surely now exist within a trio hitherto delightfully diverse in their compatibility, Alexander's own scholarly reserve as a teacher served him well. He strictly limited all conversation to the work in hand. The three of them seemed relieved as they tacitly agreed to hold to that rule. Indeed, they responded to each other's comments freely enough and when they were offering a piece of critical analysis it was almost as though the dark shadow which hung over them had lifted: almost, but not quite. Olivia remained anxious and diffident. Jude responded with confidence, much as before. Alexander noticed that the main difference was in Charlie, who no longer rushed to respond to Jude's pronouncements, either by trying to find a consensus or by smilingly and apologetically holding uneasily to his own position. These days Charlie was untroubled if Jude and he disagreed. In turn, Charlie's disinclination to rise to the bait any longer slightly took the wind out of Jude's sails. Alexander considered how even an adverse extraneous circumstance could nurture independent intellectual growth. But he also realised that it was a pity that all this had happened, from their point of view, as well, of course, as from that of his good friend, John Donaldson. He could not remember having ever had an 'Oxbridge' group before who had not left his room happily together in discussion of their common reading.

'Sir!' repeated Charlie, recalling Alexander back into full consciousness.

'Good Heavens! I was day-dreaming! How rude, Charlie! Please forgive me. It's been a long day. I'm sorry; do you mind saying that again?'

'I was just wondering – I realise that it's an outrageously patronising thing for some-one like me to say-'

'I can't imagine your being outrageously patronising, Charlie,' interrupted Alexander.

'Well- here goes. It seems to me, though I'm probably quite wrong-'

'Stop hedging your bets, boy, and get on with it,' said Alexander in weary good humour, filling up both their glasses.

'Thank you very much Sir. I was going to say that I think

that Conrad had moved on quite a bit as a writer in the four years between writing 'An Outpost of Progress' and 'Heart of Darkness.'

'Yes, you're probably right. Tell me why.'

'Perhaps it's because I read them the wrong way round. As you know, I read 'Heart of Darkness' on your recommendation but it was only afterwards that I turned up the other one. 'Heart of Darkness' is more subtle and it's restrained in its subtlety. Kurtz dies: 'Mistah Kurtz, he dead.': so what: but Marlow, the narrator and principal protagonist, lives on to compromise himself with the lie at the end, in his own way therefore capitulating to the colonial and capitalist exploitation which he deplores.'

'Yes, the irony is consummate. Go on.'

'Well, in the earlier work, the two guys dumped by their company at the grotty trading post up the river, are overcome by the terrible isolation of the Dark Continent to the point where they both lose their reason and one shoots the other and then hangs himself. It's all more straightforward. They're Kurtz and Marlow combined. Conrad separates that persona out in 'Heart of Darkness'. Killing off Kurtz allows for greater shading of the central character. Marlow is much more contradictory. He's a real explorer, not just in navigational terms but in the Modernist thing about exploring the consciousness.'

'Yes, I agree. That is a very thoughtful comparison. I think too that the irony is more sharply defined in other ways. In both, the white man is shown to be the villain. In both, ivory, which is white, is a symbol for greed. But in 'Heart of Darkness' it seems to me that the black people are totally the underdogs whereas in 'An Outpost of Progress', they have a mixed press; some of them are not very nice at all.'

'But could that be because some of them have been corrupted by the colonists? Oh, that rather means I'm arguing against myself, doesn't it?'

Alexander smiled.

'I don't suppose anything that Conrad wrote is that simple! I think that your central point is a very good one; stick with it. That sort of ultimate challenge that draws characters to destruction or near destruction occurs throughout his works. The first mate on the ship in 'Typhoon' cannot face the storm, which is again, I suppose, like Africa, a metaphor. Captain McWhirr steers the ship safely through, rather like Marlow.'

'Oh but, Sir, surely they're very different. McWhirr partly succeeds because he has a limited imagination. Marlow isn't short on that score. He sees only too clearly 'the horror'.'

'Yes, that's true too. I'm just trying to recall; I think that 'Typhoon' was written quite a few years later.'

Alexander got up to reach for the book but he was forestalled.

'I don't think so, Sir. Wasn't it written in 1903, the year after 'Heart of Darkness'?'

'You throw me. We'd better check.'

He brought the book down.

'Yes, you're quite right! Well done!'

Alexander was delighted to be corrected by his pupil. Now would be the time to write a letter to his friend, Edward Griffin, the Director of Studies at the Cambridge college where they had each gained their first class degrees so long ago. This boy was surely a winner.

Charlie thought: wow! To think that I used to be scared stiff of the sight of him and now he lets me correct him on a minor detail like that.

Charlie quickly decided that it was now or never to raise the matter which had been troubling him. However, he knew that his current excellent relationship with Scotty could not be taken for granted. He had never discussed anything outside literature with him and the famously irascible schoolmaster's response might well be unpredictable. A shade of the old apprehension returned. He quickly offered the Almighty what he liked to term one of his 'arrow' prayers.

Please, God, let me get this right. Let him not be angry with me. I've got to do this for Rev.D. You know that, Lord. Please help me.'

'Sir, for some time now, I've been wanting to ask your advice about something that has nothing to do with English. It's something rather personal which has been bothering me and I don't know how to resolve it.'

A look of benign enquiry: so far so good, Charlie thought to himself: but, Charlie Boy, remember the awful visit to Mrs Fulwell. Mr Scott is a hundred times fiercer. Get it right.

'I know that under normal circumstances it is very bad

form for a pupil to ask one teacher about another one Sir, but I know that Rev.D- er, Mr Donaldson- and you are friends and *you* must know how good he's been to some of us boys. Some of us really want to do something to help and I was just wondering if you might be able to give me any information or advice. If this is out of order, I can only apologise but my motive is to do all for the best.'

'Don't look so worried about asking me, dear Charlie. Of course we know each other quite well enough for you to do that. I would have expected no less of you than for you to be concerned about Mr Donaldson and I do have some idea of what he means to you and your friends. Naturally you will understand that there is a limit to what I can say and, more unfortunately, to what I can do. However, I have seen him a few times and I can assure you that he's in good health and living comfortably. Obviously it's a major worry for him and he misses you boys terribly. Let me ask you a question which *you* might consider to be out of order. I apologise in advance if so. Is it not difficult for you, given your close friendship with the boy involved? You must feel divided in loyalty?'

'I'm sorry to have to say it, Sir, but Jude and I are no longer friends. I feel that he was the one who broke the friendship and I have to say straightaway that I don't see any prospect of its recovery. As we're on the subject, Olivia has also fallen out with Jude, partly for the same reason, but I don't know all the details.'

'So, as far as you're concerned, your sympathy lies with Mr Donaldson?'

'Yes, definitely. I know Jude's version of the events. He's told every-one. Even if it's true, which I doubt, I think that the action which his mother and he have taken is dreadfully wrong- and so do my parents.'

'You must understand that I can't comment, Charlie, but next time I see Mr Donaldson I shall tell him about your concern and, indeed, your loyalty.'

This wasn't good enough for Charlie.

'But I want to *do* something to help him, Sir. We don't even know where he is. Is he miles away or is he somewhere local?'

'You know that I'm not at liberty to answer that question.'

Was the tone altering, Charlie wondered? Come on, Charlie Boy, don't blow it:

'I am in blood
Stepped in so far that, should I wade no more,
Returning were as tedious as go o'er.'

'If you've seen him a few times, Sir, that means he's still based locally. I know that Matron has visited him and he must have been close by then.'

'That would seem to be a fairly watertight deduction and so I fail to see the point of the question.'

'I'm sorry, Sir. I'm stepping over the line, I can tell. I'm only asking because I feel I can't just sit back and do nothing: the old maxim about evil, and good men doing nothing, and all that. Please, Sir, could I go to see him? It must be awful for him, stuck on his own somewhere with this hanging over his head.'

'I'm afraid that you can't, Charlie. That would be infringing the terms which I understand the police have imposed upon our Headmaster: 'perverting the course of justice' I believe it is called.'

Alexander saw the boy's disappointed face and felt moved.

'The trouble is, Charlie, that none of us knows how this is going to end. You and I know how we would *like* it to end, of course. (I've probably committed some technical impropriety in saying even that.) It has gone beyond the Headmaster and the College. It's in the hands of the police and the Social Services, whose wisdom might or might not be replied upon. Neither you nor I can alter the course of events. However, if you want to do something positive, might I suggest that you exercise your customary good taste to find a suitable card and write a message of good will on it? Were the article to come into my hands, I think that I could guarantee its safe delivery. But we'd need to be cautious. I think that I would need to ask you to do this without telling any-one else in the College.'

Charlie agreed but it was clear to Alexander that this concession had fallen far short of what the boy had hoped for.

TWENTY-FOUR

THE COURSE OF TRUE love in the Sixth Form at a boarding school is a crooked path, sometimes swiftly leading its followers from sublimely vertiginous heights to agonisingly obscure depths as it twists and turns its stony way towards a destination which might be quite other than that desired or even perceived by those who traverse its dangerous route. During this November, several such travellers were to arrive at the dark and deep abyss which is its nadir. One would slowly and painfully climb out of it; three others would lose their footing and fall headlong into disaster.

The first two casualties were Emma Morgan and her latest paramour, the M.P.'s son, Paddy Fitzroy-Fitton, who were caught *in flagrante* in bed together. Every-one knew that the penalty for that offence was expulsion. Not even the threats and blandishments of Lady Wolseley could dislodge Geoffrey Tansley from his clear awareness that the creation of a precedent in such a matter must be out of the question. The Conservative M.P., keen to be selected by the latest new leader of his party for a post in the Shadow Cabinet, and fearful therefore of any adverse publicity, raised no objection.

Jasper was particularly sorry to see Paddy go. Paddy had developed into a tall, handsome boy, with his mop of dark hair and his enigmatically humorous, brown, bedroom eyes, all of which had recently prompted Jasper to go out of his way to be friendly and helpful. The girls at Montague House were divided over the departure of Emma. Obviously Olivia would be shedding no tears and Victoria and her friends just about managed the decency of a frosty adieu. Others, however, railed about repression and injustice but did so in vain.

Once again, Olivia had left Mr Scott's Oxbridge class sensing an intellectual inferiority to the two boys. She knew that she might be feeling this way because she was more generally unsettled: possibly, she wondered, slightly depressed. Although she still found him intimidating, she had no quarrel with Mr Scott. She even realised that he sensed that she was nervous. She spoke the least when they met together and, when she felt that she really had to offer something, or, indeed, when Mr Scott directly asked her for her opinion, she thought that her comments were invariably banal or, at best, superficial. Terribly sensitive, she would occasionally catch the slightest hint of a sneering smirk on Jude's face when she painfully tried to engage at what she hoped to be an appropriate level. To be fair, never once did Mr Scott, notorious for his terrifyingly dextrous verbal acidity, say anything discouraging but she did wonder what he might really be thinking, behind the manner of slightly old-fashioned, gentlemanly courtesy which he adopted towards her. Even prior to the dreadful scene in the Sixth Form Common Room just before Half Term, Jude had, on a couple of occasions, cruelly suggested that the English master was just being polite. Still, Olivia *was* working hard and she *was* interested in the books and she *did* want to get into Oxford, while realising that such a happy eventuality would be an unexpected bonus. Her father had insisted that his daughter should apply to the College which both he and her grandfather had attended. She was glad that she was not in direct competition with the two clever boys as they applied for Cambridge. Mr Scott even praised her written work, while suggesting that she might advance her own opinions a little more freely, instead of those of the critics whom she read.

She had found the break with Jude deeply distressing. She knew that he had been unfaithful and that he could be thoughtless and, at worst, deliberately spiteful. She had accepted the disapproval of Victoria Summerthwaite and the other girls seriously but had wondered if her parents had been a little snobbish when, on the basis of a single meeting, they had made their tentatively adverse judgment of this, her first boy-friend. The fact was that she did find Jude physically extremely attractive. He was good-looking in his own compact, unkempt sort of way and she even liked his cheeky assertiveness, a counterpoint to her own polite reserve. She also respected the fact that Jude seemed to cope so well, given his domestic circumstances. Her respect had increased when he had laid claim to a Christian faith. Diffident by nature, and coming from a wealthy, well connected family, which still paid lip service to traditional Anglicanism, Olivia was not quite ready to follow suit in this more personal faith, as expounded by Rev .D, in which lay people prayed *extempore* and talked to each other about Jesus as a person they knew. Nevertheless, she was impressed that some-one of Jude's evident intelligence and independence of judgment should be willing to make such a commitment. She was very clear about her own subscription to a Christian morality and she appreciated Rev. D's sermons, which she knew from various sources, girls as well as boys, to be supported by his legendary kindness and wisdom. She came to respect Rev. D all the more on account of the favourable observations which Jude and his friends had repeatedly made. Although, at Charlie's suggestion, Olivia had consulted him once in connection with her work-load, she herself had never quite managed to confide more deeply in the Chaplain, partly because she was shy about discussing any sort of spiritual intimacy and partly because it had not really been possible to talk about the difficulties in her relationship with Jude. For a start, the Rev. D probably had no idea about Jude's visits to Emma Morgan, the most objectively definable source of Olivia's own unhappiness in the relationship. Their relationship had become stormy because of Jude's various inconsistencies and Olivia had to admit that, deep down in her heart, she had probably realised that it was doomed in the light of his infidelity. Nevertheless, she did love him and she had just hoped against hope that, despite all the warnings from others, he would reform.

The catalyst for the inevitable fracture had occurred on the fateful morning when the Rev D had so suddenly and, initially at least, mysteriously, disappeared. Jude had said nothing about the alleged incident to her though she had been aware of his fury at being dropped from the team, the manifest justice of which action she had thought best to keep within her own counsel. Like others, she doubted if the incident had happened at all and, even if it had done, her own sense that it had subsequently been perversely exaggerated was more than confirmed by Jude's friends. Olivia felt shocked and angry with Jude for so obviously and so coldly betraying a man who had done so much to help him and who, it was generally acknowledged by believer and sceptic alike, was a compelling force for good in the community. It had said something when the likes of Charlie, Ashley, Jasper and Victoria, as eclectic a group of pupils as you could reasonably imagine within the College, had all fallen into spontaneous agreement during that dreadful scene in the Sixth Form Common Room. At that moment, the vestiges of love for Jude had evaporated for good. Indeed, she shared unequivocally the anger of all the other people present, an anger intensified by the humiliating light in which the episode had placed Olivia herself. Rather than expose herself to the furious vituperation which would inevitably characterise a final confrontation with him, she had written a short note telling Jude that she would be seeing him no more and that, this time, her decision was final. She had then wondered if this had been a coward's way out but Vicky had insisted not; why should she, asked her friend, allow herself to be hurt any further? Olivia was surprised by the relief which she had felt in the absence of any reply from Jude.

Olivia was an only child who had been much desired but long in coming: a gift delayed, the arrival of which had delighted all the more. Her father owned and directed a chain of upmarket department stores in East Anglia, like his father before him. Her mother was the only daughter of two members of the Suffolk gentry. Much of Olivia's time was spent in the Georgian manor house in Suffolk, rather than at the pied-a-terre in Chelsea. She returned the love of her parents and her surviving grandparents with a yearning devotion which was reciprocated with the deepest gratitude. Despite this, Olivia's perceptive and generous good nature, allied to a calm but cautious disposition, meant that there was never any risk of her being spoilt. Even as a little girl, she had been treated as a friend by her elders who had sought to speak to her, as far as possible, like an adult. She actively chose to assimilate the moral and educational values of her family and her life of reading, cooking, gardening, joining her parents and grandparents at restrained adult dinner parties, riding her horse on the small Suffolk estate and attending point-to-points, would have been regarded as old-fashioned to the point of deadliness by many of the other girls at the College.

Although Olivia was more than content in older company, and, indeed, generally preferred it to that of her peers, Vicky and some of the other girls had occasionally come to visit during the summer holidays, enjoying tennis, croquet and riding together. Her parents, especially her mother, had fretted terribly about sending her dearest darling to boarding school at the age of thirteen. They had chosen Moreton partly because it had a reputation for pastoral care without compromising academic standards but mainly because of its healthy location in beautiful countryside. There were stables close by the College where their daughter could continue to ride a designated horse in unpolluted air. This was how the great friendship with Vicky had been established. Mr and Mrs Kendall-Reid were more than relieved that their lovely daughter had settled into the College placidly, working well, participating in games and, to begin with at least, making the right sort of friends.

However, two clouds had appeared on the horizon: firstly the perfectionist's increasing tendency to anxiety over doing everything properly and to the satisfaction of her parents and teachers, an anxiety which increased exponentially as a consequence of the effect of the mass of clutter, invented by modern examining procedures, upon conscientious pupils, and, secondly, the irruption of Jude Williams into Olivia's life. It seemed so out of character, Mr and Mrs Kendall-Reid had confided to each other when driving home from the College. Presumably, alas, it must be something to do with the attraction of opposites (not at all a force behind their own engagement and marriage a generation earlier). They were not ironists and Jude's jocularly irreverent remarks, during his one visit to Suffolk, about living in the world of Jane Austen ('Where are the peasants and the coachman with the barouche-landau?'), together with his arrival in the dining room, when other guests had been invited, wearing a pair of ragged jeans and a dirty t-shirt, to say nothing of his helping himself freely to the Margaux, reassuring Olivia's father that the wine was 'not bad', and addressing Olivia's parents by their Christian names, had not endeared him to Mr and Mrs Kendall-Reid.

For the first time ever, they had found themselves in dispute with their daughter. There were no threats, scoldings or sanctions from their side and no tantrums from their daughter but both Olivia and her parents were acutely unhappy that an apparently irreconcilable lapse in consensus now clouded their relationship. Her parents had met some of the other boys, who had also visited the house in a group of friends from the College. Predictably, they had taken warmly to Charlie and also, in their lack of worldliness quite oblivious to the inhibiting reality, to Jasper, who often spent weekends with his parents in their *residence secondaire* a few miles away. Why could their only daughter not have chosen a boy like that, obviously so much more suitable? Like most teenagers, Olivia had become disinclined to tell tales out of school.

Olivia was unquestionably beautiful: not merely pretty, but beautiful. Her mother deserved some of the credit for the commendable fact that her daughter was also totally devoid of vanity. Hermione Kendall-Reid had, in her turn, been modest about her own beauty and, as she observed Olivia growing into a truly lovely young woman, she had, from the beginning, praised her daughter's beauty on the one hand but counselled modesty on the other. Olivia's mother deployed her own immaculate taste to give her daughter advice but, true to form, she did so as one adult to another. This spirit of genuine freedom, allied to Olivia's gentle nature and profound respect for her wonderful mother, resulted in the good advice being taken. Olivia eschewed the fads endorsed by many of the girls at College. She was never to be seen with a bare midriff and her dresses neither rode so high that they entirely exposed her shapely thighs nor swept the ground in neo-gothic counter-statement. Her small firm breasts were modestly covered, her cleavage rarely seen in public. Her fine blond hair was swept neatly back and tied behind her head by a short ribbon. When scrambling about outside at home, or on week-end afternoons at College, she joined the rest in jeans and loose fitting blouses. Some of the boys hung around outside Montague House on games afternoons in the hope of seeing her in her short games skirt and blouse. She learnt how to parry the advances which were regularly made and did so politely but firmly. Several younger boys had even sent her notes of admiration, imploring her to meet with them. Although she did not reply to these, when she threw them away she did not do so with public scorn. She was touched that they admired her but was quite clear that it would be wrong to give false encouragement. Some of the older boys were vexed that her beauty was so absolutely unattainable and grumbled behind her back about her ice maiden's demeanour. When Olivia observed some of the other girls behaving provocatively at house dances, she moved away from the immediate scene but kept her own counsel. She was unswervingly and compassionately loyal to her friends in Montague House and in turn was loved and respected by them. As with her parents at home, however, the girls at College had expressed concern and incredulity when, from all the boys available to some-one of Olivia's attributes, she had fallen helplessly in love with Jude Williams.

During November, the combined pressure resulting from the termination of her relationship with Jude and a mounting agitation as the dreaded interview for Oxford approached ever nearer, together with the unremitting demands of the routine 'A' level work , to say nothing of the miserable, sunless weather, kept Olivia in her tidy study for long periods. She only left the House when classes, games or meals required her to do so. She even missed as many College meals as possible, preferring to cook pasta in the kitchen along the passage or microwave vegetarian meals purchased on hasty trips to the supermarket in the town. She ate an apple and a banana each day and drank several glasses of orange juice.

Olivia's principal reason for wishing success at Oxford was to please her father and grandfather. She felt a deep sense of responsibility to succeed on their behalf. Her father had not realised quite how seriously she had taken his remark about 'maintaining the family tradition.' She knew how much he was relishing her prospective success. Even though he had in no way bullied or cajoled her, she desperately did not want to let him down. Her mother, ever vigilant, had observed the difficulty and had gently taken Olivia aside to tell her that they knew that she worked very hard and would do well and that she must not think of it as 'the be all and end all' if she didn't get in to Oxford. But Olivia knew her father's great hope over the matter and, although she also knew that he would be kindness itself if it did not work out, she did not want to fail a parent who had given her so much.

The one friendship outside Montague House that gently developed at this time was with Charlie. From both sides the friendship was primarily platonic, though when Calpurnia Tansley had seen them standing together over drinks at the luncheon party for Lord Macclesfield, she had remarked to Alexander Scott about them being 'a remarkably handsome couple', which, Alexander agreed, they most certainly were. Olivia and Charlie could not possibly have been oblivious to each other's charm and good looks. However, the friendship blossomed because, by the standards of young people, they were both unusually mature in their restraint. Given the exclusion of Jude now from the trio's literary conversations, it was natural for two highly serious and strongly motivated pupils to discuss their common interests. Progress was, however, gradual. Olivia was responsibly cautious in the knowledge that Charlie had lost his closest friend and Charlie, in turn, felt that it would be cheap and unkind to invade what had so recently been Jude's territory, even despite remaining bitterly hurt by the treatment which he himself had received from his former friend and, even more, by that dealt out to Rev D. Neither Charlie nor Olivia was socially competitive. Still a little ashamed of his fall from grace with Emma Morgan, despite having long ago accepted Rev. D's admonition that if God forgives you, you jolly well ought to be able to forgive yourself, Charlie appreciated Olivia's modesty quite as much as her beauty. In her turn, Olivia was grateful for Charlie's supportive presence and his thoughtful kindness. Most days they either spoke on their mobiles or texted each other if they had been unable to achieve a significant meeting. Inevitably they discussed the debacle with Jude. Neither fully expressed the depth of their dismay, though each guessed how the other truly felt with considerable accuracy and each respected the other all the more for such restraint. Neither of them pursued the other. There were natural meetings over the sharing of books or the checking through of one of Mr Scott's increasingly fiendish critical appreciation exercises. These meetings often developed into gentle enquiries about how the other was coping, especially from Charlie's side. He sensed that Olivia was feeling the pressure on the run up to Oxbridge even more than he was and he mentioned this quietly to Mr Scott.

TWENTY-FIVE

It was a particularly gloomy Saturday afternoon in the middle of November and Jasper was at a loose end. His parents had taken off to Antigua for a fortnight and so he had been unable to wangle an *Exeat* to allow him to go home and enjoy the pampering of Mumsy before paying a visit to one of his favourite gay bars in the West End. Among other inconveniences, this had prevented him from returning from London with a decent quantity of contraband liquor and an opportunity to augment the limited supply of dope which he had left, secreted under his mattress. After lunch, he had slipped out of College and walked down to the town where he had purchased a bottle of whisky and some cigarettes.

Some time ago, Jasper had struck up a friendship of convenience with a local taxi driver, Mahmoud, whom he now called on his mobile to fulfil the usual arrangement of driving him back to a discreet point close to the College grounds. Jasper was always very generous with Mahmoud's tip, partly because it suited his purpose but also because he found the handsome, swarthy, young, second generation Pakistani terribly sexy. Even in November, Mahmoud was driving in a short-sleeved shirt and Jasper needed to exercise conscious restraint not to stroke the glossy dark fur which covered his driver's arms. Jasper guessed that Mahmoud was probably a Moslem and so it was necessary to be doubly careful not to let him know how absolutely gorgeous he was. Jasper sometimes entertained a fantasy whereby he would invite Mahmoud up to College one hot Saturday afternoon in the summer, tempting him with a swim in the lake. The scheme would involve Jasper's secret trysting place on the more remote, densely wooded, southern shore of the lake. Mahmoud would strip down to his boxer shorts and dive into the cool water with an admiring Jasper looking on, armed with a hamper full of delicious goodies, waiting to be consumed after Mahmoud had towelled himself down before drying off completely in the warm sunshine.

Mahmoud was, of course, completely unaware of this aspect of his client's motivation. In his turn he was always happy to oblige Jasper and not only because he paid well.

'He may be posh like,' he told his cousin, Mohammed, back in the cramped little office, 'but he's not stuck up like some of them up there; he treats you like a real mate, kind of; know what I mean like?'

Back at Blenheim House, Jasper had no intention of spending the remaining part of the afternoon alone with his bottle of whisky. He would try to tempt Charlie away from the endless swotting which seemed to preoccupy his best friend these days. The football match due for the afternoon had been cancelled after a night and early morning of relentless rain. The pretty thought of Charlie, Ashley, Chris and Tim returning from the field of battle, their bare limbs plastered with mud, might have provided Jasper with some diversion later on but the fields had been declared far too sodden to use. Surely therefore, Charlie, having been scheduled to play in the match, would be free to join Jasper for a warming glass of 'Famous Grouse', or two, or more, in a secret place which the latter had only recently discovered.

Jasper retreated petulantly from Charlie's irritated rebuff when the latter had been interrupted during his reading of the taxing narrative which comprises the opening chapters of Conrad's 'Nostromo'.

'I don't think you're a friend at all any more. You never want to see me now.'

'Oh, don't be ridiculous, Jasper- and stop whining. I'm not going to spend the afternoon drinking whisky under some soaking bush with you. I've set myself this to read during the next week and I've got loads of other things to do as well.'

'Well! Your loss! At times I really wonder if I like you at all.'

Charlie paused for a moment and stretched out his long, elegant form, unconsciously igniting Jasper's sense of desire by giving him a glimpse of the upper inches of a pair of red and white striped boxer shorts revealed between the waist-band of Charlie's trousers and the hem of a light blue shirt which had lost its lowest button. The sudden vision of Charlie's bare lower torso, slim and tautly stretched, prompted Jasper out of his temporary mood of aggrieved self-pity but, on this occasion, Charlie was too quick for him when Jasper lurched forward to tickle him.

'No you don't!' shouted Charlie, leaping up from his seat and breaking into a good-humoured grin. He paused momentarily before saying, 'You know you'll always like me, Jas.'

They moved towards each other and hugged. Jasper held Charlie tightly.

'Let me go, you great slob!'

'You're so *skinny*, Chips, but *so* beautiful.'

Charlie released a muted, wailing little gasp as Jasper intensified his inescapable embrace.

'Jasper, stop- for pity's sake!' exhaled Charlie in panic. 'I can't breathe. You're like a bloody python!'

Jasper kissed Charlie and released him.

'You should hear yourself sometimes, Jas. You should try not to be *quite* so camp,' rebuked Charlie, not in an unkindly way, as he struggled to recover breath.

'Oh, Chips, don't be cross with me. I *need* you this afternoon.'

'No! No! No!' said Charlie, raising the palms of his hands and moving them forward in a gesture of rejection. 'If you really love me as a friend, you'll leave me alone this afternoon. This Cambridge thing is *so* important to me; it's really getting to me. I *can't* suddenly take a whole Saturday afternoon off without warning. But, Jas, don't go off on your own with booze into the grounds. It's not wise. I do worry about you sometimes. Can't you find *something* to do? Read? Work? Stick a video on in our Common Room? Take a *walk* outside *without* the booze? It's stopped raining now.'

'All-right, Chippie- and *of course* I want you to get into Cambridge. I can see you with a teddy bear and a boater, punting me down the river. I would, of course, have one of the larger hampers from Fortnums on board and plenty of bubbly.'

'I couldn't punt *and* hold a teddy bear. Anyway, that happened in Oxford and I'm not sure that the comparison with Sebastian Flyte is entirely flattering. You do talk crap sometimes.'

'Don't be cross with me. I couldn't bear it! I'll go away and I promise that I won't go out into the grounds on my own with the Scotch.'

Jasper returned to his study and looked at the sealed bottle on his desk. A fleeting shaft of sunlight- the quota for that day- momentarily invaded the window to illuminate the dark, amber, translucent, liquid and emphasise the calming transport of oblivion which it stored. But Jasper needed more than just the whisky that afternoon. He would indeed keep his promise to Charlie. He would not go out into the grounds on his own with the drink. He knew what he really wanted. The bottle remained sealed as he sat in his armchair and hatched a cunning plan.

So…..Charlie was not available. In any case, he was too forcefully pure a character for the purpose; it would never work. But, with the soccer match having been cancelled, the boys must all be around and about. Ashley was certainly an attractive proposition but a similar objection held, albeit in a different way. Jasper went through a catalogue of names in his mind and emerged with a short-list of two. Chris and Tim were both sexy boys in just the way that appealed to Jasper. They were both smaller than he was, athletically slight in build and decidedly good-looking. Tim was slightly taller than Chris but even thinner. Chris was more fun, with a wicked sense of humour, but the quieter Tim was quite friendly too and, really, just as nice.

Let the wheel spin, thought Jasper, and see which of these two beauties I bump into first.

He tried Chris first because he guessed that he might be easier to persuade. However, Chris was not in his study whereas, next door, Tim was sitting at his desk writing a History essay. It was much less difficult to dislodge Tim from an academic chore than could ever have been the case with Charlie and so, a few minutes later, Tim having grabbed a blue fleece to put over his t-shirt, the two young men set off through the woods, round the eastern head of the lake and along the wooded path on its southern shore, Jasper having concealed the whisky, cigarettes and dope in the inside pocket of his capacious overcoat.

At one point, the path continued directly across the neck of a small headland which projected into the lake and a secondary, much less worn, track led off at a right-angle to a point where a narrow, rickety, wooden bridge connected with a tiny island upon which had been erected a boathouse, long since disused. Access was prohibited by a faded notice stating that the bridge and the island were 'out of bounds to all members of College' and a formidable, if rusty, padlock which fastened the door of the boathouse. Just before Half Term, armed with alcohol, cigarettes and weed, Jasper had been moodily wandering about on his own. He had crossed onto the island several times before but, on that occasion, he had aimlessly pulled at the padlock and, to his surprise, found that, although it was still locked, it was so corroded with rust that, with a certain amount of pressure, it gave way. He had explored the interior of the shed. It was airless and empty, apart from a few pieces of discarded junk. There were no windows but it had been well built and was surprisingly free from dampness. Once his eyes had become accustomed to the darkness, he noticed two bolts which held fast a set of double doors on the opposite wall. The bolts had slipped back fairly easily, allowing the doors to open partially. The hinges were badly impaired by rust and Jasper had taken care not to force the doors very far. A jetty, the rotting wood of which had partly fallen into the water, projected into the lake but, by this time, the shrubs between the doors of the boathouse and the immediate shore had grown sufficiently to conceal the front of the building substantially, if not entirely. With the double doors partially open to the lake and the entrance door from the bridge closed, sufficient light could enter the shed with privacy still being protected. There was, moreover, a single bolt on the inside of the entrance door. This, Jasper had quickly decided, could be a useful private domain. He had carefully shut the double doors, taken a few generous swigs of whisky, smoked three cigarettes and, when leaving, had replaced the outer padlock as convincingly as possible. During the Half Term break, he had bought a new padlock and, soon after arriving back at College, he had slipped down to the old boathouse and replaced the lock.

Tim was impressed, especially when his companion opened the doors out onto the lake, thus allowing daylight into the interior.

'I didn't think you could get into this place, Jas. How did you manage to deal with the existing padlock?'

'Ah!' murmured Jasper, putting his index finger to his nose.

But Tim was noticing the sudden blast of north wind just as much as the daylight.

'Hell! I'm absolutely freezing. I hadn't realised it was so cold this afternoon. That breeze isn't half whipping across the lake.'

'It's because you're so skinny. You're even skinnier than Charlie. Have a good slug of this; it'll soon warm you up. I can only offer you the floor to sit on.'

They sat down on the floor near the open doorway. Jasper unscrewed the top of the bottle of whisky and passed it across to his friend. He prepared a joint and, after taking a puff himself, handed it over to Tim who inhaled deeply, succumbing to the immediate relaxation which the cannabis provided. He had taken the drug for the first time at a London party during the previous February half-term.

'I'm not really used to whisky. I've hardly ever drunk it.'

'Really? Well, it's the best of the lot when it comes to warming you up. God, you're shivering! Take a good swig.'

Tim choked and spluttered as the powerful spirit caught the roof of his mouth and sent fumes down his throat and along his nose. He coughed as the tears came to his eyes.

'Easy, boy!' said Jasper, recovering the precious bottle. 'What do you usually have?'

Tim took a moment to recover.

'Beer usually.' He coughed again.

'I forgot; you're one of these sporty football plebs,' lied Jasper, but with a friendly smile.

'I have wine with my parents. They don't allow us to have spirits and, to be honest, I've never really fancied them. Still, I must admit, this stuff does warm you up.'

Jasper took a token sip himself and handed the bottle back to Tim. They took turns with the joint.

'You'd better have some more and avoid choking on it this time. Take a longer drink more slowly. You'll find it really does keep out this cold. In fact, whisky doesn't really upset you like the other spirits do. You don't get drunk very easily on Scotch.'

'Really?'

'Yah, it just makes you feel nice and mellow.'

Jasper watched Tim take a long, slow, generous draught from the bottle. He hadn't before realised quite how attractive Tim was, with his neatly trimmed brown hair and his handsome face, with its finely sculptured cheek-bones and chin, the pale blue eyes set in a sallow complexion. He was delectably slim. He noticed Tim's small feet, encased in short black socks; the laces of his grubby trainers were carelessly adrift. He's really terribly pretty, thought Jasper: so slender, dainty even: and delightfully naïve and very sweet.

'How come that a thin little boy like you is in the First Eleven?' he asked his companion.

'Well, I'm very fast and very manoeuvrable,' replied Tim in a tone of faintly injured pride at this questioning of his athleticism.

'I'll bet!' leered Jasper. 'I like slim men,' he added.

Tim was, of course, aware that Jasper was gay but, as he had never engaged in a conversation with him which had involved anything directly related to that fact, he was uncertain about how to take the compliment. In common with most Moretonians of his generation, so much more generous in spirit than their predecessors in many ways, he had simply acknowledged that Jasper was different as a matter of fact. On the rare occasions when he had given it any thought, he had vaguely wondered what being gay might be like and had felt that it must be rather sad not to be aroused by the presence of so many pretty girls all around them.

Jasper took the bottle back and imbibed a little more of the whisky, calculating with experienced practice a quantity which would help him to feel warm, relaxed, and just a little randy, but which would stop well short of inebriation and loss of control. Judging that he had consumed pretty precisely the right amount, he returned the bottle to his friend. They finished the joint.

Tim had already drunk far more and his inexperience with spirits, his smaller body mass, his failure to have gone to College lunch, the heady sensation of the cannabis and his exposure to the cold wind, now combined to have a rapid effect. He took another immoderate draught of the Scotch and, putting the bottle down, subsided under the cumulative impact.

'This stuff *is* going to my head, Jas,' he said, laughing as his speech began to slur.

'But I bet you're no longer cold. Look, you've stopped shivering.'

Tim seemed to be seeing Jasper with double vision. The lake and the sky to his right, and the trees on the opposite shore, seemed to be very slowly rotating in an anti-clockwise direction, but without the panorama ever altering. He tried to get up but the moment he had to balance on both his feet, he fell back clumsily to the floor.

'Oh, my God! I can't walk!'

But he gave a relaxed giggle as he abandoned the attempt and lay back on the floor.

'It'll help you if I rub your feet,' said Jasper, moving forward. 'It'll get the circulation going again and draw the alcohol away from your head,' he invented.

Tim shrugged his shoulders and chuckled happily.

Jasper now removed Tim's trainers and, grasping each of his exposed, bony shins in turn with his large fleshy hands, he rubbed the soles of Tim's feet.

'Is that better?'

'Yeah! Well- I s'pose so! God, I feel really peculiar. My head's all swimmy,' responded Tim with blithe unconcern as the whisky and the cannabis combined to take effect.

'Just relax, Timmy; it won't do you any harm.'

Jasper then changed abruptly from rubbing Tim's feet to tickling them. Tim shrieked. He succeeded in drawing one foot away but could not free the other one. Aware that he had now successfully trapped the object of his desire for that afternoon, Jasper held on to the bare, hairy shin with his left hand while tickling the sole of Tim's foot with his right one. His appetite now suddenly welled up into an erection and he launched himself upon the smaller youth.

'Let's see if you're as ticklish as Charlie is.'

Even if Tim had not been helplessly intoxicated, his plight would have been hopeless. Completely unable to move, he screamed and howled, laughing hysterically, as Jasper, tickling Tim as he sat on him, worked himself up into an erotic frenzy. Having slipped down the zip of Tim's fleece, he felt the ribs of his prey's warm, writhing body beneath the thin t-shirt with a sensation of blind ecstasy. Jasper moved his position to kneel over Tim's waist. He now undid the zip of his captive's jeans and, Tim's feet being free from the impediment of trainers, Jasper deftly flicked the jeans off. Now, sitting athwart his skinny thighs, he undid the buttons of his Tim's boxer shorts and, his erection stiffening and expanding into hardness, he plunged his hand inside and, through the warm mass of pubic hair, he roughly fondled Tim's penis and genitals.

'Oh, fuck! What are you doing to me, you mad git? Get off!' yelled Tim but, with his judgment of reality so seriously impaired, he was still laughing crazily and offered no resistance.

At the same time, he saw, out of the corner of his eye, the steel grey lake, surmounted by the metallic gleam of a cold silvery sky. Silhouetted in the immediate foreground, was a figure wearing a black tracksuit.

'What the Hell's going on here?' demanded Captain Clark. 'Oh, my God!'

The young officer had been taking a run along the northern shore of the lake and, hearing yells and shrieks of protestation apparently travelling across the water from the old boathouse, he had gone to investigate.

Both boys were suspended from the College that evening. The truth of the balance of blame was finally established with a fair degree of accuracy. Tim returned a fortnight later, cowed by shame and apprehension. Jasper never came back.

Charlie felt both guilt and profound distress. He joined Ashley in doing everything imaginable to support a traumatised and humiliated Tim but, despite Matron's best efforts and genuine concern, and after a frustratingly futile conversation with Bernard Bassett, who refused to confide in his Head of House and regarded an approach from him as an impertinence to be shiftily avoided, Charlie felt even more upset that the one man who could have provided Tim with effective counsel was not there for them.

TWENTY-SIX

Naturally, John did come to hear about this lamentable event during one of Priscilla's regular visits. He was greatly concerned and prayed for both boys. At his request, Priscilla had asked both Bernard Bassett and the Headmaster (through Ursula) if John might have access to Tim, when the latter returned to the College, but the law had made it clear that any such contact was strictly forbidden. He felt free to write a letter of consolation to Jasper (via Priscilla's address), whose association with the College had now been so abruptly terminated, but he received no reply.

As that dark, damp late autumn imperceptibly ceded to the yet darker shades of grey which signify the approach of winter, John observed that he had made no connections at all with any of his neighbours on the estate. During the day, almost no-one was there. It was by now already becoming dark when the schools came out and, when both parents (or was it partners?) returned from work, the various households shut themselves away eating convenience foods in front of televisions in different rooms. Occasionally, he would see two young mothers together pushing infants in prams. The house next door was empty. On the other side, a couple in their late twenties drove off before dawn to commute from Midhampton station, returning, armed with take-away meals, after dark. Opposite, an unsmiling, monosyllabic plumber drove a white van backwards and forwards and worked with tools in his garage. Could there ever be, he wondered, dinner parties in these houses, reading circles, church meetings? Or was this raw estate a place where only salesmen and relations came to visit?

He had regular visits from Priscilla, Alexander, Anthony and, less frequently, Tom Stevenson. Priscilla was not able to invite him back but the others made an effort to do so. In each case, their wives were also supportive. John had always rather liked Cordelia Scott in particular. A childless couple, Alexander and Cordelia seemed to live lives which were simultaneously independent and harmonious. A fellow Cambridge alumnus, Cordelia taught Classics part-time at the grammar school in the town. Bespectacled, thin, with greying hair neatly cropped, she ran their ménage with brisk efficiency and sat tolerantly through Alexander's occasional diatribes without concern.

In truth, John was better suited than many to cope with the solitary life which circumstance had suddenly imposed upon him. Inevitably, there was a prevailing sense of loneliness, not helped by an undercurrent of anxiety, but he was experienced in the discipline of prayer and in that he found solace. He had more time now to turn to the scriptures and there he found his faith buttressed. A verse in the Epistle of James leapt from the page one morning when self-pity threatened more than usual:-

'Blessed is the man who perseveres under trial, because, when he has stood the test, he will receive the crown of life that God has promised to those who love Him.'

He was seeing much more of Maurice Stantonbury. He worshipped at the parish church and quietly attended a weekly Bible study group in the vicarage. The other people present must have known about his difficulty but prying questions and invasive comments were graciously avoided, a courtesy reciprocated by John's tactful silences on the occasions when an inexperienced lay person might make a theological blunder in the discussion. He also went to a meeting run by a missionary society which sought to support the persecuted church overseas. He felt particularly moved by an account, accompanied by video, of attacks made on Christian churches in Pakistan. Relatives of murdered Christians told of their grief but also offered amazing pronouncements of faith and forgiveness. He took back fliers from the society's representative, wrote out a generous cheque and kept a list of names and adverse situations which was produced monthly and over which he prayed faithfully. He was not slow to contrast his own relatively favourable situation with their extremity. If any-one deserved 'the crown of life', surely it must be these courageous and steadfast men and women as they withstood the torching of their churches, the assaulting, and even murdering, of their relatives and the burning, violent, obsessive hatred of the fanatical young Islamists directing their energies so destructively. How mild was his persecution by comparison; how much easier, therefore, surely, to persevere.

One day, he decided to take the train to London. As he stood waiting on the platform at Midhampton Station, two high speed, long distance expresses thundered through. Even in the open air, the warning siren was immediately followed by a blast of air which cuffed his right ear-drum abruptly. The sense of power and urgency, as hundreds of invisible, busy people were swept at more than two miles a minute from the great cities of the North and the Midlands to London, made him seem frittering and insignificant.

Even as his own train clattered through the stations of the northern Home Counties, overtaking the streams of vehicles on the motorway, hurrying past a school where boys were playing football on a field beside the railway line, fleetingly checking off a cemetery here, a warehouse and dispatch yard there, the journey paradoxically reinforced the shockingly sudden reduction in the pace of his own life. He saw the great arch suspended over the elegantly dipping oval structure of the unfinished new Wembley Stadium. Here was a statement of progress, vitality, the future: a celebration of youth and enterprise. Only a short time ago, in his own world, John was part of all these things, but not now.

At Euston, every-one around him seemed definite and purposeful, as the different platforms disgorged hundreds of people onto the concourse. Standing on three successive escalators, he descended with the ever altering crowd into the underworld of the London Underground and had soon taken his seat on a southbound Northern Line train. As they rattled deep under the metropolis, the passengers sat in intimate anonymity, each suspended in their own meditative Nirvana, some transported electronically to another world via ipods and earphones.

The focus of John's meditation was a young man sitting directly opposite. His slim frame was clothed in a black, light-weight cotton jacket with the collar turned up and under which the round neck of a white t-shirt left exposed tufts of dark chest hair. He had subscribed to the universal uniform of the young in wearing blue jeans and trainers. A navy blue woollen cap was pulled down over the top of his head. His handsome face was fringed by the stubble of a heavy beard, left unshaven for a day or two. He had a dark complexion, signifying, John thought, the likelihood of Arab or Pakistani descent. His dark eyes, warm and sensitive, looked abstractly ahead, fixed on some private projection of the imagination. On his lap lay a small canvas back-pack, the straps of which were secured. For a moment, out of habit, John considered what he might look like in his underclothes but, again out of custom, he imposed the spiritual self-discipline inculcated by his priesthood and handed the licentious thought over to God. As the tube train whined and clattered into the tunnel out of Warren Street station, he spoke to God in prayer about his unsuspecting travelling companion.

Father Almighty, you know my feelings for young men. Like Gerard Manley Hopkins, another, greater, priest before me, I can only confess my bondage to 'the sots and thralls of lust'. I know, dear Lord, that this is not even a chance encounter; it is nothing more than an arbitrary sighting. Still, my God, I thank you for this young man's beauty and I commend him to your love and care. He has a distant look. I don't know what his attitude to you might be but, in your name, I bless him and commend him this day to the gracious care of the Lord Jesus Christ.

John reflected that the young men responsible for the carnage on the underground on the fateful 7th of July, so very close to here, possibly looked rather like this gentle fellow traveller. Who knows? Possibly that bag on this young man's lap might be packed with explosives. Still, as the train braked to stop at Leicester Square, the very idea of the pleasant looking youth opposite him detonating random mass violence seemed ridiculous. And yet, thought John, who other than God Himself knows the innermost thoughts of an individual human heart?

He had to break off from his object of meditation when they drew into Charing Cross, where John had elected to alight to spend a few hours in the National Gallery. The dark young man was carried off under the Thames and onwards into the endless, concrete, high-rise impersonality of south London.

John approached the escalator amidst the sea of people leaving the underground train.

'Oi, Mate! Who do you think you're pushin' in in front of?'

He was startled as a bulky leather shoulder gave him a glancing knock on the chin.

'Do go first if you want to.'

'What d'yer mean - '*do* go first'? I fuckin' WAS first!'

How crude and rude London has become, thought John regretfully, as he held back to let this large thug, with a shaved head and metal in his nose and eye-brows, push on ahead. How different it all was from his world of the College but, he feared, how sadly real and how painfully it reflected the times. He helped a black woman struggling with a push-chair as the rest of the world barged heedlessly past.

He had crossed the rain swept expanse of Trafalgar Square, no longer pigeon infested these days, though full of tourists digitally immortalising each other, and, having entered the National Gallery, he was now standing in front of Poussin's masterpiece, 'The Arcadian Shepherds.' The gallery had acquired a small but brilliant collection of Poussin's paintings in the form of a temporary exhibition lent by the Louvre.

In the background were the summer trees of an Arcadian landscape, framed against a moving sky. In the foreground, two of the three beautiful young shepherds, personifications of the *jeunesse d'or* of Ancient Greece, their visibly elegant muscularity draped in loose mantels of silvery beige and sapphire silk, were bent in rapt astonishment over the minatory inscription on the stone sarcophagus which they had newly discovered: '*Et Ego In Arcadia.*' The second shepherd, bearded and virile, was kneeling on his left knee, his sinewy right leg crooked before the tomb, catching the light, along with his robust back and shoulder. As his index finger pointed to the words of warning, it appeared simultaneously to come into contact with its shadow on the sarcophagus. His form in shadow assumed the aspect of the grim reaper, his powerful arm having been transmuted into a ghostly sickle, a darkly insubstantial and threatening projection of an implement which he had perhaps been using earlier in the day, the promise of the inevitable fate awaiting his manly physicality. The third swain, on the right, was wearing a scarlet mantle. He had placed his left foot on a low rock. The elbow of his left arm resting on the knee of his perfectly formed leg, he had turned his face towards the young shepherdess who, with her right hand upon his shoulder, while she stood erect, her left hand upon her hip, appeared to gaze down upon the tomb with a greater serenity. Her head modestly covered, she alone was fully clothed in a gold mantle and a sapphire robe. Perhaps she, like the women on the day of Resurrection, alone among this group, perceived a possible hope beyond the grave. The young men's exposed limbs, so strong and compellingly vital, declared the beauty of youth but the frisson of shock was immortalised in this, their first intimation of mortality. The pagan beauty of the composition disturbed John. A different painting could easily have presented the same shepherds worshipping the infant in the stable, enraptured with equal suddenness but with the revelation of eternal hope. These graceful youths could almost have been John's pupils, the landscape the parkland around the College. And death? Well, if he was to lose his position, whatever else could there be for him before that inevitable stop along the way? And, within a single flicker of the great spectrum of time, the beautiful boys would be worn and harrowed by age and responsibility and, in due course, be seen and heard and touched no more.

> 'Golden lads and girls all must
> As chimney- sweepers, come to dust.'

Moving in a sort of trance, the image of The Arcadian Shepherds held with arresting vividness at the front of his mind, John drifted into the room holding the permanent collection of Rembrandt portraits. Suddenly, he found his eyes meeting those of Rembrandt in the painter's self-portrait in old age. The piercing intelligence of those dark eyes held all the knowing, querulous bitterness of experience. Yes, they were sad eyes; they had felt and seen too deeply. John was alarmed by their scepticism. These eyes could no longer be convinced, as they gazed irritably, almost peevishly, from the pasty, glazed, blotchy complexion of the great artist entombed in swirling shadows. John's own eyes looked more searchingly into those of the painter. No, he implored silently. Please do not dismiss me. Is it all to be scorned? He seemed a puny, vacillating thing under that stern and unwavering gaze of disbelief. He retreated, reproved and unsettled.

He sat down on the low bench in the centre of the room and tried to pray. It was impossible in front of that worldly, knowing gaze. He needed to find some Christian art. In suppressed agitation, he found his way back to the early rooms, to the assurance declared by Giovanni Bellini more than five-hundred years ago, to 'The Agony in the Garden.' Here was another garden. Jesus was in the centre of the picture, half turned away from the viewer, praying to be spared the cup of bitterness but confronted by an angel in the sky bearing the chalice which denoted the appointed sacrifice of the coming Crucifixion. As in 'The Arcadian Shepherds', three men were present. This time they were the disciples, Peter, James and John, and they were fast asleep, in the foreground but low in the picture, missing the metaphysical drama so close to them. Judas and the soldiers, minute and insipid in the hollow in the middle ground, prepared to cross a neat little Italian Renaissance bridge on their way to arrest the Saviour of the World, unaware of the irony that, in their mercenary and self-protective spite, they were factors in the benign eternal plan.

To begin with, the formality of it left John cold. This was another civilisation, long since departed, with characters assuming formal poses, swathed in medieval robes, believing a simple, if beautiful, myth in a world which was about to be geometrically redefined when Christopher Columbus 'sailed the ocean blue' and which Copernicus in Krakow would very soon prove to be a mere planet in a heliocentric universe. And yet, and yet: something in the picture compelled him to retain a tenuous grasp upon his faith. In the upper centre of the composition, above the darkly defined horizon of an indeterminate landscape, the sky was being transformed by a roseate dawn. The blue of the sky was *not* darkening; on the contrary, it was becoming lighter. Then he noticed that the warm hope of the sunrise had irradiated the grass on the steep rise upon which the Saviour was kneeling. At the very moment when John had been on the verge of surrendering hope, his downward slide was gently arrested by faith and hope and divine love. The brink of the abyss receded and with it the swirling fog of fear and despair. He was not suddenly projected into a bliss of elation but his spirit found sufficient peace to rest. It was a foothold on the side of the mountain, a personal promise to take home through the heaving mass of humanity as the paths of millions intersected within a fabric never exactly repeated in pattern and incomprehensible in magnitude and variety.

'Peace I leave with you, my peace I give unto you: not as the world giveth, give I unto you. Let not your heart be troubled; neither let it be afraid.'

The words of Christ returned to him as he looked at Bellini's painting and he held on to them as he clung to the overhead handrail in the crowded tube train on his way home.

The following afternoon, after John had visited Maurice Stantonbury for a bite of lunch and a time of prayer, he walked into the town centre to buy a few basic groceries. He turned round the corner by the bank and very nearly collided with Charlie, Douglas Macintyre and two other boys, not from Blenheim House.

'How *are* you, Sir?' asked Charlie.

'We're all missing you terribly,' declared Douglas.

John again observed that the lad retained some flavour of

his clear, lilting Edinburgh accent, despite having spent more than four years at an English boarding school.

'Where are you living? You're in the town somewhere,' challenged Charlie.

'It's really good to see you again, Sir,' said James Robertson, a pleasant, tall, blond youth, whom John had rescued from a minor disciplinary scrape some months ago.

Charlie stepped forward and hugged John and then, standing back, asked, 'So- where is it, Sir? Where have they put you?'

'You know I can't tell you, Charlie,' replied John, looking and feeling anguished.

'But this is between friends. It has nothing to do with the College.'

'It is between friends; you're right. But I'm afraid it *is* to do with the College as well. You must know that, Charlie.'

'It's terrible what they've done to you, Sir,' said James.

'Have you heard about Tim?' asked Douglas.

'Yes, I fear so- and about Jasper.'

'We really could have done with you then,' said Charlie, 'and we still could. It's been a bad old time.'

They talked for several more minutes. John found himself dreading the time when they would have to part company. The town hall clock chimed. Dominic Graham, the fourth boy, exclaimed that they would be in danger of missing the minibus scheduled to take them back up the hill to the College. Dominic had also received kind counsel from John during a time of teenage Angst. Instinctively, he delved into the plastic bag which he was holding, full of purchases from the supermarket, and produced a jar of high quality black cherry jam, which he insisted John took. They all wished him the very best, each pumping his hand, and ran off to the departure point for the minibus. John walked down to the riverside and, finding a quiet bench, away from the car park and the shops, he sat down and wept. Ten minutes later, and conscious of a cutting easterly breeze whipping upstream, he blew his nose, pulled himself together and walked home. 'Home', he thought: this anonymous, impersonal box which might as well be on the Moon: is *this* really to be 'Home'?

He had just taken his coat off when the front door bell rang. Surprised and curious, he opened the door to find himself confronted by Charlie on his own.

'How on earth……'

'I've been taking the answer 'no' about this for too long, Sir. I followed you back. I'm not going to apologise.'

John stood in astonishment.

'Well! Aren't you going to ask me in?' asked Charlie, smiling.

'Yes, of course, my dear boy; I'm sorry. Come into the kitchen; I'll put the kettle on.'

'I saw you by the riverside, Sir. I'm so, so sorry about all this. It's *so* unjust. It'll very soon be obvious to *every-one* that you're innocent so it can only be a matter of time before you're back with us all again.'

'I think it could be some months before the case comes to trial, Charlie.'

'What? But that's ridiculous. My Dad wonders why the College took any notice of this slander in the first place. My parents really feel for you too, Sir. So does everybody.'

'The College had no choice, Charlie. It was taken beyond their jurisdiction. The police, operating on behalf of the Social Services, are pressing for conviction.'

They talked about the whole sad business. Charlie wanted to discuss the incident involving Tim and Jasper. John wanted to know how Charlie's preparation for Cambridge was going and about the fortunes of the First XI. They prayed for each other extempore. When Charlie had to leave, John sat still in the blankness of the gathering darkness. How he wished that Charlie could have stayed here with him. Was Bellini's dawn a false one, he wondered, a beautiful piety which started and finished in the imagination? Perhaps, as in Gethsemane, it was now *his* time to endure 'the dark night of the soul'.

He had a disturbed night. A feeling of acute loneliness set in. His faith continued to waver. He felt a shadowy dread that none of it might be true and that, if it were not true, his life must therefore have been a pathetic lie and the only certainty ahead is death and oblivion. The next morning he struggled to pray and eventually gave up trying. He considered confiding in Maurice but remembered that his friend was away at a conference all day. He could not bear to be in the house alone. He set off on a long walk into the chill, dull, grey, dampness of the encroaching English winter.

He bought a sandwich at a pub. It had once been an old coaching inn of a kind beloved by characters in Shakespeare's, or Fielding's, England but it had long since become part of a chain owned by a brewery and had been converted into a stereo-type which was repeated a thousand times across the length and breadth of the country. A bored girl, with expressionless eyes and an estuary accent strangled at the top of her throat, took his order at the bar. He sat next to a table where four salespersons (three men and one woman) affected friendship for each other as some deal was laboriously discussed. A large man in his mid-thirties, with a loud voice, ran figures through a pocket calculator. An attractive blonde young woman drank mineral water and laughed exaggeratedly at her male companions' attempts at smart remarks. Another young man, bespectacled, prematurely bald and with a florid complexion, seemed regularly to be conducting a secondary conversation on his mobile 'phone. They fell into discussing their superiors back at the various offices and the men talked about cars and motorway routes across the crowded, homogenised island upon which they existed. John sat on one of several dozen crimson mock velvet stools in a room with dark veneer panelled walls decorated with fake horse brasses, riding whips, reins and stirrups. Why on earth, he wondered, should such artefacts be placed inside a room the purpose of which was to provide people with food and drink? Two fat men in their forties leant against the bar, nurturing pints of ale and leering at the barmaid. She was wearing a pink top and tightly fitting blue jeans. Four inches of bare midriff was exposed. Her response to the men was glacial.

He was glad to leave. He set off through a sodden landscape the colour of pale shit. With the exception of the College side, to the north, the town was besieged in every direction by identical housing estates. John himself was presently living in one of these, to the south. These estates had tripled the population of the little market town during the last three decades. The half built edges of the town were now extending beyond the ring road which had been built some twenty years earlier but which already boasted significant traffic jams. Now, on foot, he was approaching the town from the east. Ahead of him, the only prominent edifice visible was the spire of the parish church, still benevolently, if bravely, paternalistic, raised on its modest elevation in the town centre. The track became a metalled footpath as he crossed a deserted playing field before entering the eastern housing estate, the streets of which were improbably named after wild flowers, the growth of which had long since been decimated by the demolition of the ancient hedgerows, extensive green belt building and, in the bordering countryside, the liberal deployment of weed-killer. John found himself walking along a road with the improbably fictional nomenclature of 'Bluebell Lane'. This led on to 'Buttercup Drive' which terminated at a confusing junction with 'Foxglove Crescent' and 'Meadowsweet Close'. At least, John thought wryly, the planners had not, albeit fortuitously, surely, made the mistake of consigning people to the 'Primrose Path'. The houses comprised identical repetitions within a strictly limited permutation of architectural design. They stood closely together in unashamed nakedness, unprotected by the garments of trees or shrubs, perched above narrow strips of lawn which directly bordered the pavement. The small areas of grass had ceded territory to attenuated asphalt drives which, in the case of the larger houses, had been laid in front of double garages. The development was utterly without distinction in its blandness and could have been anywhere in England. A self-consciously winding little thoroughfare through the centre of the estate, euphemistically christened, more in hope than in promise, 'Forget-Me-Not Way', led onto the main road which, after half a mile or so, opened onto Main Street.

John had seen old photographs of Main Street before the planning vandals of the 1950s had pulled down the elegant, brick Georgian houses and shop-fronts and replaced them with the ugly brutalism of the day. The town had escaped the attention of the Luftwaffe and must therefore take responsibility for its own architectural disaster. No better now, though, was the soul-destroying influence of the huge conglomerates and the systematic demise of the small local traders. It seemed to John that there was no shop of local distinction left. The High Street names were there, albeit in limited versions, interspersed with the big banks, building societies, estate agents and charity shops. The King's Arms Hotel had been taken over by a commercial chain which served the same food as it did throughout the land, to customers sitting at the same tables on the same chairs, by staff who wore the same uniforms and had been taught on training days to offer verbatim the same greetings and the same options. Opposite the hotel, was a run-down public house, 'The Swan', which attracted the youth of the town on Friday and Saturday nights who, after having been provided with several litres of alcoholic refreshment, enjoyed breaking saplings in half, lobbing bricks through 'bus shelters, vandalising parked cars and driving off noisily at murderous speeds into the hinterland.

As John's critical faculties sharpened in his solitude, so did his concern over his newly jaundiced view of the world.

He had been accustomed to walking through the College and its grounds, feeling a profound personal blessing in the people and the place and conferring silent prayers of grace upon those whom he met during the day, even if only in passing. He had enjoyed his occasional sallies into the little town, with its ordinary, lively bustle, its narrow alleys leading to the quiet river, the gentle incline of Church Street leading to St Mary's like the gradual within a medieval church. What was the matter with him, he asked himself? It seemed that his foothold on the mountainside of faith was truly slipping.

Then, suddenly, all such thoughts were banished by a very unpleasant incident.

'Hi there, you fucking wanker!'

'It's that poofter, Donaldson!'

'Going back home to bed with Jude Williams are you, Sir?'

'Or how about that nancy-boy, Charlie Blakestone?'

'Yeah, Rev.D! He's sweet, that Charlie Blakestone, isn't he?'

'Got it up today yet, have you?'

'Ooooh, Freddie! Aren't *you* a one?' shrieked the other boy, trying to assume a falsetto voice and waving his right wrist limply. 'D'you think he fancies *us*? He might take us home and get us to strip for him!'

People turned firstly to look at the College boys shouting the obscenities and then at the object of their derision on the other side of the street. This entirely unanticipated, public, raucous jeering assailed John like a series of physical blows. He stopped in his tracks and blushed crimson as hatred, fury and mortification competed to be first to break through the barrier of shock.

Passing pedestrians, cars and vans separated him from his verbal assailants. His first instinct was to run across the road and beat the Hell out of them. But he was fifty; he wouldn't have caught them; an undignified melée would have compounded the humiliation of the scene; he might have been accused of assault- again! He turned sharp left into the bank. The heavy, automatic plate-glass doors slid shut behind him. He sat down at an empty table near the entrance and tried to recover his composure. No-one inside the bank had witnessed the incident and no-one thought it strange that he was sitting there. He inhaled some deep breaths and tried to measure this latest shocking challenge. He knew that the two boys concerned were disliked throughout the Common Room. They had been involved in a number of unsavoury disciplinary incidents, including bullying, and there had been a rumour, as yet unproven, that they had brought drugs into the College. They were currently surviving on a 'last warning.' John himself had had no dealings with them, which made their attack the more astonishing. He had formed a vague impression that- unusually for Moretonians these days- they were the sort of boys who had never managed to shed an ingrained sense of 'us and them' in their attitude to the teaching staff. In truth, he had never much considered them at all.

Worries began to develop and compound in his mind. If this was the way in which he was going to be regarded by pupils who did not even know him personally, even allowing for the fact that these were two unusually unpleasant boys, and assuming a fair verdict at his trial, it might not be possible for him ever to return. If he did go back, this incident could not be allowed to pass. It would either need to be referred to the Headmaster or, more probably, he would call the boys in himself: yet another cloud on a horizon already laden with threat. It really was all *too* vexatious. He got up and walked back to the house in a fury. He sat down and wrote a letter to Geoffrey Tansley, naming the two boys and describing what took place, not sparing the recipient's blushes by quoting verbatim the obscenities used. He slammed a first class stamp on the envelope and, still in the speed of agitated rage, strode along the road to the pillar-box.

There can be few people who have not had the experience of posting an angry letter and doubting its wisdom soon after committing the irrevocable act of dropping it through the slit in the pillar-box. The document is then bound into the guaranteed security of The Royal Mail and, even if one waited hours for the postman to come and make his collection, one would merely find that he was under strict instructions not to release the offending missive. John's hand was raised to the dreadful aperture; the envelope was in contact with the cold hard red lips waiting to devour it. Suddenly, a text from Paul's letter to the Ephesians swam to the front of his mind:-

'Be angry but do not sin; do not let the sun go down on your anger.'

The sentiments which he had just expressed would be read by Geoffrey Tansley in the cold light of the following morning. All the experienced discipline of his priesthood now urged him to stay his hand and to delay until he might be acting from reason rather than passion.

'Father, forgive them; they know not what they do.'

My God! He of all people, a Christian priest, should be setting an example of forgiveness! What is this fierce, unaccustomed passion of anger which has come over him? The thing to do- the *right* thing to do- is to summon those two boys when he does get back and to forgive them. That, indeed, could save *them*, as well as keep his Christian conscience clear. He stepped back from the pillar-box and retraced his steps more slowly. He tore the letter into small fragments and put it in the dustbin before entering the house again.

Now that he was calmer, even the motive of self-preservation suggested that he had done the right thing. It would not be helpful if the Headmaster's course of reasoning were to parallel John's own thoughts when he had been sitting in the bank. He could just about imagine Geoffrey Tansley briskly deciding: 'probably better not to have the fellow back: can't have all the kids wandering round the College telling each other that the Chaplain's a Queer- or, even worse, telling their parents!'

Yes, he thought, as he sunk heavily into an armchair, the Holy Spirit *is* real. He has just intervened. Praise to the Lord!

He was delighted to notice that there was a Premier League match on the television. His spirits rallied as he watched 'the beautiful game'. He brushed aside the little teasing devil which tried to taunt his imagination with the pictures of Gary Hassell which he had seen in the newspaper the other day and became absorbed instead in the national excitement as two of England's great soccer teams vied for supremacy.

TWENTY-SEVEN

THE NEXT MORNING, JOHN woke later than usual to the first sunshine for many days. It suited his lighter mood. He could pray again. He organised and updated his prayer diary. He spent an hour in prayer. He brought the two miscreants of yesterday to God, offering his own forgiveness and asking for their salvation. He prayed for Charlie and Tim and Jasper, and the kind boys he had met in the town the day before (much more typical of his beloved Moretonians than the two who had caused him such grief yesterday). He prayed for Priscilla and Richard and Alexander and Geoffrey Tansley. He prayed for Jude: for repentance so that forgiveness might follow. He prayed for Simon Staveley, the disgraced politician, and for Gary Hassell, the young rent-boy who had brought the public man down. He prayed by name for those persecuted Christians in Pakistan who had been brought to the attention of the missionary society. He prayed for his own situation: that God would see him through the time of trial: that, above all, his faith would be kept secure and that he would continue to be favoured with full time service to Christ. Once again he confided in God his passionate desire to return to the College and resume his work there but, nevertheless, *'not as I will but as thou wilt'.*

He arranged his CDs and, with Advent approaching, listened to the hope, joy and aspiration so sublimely expressed in Bach's great chorale:-

'Wachet auf, ruft uns die Stimme
Der Wächter sehr hoch auf der Zinne.'

He joined in with his good singing voice, fending off a sudden threatening pang of self-pity, as he realised that he would not only miss the College Choir's Christmas concert but that he would not be conducting the annual Carol Service in the College Chapel. He supposed that Maurice had been co-opted to do that but had mentioned nothing about it out of gentleness and tact.

That evening, after dark, John was aware of a very large four-wheel-drive pulling up outside the house. It seemed to be as long as the width of the house and the miniscule patch of garden in front of it. Two tall men got out in the shadows and, within seconds, had rung the front door bell. John opened the door to find Bill and Charlie Blakestone standing in the pool of light shed from the hallway. He felt a thrill of surprise, pleasure and gratitude as he ushered them in, taking their coats. Bill seemed to fill the little front room. John himself was of average height; Bill was six foot three, two inches taller than his son and, in his burly ruddiness, half Charlie's weight again. Bill plonked a bottle of Grand Cru Lynch-Bages on the table and Charlie, with rather more delicacy than his father, set down a box full of pates, cheeses and pastries.

'Well! It's not *too* bad in here!' exclaimed Bill. John felt that, with a modest expansion, Bill could have touched every wall of the room without moving his feet, including the ceiling.

'There's a plucked pheasant wrapped in foil somewhere inside this box that Charlie's put down,' said Bill, speaking at a volume designed to communicate across rooms at least four times the size of this one. 'Susie's made a few little somethings up for you to cheer you up while that bloody school sorts out this nonsense.'

'One of Mum's fruit cakes is in here somewhere too,' said Charlie, tentatively peering in amongst the goodies. 'It must be at the bottom. She'll have packed it very carefully.'

John noticed a packet of Jackson's Earl Grey resting on the top of the box.

Charlie produced a tasteful card signed by the usual gang of boys in the year, each one adding a note of encouragement and good wishes.

'This is amazing! How kind of you all!' He was nearly in tears. 'Sit down, please. I've got some Chardonnay in the 'fridge' and I can find some Pringles or something to go with it: all very simple, I'm afraid.'

He returned with the bottle, three glasses, crisps and some olives which Priscilla had recently brought.

The conversation was predictable and Bill did most of the talking, though not until he had heard what John had to say. Charlie was quiet in the presence of his father and his teacher. Bill was, of course, scandalised by the way in which John had been treated. He declared that he would be in touch with a number of parents and together they would let 'that pillock, Tansley,' know their view.

'But it's not the Headmaster's fault, Dad, as Rev. D has just explained,' assayed Charlie. 'It's Jude and his mother and the social services in Midhampton….'

'John, you can see *he's* going to sweep into Cambridge, can't you, with all this analytical reasonableness he's suddenly found!' interrupted Charlie's father, smiling with barely concealed pride as he benignly hectored his adored son.

'We wish!' said Charlie, also smiling, though more ruefully.

'To think we've had that boy in our house as though he were one of our own. I know what I'd like to do to the little sod!'

'Dad!'

'Oh, I know, Chips, we're at the stage where parents are an embarrassing liability.' Bill winked at John. 'Poor old Mum and Dad are well over the hill: fossils buried in the past: just useful for board, lodging and an allowance!'

'Where's the logic of all this?' asked Charlie, spreading his hands out and chuckling with surprise.

'Ah! Logic! God! We're going to get an awful lot more of all this when he goes to Cambridge!'

'Dad! I haven't *got* there yet. Sir, he's so sure that I'm just going to walk into the place. 'Hi guys! I'm Bill Blakestone's son. Yep, that's right! Quake away! You're not going to send *me* home without a place, are you- now that you've heard that!"

Bill roared with laughter and helped himself to another glass of John's Chardonnay. Then he changed his tone abruptly.

'I'm just so *proud* of him, John, and you and Mr Scott, more than any-one else, have made this happen between you.'

'I think his parents have had something to do with it too,' suggested John.

Charlie was shaking his head but still smiling.

'Sir, how can I *not* be embarrassed when he goes round saying things like this? 'Here, meet my son- Chips the Wunderkind."

Both men laughed.

'The relationship between you two is something amazingly special- and you both know it,' said John.

'I think that Mr Scott does have high hopes for him,' said Bill, attempting unsuccessfully to disguise his concern.

'Dad, I MIGHT NOT GET IN. You've got to understand this!'

'Nonsense. The moment they hear what you've got to say about Shakespeare, Chips, they'll be blown away.'

Charlie shook his head and gave up.

'Anyway,' said Bill, getting his diary out, 'Susie's commissioned us to get you round for supper.'

'That's very kind. But do you really want to be allied to a master who's been suspended from duty? *Should* you be?'

John was not joking.

'Sir!' Charlie intervened, using the same tone that he had just used to his father.

'Now, John, we're not fair-weather friends in our family,' reprimanded Bill, allying with his son's seriousness.

'Well, I would, of course, love to come. It's terribly kind of you.'

'It's not kind at all; it's our pleasure. It's not going to be a once-off, either. Charlie will be there, of course. He's been missing you a lot, John. They all missed you when that other business occurred too: most regrettable. Charlie told us all about it. It's not been an easy time for any of you. How are you placed next Saturday?'

John was, of course, free.

'You OK then Chips?'

He was.

'Good: well then; that's fixed. I thought that I'd give Mr Scott a ring too, now that we've booked *you* in, and see if his wife and he might like to join us. He's been so good to our boy. And we thought we'd ask Matron, too; none of this can have been easy for her. Charlie's told me not to ask The Hound…..'

'Dad!' Charlie covered his eyes.

'Well, that's what you all call the miserable git, isn't it? I don't think they've been getting on too well, John.'

'You'll have to watch what you say if Mr Scott's there on Saturday. I don't think I could bear your indiscretions in front of *him*,' pleaded Charlie.

'Nonsense! He's obviously a man of good judgment. I bet he thinks the same.'

'But they're *colleagues*!'

Bill rose to go.

'You know, John, it's funny the way roles get so soon reversed. It used to be that parents were worried about taking their children anywhere in case they said the wrong thing. Now it's the other way round!'

John needed no assurance that the remark was made in amusement and within the total security of a relationship between father and son which could only be regarded as a paradigm.

Bill looked John straight in the eye as he took his leave and gave him a knuckle crushing handshake. Charlie rejected John's outstretched hand and put his arms round him instead.

The house felt emphatically empty and silent after they had gone. To have had a son like Charlie! To be in a family like that!

The evening at Greenvale Farm was predictably excellent. Alexander and Cordelia had insisted that John should not drive there on his own. John was not sure if Alexander could in fact drive. He had only ever seen Cordelia at the wheel. Of course, it could be that when she collected her husband from the College, it was because she was using their car during the day.

There were eight at dinner: Bill, Sue, Charlie, John, Alexander, Cordelia, Priscilla and, delightfully, Richard, whom John had not seen for so long. Charlie's younger brother was away at a 'sleep-over' at a friend's house. The elegantly appointed Georgian drawing room was just the right size for the party to stand around having drinks for twenty minutes or so before dinner. Richard made a point of engaging with John. John felt that his young colleague could not have been more imaginatively compassionate and supportive.

'John, I haven't made contact because I was instructed not to do so by Bernard. But- hey! - *All* of this lot have done the decent thing. Priscilla felt that she couldn't give me your address in the town. I can understand that; she was in a difficult position. But when Charlie Boy here found it out the other day, he passed it on straightaway. Now that Priscilla knows I'm in on the open secret, she said that I could come through to you with her one evening.'

'You mustn't put yourself at risk on my account, Richard.'

'I don't see how it can be a risk. Every-one else seems to know. Look round this room!'

John said that it would be really very good to see Richard any time he liked. They exchanged mobile numbers. They had a chat about the First XI and the boys in Blenheim House.

Sue Blakestone had gone to some trouble to provide them all with a splendid meal. Bill made sure that the wine flowed. Both Priscilla and Cordelia, as the two drivers, said that they were not worried about limiting what they drank.

'I notice that the ladies are being the self-sacrificing members of the party. It so often seems to happen this way,' teased Sue.

'I really don't mind. I drink very little,' said Cordelia.

Bill was, of course, the warmest host. Every-one, other

than Cordelia and John, the two who knew him best, was surprised at what a success Alexander Scott was at a dinner party. His relaxed and brilliant repartee delighted his host. Charlie felt relieved and happy. Who would have thought that the once most terrifying master in the school would be sitting with his parents and him at dinner in his own house, proving to be such good company and getting on with his Dad so well! Mr Scott didn't flicker an eyelid even at his father's most appalling indiscretions. Yep, probably Dad was right- as usual!

'Tell me something, Alexander: this Chaucer chappie, whom Charlie here goes on about-' launched Bill.

His son instinctively gripped the edge of the table. Oh no! I was right after all, Charlie thought; it's going to be a disaster.

'You'll have to forgive my husband's choice of language, Mr Scott,' his wife interposed serenely. 'I'm not sure that Chaucer would have appreciated being referred to in quite that way, Bill.'

'Well, he's been dead for God knows how long. What can *he* care?'

'Nothing to forgive dear hostess,' responded the literary scholar, his eyes twinkling with merriment behind his spectacles, 'and the name *is* Alexander. What about 'this Chaucer chappie', Bill?'

Every-one laughed.

Thank Goodness Scotty's already had a skinful to drink, thought Charlie.

'Why do you lot (and I include my son here) spend so much time reading all that funny old language? I picked up one of this boy's books and I couldn't make head or tail of it.'

'Well,' began Alexander, '- er, I hope that Charlie agrees with me- so many people like the Canterbury Tales because, despite being more than six-hundred years old, the characters and their situations are timeless. We can see them all again today. For example, Bill, I can think of one of the Canterbury pilgrims who is not unlike you.'

Charlie ran through Chaucer's pilgrims in panic. No, it can't be the Knight or the Parson; are there any other good ones?

'As we are all enjoying this magnificent and generous dinner here, Charlie, you must know which one I mean.'

Charlie blushed. He had guessed beforehand that the combination of visitors this evening would be too much for him to cope with all the way through and his private prediction about trouble coming from the combination of his father and his English teacher was now proving all too accurate. He had not, however, expected it to come in the form of an alliance between the two, possibly directed against him.

'Ah! Put him on the spot! That's right! Good practice for Cambridge!' roared Bill in high good humour.

Suddenly Charlie's mind cleared.

'Were you thinking of the Franklin, Sir?'

'Instant accuracy, as so often,' beamed Alexander. 'Quotation?'

Bill listened with absorbed fascination to this exchange, unaware of its modest simplicity in comparison with the customary level of discussion between Alexander and his son.

Charlie looked up and down the table.

"It snewed in his hous of mete and drink.' Is that the line you had in mind, Sir?'

'Is that right, Head of English?' asked Bill.

'Yes, of course. Charlie can deal with things very much more difficult than that!'

Charlie desperately wanted to catch his English teacher's eye but, because Matron was seated between them, it was difficult. Mr Scott must have sensed his pupil's discomfiture. At just that moment, Priscilla leant forward a little to hear better a remark being made to her by Mrs Scott, who was sitting opposite. Mr Scott took the opportunity to lean back slightly. Charlie did likewise and was as astonished as he was reassured to see the great man actually *wink* at him and gently move his right hand up and down, as if to say, 'keep it cool, lad; it's okay.' *Mr Scott* to be colluding with one in evading the idiocy of one's own father! Hello, adulthood; I've arrived!

'You know, ladies and gentlemen, forgive me, but I'm just so proud of my dear son.'

Bill's bright blue eyes momentarily moistened.

Even by his own standards, Charlie blushed deeply. There were moments when he really could cheerfully go and strangle his Dad.

'You're making him self-conscious, Bill. It's not fair. Stop it!' said his wife.

There were other moments when he could rush up to his Mum and hug her to bits.

'So much of it is due to you, Alexander. He is very, very lucky to have you as a teacher,' said Bill.

'Well, we all agree with that,' said Sue.

'Yes, absolutely,' mumbled Charlie in genuine assent.

'Anyway' said Bill, 'I hope that every-one has some claret in their glasses, including you abstemious ladies. I have a few toasts to propose.'

'But no speeches, Dad,' begged Charlie.

'Amen!' said his mother.

As Sue Blakestone smiled, the resemblance with her son was striking. John had noticed again this evening that Sue was a very pretty woman and that it was primarily to his mother that Charlie owed his own good looks. Although he had his father's light brown hair (though Bill's was tinged by now with grey), rather than the blond hair of Sue, he had inherited his mother's distinctive light brown eyes- almost amber- and her finely sculptured nose, chin and cheek-bones. She was no more than average height and, although Charlie was tall, he had her slim frame and natural elegance in movement. Temperamentally, they were similar too. It was clear that they both passionately loved Bill for all his devoted goodness but that they had long since agreed to a pact, possibly tacitly, that part of the success in loving him so much was not always to take him with ultimate seriousness.

Bill cleared his throat. Charlie groaned audibly. Every-one else laughed.

Bill was a man of strong convictions who saw people in black and white. Tonight was being given as a feast for the angels and so he was moved to toast his wonderful wife for 'characteristically putting on such a marvellous feast'. Then they toasted 'the best English master in the country who, he had been reliably informed (presumably by Charlie), was a major literary scholar at whose feet every-one at Moreton College and far beyond should be permanently seated. Matron was toasted 'for putting up so heroically with all those smelly, skiving boys'.

Then it was the turn of 'the best son any father could ever hope to have'. At this point, Bill broke down momentarily and had to extricate his vast handkerchief.

'Yes, darling,' his wife said in gentle encouragement, catching Charlie in her glance of absolute love along the table.

'And I would like you to join me, ladies and gentlemen, in wishing Charlie success at Cambridge with all our hearts. I can't believe that any young man could have worked harder to deserve it more.'

'Yes, indeed,' pronounced Alexander, defusing the sudden emotion of the moment with a helpfully concluding formality: 'to Charlie's success.'

'To Charlie's success,' they all echoed warmly.

Dear, dear old Dad, thought Charlie now. Dear God, I'm so lucky with Mum and him. Thank you.

'And now, of course, to a gentleman who is a very, very special friend of every-one here. John, we are all of us here- your friends- so desperately sorry about this nightmare that has been visited upon you through no fault of your own. Let us drink to the swift acquittal of this godly man who has done so much to help so many young people at Moreton College for so many years. May you soon be back in your rightful position, John, and with your spotless reputation seen by every-one for what it truly is.'

'To John,' every-one assented, smiling down at him as he sat in his place to accept the toast. Suddenly, he was engulfed in emotion and had to rescue his own handkerchief. At the same moment, tears filled Priscilla's eyes. Cordelia, sitting on John's left, gently squeezed his hand. There were clucks of sympathy.

'I'm glad this happens to you sometimes. It's *always* happening to me!' said Bill, moving to his left and putting his arm round John's shoulder. Charlie, noticing that Matron was on the edge of tears, put his hand gently on her arm.

John had withstood the inclination to weep quite well during his ordeal, apart from the moment on the riverbank previously witnessed by Charlie and during his visit to Maurice on the first morning; but now the dam burst; he sobbed uncontrollably.

Alexander also moved round the table and stood next to Bill behind John, resting a hand on his colleague's shoulder.

'There, there, old chap. It'll be all right. See all these good friends whom you have around you!'

The short intense storm passed.

'I'm so sorry, every-one. I'm just overwhelmed by your kindness.'

'It's been a desperately stressful time for every-one,' said Sue, smiling with sympathy, a smile exactly replicated by her son, 'especially for you, dearest John. But we're all here for you, you know.'

TWENTY-EIGHT

IN THE DAYS BEFORE the great quarrel, Charlie and Jude would, of course, as best friends, have travelled up to Cambridge together, encouraging each other as they anticipated their interviews. In the light of the recent events, however, they went separately and without contact. Each boy was staying overnight in the college to which he was applying.

Jude caught the hourly 'bus which went from Midhampton. Bill drove Charlie through, arranging to pick him up again thirty-six hours later.

'Take the pants off them, Son. They'll be glad to get a chap like you here; just you see!'

For a moment, Charlie was going to give voice to irritation but, instead, he could not help smiling at his Dad, grateful for the totality of his love and support.

'Just you tell them all you know about Shakespeare and Chaucer and remember all the advice Mr Scott's given you.'

'I'll do my best, Dad.'

They hugged and went their different ways.

It was a cold, brilliantly clear, day in early December, unusual in the Fens at that time of the year. A piercing east wind blew discarded leaves, gold, yellow, ochre and brown, along King's Parade and across the Backs. There was no height equivalent to the top of the tower of Great St Mary's this side of the Urals whence it came. High white clouds raced urgently across the wide, blue, East Anglian sky, trailing streamers as they hurried westwards.

Charlie had checked in early and was thrilled with what he saw. The visual impact of the ancient university city whetted the edge of his ambition with an even greater keenness. Until now, the literature itself had been his overwhelming concern and Cambridge had seemed merely the abstract representation of a pinnacle of academic achievement. But to *come* to this dramatically beautiful place......*Oh, God, that you might favour me by making it possible!*

The college porters had issued him with a rudimentary map, with all the colleges named. He decided to explore for an hour or so before returning to his room to acclimatise himself yet again to his essays, notes and books. He had brought a bag full of these, though, in truth, he had rehearsed pretty well everything he knew several times before coming.

Within a few minutes, he was standing in the court of King's College, looking at the Gothic might of the great Chapel, the silvery grey western pinnacles of which towered lightly into the bright sky. A woman wearing a black gown trimmed with the purple of the college colours stopped him at the north-western door. He was disconcerted to find that he had to pay for admission and he had no money with him on the brief walk out. He noticed that the fee was rather high. But Charlie was not one to give up that easily. He explained that he was a schoolboy, a candidate for admission to another college. His smile and obvious candour not only bought him free admission to Cambridge's greatest building but hearty best wishes for his success. He walked slowly down the long nave, admiring the soaring immensity of the fan-vaulting in the ceiling above, a sequence of high fountains which never fall. Sunshine came in through the eastern window above the altar. The brilliant colours of the stained-glass played across the pale stone: ruby, emerald, amber: blue as richly deep as lapis lazuli. His spirit soared with the architecture. *O, God, if only…….*

He continued his magical stroll to King's Bridge. The colour glowed in his face as the strengthening wind whipped across the river, fretting the surface of the water and tugging at a few stubbornly tenacious leaves still clinging to the riverside trees. He looked to his right at the astonishing juxtaposition of the Gothic Chapel and the classical Gibbs Building, both towering to visual advantage behind the extensive green open space between them and the river. A few tightly secured, deserted punts huddled together against the bank as they bobbed on the disturbed surface of the water. He thought of Jasper's wishfully idiotic remark with rueful amusement and wondered, for a moment, how his lost friend might be.

He returned to 'his own' college. He passed through the great early Renaissance gateway and gazed across the vast court, a pleasingly irregular quadrangle, with the medieval Chapel to his right and the old dining hall opposite the entrance, through which was a Palladian court and, bordering the river, the college's famous library. He had been lodged in a room in a further court, off the Palladian one, in the middle of which was a huge, ancient chestnut tree, now denuded of its foliage. *I could be making this* walk several times a day, he thought. I could be working in that library. *No! I mustn't!*

As he crossed the court, he considered how curious it was that this was Mr Scott's old college. To think that *he* was here all those years ago, a boy like Charlie. He wondered if the redoubtable schoolmaster could possibly have been as keyed up before *his* interview: surely not, even back then.

He sat down in his room and looked at his watch: thirty minutes until the interview. He opened his backpack and fished everything out. His nerves raced; it was impossible to concentrate. Scotty had been disappointed to discover that his friend, Dr Griffin, was taking a sabbatical term in the U.S.A.. He was unfamiliar with the name of the English don who would be interviewing Charlie. Yet again, Charlie wondered what these personages would be like. He had never felt so nervous in his life or, in a not unexciting way, so much on his own. He *so wanted* to come here. He knew that he would face fearful disappointment if he failed. *Oh, Jesus, you know how much I want this. I can't help it: oh, please, please, please!* Being Charlie, he felt very acutely too, that, if he failed, he would be letting his father down. He knew that his father would not blame him and would seek, with clumsy generosity of spirit, to comfort him but that he would be doubly hurt, on his own account and on account of his son. And then there was Scotty. He had done so much for Charlie. What a waste of effort it would all be if it didn't work out. Even the Headmaster, over drinks before the lunch for Lord Macclesfield, had, while wishing Charlie personal success, mentioned the importance of a good result for Moreton's Oxbridge ratings which had dipped in recent years. For the hundredth time, Charlie went through in his mind the names of the writers and the particular works which he felt he could talk about. After a final brief prayer of supplication, he looked in the mirror to check that his tie was straight, made sure that there were no marks on his charcoal grey suit and set off five minutes before the scheduled interview.

The room he entered was cluttered with papers and books. It was Dr Griffin's room but, in his absence, was being used for interview by two women who now sat together on a sofa opposite Charlie. One of these was Dr Collett, whose name had appeared on the correspondence inviting him for interview. The other was introduced by Dr Collett as Natasha Harkness. It was not explained where she fitted in and Charlie did not know whether to address her as Dr, Mrs, Miss, Ms or even just as Natasha. He decided to avoid calling her anything at all.

Dr Collett looked like an earth mother. She seemed to be dressed in the off-cut from a carpet warehouse. She's wearing Joseph's Amazing, Technicolour Dream-Coat, thought Charlie. The garment had no buttons. It seemed to be held together by wooden fasteners which Charlie thought looked rather like clothes-pegs. When she was sitting, the cloak completely covered her somewhat rotund frame from the shoulders down. It had a monastic hood of the same fabric. Two slides, decorated by yellow sprigs of early winter jasmine, held her quite long, straight brown hair vaguely in place. She sat with her legs tucked beneath her on the sofa.

Natasha Harkness could only have been five or six years older than Charlie. She was dressed entirely in black and this, together with her dark hair and eyes, lent her a somewhat Gothic aspect. She was slim and had very long legs, clad in black tights. Her short, tightly fitting skirt rose up her shapely thighs in a way which Charlie could not but find slightly distracting, especially when she persistently crossed and recrossed her legs. He guessed that, were she to stand up, she would be very tall. Her black top left a naked space above the skirt. It seemed to Charlie that she was not wearing a bra. She had glasses with metal frames and small round lenses. She had a pale face and did not smile.

Beyond being told to sit down and advised of the names of his two interlocutors, there had been no welcome. They had not risen when he entered and Charlie's expectation of shaking some-one by the hand while confirming his identity had been still-born.

'Do you want to start with this one, Natasha?' enquired the earth mother.

Without looking at him and appearing instead to focus on some papers which she held in front of her, Natasha Harkness asked Charlie which contemporary women novelists he had read.

'I haven't read many, really. I suppose I must have read *something* but I can't think of any at the moment.'

'Can you name any?'

He didn't think he could; or else his mind went blank; he didn't know which it was, but he already felt himself blushing with nervous apprehension. All my work, he thought, and she's got to ask about this!

'So, you mean to tell us that you haven't heard of Jeanette Winterson or Margaret Atwood or Kate Atkinson?'

'I have heard of two of them but I haven't read them.'

'But you couldn't bring their names to mind?'

'No.'

Charlie noticed her skirt rising another inch up her thigh as she wrote down some presumably hostile observation. It was maddening that, already now unsettled, this provocative image persisted in teasing him yet further. She would be hotly attractive if only she were in a less frighteningly powerful situation. But, contrariwise, he also wondered if perhaps her sexual potency was accentuated for him by the very power she was able to wield. Would *she* be teaching him week by week?

'You *must* be aware of *some* contemporary woman novelist, surely,' asked the earth mother, a look of benign incredulity, when confronting such vacuous ignorance, filling her round face.

'Yes, I am; I'm sorry. My mind went blank.'

'So?'

'I've read Jane Smiley's 'A Thousand Acres'.'

'And how did you come to that?'

'My English master suggested that it was an interesting modern take on 'King Lear'.'

'Have you read any contemporary woman writer *not* suggested by your teacher?' asked Natasha Harkness. Now she looked at him with her beady dark eyes through the pebble lenses. As she did so, she crossed her legs in the other direction. Charlie could see a long way up the underside of her left thigh.

'Er…um…'The Shipping News' by…….'

'……E Annie Proulx. Yes, well, every-one's read that- or, at least, seen the film.'

She turned her gaze away from him and conferred a knowing conspiratorial smile on her colleague.

'I haven't seen the film but I have read the book,' said Charlie, bridling.

'Ah,' she said, now looking him up and down.

Charlie sunk further into the armchair. He could feel a broken spring through the fabric uncomfortably pressing against his left buttock. Her look was sufficiently penetrating to make him wonder if his flies were undone. To his annoyance, he became aware that he was blushing even more. He tried to wrest the initiative.

'Of course, I have read *classical* female novelists.'

'You're going to say Austen and the Brontes.'

'Well, er, yes. Is that unreasonable?'

The women both laughed a little but not in a way that suggested that they were engaging with him.

'Tell us, then, how you find Austen's lesbianism communicates through the novels,' demanded Harkness.

Charlie was seriously discountenanced. Was this some ridiculously outrageous provocation which he was expected to sweep aside or- horror of horrors- had some new evidence just appeared, proving Austen to be a lesbian, about which he was entirely ignorant? He thought the wisest course was to ask.

'Oh, she was a lesbian; there's no doubt about that and her writing clearly points in that direction. There's nothing wrong with that, of course: on the contrary. Do you have a problem with it?'

'I don't have a problem with a person being a lesbian….'

'I'm glad to hear it,' interrupted the earth mother.

Wow, thought Charlie! They're sitting rather close together; I wonder: surely not! He decided to battle on.

'But I *do* have a problem with any insistence that lesbianism is a prominent concern in Jane Austen's novels.'

'Do you now?' quizzed Harkness. 'Brave talk coming from a seventeen year old boy from a single sex boarding school! Go on.'

'Moreton is co-educational!' declared Charlie, scandalised that they should not know.

'Is it really? I'm not really familiar with public schools. I beg its pardon. But, go on; tell me why we're all wrong about the lesbianism in Austen's writing.'

Charlie, ever sensitive to tone, could not fail to detect the note of scorn as she gently swung her long, slender right leg to and fro as it rested on her left knee.

The armchair in which he was sitting was low as well as uncomfortable. This did not assist their relative dramatic status from his point of view. His own thighs inclined slightly upwards to his knees. He pulled his trouser legs up as he took on the faintly mocking question. When looking at her, it was impossible for his eye not to run up her legs.

'Well, no criticism or biography of which I am aware remotely suggests lesbianism….'

'What criticism or biography have you read?' asked the earth mother.

'Er…. Lord David Cecil and Marilyn Butler.'

'David Cecil's book is for coffee tables,' said Harkness.

'And Marilyn Butler is very political in interest and now very old hat,' added the earth mother, wearing an injured smile, as if appealing for a basic modicum of elementary good sense.

'Well, these were the books in our school library and, anyway, my own response doesn't point in that direction either,' said Charlie, now, at last, becoming sufficiently irritated to find the guns of determination and stick to them. 'Anne Elliot sustains her love for Captain Wentworth for nine years and if the relationship had not worked out, it wouldn't have been because she's a lesbian. It would have been because she would finally have succumbed to social pressures, as personified in her selfish, snobbish father.'

The earth mother took an inward breath prior to interrupting him, a signal to which, in all his life, Charlie would have hitherto conceded but, thrown onto the defensive and feeling antagonised by their unfriendliness, he carried on. What the hell? They hate me anyway (Heaven knows why) so I might as well give it to them

'Fanny Price and Edmund Bertram might not be the most exciting couple in the world but, on their own terms, they seem pretty obviously to be in love and, again, there is plenty of time for them to think about it. They are both cautious and intelligent people and they face down real opposition from Sir Thomas Bertram, something which they certainly need to consider before proceeding. Elizabeth Bennet *does* fall for Darcy. No-one would be able to tell *her* what to do, would they? She wasn't going to replicate the horror of her friend, Charlotte Lucas, by marrying Mr Collins. Elizabeth is the central character in the novel. If the message is lesbian, which of the other female characters are you suggesting she might be in love with? If you ladies want to take a *feminist* approach (which, I know, is not the same as a *lesbian* one), I suppose you could point to the hapless Lydia at the hands of the unscrupulous Wickham but, it seems to me, that she is as much to blame as he is and both her parents invite the reader's disapproval too for their different kinds of incompetence.'

The two women turned to each other and smiled. He did not feel included in their merriment. He tried to tell them the other novelists which he had read. They seemed uninterested. When he attempted to introduce Conrad into the discussion, Harkness dismissed the novels as 'blokes' books'. Time was, not so long ago, Charlie would have questioned his own judgment; now, however, he began to feel anger and contempt.

'It's all-right; we can see that you've been well drilled by your school,' said the earth mother, smiling and using a tone which might have reassured a five year old.

The remark infuriated Charlie but he was careful not to show it. Yes, he had had the privilege of brilliant (perhaps even great) teaching but this teaching had given him the independence of judgment which he felt he had, admittedly under provocation, just rather effectively demonstrated.

The fact that his comments had been spontaneous proved his point and disqualified the slander just made. He began to wonder whether, after all, he really wanted to come here.

Next, they produced the unseen poem which Mr Scott had warned him to expect. Charlie was allowed ten minutes to look at it while the two women quietly moved papers around and whispered to each other.

At the first glance, he considered that he might have known that he would be confronted by a female poet. He had not read any of Sylvia Plath's works and feared the worst. But, as he read 'Blackberrying', he thought that it was rather good and, moreover, that he could give a good account of himself when commenting on it. He explained how he saw it to be an inversion of conventional expectation. Walking down a path towards the sea, collecting blackberries, was normally a picture of routine innocence and relaxation. However, the poet had effectively turned it into an episode embodying threat, ugliness, developing paranoia and the promise of death and oblivion. He indicated the surprise of the minatory diction: 'heaving', 'squander', 'cacophonous', 'intractable', the simple and contrived ugliness of the similes:-

'*Blackberries*

Big as the balls of my thumb, and dumb as eyes

Ebon in the hedges',

the shockingly surreal metaphorical inversion when the flocks of choughs are described as

'*Bits of burnt paper wheeling in a blown sky*'

and the almost horrific bathos at the end, where the arrival at the sea, instead of providing fulfilment, presents '*nothing but a great space*'.

'Yes, thank you,' responded the earth mother. 'That's quite a sensitive reading.'

'It's a pity she was a manic depressive,' said Charlie, relaxing a little for the first time. He had enjoyed analysing the poem, rather than the vague and hostile sparring earlier. 'I suppose that it was shortly after this that she put her head in the gas oven.'

'That, of course, was a direct result of the brutal treatment of her husband,' snapped Harkness.

'Was that altogether the case?' asked Charlie, having dropped his guard. 'I thought that, since Ted Hughes' death and the revelations from the diaries, the blame was more equally spread. She must have been Hell to live with.'

'That is a chauvinistic remark,' hissed Harkness. 'Why do you think that there are so few great women poets in the canon?'

'I suppose,' responded Charlie, 'because it was for so long a man's world. Who knows what we have all missed as a result?' he added diplomatically.

Unfortunately, the remark was received as sarcasm.

'You public school boys are very smooth, aren't you- very assured,' commented the earth mother in a tone less friendly than before.

'Anyway,' said Harkness, 'given what you have just said, would you not agree that it is time that society corrected the balance?'

'That would seem to be right,' said Charlie cautiously, sensing the danger and wondering with a faintly sickening sensation if that was her way of saying that she had made up her mind not to admit him.

He left the interview dissatisfied. He had no real sense of how it went but he felt angry and confused. He had detected a bias against him. Every piece of discussion had involved women writers. Even when he had commented well on the unseen poem (as that earth mother herself had admitted), they seemed to turn it against him personally. Chaucer, Shakespeare, Keats, Dickens, Conrad- all writers he had been longing to answer on- had not even been mentioned. Perhaps they were just testing him, pushing him to the limit. On the other hand, perhaps they really didn't like him. And why should that be? Was it just because he was a white English boy from a public school? He had, of course, heard of this alleged bias but he had given it little credibility, feeling sure that Cambridge University would exalt itself above any such fashionable prejudice. Now, in reality, he was much less certain of that.

He was in low spirits when he attended at interview with the Tutor for Admissions. Dr Campbell was a middle-aged gentleman wearing a suit whose appearance and manner conformed more readily to Charlie's expectations. The usual questions came, anticipated and undemanding- why Cambridge? Why this college?- and, after the fifteen minutes was up, Charlie was beginning to recover hope. At the end, however, when they were shaking hands, Dr Campbell vouchsafed pleasantly that the *real* decision lay with the Director of Studies in English. He, Dr Campbell, just screened candidates more generally and processed the administration of admissions. Charlie obviously had much to offer the college in so many ways but English was one of the most competitive subjects. Much would depend on the verdict of his colleagues. It was confirmed that Charlie, like nearly all the candidates, was asked to stay until the following afternoon in case he was transferred to a different college for another interview tomorrow morning.

So, back to square one, thought Charlie as he returned to his room. He got out his mobile and 'phoned home. He was relieved that his mother answered; his father was out on the farm. He told her about the discouraging interview with the women. His mother insisted that it was surely impossible to judge and suggested that they were quite possibly testing the candidates for their mettle. Charlie was grateful but unconvinced. He 'phoned Rev. D. Rev. D paused before offering a judgment. Then he said that he had no idea what it could all mean but that he knew that Charlie had, like Rev. D himself, prayed for the entire matter and that it sounded as though Charlie had done his best and made a good fist of it. It was, therefore, in the hands of God and, if it was not God's will for Charlie to go to Cambridge, he would end up somewhere else just as good and that would be the place of God's choosing. He reminded Charlie that he, Rev. D, would not freely have chosen his own present situation but that he had no choice but to have faith that God had permitted him to be put through this trial.

Charlie met some of the other candidates when he went to have dinner in Hall. He sat next to a sweet and pretty blond girl called Sarah who came from Nottingham and was applying to read Mathematics. A pleasant boy of Pakistani descent, Karim, sat opposite. He was from Leeds and was applying to read Medicine. Sarah and Karim both attended state schools and wanted to know what it was like being a pupil at a boarding school. The three of them compared their experiences at interview. Charlie shared his misgivings. Sarah said that it was difficult to judge in Mathematics; it was all so impersonal; it must be very different in English. Karim felt that, like Charlie, he had been given a fairly severe grilling and he feared that he had been slow on the uptake in at least one question. Charlie liked both Sarah and Karim and felt better for their company. He suggested that the three of them might go out for a quiet drink in a local hostelry. Sarah said that she didn't usually go out to pubs and Karim explained politely that he was a Moslem and didn't drink alcohol. When Charlie honestly admitted that he too seldom went out drinking in the evening ('not exactly an option at a boarding school in the middle of nowhere'), Karim suggested that the company might do them all good rather than moping in their separate rooms and that, after all, no-one need drink very much and he, Karim, was perfectly happy to drink coke. They ended up furthering their acquaintance in a pub' on Bridge Street. Sarah said that she had never been out with *two* boys like this before and that it was 'really nice' to meet Charlie because she, in her self-confessed ignorance, had thought that all the people at public schools were posh snobs but that Charlie was 'really really sweet' and showed how wrong you could be. Karim agreed that stereo-types were very dangerous.

'Take me, for instance. Just because I'm a Paki, I got beaten up a few months ago on my way back from school. I won't repeat the names they called me. My family's quite religious. My Dad's quite in with the Imam at the local mosque. We don't have many friends outside the Pakistani community in Leeds. Of course, I've got other friends at school but I couldn't really invite any of them home. But, yet, here I am with you two and you're really nice guys and this has been the best part of the day here.'

Charlie was truly grateful to them for their company. Sarah was pretty, obviously bright, and appreciative. Karim clearly had a great deal to him as a person. Although he was far too polite to mention it, Charlie liked Karim's Yorkshire accent with its broad vowels and clear enunciation. The three of them drank coke. Charlie bought the first round and Karim the second. Charlie suggested that they swapped mobile numbers so that they could be in touch about the results. He added that he really hoped that they would all be successful.

'I'll tell you this, mate,' said Karim, looking Charlie directly in the eye, 'if we meet up here next Autumn, I shall know that I've got a good mate from the beginning.'

'Agreed. Me too,' said Charlie.

The two boys stood up and smacked the palms of their hands together.

They looked down at Sarah who was still sitting.

'And you too, Sarah,' said Charlie. 'What do you say?'

'Oh, yes,' she said. 'Oh, I *do* hope we all get in.'

They walked back together, little Sarah safely between the two tall, handsome boys whom she had first met just some three hours ago. The temperature had fallen. There was a light dusting of snow on the pavements and snowflakes in the atmosphere settled gently on their hair and coats. They agreed to meet for breakfast the following morning.

Charlie felt a twinge of loneliness when he was alone in his room again. He sat down and prayed. He gave his concern to God, trying hard to agree to accept the undisclosed divine will with good grace. The sheets on the strange bed were chilly. Outside, in the intermediate distance, a siren wailed in the December darkness as an ambulance sped to the Accident and Emergency Department at Addenbrooke's Hospital.

TWENTY-NINE

While Charlie was engaging with the earth mother and Harkness, Jude was being interviewed at a different college not far away.

'So- why I should I take a white, middle-class public school boy with all the advantages which you've had?'

It was a one-to-one interview. Jake Willard was the young, recently appointed, Director of Studies in English. Long hair was returning to fashion; stubble was still in. Jake sported both. Despite the coldness of the day and the room, his athletic form was clad in a short-sleeved white t-shirt with horizontal green stripes and a pair of thin black chinos. Jude wore a suede jacket over a white polo-neck and a pair of stiff new jeans, the legs of which were too long.

'I can't help being white; surely that's obvious- but then I didn't ask the question. I'm *not* middle-class. I come from a one parent family. My father walked out when I was born. My mother works her butt off as a receptionist. We live in a house owned by a housing association. I *hate* public schools. I didn't ask to go to one. My mother took the decision. I got a scholarship to Moreton. Twelve year olds are not normally in a position to control events, even when they're at the centre of them. I'm surprised to have been asked this question because I expect that all this hard luck stuff's been written down on the school reference. If you consider that this is a catalogue of adolescent advantages, that's up to you.'

This was not at all an impassioned speech. It was delivered in a weary monotone to match the cynicism it contained.

Jake was impressed. He grinned amiably. Jude remained expressionless. He wasn't going to be soft-soaped or tricked. He had an agenda too. If this place was going to be a mere extension of Moreton, it could go to Hell so far as he was concerned. Still, this guy seemed nice enough- a lot better than he had expected- even if he had started with a dumb-arsed question like that.

'So-you've not enjoyed your time at public school?'

Who's supposed to be the bright one round here? thought Jude.

'That *is* the impression I thought I'd conveyed,' he said, allowing himself now a judicious little smile. 'I mean- I have to say- it wasn't *all* bad. But I'll as sure as Hell be glad to get out of it.'

'I'm intrigued. I went to a London comprehensive myself. What specifically has turned you off so strongly?'

'Oh- all the rules, the details, the petty inflexibilities. You must imagine, surely. You still get punished if you wear the wrong colour of socks or turn up two seconds late for a house meeting. It's all so bloody regulated. Breathe at the wrong moment and you're sent off for a run round the field.'

Jake chortled.

'And, frankly, I don't like the class thing,' continued Jude, warming to his theme and making a shrewd guess that it was appealing to his interviewer. The sod could, of course, be double bluffing but, dressed as he was, and with a more than perceptible London accent which, though possibly self-consciously sustained, could surely not be pure invention, Jude considered the possibility of such duplicity unlikely.

'Do they make you feel a bit like a fish out of water? Thick, rich kids, with assured financial futures?'

'Yeah, that sort of thing. I mean, I wouldn't want to *over* state it but- well- it's not really been for *me*.'

'What about the teaching? Has that been pretty crap too?'

Yeah, I can see why this dude's got the job, thought Jude. There's no point in lying. He must know.

'No, I can't say that. I can see where you're going. This is where you can start accusing me of having an educational advantage after all! Much of the teaching was okay. There are *some* pompous pratts in a place like that, of course (like my housemaster), but there is some good teaching too. I've had a very good English teacher.'

'English teachers are usually the ones who get on with rebellious sorts like you. Is he young and trendy?'

'Like you, you mean?'

Jake Willard raised his eye-brows and said nothing.

Oops, thought Jude; I've miscalculated.

'Sorry, that was a bit cheeky.' Jude broadened his smile. 'No, Mr Scott couldn't be more different from that stereo-type.

He's quite an old guy: remote and can be *very* scary but he's got a mind like a razor and he *does* teach you to think for yourself. What I've been really impressed by him is that he *lives* for literature. Personally, I don't know how he puts up with the dump. He's the only teacher there whom I respect but I wouldn't take any liberties with him. I think it's widely agreed that English is the strongest subject at Moreton: possibly along with History.'

'It's interesting to hear about these places; they're another world for me.'

'And for me too, I hope, before long.'

Jake pulled up his t-shirt to scratch his stomach. At the same time, he picked up Jude's file and, opening it, crossed his legs and rested the file on his knee.

'So, Jude: I've got the list of what you've read here. It's not bad: a bit conventional but, from what you've said about your school, I suppose that's not surprising.'

Jake had a deep voice. It complemented the London accent, the muscular body and the casual attire to make Jude consider that his interviewer would be well suited as an undercover cop in one of the rash of studiedly 'cool' police dramas that had recently spawned across terrestrial T.V.. Jude was coming to like him; he'd probably be very useful in a football team.

'I see that 'Wuthering Heights' is on the list. Would you like to talk about that, or should we try something else?'

'I had a great argument with a friend of mine at school (to be exact, a former friend- we fell out about something else) about that book.'

Even as he said it, so unguardedly, there was a sudden, unanticipated moment of regret as he recalled the happy times with Charlie, the only person in his life whom he could ever have described as a 'best' friend.

'Really? Tell me about this argument.'

Jude rehearsed both sides of it faithfully enough. When this friend had swallowed some critic's statement about it being 'the most truly romantic novel in English literature', he, Jude, had countered by saying that it merely represented the rantings of a hysterical, sex-starved woman, fantasising in the bleak middle of the Yorkshire moors in the days before it had been impossible to escape elsewhere by train.

'That school can't be *all* bad if the pupils can get together freely and have a discussion like *that!*'

'I didn't say it was *'all bad'*.'

Jake Willard then asked him who his favourite pilgrim was from the descriptions given in The Prologue to the Canterbury Tales.

Jude had never actually considered this. He thought for a moment and then declared that it was the Reeve. Jake seemed amused and perhaps a little surprised. When asked to explain his choice, Jude surprised himself by finding that he could recall a few lines with reasonable accuracy. He liked the Reeve because:-

'Ther was noon auditour koude on him winne'

and

'Ther koude no man bringe him in arrearage.'

He admitted that he liked the idea of the young lord being fooled by his factor, even to the point that he gave the aristocrat presents taken from his own property.

'He's a pretty nasty character too, though,' suggested Jake. 'After all, all the other folk working on the estate *were adrad of him as of the deeth.*' What death was that?' he suddenly asked.

'The plague, wasn't it- the Black Death?'

'Yeah. Date?'

'Oh, you've got me there: middle of the Fourteenth Century?'

'Yes, that's good enough: 1348 till 1351.'

'I suppose the other one that quite amused me was the Maunciple but perhaps this isn't the place to admit that!'

'Ah, I see. You're saying that because he outwitted all those clever legal scholars?'

Jude did remember the relevant quotation and was delighted to have grabbed such an opportunity to demonstrate this. Before the interviewer could go any further, he quoted again:-

*'Now is not that of God a ful fair grace
That swich a lewed mannes wit shal pace
The wisdom of an heep of lerned men?'*

'Yes, well, I'd hesitate to suggest that that sounds a bit like our Domestic Bursar here in this college,' said Jake, chuckling.

The discussion moved on to 'Sons and Lovers.' Jude was candid. Personally, he could see the problem that Paul

Morel had with his mother; perhaps, of late, he could even empathise with it. He couldn't be bothered with Miriam and he, Jude, would have pursued the interest with Clara. (He had in fact, when reading the book, substituted Olivia for Miriam and Emma for Clara in his own mind.)

'Would you have done that even if it meant getting beaten up by Baxter Dawes?'

'I might have attempted some crafty evasion.'

Jake offered another friendly snigger.

Jude couldn't believe his luck when he saw the unseen poem that he was given. It was from A.E. Housman's 1926 collection - 'Tell me not here; it needs not saying' - and they had already done it as an unseen with Mr Scott. Obviously, he kept quiet about *that!* He knew where the trap was, a trap which both Charlie and he had avoided but through which, to his undisguised amusement at the time, Olivia had fallen as unceremoniously as Guardiano does when he goes through the bottom of the stage at the end of Middleton's 'Women Beware Women.' 'The enchantress' at the beginning of the poem is, of course, nature and, once one has turned that key, everything else falls into place. Olivia had taken the personification as an actual lover of the poet and had screwed the whole thing up as a result. Jude remembered suffocating his own dreadful impulse to have an attack of the giggles, contrasting this with Mr Scott's inscrutably polite patience and Charlie's fixed smile of friendly encouragement as Olivia disappeared into a perspiration of blushing confusion.

After a few minutes, it was clear to the young don that Jude had mastered the poem with accuracy and sensitivity and he wound up the interview in a friendly, blokish manner which suited Jude quite well.

'Can't give any promises, Jude. Plenty more folk to see, I'm afraid, but we'll let you know as soon as we can. Whatever happens, though, good luck! I've enjoyed our meeting!'

That particular college did not keep people overnight. The candidates would be called back if required. Jude found a large music emporium near the market. He didn't have any spare cash to buy anything but he liked mooching around in the warmth and brightness amongst the vast CD collection, immersed in the polyphonic beat of the bass. Then he caught the 'bus back.

As he travelled through the dull countryside east of Bedford (neither Home Counties, nor Midlands, nor East Anglia, rural but cluttered and always threatening to break out into development), Jude's pattern of thoughts surprised him. For the first time for ages, he was neither at school nor at home nor in a car being talked at by either his mother or Mike. Sitting alone in the moving 'bus, he considered that the interview had, above all else, redefined with a new vividness the three people with whom he had worked so much of late: scholarly, meticulously scrupulous Mr Scott, whose devastatingly sharp judgments and shafts of acid humour Jude greatly admired, Olivia, whose beauty and goodness had both attracted him but for whom, he had to admit, he was just not good enough and, most of all, that erstwhile best friend, Charlie. He found himself wondering how Charlie had fared on the same day. Jude felt that he was sure to be successful. Charlie never put a foot wrong and his safe intelligence, earnest thoughtfulness and utterly clear sincerity could not but fail. Jude realised that he really wanted Charlie to get into Cambridge. Charlie deserved it- more, in fact, than he did himself. Charlie had worked so hard and would do so well when he got there. Above all, Jude knew that Charlie himself really wanted it. He, Jude, was less bothered. It would be nice, of course, and that Willard bloke seemed quite a good guy, but Jude had other things to think about. The whole mess at school couldn't just be shut away in the way that his mother seemed to think. He was cut up about the break with Olivia. He had felt ever more certainly that he *did* love her. It was just that he couldn't kid himself by meeting her high standards. He simply wasn't good enough. And- God knows- he did miss Charlie. Charlie had, more than any-one else, picked him up and sorted him out, dusting him down and so often standing between him and trouble. And he, Jude, had said those foul things to Charlie. But it was all too late; it couldn't be taken back. The fracture had come because of the Rev. D business. Charlie would never forgive him for that. And why should he? In the end, wasn't it a mean, low trick to have played on a man who, from whatever motive, had given his life to helping boys in such a positive and enlightened way? Why had he let his bloody mother drive it on? He couldn't go back on it all now. The fact was that Rev. D *had* touched his bare leg and that, pure and simple, was what the whole fuss was about. But SO FUCKING WHAT? He had got himself into a corner and wronged everybody but it was all too late now. He couldn't get out of it. When he got back, less than an hour later, he would happily have withdrawn the whole thing. But it wasn't up to him now- or even his stupid, mercenary mother. The police, at the instigation of some P.C. airheads in the social services, were in charge of the prosecution. He knew that Charlie would forgive him for his outburst against him personally but he also understood his former friend well enough to know that he would never forgive him for hurting some-one else so badly and so unfairly. Moreover, dear, honest, naïve Rev. D had actually admitted that he had done it!

If he had denied it, Jude could have said that he, Jude, had made it all up in a sudden fit of pique which he later regretted.

He hovered for a few minutes at Midhampton 'bus station and then wandered round the shopping mall. He bought a baked potato with a grated cheese filling and ate it, sitting on a stool looking out of a plate-glass window. A line in another poem which he had prepared with Scotty, Charlie and Livvy came into his mind as the file of shoppers drifted past:-

'A cut-price crowd, urban yet simple.'

Yep! All very different from the bloke he had just met at Cambridge, from Mr Scott, from Livvy: *very* different indeed from Charlie.

He couldn't put off going home much longer. He knew that he'd have to go through the agony of trying to tell his mother how it had all gone and of not showing overt exasperation when she pretended to understand what he was talking about. Even worse would be the simpering, patronising observations of Mike who, would, of course, show off to mother and son by demonstrating how he, Mike, would have outwitted that English don at Cambridge at every turn, having the advantage of an education at 'the university of life'. Mike had moved into their home at last, prompted, philanthropically of course, by the need for Lynn to have a man around to support her and her son, during the crisis of litigation which had now engulfed them. Jude kicked a concrete waste bin as he left the mall.

THIRTY

Christmas came and went with its usual range of emotional challenges and opportunities. The joy of happy families was even more positively experienced when their energy could be diverted from the disparate demands of work into the harmony of celebration. The underlying divisions within less happy ones festered into a more intense misery or were detonated into active conflict. Even the most self-sufficient single people were in the hands of others as arrangements were made for them; they were thankful for any inclusion which could dispel the spectre of loneliness on the one day of the year when the collective consciousness impelled fellowship.

Richard went to friends of his parents who lived in London. He was grateful for their hospitality but, through no fault of his hosts, felt that he was a stranger within the intimacy of an unfamiliar family and was unable to ward off a wave of homesickness as, looking out upon a cold grey London, he spoke on the 'phone with members of his own family who were relaxing in the heat by a swimming pool back at home. Priscilla went to her friend in Cheltenham, two lonely women who had made the best of it together for several Christmases now. John joined Maurice, Pauline and their daughter for Christmas lunch at the vicarage after the morning service. Jude simmered with rage during the nights at the thought of Mike sharing his mother's bed in the next room. He pointedly refused to obey the interloper's blundering attempts to assume authority and walked out of the house in the middle of Christmas dinner when Mike instructed him to 'go easy on the wine.'

In contrast to these compromises and failures, and the cloud of the impending result from Cambridge notwithstanding, there was festive joy at Greenvale Farm. The interior of the unspoiled Eighteenth Century brick farm-house, set in its own walled garden with fields surrounding it, was festooned with natural greenery in much the same way as might have been done for the Christmas celebrated by George Eliot's Tom and Maggie nearly a century and a half earlier. Charlie and his younger brother, Harry, had decorated the tall Christmas tree, freshly cut from a nearby fir plantation. Sue Blakestone's culinary skill was matched by her tireless enthusiasm. Granny sat contentedly sipping from her thimbleful of Amontillado, quietly thrilled with her precious daughter, dearest son-in-law and her two wonderful grandsons, about whom she boasted unashamedly to all her friends. Dolly, Sue's former home help, long since widowed and reluctantly forced into retirement by the onset of arthritis, had joined the family on Christmas day for many years. Bill fetched both old ladies after the family had attended the morning service in the neighbouring village. His younger sister and her husband and two daughters drove through from Warwickshire. The girls were fifteen and thirteen, between the ages of the Blakestone brothers. They both fell madly but silently in love with Charlie each time they saw him, a secret which they shared with each other but no-one else. A log fire fizzed and blazed in the sitting room. Presents and hugs of gratitude were exchanged. Every-one helped.

Charlie received a call from Olivia on the twenty-eighth

of December. Oxford's results generally come before those of Cambridge and are usually out in time for Christmas. Perhaps it was fortunate that Olivia's letter had been delayed in the seasonal mail in view of the disappointing news which it contained.

'I'm not really surprised, Charlie, and, honestly, it's a relief to have got the wretched thing over one way or the other. I was never as good as Jude or you and I can't imagine that Mr Scott will be all that amazed. The biggest problem is my father. I can see that he's dreadfully disappointed. Don't get me wrong. He's not complaining openly or anything, or even hinting that I've let every-one down, but I know that I've broken the family line in not getting in. I actually overheard my grandfather saying so. I think that he's probably even more fed up than my father. I really hope that, of all of us, *you* make it; I'm sure you will.'

Charlie commiserated with genuine warmth on his friend's account. Moreover, much of what Olivia had said sounded like a minatory harbinger of his own possible fate, including the bit about their respective fathers, even though there had been no history of Oxbridge admissions in Charlie's family. Additionally, and significantly, there was one critical difference between Olivia and Charlie. Charlie desperately *wanted* to get into Cambridge. A hard, though not unworthy, seam of ambition had developed over the last few months. Charlie and Olivia had both always been earnest and industrious pupils but, whereas Olivia had remained in that mould, Charlie had an arm which stretched high for the glittering prize.

He had another week to wait. He was fast asleep when the postman came. When, in the middle of the morning, he had finally got up, taken a shower, dressed and wandered downstairs, he saw the envelope with the Cambridge postmark left tactfully by his mother on the Pembroke table in the hall. Suddenly alert, he braced himself against the moment of destiny. He shot an arrow prayer heavenwards.

Dear God, this is it! You know how much I want this. If you give it to me, I promise that I'll do my best and I'll try to serve you in Cambridge. No, I'm not making conditions; you know I'm not doing that, Lord! I'm almost too scared to open it! Oh, please! Please! But'- Charlie closed his eyes for a moment and exhaled- *'I've got to accept what you've decided. Whatever it is will really be best, I know. But you know how I feel.'*

He was trying to be mature and courageous as, in agitation, he sought to apply his chosen life-view to this, the most severe challenge which his young faith had yet confronted.

The letter of rejection, signed by the Tutor for Admissions, was a perfunctory pro-forma. It defensively advised of 'an exceptional number of able candidates this year' and 'sincerely hoped' that Charles would 'soon be offered a place at an alternative university' where he would be enabled to 'fulfil his academic potential to a degree which would satisfy him.'

Rationally, of course, Charlie had always been aware of the possibility of this eventuality. Statistics alone advised it and he had not been sanguine about the interview. Emotionally, however, he had set his heart upon succeeding with a sustained and relentless determination the full force of which now hit the immovable obstacle as an express train might run into the buffers at full speed. He felt as though he had been punched in the solar plexus. He was completely disorientated by the shock and sat down heavily at the bottom of the stairs with his head in his hands.

Like most parents these days, Bill and Sue had conceded to the lie-in which teenage children seemed to regard as a *sine qua non* during the holidays, reasoning with sensible charity that their son permitted himself insufficient sleep during the school term and that there was leeway to be recovered. Sue had restrained Bill from waking Charlie when the letter had arrived. Knowing all too well that it represented either triumph or disaster, she had insisted that their son should initially encounter whichever of Kipling's two impostors awaited him in his own time and in his own way. Normally, Bill was out and about on the farm without interruption between an early breakfast and lunch-time. Today, however, he had persisted in returning to the house again and again, getting in her way in the kitchen. He was back now. Neither of them had heard Charlie coming down and opening the letter. They were both, for different reasons, anxious. Sue was only too aware that she would have two very unhappy men to deal with in the event of rejection. It was a moment of extreme options, devoid of synthesis. Unusually, she too was feeling the strain. Exceptionally, she had snapped at her husband. Like the proverbial wounded bear, he had looked down at her unhappily, saying that he 'only wanted the very best' for their dear son. She had nearly capitulated but judged it best to remain firm and tight-lipped until either euphoria or desolation swept through the house.

Bill went out into the hall yet again to see if the missive had been moved. As soon as he saw his son sitting silently at the foot of the stairs with his head in his hands, he did, of course, realise the outcome.

Charlie looked up at his father, shook his head and could do nothing to prevent the tears from running down his face.

'Show it to me, son.'

Charlie handed the hateful document across without getting up.

'THE BASTARDS! THE SODS! WHAT SORT OF A LETTER IS THIS?'

Sue came flying out of the kitchen, still wearing wet rubber gloves. Narrowly avoiding a collision with her husband, she sat down on the stair next to her son and put her arm round him.

'Oh Mum,' moaned Charlie softly as the tears, now generating with greater intensity ran scalding from his eyes. Although Charlie could, like his father, feel very deeply, he was less accustomed than Bill to yielding to tears but, now that they had come, he abandoned himself to them totally. He rested his head on his mother's shoulder. Sue cradled him in her arms in a way that she had probably not done for at least ten years and rhythmically patted his upper arm. The contagion spread and she too burst into tears.

'I'LL GO OVER THERE AND BLOODY SORT THEM OUT! WHAT THE HELL DO THEY THINK THEY'RE DOING?'

Bill looked at the chilly little sheet of paper again in furious disbelief. Its three sentences had reduced the same number of people to the nadir of distress and all around the country the first week of the New Year was being similarly blighted in six times as many families as were presently uncorking the champagne.

'They COULD NOT have HAD a whole string of better folk than our Charlie! It's PREJUDICE! That's what this is: PREJUDICE!'

'Oh, Bill, do shut up for Heaven's sake! This isn't helping at all!'

'Dad, I'm sorry!' wailed Charlie.

'It's not your fault! You worked so DAMNED hard!' shouted his father. 'How DARE they do this to you?'

Sue got up, her voice steady, despite her tears. She stood in front of her husband who towered massively over her.

'Bill! Stop this at once! Our concern must be for Charlie- not for you in your rage. Now, pull yourself together!'

His angry red face looked down at her and froze. He turned abruptly away and went into the drawing room with the offending letter dangling from his great hand, a fragile and deceptively insignificant scrap of paper.

After a few minutes, Charlie intimated that he wanted to be on his own and that he intended to go for a long walk. His parents united again in worry but he assured them glumly that he would 'be okay'. While he was in his room pulling on a thick jumper, his mobile rang.

'Hi! Is that Charlie?'

'Yep?'

'Oh- Hi Charlie, it's Sarah. Er....we met in Cambridge. I

don't know if you remember.....'

'Hi, Sarah. Of course I remember. How are you?'

The requirement to speak normally to some-one on the 'phone necessitated Charlie's having to find a handkerchief and discreetly blow his nose.

'Fine, thank you.' Her voice was high-pitched, gentle, diffident. 'Um....Have you heard from them yet?'

'Yes- I didn't get in,' he responded with unavoidable terseness and could only just about bring himself to add 'How about you?'

'Oh! I'm so sorry to hear that Charlie. Oh dear: that's horrid.'

'Yeah- well, it's the way it goes, I guess. I've only just found out. But- you haven't told me; how about you?'

He had, of course, guessed correctly. Why otherwise would she be 'phoning? You don't 'phone round the country telling every-one that you've failed! But it would have been impolite to take the shine off her success with some remark of surly anticipation.

He could almost feel her blushing across the airwaves as, with apologetic restraint, she confessed her fortune.

'But I'm really really sorry that you haven't got in, Charlie. I'm really really surprised. I thought, of all of us that night, you were the one who was going to make it. I guess English is so competitive. It's much easier to get in for Maths.'

Charlie didn't know whether this was true or not but he did, of course, reject any such self-deprecating hypothesis. Sarah asked if he had heard from Karim. She said that she had been going to 'phone him too but, after this, perhaps she would wait a bit.

'It's such a pity, Charlie. I was really really looking forward to the three of us meeting up again when we- er- all got there. I'd felt that I'd got two friends to start together with.'

'Me too,' said Charlie, trying hard not to let his emotions take control again.

They agreed to keep in touch: perhaps, with Karim, meeting at some unspecified future time. At that moment, they might even have believed in such a possibility; of course, it would never happen.

Both his parents were downstairs, hovering over him in a fully recovered alliance, as he pulled on his gum-boots, warm fleece, scarf, woollen hat and gloves to brave the cold outside. He really didn't want them fussing round him at this moment but, aware that they had been there for him at the immediate impact of disaster, he certainly wasn't going to turn on them with any expression of nasty bad temper. He knew also that he *would* want to talk it all through with them in the intermediate future. When he saw their worried faces, he said as much as he left the house.

Greenvale Farm was in a shallow valley. Charlie followed a track across a gently rising meadow, through Hexen Wood and across another meadow, which rose more steeply, to the public footpath which ran for several miles along Bleaklow Ridge. Even as he left the walled garden round the house, he could feel the edge of the east wind cutting into the right-hand side of his face. He pulled his woollen hat down over his ears. A country lad, he was untroubled by weather and he had become increasingly used to solitary walks during the school holidays, often using these to think literary issues through or test his memory in poetry. Even now, as he entered Hexen Wood, he thought of himself as an ill-fated character in 'King Lear', crossing the inhospitable heath:-

'Child Roland to the dark tower came.'
'Now stab and end the creature- to the heft!'

He had recently discovered a new pleasure when Mr Scott had, in passing, attracted his attention to Browning's extensions of Shakespeare's characters in the poems featuring Edgar and Caliban. Now, this encouraged him to project his feelings onto a landscape of the mind as he half identified with Edgar, cast out from his rightful inheritance onto the blasted heath. In his imagination, he fused 'King Lear' and 'Macbeth' together as he made his way with bleak courage to the trysting place to meet with two witches assuming the forms of the earth mother and Harkness. Or, perhaps they were Goneril and Regan and, allowing for a vagueness in generation, he was the wronged *Mitglied* of the family, denied his place at Cambridge. It cheered him a little to objectify his misery and create such fantasy. As a child, more than five years older than his brother, he had played increasingly elaborate solitary games of the imagination. He had joined the children in Enid Blyton's 'Famous Five' in their explorations. Then he had teamed up with the Swallows and Amazons, turning the gentle, undulating countryside around the farm into the grand fells of Lakeland. Once, he had taken the 'bus into Midhampton with the deliberate intention of wandering through the streets of terraced red-brick houses near the railway sidings in an attempt to recreate Alan Garner's Manchester in 'Elidor'. And, of course, he had willed the heavy old oak wardrobe in his bedroom to open out into Narnia. This area of his life was so secret that he shared it with no-one, not even his parents. When he had first gone to boarding school, it had been a natural pleasure to team up with other boys and girls to explore the grounds of the College. In innocent make-believe, Charlie had coined his own private names for any location on the estate hitherto innominate.

Now, he was in the middle of Hexen Wood, fast approaching a spot long since cherished as ultimately dreadful in his imagination. The wood was on a plateau, half way up the hill which was crowned by the ridge. In the middle of the wood was a clearing in a hollow. When, many years ago, Charlie had first ventured into Hexen Wood on his own, he had suddenly and unaccountably felt extremely frightened when he had come upon this indistinctive landmark and had run back to the house in tear-stricken panic. He had still hurried through the clearing on subsequent visits, averting his eyes until he had picked up the path again at the other side. Irrational though it was, he had felt a compelling certainty that this was an evil place and that something appalling had occurred there. Not until he was twelve did he find out that a man had been brutally murdered at precisely that spot some one-hundred-and-thirty years ago when, one dark winter's night, he had been carrying a significant sum of money between the farm and his home in the first village to the west below Bleaklow Ridge. The discovery had shocked Charlie but had also served to confirm him in a certain confidence in the intuitive power of his imagination. Here was a place where witches had reputedly held their covens three or four-hundred years ago, a location which served as a metaphysical junction for natural and supernatural evil. Even now, as an intelligent young adult, Charlie could not dispel a frisson of almost enjoyable apprehension as he hurried through. *'There to meet with Macbeth.'*

He reached the ridge, breathless after the energetic climb in the cold. At this elevation, the east wind was wailing with mournful malevolence as he stood against it. He looked down over the wood, which always appeared less threatening from above, and then over the quiet meadows and outhouses of the farm and over the home where he had lived all his life. He felt an aching love for it, even as the wind buffeted him. Here was the certainty of security. Within those hallowed walls were his loving parents and his little brother whom he also loved and the various dogs and cats so precious to him as a farmer's boy, a son of the soil, however widely his fancy roamed or his intellect examined. 'Bugger Cambridge,' he could hear his father soon saying and being reprimanded for his bad language by his mother. Charlie smiled faintly as the tears started again, the icy wind now tearing the salt water across his face as his nose began to run. Already the tears of harsh rejection were being transubstantiated into the tears of belonging, the tears of profound affection. At this moment, he knew that he was not a tragic character. Indeed, had not Edgar won out in the end, as 'the wheel turned full circle'? And he, Charlie, had not been disinherited from the modest palace which was his home. Had not Raskolnikov been redeemed? - and he, Charlie, had not murdered any-one! It was Svidrigaylov who had committed suicide- or Decoud, who didn't have a home and family in the English countryside.

A spiteful gust sliced into his left cheek. Threatening dark clouds tumbled over the landscape, dwarfing the farmstead below. Would all this pass too? Certainly, it would, one day.

Charlie had been devastated by two deaths in the past: those of his grandfather and the favourite labrador who had accompanied him as he had set out on his expeditions with the Famous Five or the Swallows and Amazons.

Circumstances had moved on at school too. Jasper had gone: poor Jasper. They had met once since, at a pre-Christmas party in London, after which Charlie and several others had crashed out for what remained of the night at Ashley's. Jasper seemed to be doing nothing at all beyond becoming promiscuously involved in the gay scene and, Charlie feared, possibly approaching a point of no return in heroin addiction. He had lost weight and looked dreadful. Charlie still grieved too over the fracturing of his greatest friendship at school. He found it impossible to forgive Jude for what he had done to another person, especially to some-one like Rev. D. In any case, judging from the outburst which had represented their last significant conversation, Jude did not seem to want forgiveness or even feel that he needed it. And now, Rev. D was no longer at College for them either and might never be there for others in the future, for boys like his little brother. In a few years' time, the College would be full of people whom Charlie did not know, strangers usurping the special places which had belonged to him and to Ashley and Tim and the others.

The inhospitable January sky darkened as a vast, swirling cloud of charcoal grey swept overhead. Even at midday, lights from the farm bravely sparkled against the suddenly gathering gloom. A squadron of snowflakes, sparsely spaced, stung his face as they flew past horizontally in a crazy fury of purposeless haste.

Was he looking down at the past, Charlie wondered? He saw his father emerging from the back of the house, pulling his hood up over his head and walking towards the nearest barn. From this distance and height, the big man was reduced to the proportion of an insect within the immutable immensity of the land and the sky. Was the comfortable security of childhood, hitherto taken so totally for granted with such blissful ease, slipping swiftly and irretrievably away? As he turned to walk along the ridge, was this the bleak wind of a frightening and indeterminate future? Where was God, he began to wonder with sad alarm, amidst these *'impetuous blasts of eyeless rage, catching in their fury, and making nothing of'* this *'little world of man'*? Are our lives merely the business of *'outscorning the to-and-fro-conflicting wind and rain'*?

Uncertain of purpose but firm of tread, Charlie set off along Bleaklow Ridge, facing the east wind head on as it howled and stung, whipping the snows of the Urals, Poland and the Lunenberg Heath into the frenzied storms of the North Sea, snatching the icy message from Cambridge, before its arrival, unwelcome and uninvited, at Greenvale Farm. It brought with it the warning horns of express trains on the main line as they approached Midhampton station, a repeated, haunting, siren sound of danger ahead.

When he got back, more than two hours later, two messages awaited him. Alexander Scott had 'phoned his parents with genuinely felt commiseration. When Charlie returned the call, he learnt that Jude had been successful. He bravely and generously acknowledged his former friend's intellectual superiority, something which, despite his teacher's sincere assurances that he, Charlie, was the true scholar, the one with the vision and the commitment, he nevertheless had always genuinely believed. Mr Scott told Charlie not to underestimate his own intellectual power.

'Charlie, it is possible to be both passionate and intelligent and, whatever, they might have thought at Cambridge, you *have* both these qualities.'

The other message awaited him on his mobile. Karim had also been accepted and wanted to know how Charlie had fared. Karim very much hoped that they would be meeting together as fellow students next autumn. Charlie dutifully 'phoned back. There was a compassionate warmth and understanding in the deep, softly distant, Yorkshire voice. As Charlie recalled Karim's seriously humorous dark eyes and the embryonic friendship struck up as their palms had closed together that night in the Cambridge pub', he felt his loss with renewed acuteness and, accept it though he knew he must, he could not believe that it was fair.

That was his message to God as he dropped to his knees by his bedside.

THIRTY-ONE

Jude received the letter from Cambridge phlegmatically. For him, it was a piece of information which had the advantage of sorting out where he might be going next. He felt no special excitement at the news. It merely decorated the edge of his present primary concerns.

His mother, however, was euphoric. She was bursting with vicarious pride at her son's achievement.

'That fucking school should be proud!' she exclaimed to both Jude and Mike. 'Jude's got into Cambridge despite them!'

Jude considered privately the teaching of Mr Scott but said nothing.

Mike joined in possession of the triumph.

'I'm really proud of you, boy! This calls for celebration!'

He popped the cork of some insufficiently chilled Australian sparkling wine.

Lynn hugged her son. Jude hated physical contact with his mother. He could smell the body mist which was currently being discounted at various high street multiples. But he stood passively, allowing her lips to roam in salivation across his face.

'Just think, Lynn,' said Mike, in his slightly whining,

nasal, flat, Midland voice, 'We'll be able to drive over to Cambridge of a weekend and take him out for a pub' lunch and swank about with our lad who's actually a student at the university! That'll be something again, won't it?' He leered at them both.

The clumsy remark was intended to embrace both Lynn and Jude in proprietary affection. The effect on Jude was, of course, the reverse but, again, he kept counsel and merely smiled awkwardly. When his mother finally released him, he said that he needed to go out for a breath of fresh air to take it all in. As he intended, the sarcasm was lost to both his listeners.

After he had gone, Lynn and Mike both agreed that he 'seemed to be settling down and accepting things.' Lynn felt certain that in this New Year everything would now be all-right at last. Her brilliant son had excelled himself in achievement. Moreover, she had pretty well decided that she would settle for Mike. He might not be the most exotic of partners but he would stand by them and, with his bulky male presence around her, she would not be left on her own. She also felt confident that she would gain satisfaction, both emotionally and financially, from a successful prosecution against that toffee-nosed school with its hateful institutional snobbishness; it would be good too to see that creepy priest cringing in the humiliation of public ignominy.

The east wind cut between the concrete and glass edifices of the town, blowing dust into Jude's face and sweeping long dead leaves and occasional pieces of litter across roads and pavements. He entered the shopping mall and called at Smith's to buy a pad of paper, a packet of envelopes, a cheap ball-point pen and some stamps. He went into a fast food joint and bought chicken nuggets and chips. He sat at an individual table facing a wall.

He shucked off the cellophane wrapping of the note-pad and started to write a letter. He put the date but no address at the top of the page.

<u>To: Rev.D, Charlie & Olivia.</u>

I am sorry to write a combined letter to all three of you but, since I want to say broadly the same thing to you all, I hope that you will forgive my photo-copying this and then sending it to you separately .

I know that it is too late to make amends, and that I can't expect any of you to forgive me, but I am writing to offer my sincere apologies to you all.

REV.D: You and I both know that what I did was totally wrong and that it was motivated by spite, ignited by temporary rage after I was dropped from the First XI. You were quite right to drop me, Sir, because my behaviour was deplorable and I was able to see not long after the event that you had no choice but to act in the way that you did. I am certain now that I would have done the same in your position. I want to state unambiguously that, when you applied the cream to my leg, the action was taken for medicinal purposes, as a consequence of my scratching my shin (rather badly) NOT on the football pitch but the previous night when I had been breaking bounds. I deeply regret that I misrepresented it as something different. As I write now, I cannot believe the depth of my ingratitude when I consider all that you have done for me. I can, of course, expect nothing from you at all but I would like you to know how very sorry I am to have caused you such immense distress.

CHARLIE- Mate!- my very best and truest mate!- believe me, I'm fighting back the tears when I try to write this bit. You can't believe how much I hate myself for the things I said to you that day. I don't expect you to believe me now- it's all too late- but, again, I'm just so, so sorry. What more can I say? I was so lucky to have you as a friend for those years; no-one could have had a better friend. I owe you more than I can begin to say. This next bit might sound like gloating but it isn't. I just thought what a stupid, unfair world it is when Scotty told me on the 'phone that you hadn't made it to Cambridge. Well, mate, it's their silly loss. Honestly, I'd willingly give you my place: really, I would. I know how much it meant to you. Give Scotty my best wishes (I don't suppose he'll want them!) and my thanks. I know you'll think this is just so insincere after all that's happened. All I can say is that I mean it with all my heart. (What heart? I hear you say). Ah well, I know I've done too much damage to put it right. You gave me some of the happiest moments in my life, Charlie- that's what you did for me. Thanks Mate.

LIVVY: You never thought you'd hear from me again, I know. I've treated you like shit and I'm sorry for it. Yes- I know- you've heard all this before. I did mean it when I said sorry before but I guess I was just too weak to do the right thing by you. I did try, honestly, but I kept failing: the story of my life really. I'm not talking about academic things or sport; I'm meaning the important, deep things: things of the heart, things of the spirit. You won't accept the apology, I know- and why should you? But I need to make it, Livvy, and here it is. I'm sorry to have treated the most wonderful girl in the world the way I have treated you. I didn't deserve you and now I've lost you for good. It's all my stupid fault. Thanks for putting up with me as long as you did. Find an HONEST guy- some-one who DOES deserve you. (Charlie?........!)

TO ALL THREE OF YOU:

Now a bit about me. Let's face the truth. I don't fit in at the College- never have, really. I'm not saying it was wrong for me to go to Moreton College because I met you three there and some other great people as well. And the football was really GREAT! (Give my best to Ashley; it was good to have some-one at that place who was even scruffier than me!). The English with Scotty was really special too. Even now I'm too scared of him to write directly! But, as I say, I didn't fit in. In the end, something was inevitably going to go badly wrong. I'm just sorry that I hurt other people as well as myself. (This 'S' word is turning up a lot in this letter; perhaps I'm making up for all the times it should have been said before!).

As I'm sure Rev. D already knows- and probably Charlie & Livvy will have worked out too- it isn't just at school where I don't fit in. The same can be said about home. My Mother wants the best for me and she's really ambitious for me but- how can I put it?- we really don't live on the same planet and, now that Mike's going to move in, I don't really see how I can stay. I'm glad she's got somebody to care for her though and, if she likes Mike, I guess that's the important thing. Best leave it at that.

And, so, finally: where does God fit into all this? I've asked myself that question so often recently. I wish I could come up with the answer you might want, Rev. D, but I can't. I've so wanted God to change me and make me into a better person but it hasn't worked. I can't relate to other people or treat them the right way. I guess I'm some sort of misfit- or perhaps I'm just bad. And so: either God doesn't exist at all or, if He does, He doesn't want me. Either way, it's bleak and I can't see beyond those alternatives- not for me, myself, anyway.

Anyway, I'm not going to pester you by inflicting any more of this on you. I've given you all enough trouble already. I'll sign off by writing 'SORRY' yet again.

So long,

Jude.

Jude addressed three envelopes, all to Moreton College, and stuck first class stamps on them. His handwriting was clear and well formed. He found a shop which produced photocopies and walked out of the shopping mall. He crossed the main road to the station where he posted the letters. He sent the original to Charlie and copies to the other two. He lit a cigarette, inhaling deeply as he smoked. He enjoyed the immediate relaxation which the nicotine induced. He entered the concourse and bought a ticket to London. He descended the stairs to the platform. A train was due fairly soon and there were many people waiting. A voice came over the tannoy with muffled urgency, warning passengers to stand back from the edge of the platform when the rapidly approaching high speed train passed. Feeling calmly elated, Jude timed his move with all the instinctive, balletic precision which he had found so natural on the football field as he now stepped forward to engage with his destiny.

THIRTY-TWO

The mess on the railway line was forensically examined and then cleared up in time for trains to be running normally again during the evening rush hour. The tide of life, both on the main line and at the College, soon covered and eradicated the temporary interruption. In a few weeks' time, boys and girls would be sending each other Valentine cards. Express trains were still hurtling through Midhampton station. The recorded announcement to stand back from the edge of the platform had not changed. Geoffrey Tansley still drank plenty of gin.

So far as John was concerned, Jude's letter meant that The Crown Prosecution Service decided not to further a charge which a deceased complainant had withdrawn immediately prior to death.

The question of John's reinstatement at the College did not, however, turn out to be the simple matter which might have been expected. Bernard Bassett was most unhappy at the prospect of John returning to Blenheim House and he foresaw with dread the incessant whining of Delia over this matter whenever he would be coming back after a long day's work. With furrowed brow and much pushing up of his heavy spectacles onto the bridge of his nose, he discussed the problem with Cressida Fulwell. She did not want John back either. Apart from anything else, it would represent a signal political reverse. They took their case to the Headmaster.

'What's all this about?' Geoffrey Tansley asked with some exasperation. 'The man is in the clear. The poor wretched boy's penultimate action was to write that fact in a way that is beyond dispute.'

'I agree with you, Headmaster. That's not in doubt.'

'Well then Cressida, ç'est ça, n'est çe pas?'

'It's just that….er…..I don't quite know how to put this……'

'Go on! Spit it out!'

'It's just that, although John Donaldson must now be regarded as innocent…..'

'Correction: not 'regarded' as innocent: '*is*' innocent.'

'Yes, indeed, Headmaster, as you say, '*is*' innocent….'

'Well… what, for Heaven's sake?'

'People will always say that there is never any smoke without fire. John has now got stuck with the reputation for being gay and, given his particular role as Chaplain, this might inhibit boys in particular from sharing…… er…..intimacies with him which they might otherwise have been willing to disclose.'

She paused, trying to gauge her irascible superior's response.

'I hear what you're saying.'

'And, desperately disappointing though it may be for John Donaldson not to come back to Moreton, I suppose that one has to consider the reputation of the College more widely. We know that there have been unfortunate references in the press and one can't help wondering what parents- present and potential- might think. It might be a question of balancing loyalty to a colleague against adverse gossip and its effect on recruitment and, of course, onward from that, on revenue.'

He sighed. Cressida was aware that she was moving into more hopeful territory. She found it hard to believe that Geoffrey Tansley could feel any significant emotional or moral commitment to a professional inferior, especially if there might be any risk attached.

'The Moreton parents are very conservative about such matters,' she continued. 'It's a pity that more of them aren't more enlightened but I suppose that, as fee-payers, they call the tune- at least to a certain degree. Forgive my being so frank, Headmaster, but, as you've said before, a Deputy Head is here to offer suggestions and, in this case, to counsel caution.'

'And, in all honesty, Delia and I are not happy to have him back in the House, Headmaster. It will be very difficult after all this,' added Bernard Bassett, assaying a tone of genuine regret.

'What you both say does certainly have to be taken into account. I have no choice but to do that but it would be a case of wrongful dismissal, you know. The College would lose and we would find ourselves paying hefty compensation. That might not be good for publicity either- or finances.'

'Yes, I am aware of that difficulty. It is not at all an easy decision for you,' said Cressida, not quite clucking with sympathy.

'Mind you,' responded Geoffrey, ruminatively, 'a new,

cheap, young Chaplain, straight from College, or being rescued from the pittance paid to a curate, would bridge the immediate shortfall in just a few years.'

'Gosh,' said Cressida, trying hard to conceal her disingenuousness, 'so, in the intermediate term, there would not really be any financial loss at all.'

'No,' said Geoffrey, shaking his head and shrugging his shoulders. 'It's a thought. Anyway, you'll both have to leave it with me and I'll need to discuss it with the Chairman and the school solicitor.'

'That seems absolutely right.'

'I haven't yet decided, of course.'

'No, indeed, Headmaster: I think we both fully appreciate that, don't we Bernard?'

Cressida was becoming more accustomed to the Headmaster's scorpion-like backlash at just the moment when one of her schemes might show signs of prospering.

Geoffrey Tansley then poured himself a large gin and tonic and, alone, paced about the room. He rather liked John Donaldson and certainly respected him. He was convinced now that the Chaplain was indeed gay but John had never come out of the closet and the letter written by the unfortunate boy most certainly absolved him even of the suspicion. If Donaldson were ever to declare his sexuality, let alone act upon it, that would be the end of him but, surely, Tansley thought, he is too experienced and canny a schoolmaster to make so cardinal a blunder. In any case, this particular Chaplain's strongly held evangelical convictions would almost certainly prevent any actual buggery. Nevertheless, the issue of rumour and reputation *was* a factor and he had not, in fact, required Cressida Fulwell to point it out. An adverse view of John Donaldson would, of course, be ill conceived and unfair but, although the Headmaster did indeed think well of John, freedom from any kind of future hassle affecting him personally was one of Geoffrey Tansley's most cherished principles. Moreover, the very nature of the Chaplain's work required emotionally charged one-to-one conversations. After all this, it would only require another false and malicious accusation to put the whole place in the shit once again, with his, the Headmaster's, judgment coming under particularly unfavourable scrutiny. How his Deputy would then be able to crow about the warnings she had given, with that nonentity Bassett as a witness! Tansley was well aware that, within the Headmasters' Conference, two headmasters had fairly recently paid the heavy price of dismissal as a consequence of conniving deputies who had then been given their jobs. Oh damn and blast it all, he thought, pouring out a second stiff gin and tonic, this is all just as complicated as ever it was. Perhaps, in the end, the safest thing would be to recognise that any sense of personal commitment to any colleague can, at best, warp judgment and, at worst, invite error. Maybe the place did need a breath of fresh air and the appointment of some new young whiz-kid to the Chaplaincy, maybe even a woman, would show how dynamic, innovative and dispassionate in judgment he, Tansley, could still be in his performance as chief executive. There would be an outcry, of course, but an occasional display of ruthlessness to a Common Room currently rather too given to grumbling and whingeing was no bad thing either.

His private 'phone rang. Calpurnia was checking that

he had remembered that they were soon due to set out to have dinner with the Lord Lieutenant of the county. Before leaving, he telephoned the Chairman of the Governors in the hope that it might be possible to arrange an appointment the next day.

Sir Edward Moncrieff's chauffer parked his employer's new, midnight blue Mercedes across the front steps of the main entrance to the College. Mecedes-Benz surely missed a marketing opportunity with their magnificent machine thus publicly framed against the recently restored Vanbrugh portico.

Sir Edward found his own way down to Tansley's study. Alerted to his arrival by the porter, Ursula had hurried out the Head of Design Technology who had, at length, been trying to persuade the Headmaster that he required another member of staff in his Department.

'You know Dave Easton, our Head of Design Technology, I think, Sir Edward?' hinted Geoffrey Tansley.

Although they had in fact met more than once, Sir Edward clearly did not have a clue about the identity of the bearded, heavily bespectacled, somewhat unkempt figure to whom he was being introduced again.

'Yes, yes, I'm sure we've met before, of course,' said the Chairman. 'Design Technology, eh? It was all Woodwork in my day. It was taught by a curious character- I can't remember his name…..'

'It's all very different now!' mumbled Dave Easton into his beard, slightly offended by this off-hand anachronistic reduction of his subject and smarting with annoyance that the arrival of the Chairman had almost certainly finished his hopes for recruiting a new member of staff for at least another year.

'Oh, I'm sure it is- and I suspect a damned sight more expensive too!' said Sir Edward, smiling coldly, his eyes glinting with hostile humour at a person whom he took to be a glorified workman.

Never one to miss so obvious an opportunity, the Headmaster said 'It's funny you should say that, Chairman; Dave has just been trying to twist my arm to employ another teacher in his department!'

'I take it that you're resisting, Headmaster, the school finances being in the state they are! That latest percentage rise in staff salaries has knocked us back a bit!'

The remark was made humorously, but also calculatedly, and it had entombed in concrete the luckless Easton's cherished hope.

The Chairman and the Headmaster sat down to discuss the Donaldson affair. Sir Edward was more than acquainted with John Donaldson and held a genuinely high opinion of him, as did, not insignificantly, his wife, Lady Francesca. Having expressed once again his own warm appreciation of his Chaplain, Geoffrey Tansley, seeking to adopt a tone of shrewd caution enlivened by a hint of innovative insight, tentatively floated the notion of change that he had been considering. In so far as Sir Edward's cold banker's eyes could ever look surprised, they certainly did so as he responded initially to such a proposal. He looked very thoughtful indeed when they broke off the conversation as Ursula brought coffee and biscuits in. As he collected his thoughts together, he wondered about the reaction of Old Moretonians, of the other governors, of the Bishop, even of the Common Room. He mentioned that his wife and he had often met influential parents who had warmly applauded the work of the Chaplain.

'Of all the men to go for, Geoffrey, other than Alexander Scott, I can hardly think of a more risky target.' His voice was grave, his eyes an unsmiling mask.

'But what about the problems which I've outlined? Are the risks not even greater?'

Geoffrey was slightly surprised by the Chairman's reaction. After all, as Chairman of Delmundo's Bank, he must have sacked loads of people over the years with the same indifference demonstrated by Fortinbras towards his soldiers when invading Poland.

'There are risks and certainly, if there were to be another allegation in the future, that would present a considerable difficulty.' Sir Edward looked at his watch. 'Look, old chap, I'm lunching in Oxford with the Warden of All Saints. (I'm giving Freddie a hand with some appeal or other). You're the Headmaster and I think I must leave you to make the judgment. That's what we pay you that huge salary for.' (Wintry smile). 'There are risks either way. You must assume responsibility for calculating them.'

Tansley looked worried. He had wanted more definite support.

Sir Edward rose.

'Here's an idea, Geoffrey- but, be clear, I'm still leaving the responsibility with you. How about this? The tragedy has just happened- and it is ghastly. It is a terrible thing to have happened to a talented boy and presumably the place is still in shock, even if the boy concerned had not exactly made himself a favourite, even amongst his peers, from what you tell me. Now, John Donaldson has not yet been reinstated and, under the circumstances, you are certainly right to have the local vicar taking the Memorial Service next week. (I understand that the funeral has been a private affair). Obviously, John must be kept away until all that is over. Why not write him a letter pointing out the difficulties which you have identified and suggesting that it might not be in the College's best interests for him to return? Do that as a preliminary move and see what the reaction is. You will not have burnt your boats either way. John Donaldson is so loyal to the College that, although it will undoubtedly hurt him very much, he might agree that it would serve the wider interest. You would then get your way without firing one of the most respected masters at the College.'

'Thank you, Edward. That sounds a brilliant idea.'

'It's just a thought. He may not wear it, in which case you will have to weigh up the risks between keeping him and initiating proceedings for dismissal. You'd never win, of course, but I imagine that you will have made some sort of approximate calculation of the finances involved and you would still get your way in that we would be talking about compensation rather than reinstatement. If you do decide to write the letter I've suggested, I think that I can safely say that the governing body would expect to make him a handsome payment as a gesture of gratitude for all that he has done for the College. Don't quote a figure but do feel free to state the principle. As I say, you must take responsibility for this yourself and so obviously you will not be telling him (or anybody else) that the idea came from me. Indeed, you don't need to follow the suggestion through at all. I've only just thought of it and it may be a very foolish idea. You're the Headmaster and it is for you to get it right! Now, I really do have to go. Take this one carefully, won't you.'

The College had, of course, been shocked by Jude's death. To begin with, the news had filtered through as an accident but the receipt of the three letters left no doubt about the matter. John, shut up in the lonely little house, was profoundly distressed. Falling to his knees, he asked God how a boy of Jude's intelligence, and not insubstantial education in the Christian faith, had so completely failed to understand that, of course, repentance is followed by forgiveness. Why had Jude denied John a chance to reply to what he had written? The boy would have been alive, forgiven, reformed: morally and spiritually able to construct a good and vital life on his huge academic success. Even if Jude's faith *had* run into the crisis described in his letter, or, indeed, had been lost altogether, surely the most preliminary judgment would have informed the boy that John's only response to such an eloquent and palpably sincere statement of repentance would have been forgiveness. John wept as he thought of Jude's young male beauty so violently smashed into unrecognisable fragments by the blind, mechanical, unimaginably destructive force of the train.

John had Jude's letter photo-copied and Priscilla delivered the copy in a sealed envelope to the Headmaster who had, in fact, already received a copy of the one sent to Charlie. At least, John thought, he would be able to resume his duties soon, though, in all sincerity, he was appalled that such compensation came as a consequence of that poor boy's rash and desperate act.

Great therefore was the further shock awaiting him when the letter from Geoffrey Tansley arrived. He trembled in a mixture of fear, incomprehension and anger as he found his way to the vicarage and, having shown Maurice Stantonbury the offending document, traipsed miserably to Timothy Watson's office on Market Street. That evening, he had been invited by Sue and Bill for an informal supper at Greenvale Farm. There were only the three of them. It was inevitable that the topic came up quickly as Charlie had received the same letter and had shown it to his parents. After the horror of Jude's suicide had been shared, the assumption was made that John would be returning to his post. The Blakestones were incredulous when they heard about Geoffrey Tansley's letter to John and Bill vowed that he would act.

On the morning following the Memorial Service for Jude, Geoffrey Tansley was surprised to be confronted by an anxious looking Ursula rising from her seat in the outer office. It was unprecedented that the Chairman of the Governors should call unexpectedly first thing in the morning, even before the Headmaster had arrived for work.

During the two previous days, Sir Edward had received three unwelcome letters. The first one had come from Timothy Watson, writing on behalf of his client to state, very briefly, that the Rev. John Donaldson had authorised him to acknowledge the letter received from the Headmaster but that his client would not be offering to relinquish his post as a consequence of the grounds for his original suspension from his duties no longer applying.

The second letter had come from the Bishop. This complained that the ecclesiastical authorities had not been consulted in the first place (when the original allegation had been made) and claimed that it was not in the Headmaster's gift to dismiss the Chaplain of the College as the latter was ultimately answerable (in this world at least) to the Bishop. The Bishop continued by saying that the circumstances surrounding the attempt to remove his priest from office, as reported by the Rural Dean, could in no way justify any such action and that the ecclesiastical authorities would take whatever steps were deemed necessary to prevent it.

Clearly displeased, Sir Edward continued to explain that the third letter had come from a parent, Mr Blakestone, whose son was currently the Head of Blenheim House. This letter, the longest of the three, eulogised John Donaldson and stated that all the help which he had given his son had been repeated across the school and that he, Mr Blakestone, would now be spending considerable resources of time and energy to mobilise the opinion of Moreton parents more widely in a determined effort to prevent the Headmaster from taking action which would not only be unfair and injurious to the Chaplain but which would rob the College of one of its most gifted and benignly influential masters.

Sir Edward removed his half-moon spectacles and handed the documentation across to Geoffrey Tansley.

'I am afraid that you will see that you yourself come in for some criticism in the Blakestone letter, Geoffrey, and so does the boy's housemaster. Now, I can understand that a Headmaster might, almost inevitably, seem remote to parents but there must be some concern over the comments made about the housemaster when the father of the Head of House complains that this Bassett fellow is incapable of relating to the senior boys in the house. What's Bassett like? How did he come to be promoted? Are you satisfied with him yourself? What has your appraisal scheme thrown up about him?'

Decidedly thrown by the barrage of attacks which had been fired from so many different directions, uncertain about the way which the Chairman might jump, and unsettled by the delay of his early morning coffee, Tansley underwent the rare experience of being temporarily lost for words. Perhaps the easiest way to begin would be to pave the way towards the sacrifice of Bassett who had been particularly useless during the whole sorry episode. While he read through the letters, the Headmaster answered Sir Edward's last question.

'I have to admit that Bernard Bassett has been disappointing. He's a complaining sort of chap and he seems to be driven on by a ferociously ambitious wife. I had hoped for better things but perhaps it's not working out for him at Blenheim. I'll look into it, as you suggest.'

'I really don't want this Blakestone man to be organising a barrage of letters to me from parents and I must confess that I'm not altogether thrilled to be receiving what amounts to a reprimand from the Bishop. You know that he's tipped for Canterbury next time round?'

'Forgive me, Edward, but it was your idea.'

'But your judgment and your responsibility. I don't know what on earth you wrote but the Chaplain does seem to have been under-estimated. As I think I've mentioned before, I've received more complimentary remarks about John Donaldson from parents here than about any other master at the College, with the possible exception of Alexander Scott- even then, at a guess, I think it's probably level-pegging. You can read yourself what Mr Blakestone writes about those two. He does seem even-handed- which, I suppose, makes the criticism of Bassett the more serious.'

'Well then, Edward, as we said at the outset of your….er…. this plan, it was only an option offered to John which he was free to reject. I must confess that I'm a bit surprised by the vehemence with which he has decided to do the latter (involving solicitors, bishops and parents) but I shall write immediately to acknowledge his decision and to welcome him back in the warmest possible terms.'

'A wise decision, I have to say, Geoffrey. I think you have little choice. And, anyway…..' (with a rare display of unveiled frankness) *he is a good man!* I am sure that he will honour your request not to discuss your earlier manoeuvre further. Tell him that I think that you are doing the right thing in having him back *toute de suite*. Tell him, too, that, in the light of all the horrors he has gone through of late, Francesca and I, and some of the governors, would be delighted if he could join us for dinner here at the College before the next plenary meeting. You can fix that, can't you?'

'By all means, Edward. What a good idea!'

Sir Edward hurried out to his waiting Mercedes just as Cressida Fulwell arrived for her scheduled daily briefing with the Headmaster.

'So, what have you got for me today, Cressida?'

'Isn't it rather early for Sir Edward to have paid a visit?'

'Yes. The circumstance was unusual.'

Cressida paused but, when no further information was forthcoming, she proceeded to the only item of business on her agenda.

'Now that the Memorial Service is over, Bernard has been at me a bit, wondering what your decision might be over the Chaplain. Hard though it will be for John, it seemed such a good idea of yours to have a change- even apart from this dreadful business.'

'Yes, I have decided. I am about to write to him, asking him to return with all speed and assuring him of the warmest possible welcome when he comes back. I intend to announce this to the Common Room at Break today and to the College in Assembly.'

The Deputy could only issue an inarticulate murmur of disappointed surprise, so abrupt and unexpected was the shock of this announcement. Tansley was in a foul mood and was rather satisfied to observe the effect of his words.

'I can see that this doesn't please you but you've never liked John Donaldson and I can't allow a longstanding grievance, personal to you, to cloud my judgment when dealing with a much valued Chaplain and colleague.'

'I feel that that's a little unfair, Headmaster. I have always had only the good of the College in mind.'

The unanticipated, unsmiling savagery of the rebuke was sufficiently painful to bring tears to her eyes.

'I'm sure. Was there anything else?'

Reaching for her handkerchief, Cressida just about managed to say that there wasn't.

Tansley's tone softened and he leant back in his chair.

'In that case, there's just one thing from me. You've done four years here and I have been (and am) very grateful to you for many aspects of the no-nonsense modernisation which you have helped me to introduce. I feel now that it is time that you start looking for a new opportunity. By the time you find the right thing, you'll have done five years and that's just about the right length of time for an ambitious, go-ahead Deputy. You might think of going for a headship at a minor school somewhere. I'd certainly support you.'

'You want me to go? I can't believe that I'm hearing this!'

'I think that it would be in your own interest, Cressida, honestly. You need to move onwards and upwards, as they say.'

His tone was now almost kindly and was accompanied by a compassionate smile.

Now, she gave vent to an angry outburst.

'I want to go in my own time and choose the right sort of place. And I don't want a *minor* school.'

Tansley remained calm but he stopped smiling.

'Of course, of course. But, as you are choosing to make an issue of what is, in fact, good advice, I'm afraid that I have to tell you that it does not please me that you have pretty persistently set out to wage a vendetta against some of the most senior and trusted members of my Common Room and I would advise you that, when you do move on to higher things, you learn a little about the ancient art of diplomacy. Now, I can see that you're upset, and I'm sorry about that, but you must go away now and consider carefully what I have said and leave me to get on with things here. Ursula tells me that she has a list a mile long.'

Later that day, Tansley received a visitation from Bernard and Delia Bassett. Bassett had received the announcement in the Common Room with consternation and openly complained that he had 'not been consulted, let alone informed.' His wife was rude to the Headmaster, telling him that the way they had been treated was 'disgraceful'. Weary with the whole business and more sick of the two of them than of any-one else at that moment, Tansley lost his temper. He told them that if they were not happy with John Donaldson returning to Blenheim House, they were free to pull out. The house down in the town, currently inhabited by John, would fall vacant. He then pressed home the complaint made by 'several parents' that Bassett was not offering an appropriate level of support to the boys in his house, especially those in the Sixth Form. He accused the housemaster of failing to understand 'the disturbed genius' of Jude Williams and, less fairly, alluded to the Jasper/Tim episode.

This drew a furious response from Delia but she was only able to get the first two words out of her mouth. 'My husband……..'

Tansley was able to take the gloves off at last, after all the shadow-boxing of a very trying day.

'It is *not* for you, Madam, to speak for your husband here in the Headmaster's study. Frankly, it is a gross impertinence that you come here at all. You have nothing to do with school business and I do not intend to tolerate your interference, to say nothing of the inappropriateness of your tone.' Then, turning to Bassett, 'I shall be putting it in writing that you must make this arrangement work or find another job. Now, I have nothing more to say on the matter and I certainly want to hear nothing more from you about it.'

The following September, Bernard Bassett left the College to take up a post advertised in the Times Educational Supplement as 'second in an expanding History Department' in a recently opened, small, independent day school in the West Midlands.

THIRTY-THREE

On a freezing St Valentine's Day, the members of the First XI were practising on a field which had patches of snow and ice.

John and Richard stood on the touch-line. John wore a scarf, overcoat, fur hat and gloves. Ashley and Chris had teasingly persuaded Richard to wear his football strip so that he could run about the pitch with them. John's young colleague had, however, felt that he should spend at least part of the time talking to his good friend, the reinstated manager of the team. Richard was in agony with the cold. He had never experienced anything like it. A Siberian blast tormented his bare arms and legs and mocked the thin football shirt which attempted a hopeless gesture of protection. He had taken a tumble on the icy grass before retiring temporarily from the fray to stand with John. His teeth were chattering.

'I've never felt so cold,' he stuttered in manifest discomfort. 'I thought the English rain was bad but this is bloody dreadful.'

John could not decide whether the tears being whipped from his eyes resulted from intense pain or the effect of the freezing wind on his tear-ducts.

'You shouldn't have let these boys talk you into wearing shorts and a football shirt,' laughed John. '*They've* been used to this each winter; *you* haven't. Do you want to go in and put something warmer on?'

Richard might have been just about to capitulate when Ashley and Chris ran up.

'Not thinking of chickening out, Sir, are you?' asked Ashley, with a broad grin. He had even less flesh protecting him than Richard but seemed oblivious to the freezing temperature.

'Oh dear! Your teeth are chattering, Sir,' teased Chris. 'Do you think you should go back to Matron and go to bed with a nice hot-water bottle?'

'Sh-sh-shut up and p-p-p-piss off!' stammered Richard, smiling despite his misery, conscious that he could not be marked down as a wuss.

'Tut, Tut!' commented Charlie, who had come up to join in the fun. 'Is our Australian teacher not able to cope with the cold?' Do you think that maybe he needs a bit more toughening up, lads?' he joked with mock concern.

'Yeah, it's not all about lying around a swimming pool with a few chilled tinnies when you're back here in Old England,' added Chris.

Richard lunged at him but Chris easily dodged out of the way.

In due course, the arrival of Priscilla by car alleviated the situation. She produced a flask of hot tea and pieces of chocolate sponge cake for John and Richard. She ignored the boys when they jokingly complained about favouritism. When the practice ended, she drove John and Richard back.

There had been the annual exchange of Valentine day cards within the Sixth Form that morning. Olivia had received several cards, including one from Charlie. His handwriting was so familiar to her that even the single question-mark had given the identity of the sender away. She did, of course, play the game by pretending that she had no idea who this might be.

Ashley had sent several cards, including one to Victoria Summerthwaite: 'from one of your male slaves: the one who's so cool that it hurts!' The recipient had initially snorted with amused contempt but had then rescued the card a few moments after she had slung it into the waste-paper basket and, smiling, placed it at the back of her desk.

Richard, to his embarrassment, had received a large number of cards from the girls whom he took for swimming, some of them displaying pictures of scantily dressed hunks and containing messages suggesting flattering comparisons. A couple had been smeared with lipstick; others were festooned with a plethora of 'love and kisses', the repeated phrase accompanied by a sequence of crosses. He did not feel that he could put these tributes up for display but he also felt that it was mean-spirited to throw such appeals to his limited male vanity away. In the end, he decided to put them in a drawer inside his desk. He had, he thought, successfully identified Rosie's card amongst the others. He singled this one out and put it on his desk. The flowers which decorated the one which he had sent in exchange had been as predictable as the rhyme inside. He had crossed the second line out, writing 'Who cares about the violets?' beside it.

John had had a number of important meetings with

pupils since his return a fortnight or so ago. The day after he came back, a shame-faced youth slunk past him in a passage, clearly, it seemed to John, attempting to avert identification. John suddenly made the association with the unpleasant incident in the town, involving the obscene remarks made in public. He called the boy back, took his name and instructed him to come with his friend 'without fail' at a time arranged later in the day.

When they duly arrived at the appointed hour, he kept them standing. He reminded them of the incident and asked them if they would care to repeat what they had said. Mortified, tongue-tied and plainly all too fearful of the consequences, they stammered out the facile apology which they had cooked up on the way and which John was quick to dismiss as an all too obvious apology of convenience. He enforced his advantage with the time-honoured ploy of finding minor irregularities with their uniform, an easy task in their case.

'In any case, I didn't ask you if you were sorry or not; I asked you to repeat what you had said to me down in the town centre. I am sure you remember it; I certainly do.'

Uneasy shuffling of the feet, sniffing, a shifty exchange of glances.

'Come on; I'm waiting. Perhaps you'd prefer it if we all adjourn to the Headmaster. I'm sure that *he'd* be fascinated to hear it too.'

Hard swallowing: a sudden preoccupation with an indeterminate spot on the carpet. Eventually, the one called Freddie, blushing furiously and scratching his right ear, said, 'Sir! We can't say those things, *not in here!*'

'Ah, I see! *Not in here*, within the hallowed walls of my study back at the College! But it was all-right to insult me with obscenities, shouted across a busy street, full of people shopping, in the town centre?'

Freddie shook his head slowly and, sniffing in an effort to control the incipient tears, mumbled to the carpet,

'No, of course not. It was an awful thing to do.'

'And what about you?' John asked the other boy who grimaced with misery at the challenge. 'Tell me, what would you do in my situation if you were me and I were you?'

He deliberately held back any use of their names.

The miscreant glanced furtively round the room, as though looking for an avenue of escape, or, perhaps, desperately hoping that the bookcases, filing cabinets and chairs might suddenly, if inexplicably, come to his rescue.

'I'd- I'd expel us, Sir!'

'Ah, so you are capable of some judgment! Yes- well- I expect that that's what the Headmaster will do when he hears about it.'

Freddie could stand it no longer. He burst into tears.

'Oh! Sir! I'm so, so sorry! I know it seems like an apology of convenience- as you say- and I am really scared- but I'm *really* sorry too. We should never have said those things.'

He searched his pockets for a handkerchief but couldn't find one. John did not point him towards a box of tissues on the table behind him. Freddie wiped his nose on the sleeve of his white shirt.

'It *is* an apology of convenience, I'm afraid, as I've already said. Tell me, when you said '*not in here*', are you suggesting that it is all-right to speak to people in the way that you did in other circumstances: when the victim appears to be defenceless, for example, or when you have an opportunity to entertain yourselves by inflicting the maximum possible humiliation on some-one in a more public situation?'

'No Sir,' breathed Freddie, appearing as though he was about to collapse, and the other boy, looking at John beseechingly, gravely shook his head.

'I'm also *personally* sorry, Sir,' said the other boy, finding words at last. 'It was a horrible thing to do. I can't think what came over us.'

'Apart from anything else, it was very cowardly. I can't help but notice that there is a difference in your attitude '*in here*', now that I'm the one who has the power to control the situation.

'Yes Sir.'

'Are you aware that what you did is actually a criminal offence? Making allegations about people's sexuality could land you both in front of a juvenile court prior to doing time in a detention centre.'

One said yes; the other one said no. John felt a shade guilty that he might be enjoying himself a little too much and he was beginning to feel sorry for them, especially for Freddie who now looked as though he might expire at any moment.

'In any case, to make unwarranted assumptions about another person's sexuality is wrong. You know nothing about mine. In fact, I'm a celibate priest but I don't suppose that such a concept can mean much to you.'

Freddie shook his head; the other boy looked blank. John explained celibacy and added that, in its application to him, it was none of their business.

'It's clear to me that you are the sort of chaps who would go round gay bashing if, for whatever reason, you did suspect some-one of being homosexual.'

'No! No! We're not! *I'm* not!' said Freddie mournfully.

John now told them to sit down. He passed Freddie a tissue. These simple gestures unleashed a cascade of tears from Freddie. However, John had not finished.

'Your spontaneous behaviour down in the town that day suggests exactly the opposite. What I've just said about you *must* be true. You are the sort of louts who will enjoy humiliating and beating up people whom you might guess, rightly or wrongly, are queers, aren't you? Just imagine for a moment how hurtful that must be to a recipient of your attentions, whether they are homosexual or not. What if some random thug saw you two together and shouted such accusations?'

The second boy raised his hands in surrender. Freddie looked tearfully mystified.

'No, listen to me; I haven't finished. You absolutely cannot go around saying things like that *to* people or *about* them. In any case, even if a person is homosexual, it is a biological fact. Some people are tall; some people are short; some people are black; some people are white; some people are naturally stupid; others are very clever. How people might *behave* with their sexuality, be they homosexual *or* heterosexual, is a different matter. You then enter ethical territory; but the condition itself is a matter of fact and it is not for you or any-one else to make a moral judgment of that.'

'I understand that now,' said the second boy 'and I'm sure that Freddie does too.'

Freddie quickly confirmed this fact.

'You both say so but, of course, that is what you *would* say, given that you are in very hot water at this moment.'

Freddie began to collect himself.

'Sir, Jason and I now realise that we got it badly wrong. The way you've explained it shows how stupid as well as how hurtful we were. I can't speak for Jason but I certainly will never ever do anything like that again. Again, I can only say how very, very sorry I am.'

Jason was quick to align himself with this affirmation.

'It really is all too easy for you to say this under your present circumstances. I now need to consider what to do. It is so serious that the only course of action open to me, both personally and as a master here, is to refer it to the Headmaster.'

Now it was Jason's turn to cry. Freddie remained silent and shredded the damp tissue he was holding. He shook his head and sighed mournfully.

'BUT.....'

The word hit them both like a pistol shot. They looked at him with a new desperate hope.

'I am a Christian. I have to consider what Jesus would do and, of course, he would *forgive*. Though I have never behaved the way you have, I myself have, like every-one else, been guilty of wrong thoughts, words and deeds. I can think of them now; I don't need to think very hard. If Christ forgives *me* for these, I must forgive *you* for your wrongdoing to *me*. Otherwise, I would be a hypocrite and might as well resign my post in the church. Jesus actually forgave the people who were crucifying Him, you know. He did that from the Cross itself. Forgiveness does, however, depend upon true repentance: being *honestly* sorry and, indeed, *changing*. You do both *seem* sorry at the moment. I don't know whether this is an act to try to appease me or, even if your sorrow is genuine, how long it might last but I think that God requires me to give you the benefit of the doubt and so, unless anything else happens, I shall keep this matter between us. I shall want you both to write something for me in which you give an account of your present attitude to homosexual people and I also want you to write a promise never to treat any-one else like that again. As I've said, you can have no idea of how hurtful your silliness was. I was very unhappy at that time. We'll leave it at that but don't let me ever hear of you treating any-one else like this.'

They left, full of tearful gratitude and relief and repeating their apologies yet again. John sat back heavily in his chair, not ultimately knowing whether or not they were at this moment descending the stairs changed boys or smirking to each other in congratulation at having successfully pulled off a narrow escape. He committed them in prayer.

How focused John was now! How purposeful! How confidently he could manage in his appointed slot in the world! But how far, he wondered more than ever before, *was* the College the *real* world? Was that unwelcoming territory of reality not rather to be found in the bland little house on the estate on the margin of the town, surrounded by salesmen and single mothers with young children, a representative location of where so many millions of ordinary people lived? Or was it the purposeless track across the dull, blank fields, arriving at the stereo-typical pub', eating the same pre-packaged microwave meal that others were consuming the length and breadth of the country? Or was it the selfishly assertive brashness of the infinitely revolving crowd on the moving escalators at London's Euston Station? Or, in the end, was it the memento mori discovered by *la belle jeunesse* in Poussin's '*Et Ego in Arcadia*'? Perhaps, even here, within the protection of the College estate, the reality was darkly tragic. Was the slightest of the youths in the painting, the one to the right, turning towards us in concerned surprise, his left hand pointing to the inscription on the sarcophagus, to be identified perhaps with Jude, recognising death and oblivion as the only certainties? Had Jude turned away with a similar expression of surprise as he had committed himself to the unanswerably final encounter of his shattering demise?

No, he had to hold faith. Ultimately, it was the same here as elsewhere. Christ Himself witnessed these scenes of sterility and devastation as He hung on the Cross after He had wept over Jerusalem. How fortunate he, John Donaldson, was, that, despite his own shortcomings, he should be given this further opportunity to offer prayer and counsel to the young, his single talent well employed. Dawn will break upon Gethsemane.

John's next appointment, not, this time impromptu by arrangement, was with Tim. It had been at the boy's request, albeit encouraged by Charlie. Tim had benefited from no adult counsel since his humiliation, desperately challenging to a seventeen-year old boy, but his self-respect had just about survived through the different ministrations of Ashley and Chris on the one hand and Charlie, somewhat (though not altogether) differently, on the other. Matron had offered to talk it through but Tim was far too embarrassed to discuss it with a woman. His parents had been shocked and seemed to think that their errant son had more responsibility for the incident than was in fact the case. John said nothing that had not been said before by Tim's friends but a hopeful message given from the *adult* world came to the boy like a beneficent emissary from outer space. John told him that, apart from accepting alcohol to a degree which had disabled him and smoking some cannabis, he was a blameless victim in the whole unfortunate affair. By the time the School Chaplain had finished with him, Tim walked away believing that what his close friends had said was true and he could look the world in the eyes again. When talking it through with Tim, John had seen again that Tim, with his slim good looks, was an attractive boy but this, absolutely, did not interfere with his mission. He prayed over the boy and helped Tim to reaffirm his own faith.

Earlier that same day, John had received a visit from Charlie and Olivia. Jude's shocking suicide had affected them predictably. Charlie, by dint of persistence, had finally persuaded Lynn Williams to allow them to attend the funeral, the only representatives of the College present. It had been a horrible affair, held in Midhampton Crematorium, sandwiched into a strict time slot between two other funerals. There were very few people present, mainly because Lynn had refused point blank to allow any-one else from the College, pupil or teacher, to come. Oblivious alike to her own shortcomings and the subtle complexities inherent to her child's character, she needed a scapegoat and invented one in the College. The pathetic, mean little ceremony was conducted by a strange, impersonal priest. This had particularly upset Charlie when he thought of what the Rev. D would have been able to do. Olivia had quietly wept at the ghastly moment when the coffin disappeared into the furnace, sentimentally serenaded by clichéd, sub-Christian, piped music. Lynn had howled in utter despair at that awful second, so terminal in its symbolism, brushing away Mike's attempt to pat her on the arm. There had been no reception afterwards.

'Why couldn't he have waited until we had all replied to his letters?' Charlie asked yet again. 'Why, Sir? Why, oh why?' John and he had met in the interim and Charlie had asked it then. John repeated his answer.

'Charlie, I've tormented myself by asking the same question again and again. God alone knows.'

'It's just so weird that a person who in so many ways was so rational should go and do something so catastrophically impulsive. I know he was impulsive too. Oh, I don't know. I don't understand it. It's so confusing.'

'We'd have all forgiven him,' added Olivia. 'So far as I'm concerned, there wasn't *that* much to forgive: certainly nothing to justify what he did!'

'You must try to explain it Sir- just a bit at least.'

'Charlie, Charlie! That's such a Charlie request! "There are more things in heaven and earth, Horatio, than are dreamt of in your philosophy."'

'I'm sorry. I know; I'm being unreasonable.'

'The tragedy is,' said John, 'Jude repented but was unable to accept forgiveness. In that, he missed the essence of the Christian faith.'

'Do you think that God forgave Him?' asked Olivia.

'Committing suicide is a mortal sin. Jude had no right to do such a thing. So dreadful an act rejects God's forgiveness in Christ.'

Both young people sat in a strained silence.

'But, mercifully, God is the judge, not us, and we cannot ultimately penetrate the divine mystery,' concluded John.

The harsh winter yielded grudgingly to a late, capricious spring and then to a gentle, sunny summer. Both Charlie and Olivia gained top grades in all their subjects and went on to read English at university. Olivia went to the University of Durham and Charlie went to Bristol where, three years on, he took one of that distinguished university's top first class degrees.

Despite Geoffrey Tansley's rearguard action, the old order was inexorably forced to submit to the new world of measurable performance criteria, norm related assessment objectives, exhaustive record keeping and codes of health and safety which, in their pathological fixation with sanitised risk assessment, systematically annihilated swathes of educational opportunity. Information Technology increasingly became the master instead of the servant.

Alexander Scott retired the following year, a little earlier than would otherwise have been the case, his agile and well informed mind thus lost to the young. John Donaldson continued until the age of retirement, increasingly confident in his belief that, whatever the vicissitudes of fashion and situation, the truth which he held dear was 'the same yesterday, today and for ever.'

About the Author

PETER FARQUHAR WAS BORN in Edinburgh and grew up in London. He graduated in English from the University of Cambridge. He has extensive experience in teaching, including having been the Senior English Master at the Manchester Grammar School and Head of English at Stowe School near Buckingham. He currently lectures at the University of Buckingham.